*"Jasmine, I must speak
with you,"* said the duke.

Jackie lowered her dove-gray eyes, her heart beating furiously. She prayed that he would not recognize her—a stunning, silver-haired vision—as the young court page who served him. For her plan of vengeance to succeed, she must seduce this arrogant man, and then abandon him.

He took her hand in his. "I beg you to allow me to call on you tomorrow."

"Sir, this is not seemly," she demurred, but when she disengaged his hand, he suddenly caught her in his iron grip.

"No!" she protested, fear surging through her. His hold loosened, yet when he stepped closer, she shivered, even as heat rushed over her.

She ached to feel his arms around her again, and thoughts of her scheme were lost. All she knew was that she must have this man.

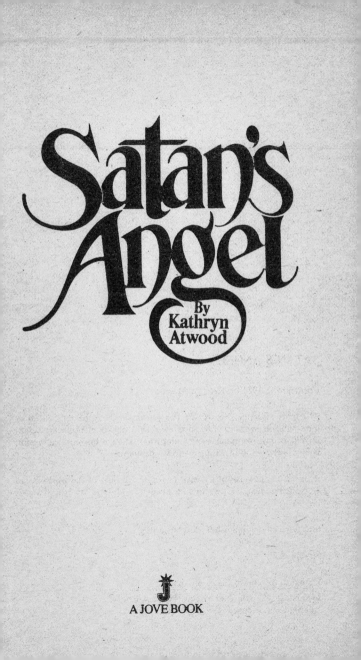

Satan's Angel

By
Kathryn
Atwood

A JOVE BOOK

SATAN'S ANGEL

First Jove edition published December 1981

First printing

Printed in the United States of America

Jove books are published by Jove Publications, Inc.,
200 Madison Avenue, New York, NY 10016

*To my mother,
with love
and to Melinda,
who nagged*

Chapter
One

"OH, LOVE ME, Jack, love me!" The Frenchwoman's passion-frenzied hands, so small and dainty in repose, now resembled the claws of a silver bird of prey tearing at the tender skin of his back, as Jack O'Connell, Irish soldier of fortune, rakehell, gambler, thief, cutpurse, occasional highwayman, and all-around rascal, strove with all his might, bull-like strength, and not inconsiderable will to obey his rapacious mistress.

She twisted her compact body from side to side as she felt the sly tendrils of fanning fire spread throughout her belly and down her legs, which were entwined about his tanned ones. His thrusting manhood drove deeper into her yearning and hungry body, seeking the cup of Love in which to pour the wine of Lust.

She arched her back to welcome the conqueror. A million blazing suns burst inside the writhing woman, and in her ecstasy she cried out loudly and passionately. His sobbing moan of abrupt and thunderous release mingled with hers as their illicit love culminated in a towering conflagration that threatened to consume both lovers.

1

"*Mon cher*, you were magnificent," she whispered, her voice deep and husky from the heat of love. Victorée Héloïse Constance de Marchaud, only daughter and child of Raoul François Pierre Christian de Marchaud, comte de Saint-Martin, sighed deeply. Her long pink tongue flicked briefly between her even white teeth and sensuously licked her red, kiss-inflamed lips. She let her heavy eyelids droop, the long white lashes caressing her cheeks.

He bent his head, pressing his hungry mouth down on hers. As his tongue explored the pink cavity of her mouth, caressing the pearllike teeth, his eyes moved beyond the top of her head, beyond the vast bed, and were caught by the gleam of something on a marble-top table next to the bed.

When he had first furtively entered the silent Hôtel de Saint-Martin hours ago to make love to this beautiful albino, the darkness and his desire for her had spread a canopy over him, blinding him to all but her aroused self. Now, by the light of a single flickering candle, lit in the stillness between the storms of their love, the Irishman could see beyond the curtained bed. Everywhere he looked richness, bespeaking a hedonistic comfort, pressed itself upon the impoverished Irish second son of a seventh son.

The gray light of dawn crept in past the golden-draped windows, and distant sounds of a city awakening could be heard. He squinted to bring the gleam into focus, and pleasure filled him as he saw a miniature oil of his love's face and upper torso. In the portrait she wore a décolleté emerald gown, its plunging neckline baring the snowy whiteness of her shoulders and half the smooth globes of her perfect breasts. Her silver hair was caught at the nape of her neck and flowed in silken ringlets across the exquisite perfection of her creamy shoulders. A slight half-smile played across her full, sensual lips. An unconquered sexual challenge gleamed in her pale eyes. It was a portrait that had captured the deep womanly essence and the true soul of its subject.

But Jack's larcenous gaze did not remain for long on her heart-shaped countenance. Instead his attention was entrapped by the clever frame embracing the beautifully executed portrait. Constructed of beaten gold, it was encrusted with gems of all shapes and sizes. Diamonds, rubies, sapphires, topazes, pearls, emeralds, garnets—from the size of a pea to that of a small bird's egg, a king's ransom beckoned to him from the

oval frame. It must be his. But how to obtain it? he wondered, his mind feverishly attacking the problem. He must—

He grew aware of muffled, thudding sounds. Abruptly, her
silver head jerked around, and with a resounding, teeth-shaking
crash the door to her bedroom burst open. A dark man looked
straight at the bed and at the two lovers in it.

"Bastard! Remove yourself!" a deep voice shouted, and in
three great strides Raoul de Marchaud, comte de Saint-Martin,
crossed the length of the room and reached the bed of love.
With a talonlike grip—not unlike his daughter's, Jack realized—
the nobleman seized the ginger-haired Irishman and roughly
jerked him from the bed. He fell with a bruising thud to the
polished wooden floor and lay stunned for a few moments.

With a groan Jack, shaking his head, raised himself on an
elbow. Above, his hands clasped behind his back, loomed the
comte.

Jack wet his lips nervously. With a snap of imperative
fingers, the comte beckoned to a shadow in the hall. Jack's
green eyes widened as he saw a hulking statue of a man
shuffle into the room, his shaggy head bent over his broad
chest. In the giant's shovellike hands rested a large black
oiled whip, the look of cruelty plaited into its twisted leather.
The giant, a fawning idiocy in his staring eyes, smiled, his
scarred face contorting with painful effort. The comte's swarthy
hawklike face, with its slanting cheekbones and black eyebrows, frightened Jack in its sudden alienness. This was no
ordinary outraged father who could be gently lulled with
quick Irish words.

The immediate flush of anger had receded from the French
nobleman's face to be replaced by a blackness of spirit, a
grim, expectant amusement. "I spit on you, dog. You dare to
touch my daughter, do you? I shall teach you a lesson, jackal,
that you shall never forget! A lesson from the pits of hell!
Rise!" He kicked Jack in a sinewy thigh with the pointed toe
of a diamond-buckled shoe.

The comte took the giant whip from the mute servant. The
Irishman scrambled to his feet hastily, making a sweeping
grab with frantic hands at his clothing in a heap beside the
bed. And as he did, he lost his balance, stumbling slightly
against the bedside table. He regained his footing, a wad of
clothing in his hands. He dodged the intent comte, who

lashed out with the giant whip. It gave a mighty crack, and
Jack jumped as the steel-tipped end savagely tore at his bare
legs. The comte rumbled with dark laughter.

The aristocrat struck out again with the cruel weapon, and
Jack sprang forward on the balls of his feet. Then the comte
tossed the whip to Carel, the giant, and instructed, "Whip
him."

As he raced from the room for his very life, Jack threw one
last look over his shoulder at Victorée. The Irishman's last
glimpse of his albino love was of her kneeling on the crumpled, soiled sheets, tears coursing down her ivory-pale cheeks,
her light eyes dark with misery, her waist-length hair tousled,
and one beautifully kept hand clutching at a sheet to cover her
bare form, yet failing completely as one quivering young
breast remained unsheathed.

Then he was being whipped through the great Hôtel de
Saint-Martin, a hundred agonizing fires burning at his heels,
his thighs, calves, buttocks. Past the long wood-paneled gal-
lery of disapproving and grim-faced ancestral portraits he ran,
ever aware of the giant gaining behind him, and the potential
maiming. Past silver and gold candelabra, across deep multi-
colored rugs imported from the East, under crystal chandeliers unlit now in the silent hours of the morning, he sped. He
caught glimpses of untapped riches and luxury, and he mentally
cursed himself and the father for spoiling the intended appro-
priation. Jack's head ached with the thought of all that
unliberated wealth, none of which he would now ever possess.

Yet somehow, Jack knew deep in his soul, he was lucky to
be alive.

In the courtyard of the Hôtel de Saint-Martin Father Liam
Dougherty, his reddened face bland with good-humored pa-
tience and a recent nip of warm spirits, awaited his good
friend's inevitably precipitous arrival. The birds had begun to
sing their morning songs. The city was waking, and gladness
filled the priest's heart. It did him good to hear the sounds
that signified the beginning of a day: the rumbling of heavily
laden wagons on the way to the open markets, the pleasant
greetings tossed back and forth between the early risers. He
smiled. Ah, it was a good thing, mornin'. Father Liam, a
stocky cassocked figure, looking heavier in his somber robes

than he actually was, leaned against his saddled horse, who stood foursquare with well-bred quietness. In one hand the Irish priest held the reins of Jack's sorrel mount. In the other hand, plump-fingered, agile, deft, he held a quirt, and he had amused himself these long hours by flicking pieces of lint off the black of his priestly robes. He shrugged his soiled cloak closer around his body and shivered in the cold morning air.

He waited for Jack O'Connell, as he had awaited many similar mornings in the last four years of their acquaintance. How many times had it been? his idle mind wondered. Always Jack had a foolproof plan, and how often had a husband, a father, son, uncle, brother—yes, even a lover—burst in upon the indiscreet couple and then with all due haste tossed Jack out into the street? Too many times to count, Father Liam decided and, with a look of piety upon his youthful face, told himself that while he might take a wee nip now and then, he could indeed console himself that he had never yielded to the ever-pervasive temptation of Eve. Hmm. Now that he started thinking about it, Jack *never* did leave by the front door. 'Twas always by the back.

Liam glanced at the hôtel, its marble and wooden facade still shuttered in somber sleep on the cool morning of March 24, in the year of Our Lord 1671. He stamped his booted feet to drive out the encroaching coldness and to quicken the circulation in his numb toes. The two horses, disturbed by the priest's motion and the sudden noise, nickered softly and pawed the ground.

Making up his mind, Father Liam moved quickly through the courtyard and around the great hôtel to the back, where it overlooked a narrow and dirty alley.

" 'Twill not be long, me dears," he whispered in a clear brogue, and he watched with growing interest and amusement as the back doors of the Hôtel de Saint-Martin were thrown open and out was thrust a very naked Jack, what clothes he was not clutching tossed out after him as an afterthought. Jack stumbled down the steps and fell with little dignity at the foot.

The horses moved slightly, fretting at the sudden activity. Liam moved to quiet them.

"May the Lord's blessin' be 'pon ye," Liam, his blue eyes crinkling into a wry smile, slurred. It was a blessing he had repeated a hundred times over.

A dark man with a face like a savage bird of prey strode down the steps to the naked man, followed by a giant holding a whip, quite wicked in appearance. In one smooth fluid movement, revealing the incredible strength masked by his careless aristocratic appearance, the dark man gripped Jack around the throat with one mighty hand and lifted him like a squalling, struggling puppy off the ground. Liam, from his vantage point, could not hear the man distinctly, only a low, threatening tone. But some instinct warned the priest, and he pulled out his pistol from his saddle holster and prepared it. The man shook Jack several times, then savagely flung the terrified Irishman away from him, turned, and strode back into the hôtel. The doors slammed shut with a final thundering dismissal. The big servant threw down the whip and flexed his fingers. A snapping sound resounded through the alley. He bent over Jack, who lay stunned for a moment before dizzily trying to rise to his feet. The giant's hands snaked around Jack's throat, wet mewling sounds indicating the mute's pleasure. Liam cocked the pistol and, murmuring a prayer for the man's soul, fired. The ball charged into its meaty target, knocking the man backward, his hamlike hands releasing Jack's throat. The giant did not rise.

The Irishman shakily advanced on wobbly legs. "Oh, Liam," Jack whispered, his voice hoarse. "I was ne'er more glad to see ye with me own two eyes. I thank ye fer savin' me ould miserable hide." He trembled. "I think we'd best leave, soon as I pull on me britches." Jack's green eyes showed white, and deep lines of fright were etched on his face. Around his throat were the vivid red-purple marks of a bruising hold. He pulled on his breeches, buttoned up his linen shirt and satin coat, and hastily pulled on his boots. Something small and shiny glinted in his hands for an instant and then was gone, tucked out of sight inside the linen folds of his shirt.

As he was dressing he seemed to regain his composure. The two Irishmen mounted and then rode quickly out the alley to the street. Jack looked back at the now quiet Hôtel de Saint-Martin. "Well, me love will soon forget me." He released a deep, tragic Irish sigh, and Liam rolled his eyes heavenward.

Liam, though curious, asked no questions, for he knew from long experience that when Jack was quite ready he would tell all, his honest heart compelled to confess. Jack, though, seemed embarrassed. "To be sure, all would have worked out so well, Faither Liam, had it not been fer the brute o' the faither." Jack emphasized his words with a nod of his head. "Yet am I well pleased that I shall not be able to ferget me lady," Jack pursued, a slight smile playing about the corners of his mouth.

"And how be that, me friend?" asked Liam, suspicion aroused.

"'I have a wee token o' remembrance, given me as a boon fer me love an' diligence, an' desirous care." He reached into his shirt and pulled out a small object. It was a miniature oil portrait of a woman, the woman in the hôtel, Liam surmised. A stray beam of the rising sun struck the oil, and with the brilliance of the gold frame and the jewels embedded therein the token of love quickly took focus.

"I shall cherish this fer the remainder o' me miserable life," Jack declared in a clear strong voice. He lifted the portrait to his lips and pressed a fervent kiss upon the lady's face. A sardonic smile quirked Liam's mouth. Aye, a token of Jack's love—his love of riches. But little matter, the cleric thought. After all, his friend had left this escapade richer than he had entered into it. "An' the Lord be blessed," he murmured to himself, crossing himself with a great show of faith. And he intended to see they kept those riches for a while. Reaching over, Liam plucked the portrait from Jack's hands.

"Hey!" the red-haired man exclaimed.

"Now, now, Jack," the priest crooned. "This be a wee bit o' insurance 'gainst lean days. If I know ye, an' I do, ye'll be wantin' to spend all these lovely gems in one spot an' on one whore. But I'll be seein' to it ye don't."

Jack was furious, calling the priest a thief and many other similar although far more unpleasant names, but Liam, seemingly deaf to his friend's angry barrage, refused to bow to his will. He slid the oil out of the frame and placed it in his Latin missal to protect it. As he rarely consulted the missal, the painting would be safe enough.

Then Liam, bidding Jack to look the other way, hid the frame. "If ye be short on money, ye may come to me, an' I'll pry loose one o' those pretty baubles. But not befer," the priest said firmly. He knew, too, that when the gems were gone, the frame would be melted down. And after that? Well, let after that take care of itself!

Jack grumbled but said nothing more of it. With a jangling of their spurs the two horsemen urged their steeds to a rapid, jolting trot, leaving behind them the awakening city of Paris.

Chapter
Two

DOWN THE FORMAL length of the candle-lit banquet table Raoul de Marchaud thoughtfully studied his beautiful daughter. In the past several months she had grown paler, and tonight she appeared even more wan than before. Yet, he thought with a touch of pleasure, there was nothing surprising in that appearance. In the four months since he had whipped that bastard Irishman from her bed, Victorée had not been allowed to move from the Hôtel de Saint-Martin. Her exercise had been curtailed to walks in the formal garden, and her social life had been completely stopped.

"What is wrong, *ma chérie*?" he asked, his tone giving the endearment a sardonic twist.

Victorée shuddered, put down the crystal goblet filled with red wine, and pressed a hand to her abdomen. The heat of the closed room in July was stifling. Beads of perspiration broke out on her high forehead and ran in shallow rivulets down her face. Absentmindedly, she brushed away the moisture.

"It is n-nothing, *mon père*. I—I—" She paled even more and, gulping convulsively, bounded up from her chair, dress and jewels flashing in the artificial light, and ran from the room.

9

With a frown the comte de Saint-Martin settled back into
the carved chair and contemplated his daughter's unusual
behavior. For a moment he stared into the verdant depths of
the baguette-cut emerald on his finger, then quickly drained
his wine. Burning with a regal fire, the liquid seemed to
motivate him to action. He slowly rose, straightening the
folds of his wine-colored velvet coat, then walked with a
deliberate tread out of the large dining hall.

The hawk-faced man strode down the corridors until he
reached her room. He stopped, remembering that late winter
morning some four months ago when he had been awakened
by her loud, lustful cries. Thinking at first that thieves had
entered the hôtel, the comte had clambered hastily into his
clothes and rushed to Victorée's room. And then when he had
burst in, he had found . . . that man . . . and his daughter.

The look of cunning on the girl's fair face had not been
missed by her father, and for a moment, with a wrenching of
his heart, he was reminded of Victorée's mother, the silver-
haired Elaine de la Vallière, whom he had discovered in
similar circumstances seventeen years before. He recalled in
an instant all the emotions of that long-ago spring day—his
pleasure in having cut short his journey to Nice, his unexpected return to his Paris home, his anticipation of once more
seeing and touching his newly wedded bride. And then the
sickening shock, the shame, the overwhelming despair, the
hatred coursing through him when he found his beautiful
Elaine and the illiterate son of the head groom in bed, their
naked bodies gleaming with the shine of sweat and love oils.

In those days his temper had been unrestrained. He was a
de Saint-Martin, a man whose family had been nobility in
France for centuries. A de Saint-Martin had sailed with the
Conqueror on his journey to England, and one had stood at
the royal side of that great emperor, Charlemagne. He was
someone. And Elaine had dared to mock him, had spurned a
thousand years of tradition and breeding, choosing in her
ill-bred lust this hard-muscled boy whose face lacked a spark
of wit and intelligence. Like an erupting volcano, de Marchaud's
temper had been unleashed. With a roar he had thrown himself across the room to their bed and with a mighty effort
gripped the neck of the stunned boy and given it a sickening
twist. The stable boy's brown eyes had bulged, his tongue
had protruded from his slack mouth. The body had jerked

convulsively, then gone still. "Quiet, you bitch!" the comte had screamed at the sobbing woman. "Slut!" De Marchaud had spit into her face, shocking her into terrified silence. "I shall teach you a lesson, she-dog. You shall never stray from me again." He had loomed above her, his hawklike face transformed into a mask of evil, then dropped his satin breeches. She had cowered against the pillows in terror, whimpering for his forgiveness, and then he had thrown himself upon her, savaging her with the force of his love turned to hate. And when it was over, he rested on one elbow and looked with contempt down at her bruised face as she lay cringing on the silken sheets, and he had vowed that she would never remove herself from his side or the sight of his handpicked servants. After that day Elaine had become a different woman, transformed from a laughing, spirited girl into a cowed, eager-to-please mouse, who rarely ventured out of the hôtel and then never without the constant companionship of two large, brutish guards who delighted in tormenting her. And in the course of a year she had produced a child and died with a certain amount of relief both to herself and to her husband.

He was a fool, Raoul de Marchaud thought bitterly to himself, to think the daughter would grow up to be different from the mother. With a shudder, the comte brought his mind back to the present.

He knocked at Victorée's bedroom door, a sharp, penetrating rap. Silence answered him. He smiled grimly, his thin lips stretching unpleasantly. The comte pulled out a key from an inner pocket, inserted it, and then entered as the door swung open. Quickly Raoul de Marchaud glanced around. The gold and sepia room was empty, but the window, shutters ajar, was open, the curtains moving in a slight breeze that brought with it the heady aroma of flowers in bloom. He crossed to the window and looked out into the moonlit garden. His daughter, her white hair a beacon in the night, had changed into a simple dark dress. She had hitched up her skirts and was slipping with stealth across the garden in the general direction of the stables. He laughed unpleasantly, although no sound came out. Moving to the bellpull, he gave it a sharp tug. In moments a sober-faced servant, an older man with a fall of white hair, appeared.

"Send in Carel."

The servant bowed. "Very good, monsieur." Soon the

large brutish servant with the scarred face appeared, grinning,
though the whites of his eyes showed in fear. He had suffered
Raoul de Marchaud's wrath for permitting the Irishman to slip
free four months ago. The wound that Carel had suffered
from Liam's pistol had only been a flesh wound. It was the
other wound, the one of the mind that the count had inflicted,
which still pained him. Carel ducked his lumpish head as
though expecting a blow to his ears.

De Marchaud did not turn. Keeping his velvet-clad back to
the mute Slav, he commanded, "Bring her back, Carel." The
man started to leave. "But," the nobleman warned, raising
an admonitory hand, "do not hurt her."

Carel shambled out. From his vantage point in the darkened room, de Marchaud watched as the man loped across the
garden, trampling tender flowers in his haste to reach the
fleeing girl.

The comte heard the young girl give a shrill cry as she
slapped the big man's face. Carel made mewing sounds, then
grabbed at her, ripping her dress in the process. He grinned,
then slung her with little effort over his beefy shoulder. She
beat at his impervious back with her tightly balled fists and
hissed at him, cursing him and his parentage fluently. He
appeared not to hear, nor to feel her blows and loped back
into the hôtel. The cursing grew steadily louder until Carel
appeared with the girl still slung over his shoulder.

"Set her down, Carel," the dark nobleman directed.

The brute gently placed her on her feet and brushed at her
clothes with a clumsy paw. She turned on him, slamming a
fist into his abdomen. A trickle of saliva drooling from the
corner of his slack mouth, he grinned at her and, like a giant
watchdog, waited for his master's next command. Victorée
backed away.

"That's enough, Carel. You may go to the kitchen now
and claim your reward."

Happily, Carel shambled over to the comte and, taking the
manicured hand with the emerald ring, stroked it with one
meaty paw and made pathetic noises of gratitude. He released
his master's hand and turned and, passing Victorée, gazed
adoringly at her. She frowned, then drew further away. The
servant closed the door behind him, and father and daughter
were alone.

De Marchaud moved about the room, lighting candles. He

then turned and looked at his daughter. Her white arms were folded, and her head was raised proudly. She disdainfully looked back at him. "Pull down your skirts," he commanded.

"No!" Her tone was defiant.

"You wish to show off your so-pretty derrière, my sweet?" A light flickered momentarily in his dark eyes. "Then an arrangement more to your liking could be established. There is a certain brothel in Paris. La Ruine des Femmes." Her pale eyes widened with fear. "Ah, I see you have heard of it. Then its reputation has reached even your sheltered ears. Good. I shall not have to bore you with details you already apparently know—and appreciate. You do know that a woman sent there does not stay long? Wives and daughters who misbehave are sent there for varying lengths of time to, shall we say, study. It is said that their courses do not require any longer than a week. They learn quickly—oh so quickly—return home, and do not ever question their lords again."

He moved across the room and sat in a gold velvet chair, one leg outstretched. He regarded the wheat-colored hose, the maroon garter, the diamonds on the shoe's buckles. "Carel worked there once, long before he entered my service. He has not forgotten his old ways."

Victorée licked her dry lips. Her voice was hoarse when she finally spoke. "Y-you don't have to send me there, *mon père*. What do you want of me?"

"Ah, so obedient now—and such a fast learner!" He chuckled. "Why were you trying to leave tonight, my sweet? Do I not give you money and presents, everything your greedy heart could possibly desire?"

"Yes, *mon père*," she replied dutifully.

"Well, then, child?"

"I had to leave secretly, *mon père*. I have to—I must go to the country. At once," she said with a note of agitation in her husky voice.

"And why?" he pressed.

Her pale eyes slipped past him and looked out through the window at the night. "To m-meet a lover, *mon père*. W-we agreed to rendezvous—"

Instantly, Raoul de Marchaud was out of his chair. He raised a hand and slapped her face, the heavy gemstone on his finger leaving a red welt on the tender skin of her cheek. She cried out and raised both hands to her face. A sob broke from her trembling lips.

His lip curled in derision. "I am not impressed by your tears or sobs, my sweet. In my time I have seen far better actresses. Do not lie to me, Victorée. I want the truth out of you. I shall systematically beat you until I have it. Do you hear?" He smiled grimly, his eyes dwelling cruelly on the swelling mark. "Or, perhaps I shall call Carel back. He will be so willing to teach you manners—he knows some delightfully elaborate practices, all of them quite quaint, none of which will show on your pretty body." She cringed, tears now falling down her cheeks. "The truth, my daughter?"

"The truth, *mon père*." Her voice was husky with emotion. "I—I—" She whirled away, at last pulling her skirt down and straightening the folds of the simple material. "M-may I sit down?"

With a sweeping gesture of one slim hand he indicated a chair. She sat and stared at the wooden floor. Her foot moved convulsively. "I am with child."

The air whistled through his clenched teeth. "So. Who is the father?" He leaned back and steepled his fingers. "Let me see." He tapped his fingertips together and pursed his lips thoughtfully. "Hmmm. It must be the Irishman. There has been no one else since that unfortunate incident four months ago. Before? I do not know about that, but I do believe, my beautiful and wily daughter, that he was not the one to take your maidenhead."

"N-no, he did not. But he is the father."

"But still this revelation does not clear up the mystery of your intended journey to the country. Well, Victorée?" He smiled patiently at his daughter.

"I—I was going to the country, to our estate outside Chartres. There is an old woman there—Ulrica is her name—who makes . . . potions . . . to rid one . . . of unwanted . . ." She could not bear to say the word, and her voice trailed off. Victorée did not move her gaze to meet her father's intent eyes.

"Ulrica, eh?" His eyes took on a faraway expression, and for a few moments he said nothing. With a visible effort, he returned to the present. "I see that even young as you are, you have had wide experience. How many times have you found it necessary to visit the old witch?"

"Twice, *mon père*."

"The truth?" He snapped, his fingers curling.

Victorée watched his face fearfully. "Yes!"

"Just a pretty sixteen, and already my daughter is acting like a painted Paris whore. Ah, you women are all alike. First your mother, and now you. You are no different, no different at all." Sighing heavily, he rose stiffly from the chair. He paced slowly in front of the fireplace and the silent girl, his hands clasped behind his back.

Minutes ticked by. "*Mon père?*" she ventured.

"What do you want, slut?" His eyes were bright.

Victorée cringed at his tone. "*Mon père*, what am I to do?"

"My dear, you should have first thought of that before you lured the Irishman to bed." De Marchaud paced a few minutes longer, then faced her. "Victorée, you shall not drink that potion, or any that the old witch prepares for you. You might die. Your death would ruin my carefully constructed plans. When you reach the age of seventeen you are to marry the duc L'Este du Plessis. Nothing must impede that marriage, a most politically expedient one. I wish our two houses joined as one. There must be no hint of scandal, Victorée. Do you understand? Therefore, we shall take the route wherein lies the least risk for you, my pretty young brood mare."

"What can you mean, *mon père?*"

"You shall bear the child."

"No, *mon père!*" she wailed. She jumped out of the chair and threw herself at his feet. "*Mon père*, please, no! I do not wish it. Please!" The sound of her uncontrolled sobbing rose as she dropped her white head upon his bejeweled shoes.

No human emotion could be traced upon the comte's aging face. He spoke: the words were comforting, the tone was not. "There, there, my sweetling. When you have been delivered of this unwanted burden, I shall dispatch a servant, perhaps Carel, to tie that loose end of this very messy knot. And then you and I need not worry about an unwanted 'niece' or 'cousin' coming to us later or living quietly on the country estate. Is this not better?" He reached down and roughly grasped her pointed chin with his hand and lifted her tear-stained face. "This is better, *ma chérie*. Believe me."

Hesitantly, one of her hands touched his. "If you say so, *mon père*," she whispered meekly.

Idly Raoul de Marchaud, comte de Saint-Martin, stroked his daughter's silver hair. "I say so." And his voice was final.

The snow lay heavily upon the ground one day late in December. The winter sky was overcast, and a bone-penetrating chill had settled into the large house, not to be cast off by a roaring fire nor a shawl pulled tightly around the shivering shoulders.

Victorée, alone in her bedroom on her father's country estate outside the town of Chartres, languidly watched the snow fall in large flakes. Snow blanketed the sculptured greenery, shaped and trimmed to give the appearance of leaping stags. It gave the trees and bushes a strange look, almost as though the animals had been frozen in midstride. Perhaps, she thought, those hideous forms were indeed once real animals.

Rising with care, Victorée waddled away from the window. Suddenly a pain stabbed through her, and she caught frantically at her side. She pressed hard at her flesh, but the pain would not recede. A moan escaping her red lips, she slipped into unconsciousness as she fell to the floor.

She awoke to the twin rhythms of pain in her abdomen and head. She lay in the wide maple bed, tall white tapers blazing all around her. Victorée blinked in the yellow, tallow-filled air. A woman of undeterminable years, yet obviously aged well before her time, huddled in a petit-point chair and snuffled, passing at her nose with the back of one gnarled hand.

"Ulrica," Victorée whispered, fighting the agony in her body. "What has happened?"

Ulrica's hair, long and gray, hung like greasy lengths of rope. Her wide-set eyes had once been a cornflower-blue, but now they were fading into an unhealthy white and were rheumy. High slanting cheekbones gave her face a thin look. Her nose, surprisingly, was long and straight, not a peasant's nose. Ancient rags, brown and gray, were her clothing. She had pulled the shreds of a once-white shawl around her bony shoulders, and upon her feet were the simple wooden sabots of the French peasant.

"You'll be having a *bébé*," she said at last. Despite her proficiency in French, the old woman gave the last word a strange foreign twist. With great effort she rose, shuffling over to the bedridden noblewoman. Gently, Ulrica touched the young woman's forehead. Her skin was hot, the face flushed. It would not be long.

She hobbled back to the chair by the fire and rubbed her hands together, seeking to warm their very depths. Aye, she must indeed be careful—for her Lord's daughter would be born this day, just as He had foretold her in the dream. And she herself would help in the birthing, an honor which was only right.

Victorée whimpered, and the old woman was drawn out of her thoughts. Ulrica peered at the girl, then fitfully rubbed a claw across her eyes. " 'Tis all right, sweetling. My Lord and Master's child will soon be here.'' She sat, her hands gripping the arms of the chair, rigid, staring at the orange and yellow flames of the fire.

Victorée tossed about in her labor. Fevered dreams drifted through her head. Her father was not in Paris; instead he had traveled on a large, soot-colored steed, shod with shoes of blazing steel. In one hand the hawk-faced man brandished the cruel bullwhip, newly oiled, that he had used on her red-haired Irish lover. In the other gauntleted hand he held, white-hot, a glowing iron rod. He moved forward, and his eyes were bottomless emerald pits, and he was thrusting that burning, searing iron into her and she was on fire, she was burning, and oh, *mon Dieu*, how she hurt! *Don't, mon père! Don't, please! I shall not disappoint you.*

Drenched in sour sweat, panting, she heard in the distance the church bells ringing out a joyous peal, and then nearby, the sharp squall of a newborn babe as the pain gave one final bone-splitting thrust. Victorée opened her eyes wearily. Her long white hair trailed wetly across her face. She tried to raise a hand to push it away, but she was too tired.

Ulrica held a white-skinned baby in her arms. She cleaned the child and then wrapped it carefully. ''Aye, it's a little girl. Born on Christmas Day.'' Demonic, ironic laughter rang through the room, rivaling the exaltation of the church bells.

Sapped of strength, Victorée managed to turn her head to the wall and let her eyelids, heavy with fatigue, droop. ''Take it away.'' She heard a grunting noise and knew that the mute Slav servant, Carel, had entered the lying-in room.

''I will take care of the *bébé*,'' Victorée heard the old crone say. She then spoke in a language unfamiliar to Victorée.

Carel shuffled to one side of his mistress's bed. Whimpering, he pawed at the heavy blankets covering the young noble-woman's exhausted form.

"Get away," she said wearily. "Leave me alone." She looked at Ulrica. "You will destroy the child?"

Ulrica stroked the child's eyebrows. "Like the wings of a raven," the old woman whispered reverently. The baby's eyes were an unfocused pale blue, which, with the eyebrows, gave the baby's face an expression of continual surprise. She gently stroked the wispy white hair.

"Ulrica!"

"Aye." She smiled slyly at the young woman. "I'll take care of the child."

"Y-you are to show Carel the b-body after it's done. Is that agreed, old woman?"

"Oh, yes." She grinned happily around the gaps in her mouth. "But first my payment. Payment for the deed and to seal my mouth."

Victorée, regarding the half-wit brute, thought she knew a most effective means of silencing the crone. The servant tugged at his too-short vest and goggled at the child, who screwed up her miniature face to cry. He drew back in dismay. Quickly the old woman placed a hand over the child's mouth and whispered something into her tiny ear. Instantly the baby quieted and fell asleep. Victorée felt a shiver of alarm run through her. She could do nothing about the old woman. Her father would not approve of any devia-tion from his original plan—and she was far too frightened of him to make an independent move, anyway. She sighed and indicated the large maple dresser along one wallpapered wall.

"In it you will find a small purse of gold. It is yours to keep." The old woman started toward the dresser. Victorée raised one imperative hand unsteadily. "When the deed is finished." Carel whimpered and clung to the old woman's skirts. She ignored him.

"You'll see the body—or at least this one will. Send him to me in an hour's time."

"Why can't you do it here?" the girl demanded.

"In front of you? It would not be a pleasant sight, mistress, to see the life choked from the child. . . ." The albino woman shuddered. "I do not think you would like that."

"No," the girl said quickly. "But, *mon Dieu*, remove it before it cries. And be careful."

"I will be, I will be," the old woman assured her. "Old Ulrica will do it proper. Yes, yes. She will, will she." Quickly, the old woman bundled the child up and slipped her under a dark cloth in her basket. No one would ever know about the precious bundle she carried as she walked through the country house, past the silent loyal servants. Ulrica left the room and Carel followed at her heels, but he stopped as she left the house. He stood watching for a moment longer, then wandered down to the kitchen.

Down the mile-long walk past the line of stately poplars Ulrica rushed. As she hurried down the snow-covered lane she giggled aloud, then glanced furtively around lest anyone should hear. But no one was out in the snow that Christmas Day. Her Lord had come to her in a dream the very night before the birth. "A child, a girl, will be born tomorrow. My daughter. You will raise her as befits my child," he had instructed her. "You will name her"—and he had paused, a great smile on his black face revealing ivory tusks—"Angel!" Old Ulrica had laughed long at the irony and had fervently agreed to do her Master's bidding.

When Ulrica reached her ramshackle hut, she pulled the silent child from the basket. "You wee little one," she crooned, lifting the child carefully. Without hesitation, she pulled open the soiled bodice of her ragged dress and offered a withered teat to the newborn baby. The child did not move, and Ulrica looked sadly at her breast. "*Ano*, there's no milk for you, little imp. But I shall steal you a goat, and you'll grow up strong and healthy on the nanny's milk.

"You are my little Angel. And they will never, never know about you. You'll be hidden here, my dear." Ulrica gave the baby several sips of a weak tea she had prepared beforehand, long before she had wound her way up to the large country house, and then, taking the child into the hut, tucked her warmly out of sight.

Some time later Ulrica heard a loud crunching noise and saw Carel, a coating of white snow on his hair and body, shambling toward the hut. Once he lost his footing on a patch of ice and, falling, skidded down a slope to land headfirst near the mire. He picked himself up and lumbered into the hut, looking with curiosity at his surroundings. Wrinkling his broken lump of a nose at the stagnant odor, he grunted at the old woman. She moved away from the great black pot set over the small fire. "It's done, all right." The crone held up a nasty concoction of bones and raw meat and blood. Blood had spattered on her dress, staining it even further. "Do you wish some? 'Tis sure to be a tasty tidbit!"

Carel cowered, shaking his furry head, then, taking courage, he touched one of the fragile bones. He held his hands about ten inches apart.

"Is it the *bébé*? Of course, it is, you dolt! What else would it be? A dead rabbit?" He shook his head slowly from side to side like a child and reluctantly pulled out the purse of gold. Carel tossed it to her, and the old woman grabbed it agilely with one gnarled hand. She stuffed it inside the open bodice of her dress.

"Tell your mistress the deed is done. She need not worry about the child. Old Ulrica keeps her word."

The manservant turned and stumbled out of the marsh, away from the crazy woman, the noisome odors, the strange sounds rising off the swamp. She watched and waited until he was out of sight and she was sure he would not return, then tossed into the frost-covered mire the bones and body and blood of her newly sacrificed rabbit. Ulrica cackled with laughter, the eerie sound rising from the snow-covered land, and then entered the hut to tend her Angel.

Chapter

Three

"YOU POXY WHORESON!" the shrill piping voice exclaimed. Liam, startled, his mouth agape, looked at the dark shape, which until a moment ago had lain still in the middle of the old Roman roadway. Mistaking it for a lump of mud, he'd urged his mount to jog past it. Then suddenly it had risen, startling both rider and weary mount. Having sipped a little more freely than usual the nectar of the gods, Liam was none too steady, and his trembling hands were loose upon the reins. As his horse reared from the mud-streaked shrieking creature that arose from the broken stones, the priest's arms flailed frantically, imitating closely the actions of a small windmill. Within a matter of seconds his efforts to retain his precarious perch failed, and with a bone-jarring thud he landed on his posterior alongside his pawing and snorting mount, whose sides heaved with fright. Liam glared at the frightful apparition, who had come into focus as a small child, a little girl by her looks—although, if the truth be known, Liam thought, he was none too sure.

"Sweet Jaysus, look what ye've gone an' done now! Aye, a hard time I'll be havin' quietin' Shannon down—what an' ye've gone an' scared him silly, the poor foolish beast. Ah, Holy Mither o' God.'' With a heartrending sigh, Laim rose to his wobbly feet, dusting off his stained cassock. He looked blankly around for the horse, who stood behind him and playfully pushed at the cleric's back with his muzzle.

A sudden expression of cunning passed over the child's gamin and dirty face, transforming it into the very mask of slyness. ''I curse you in the name of my father, the Lord of Darkness, Satan!''

At this hideous pronouncement out of the mouth of such a small tot, Liam quickly crossed himself. The child recoiled and then waited with an air of expectancy, obviously believing the sky would cloud over and lightning would strike the priest where he stood. But nothing happened. The slight breeze continued to blow, ruffling the child's long tangled locks, the sun still shone warmly, and the man just stood there, his hands on his hips. She frowned and stamped her foot impatiently.

Something must be done, Father Liam decided, and then taking a practical turn, he quickly upended the filthy child—but holding her at arm's length, for upon his soul he'd not smelled such a ripe scent since he'd left Venice a year ago—and shook her in short jerky movements so that her teeth rattled in her head. Then he cast about and, spying a mud puddle spanning the width of the uneven road, gently dropped her in headfirst. Such treatment appeared to charm the wild creature, for when she emerged from the puddle, broken twigs twisted in her tangled hair, brown goo dripping in great globs off her pointed chin, she greeted him with a brilliant smile, as warm and open and inviting as the sunshine on a spring day. She gave a little skip, hopping first on one foot, then the other, and shook her arms over her head, the motion pulling up her soiled rags to reveal a naked muddy bottom. Liam, sighing, looked in the other direction. What a little pagan she be, he thought.

She clapped her tiny hands together. ''You are not afraid of me, m'sieur. That is good. I usually frighten everyone. I am a great ogre. For this I even forgive you for almost stepping on me with your horse.''

''The likes o' ye forgive me?'' hiccuped Liam at the sound of royal condescension in the childish piping voice. '' 'Twas all yer fault—what with ye rearin' up from the middle o' the road where ye'd no business in the first place, spookin' me poor Shannon. An' me almost breakin' me neck from the fall! Brazen as a Blade ye be, imp!''

"*Alors, c'est la vie,*" she said, smiling. "If you had not been so drunk, you would not have fallen.'' Shrugging in the age-old Gallic fashion, without further ceremony she squatted at the roadside and vigorously scrubbed her stained face with a handful of grass. She brushed at her bottom with her hands, then sniffled and dabbed a hand across her straight nose.

Father Liam Dougherty, swaying in the center of the road, glanced down its deserted length and blinked drunkenly at the verdant countryside. Everywhere he looked he saw trees unfolding their new foliage, flowers blooming in a riot of bright colors. Ah, 'twas spring again. A lovely time to spend in France, he remarked to himself. It had been on the high side of five years—almost six, he amended—since last he and Jack had ridden through France. The years had been good. And bad. Life was a series of rather interesting escapades and romantic entanglements for Jack to fall into—and then as quickly fall out of. And with a little help from his priestly friend, who looked the other way, or held a furtive hand out behind his back, Jack prospered. Ah, Jack . . . Liam paused, running a hand through his straw-colored hair. He gazed about the unfamiliar countryside with bleary bloodshot eyes. Where *was* Jack?

"Where be we, child?" he inquired of the grubby girl, bending down.

"We are in my home, m'sieur," she replied prettily, glancing out the corner of her light-colored eyes at Shannon, who, his nerves now calmed, had begun cropping the long lush grass growing alongside the road. The little girl licked her lips.

"But where be that?" Distress began to show in the priest's voice.

Impatience seized her. "I do not know, stupid sir. Kindly do not plague me." She turned her back on him and marched off to the right, across a small lea to where a marsh began. A chill wind blew off it, scudding thin gray mists before it. Liam shivered and thought wistfully of the inn and its warm and cheering taproom some miles back where he'd passed such a pleasant afternoon. He was far gone in his ales, and he had no practical idea as to where—or how—he could find

Jack. Where was their rendezvous point? They'd left Milan together, riding north. Once they were out of the city they had separated, and Jack had said to meet him in . . . in. . . . The priest sighed. All he knew was that it was in France, their meeting place. Still, to ride on was imperative, for he had faithfully promised to meet his friend after their disastrous flight, and now he was three days overdue in wherever he was supposed to be. Oh, how he regretted the time wasted, simply wasted, at that tavern. Yet . . . yet, it had not all gone for naught. He belched softly with fond remembrance of the fine dark wines he had swilled and the light ales, as tasty as ever he'd had, and—With a small rustling noise at his feet, his attention was brought back to the child.

She had returned and now stooped by a puddle and playfully splashed water on her face. The dirt ran down her face, and as the child's features emerged from a week-old coating of grime and mud Liam, even in his drunken fog, felt a prickle of curiosity. No lumpish peasant child was she. Her silvery gray eyes, wide-set and accentuated by wing-swept black eyebrows, the patrician nose, the heart-shaped face, the fine texture of her skin, the haughty set of the queenly little head crowned with a glorious silver-white mane, albeit dirty at present, bespoke noble blood. She was an odd-looking child to be sure, but lovely, he decided, simply lovely. His heart softened toward the waif. Some noble by-blow, no doubt, Liam thought sympathetically and instantly offered a prayer for the child and her misfortunes, which he was sure she had suffered.

"Tell me, colleen, where do ye live?" the priest asked her.

"Out in yon marsh with my protectress and her familiar." The little girl pointed with her chin toward the east, where a foul green-gray cloud hovered. "She is a very fine witch, you know," she continued in a confidential tone and with a conspiratorial wink. "I have been given into her care by my father, Lucifer, until I shall come of age."

"Dear me, little one, 'tis all very interestin', all this about the divil an' a witch an' a familiar. Ye have a right vivid imagination." He sighed and reached out a hand to touch her tousled hair. She ducked and stuck her tongue impudently out at him.

"I have been warned never to trust those such as you," she growled in a low, husky voice, casting her gray eyes about.

"S-such as me?" he stammered drunkenly.

"*Oui*, the spawn of the dead Church, the baby-killers, the eaters of human flesh." Her fine features screwed into an alarming sneer, and the good priest felt terror spread through him.

"Me wee agate, ye must not say such things." He glanced quickly over his shoulder and made the sign of the cross. "Old Nick might be around. Do ye not know o' the terrible story o' the Blades?" The child shook her head.

"Many years ago befer ye be born, there came across to me home a most heartless tale o' an Englishman, name o' Blade, who kidnapped a highborn lady, a right sweet one she be, too. This monster ravished her, killed her brothers an' father, who tried manfully to protect her virtue. He gained the lands o' her dead menfolk, an' quite extensive lands those be, too. She found herself, poor heart, with child, an' when the child be born, a dark thing to look 'pon—aye, some whispered it be the very child o' the divil—well, broken o' heart an' spirit, she killed herself. The father died a few years later. Broke his neck when he be thrown from a hell's spawn o' a horse, an' sure it be God's judgment 'pon him.

"So ye see, child," Liam concluded in lofty tones, "it don't be paying fer ye to mock God an' invoke the divil. Now, what be ye thinkin' o' that wicked tale?" He reached forward to give her a reassuring pat, for she had remained completely silent during his story.

The girl recoiled, flinging her arm over her eyes. She huddled in the center of the road and moaned piteously, like a drowning kitten. "What be wrong, little one?"

"Your hand!" she shrieked. "Your hand—you are burning me! Help me, Father of Darkness, help me, Father! The Black Boy is taking me from you!"

Liam felt a coldness prickle his neck and wondered if the child were possessed by devils. He started to make the sign of the cross again but hesitated, remembering all of a sudden what his dear old sainted mother, may she rest in peace, had told him once long ago, years before she'd passed on. She had said that most "possessed" children didn't need devils driven out of them; they simply needed firm disciplining. "E've applied t' brich t' me daughters an' sons, an' ye don't be seein' none o' 'em speakin' o' divils an' such." And that was true, Liam reflected, for of his thirteen brothers and sisters, ten of them had found a higher vocation and had entered the Holy Church as monks, nuns, and priests. Of the three remaining outside the Church in the laity, why, they'd led exemplary lives, lives almost like the saints of olden times—except, of course, for the oldest, Black Michael, God rest his wicked soul, who was hanged as a horse thief.

He stared in bewilderment at the little silver-haired girl who was running back and forth in the dirt and mud, screaming and clawing at her hair and face. She flapped her arms about in a great frenzy. He made up his mind and, bending down, picked up the fighting bundle. He placed the kicking child over his shoulder, then brought a firm strong hand down on her bare bottom. She screamed in protest. He continued to spank. She screamed and screamed and screamed. And, finally, no sounds came from her. Blessed silence reigned. "Ye can be let down if ye've had enough o' that screamin' an' such. What nonsense fer a young lady to be carryin' on with." He heard a sniffle. "Be ye finished?"

"Yes, m'sieur," she said in a meek tone. For good measure, he gave her one more slap, then set her down on her small feet. She dropped her gaze to the road and, with both hands, rubbed her sore bottom.

"What be yer name, child?" Father Liam asked in a firm no-nonsense tone.

"Angel."

Angel, indeed! thought Liam ironically. "Devil's Spawn" might well be nearer the mark! "Well, Angel, what be the names o' yer parents?"

Her voice was tear-filled. "I—I have no mother. She is gone these many years, m'sieur. And my father is Satan."

"Indeed." She quavered at the tone of the single word. "What do ye do, child?"

"I run in the woods, and swim, and gather herbs and fire sticks for Old Woman, and climb trees and—"

"An' jump up out in the middle o' the road an' scare poor strangers to death!"

Angel looked up briefly, a twinkle of amusement in her gray eyes. "Oui, m'sieur, but that is all I really do." She shrugged, a quaintly philosophical gesture in one so young. "I like what I do. I am going to grow up to be a witch like Old Woman."

Liam felt a tug of pity that so bright and charming a child

should be raised as a wild creature by a godless witch. It was obvious that she had had little or no contact with the world, as she kept babbling on about Lucifer even in the face of the priest's crucifix and cassock. However, it seemed she had been taught that the sign of the cross was an awful thing to behold.

"First, me child, ye must call me 'Faither Liam.' Now that this be settled, come along, wee one, an' I'll take ye home."

Catching the trailing reins of the grazing Shannon, Liam Dougherty attempted to swing up into the saddle but, missing the stirrup, stumbled against the bay's soft flank. A muted giggle sounded from behind him, but when he whirled unsteadily, his gaze strict and stern, a sober little face was upturned toward him. He righted himself with some difficulty, patted the horse soothingly, and then with careful dignity mounted. Liam reached down for the little girl. She hesitated, gazing deep into his clouded blue eyes, and, seeming to make up her mind, held out her arms.

Once the girl was seated in front of him, the priest said, "Tell me, darlin', how do we be gettin' to yer home?"

"Across the marsh," Angel stated calmly. "This is a very fine horse." She gently patted Shannon's shaggy neck, and the horse nickered in response. "I am very fond of horses."

"Well, Shannon be right fond o' little ladies, an' he moves like glass, so ye'll have a smooth ride."

"You go straight through this path," the little girl directed, leaning back against the priest's chest. "Then take the cut here and follow the trail. Don't stray, or we'll go down in the bog before you can say 'Devil's hoofprint!' "

Liam felt alarm expand through him. Aye, Queen of Heaven, this was no place for a wee one—much less a poor priest such as himself—to be! "Be that so, darlin'?" He clutched her tighter in front of him, and she squealed with excitement.

"What's glass?" Angel craned her head around to peer at the man.

"It be like water in a clear pond—only it be hard an' not wet at all."

"Oh." The girl seemed satisfied with the priest's answer. Now it was his turn to ask questions. "Where did ye learn to like horses, wee one? Ye can't be seein' many where ye be livin', can ye?"

"We often have them," she replied confidently. "Old Woman finds them in the marsh."

"Ye have them?" the priest asked cautiously.

"*Oui*," she said in a matter-of-fact tone, "in a stew—with onion grass and wild cabbage." She patted her stomach and smacked her lips loudly. "Very good," Angel declared in a queenly manner.

Bile rose in the drunken priest's gorge, but he successfully fought the nausea down. Well, of course, it was only logical, if not particularly natural, that the poor child and her guardian would eat whatever animal strayed into the marsh. And it was rumored that the Frenchies ate almost anything, edible or not. But still, a horse . . . horses. . . . Sweat broke out on his forehead. He decided to change the subject and asked her about the land nearby. Angel gladly answered the priest's questions and regaled him with stories of the marsh and its denizens, two-legged and four-legged.

Guided by the silver-haired Angel's delicate and imperious little hand, Father Dougherty spurred his bay mount through the marsh in the deepening twilight. As they rode, tendrils of noisome white mist rose and crept across their path, and the wailing cries of night birds cut through the gloom. Suddenly, through the bleak air, a fitful red glare appeared. Shannon shied, and Liam reassuringly patted his mount. As they drew nearer odd murmurings grew audible, and in spite of himself Liam felt a superstitious chill run through him. At last they broke free from the clinging mud and marsh grass into a dry clearing.

Set back a few hundred paces from the marsh, a primitive hut, made of thatch and broken boards gray with age and cast-off pieces of firewood, leaned precariously against a rocky cliff. In front of the hut—if it could indeed be honored with that appellation, thought Liam—a goat, appearing to be all skin and bones and floppy ears, nibbled halfheartedly at the rank grasses struggling to grow in the clearing. To the goat's left burned a flickering fire. An old woman sat crouched near the red and yellow flames, her lips moving in an endless meaningless babble. Liam noted that her eyes were the milky white of the near-blind and that her gray hair grew out of her head like greasy spikes.

"Stefan? Georgi? Katya?" she called in a hopeful tone, her voice cracking with effort.

Angel put her fingers to her lips and, leaning close toward the priest, whispered, "Those were the names of her babies. Long ago they were torn away from her. They were hurt by the Christians—their eyes were put out and their arms and legs broken. And then her husband and her babies were put to the torch. And it was after that that my father first came to her."

The priest shivered and crossed himself, murmuring a prayer. "Why—why were they killed?"

The little girl shrugged. "Who knows? I think it was because they were the wrong sort of Christian. It is hard to understand. The Christians always seem to be fighting one another. She does not speak much of it. Just when the moon is full." She glanced up at the rising yellow moon riding eerily through the rough sea of clouds. "Like tonight. She is very strange. I think she will probably put a curse on you. I am quite sure your nose will fall off. No doubt you will melt down into a puddle of slimy grease." Liam frowned deeply at the obvious glee in the child's voice.

Halting his horse, Liam slid to the ground and reached up for the child. As soon as Angel's sabot-clad feet struck the ground, the old woman's incantations ceased.

"Angel, is that you?" The fire flared up, the light reflecting on Father Liam's golden crucifix. With the speed of a striking serpent, the aged crone scuttled around the fire, a dagger clutched in her clawlike hand.

"Angel! Fool! Whelp! You have brought a servant of the Unmentionable!" Her gnarled hand flew out to strike the child, but Liam stepped in front of Angel to intercept the blow. "Fool," Ulrica hissed, backing away, jerking her arm from his grasp as though his touch were that of a brand. "Priest of a dead god," she sneered. "Leave before I place the curse of Satan upon you. Your insides will bubble and twist, and never again will you know peace of mind. You, whose brain is full of ale. Your skin will melt and rot, running in great droplets down—"

Liam raised his hand. "May the Lord have mercy upon yer soul, ould woman."

She recoiled but was silent. The goat continued its audible munching. Ulrica drew herself up to her full bent height and, fingers curved like talons and still clutching the knife, leaped at the priest. In his mind Liam saw the image of a great gray

spider. Panicked, he started to dodge, then thrust out his arms
and pushed her. Howling curses, the old woman fell to the
dirt at his feet. Angel stared, wide-eyed, her mouth hanging
open. Before Liam could move to the child, a black demon
erupted as though from the fire. Sparks scattering before its
rush, eyes glazed red from the firelight, the cat leaped for
Liam's face, claws outstretched. He flung out an arm to
deflect it but succeeded only partially. One paw ripped open
his right cheek. Whirling, Liam threw back a fold in his
cassock and drew his sword, a weapon he had taken to
wearing since his feet first touched the road of illegal activity.
Before the feline could move again, with a whistling slash of
his gleaming sword the priest separated head from body.
Before the Irishman's terrified eyes, it seemed, a thin white
mist, terrible to behold, formed above the body of the cat and
blew away, keening, into the abysmal darkness. A piteous
weeping arose from the old woman. Father Liam whirled and
brandished the steel blade in front of her aged eyes.

"Where did ye come by this child, ould bitch? Speak, or
I'll split ye where ye lie!"

"She is the child of my Master," the old woman crooned,
rocking back and forth. "Can you not see it in her fair face?"
Puzzled, Liam turned to study the girl, who was still watching with widened eyes. The only discordant feature in her
piquant face, aside from her terror, were the black eyebrows.
And she had the devil's own temper, the man thought ruefully.

On an impulse, Liam staggered to the hut and entered. The
walls kept no cold wind from entering, and through the crude
roof above he could see the stars blinking. The stench was
overpowering, a blend of urine and excrement both human
and animal. In one corner was heaped a filthy straw pallet,
stained with muck and fairly alive with crawling vermin. It
was the only bed. No other furniture stood inside. In one
corner lay a cracked pitcher and a few stubs of yellowish
candles. Choking on the foul fumes and the heady liquor he
had consumed in awesome quantities earlier that day, the
priest reeled back into the yard.

The old woman cackled. "The perfume of the Lord of
Darkness is not for all, priest."

"Be still," he commanded, his voice harsh. Tugging thoughtfully at his light-colored hair, he studied the wide-eyed child
in front of him. Angel stood, her beauty not concealed even

by the grime. She tossed her head, her silver hair sweeping back, and stared without fear at him.

What a little lady she be, he told himself. *That child be no peasant, Liam. Ye must be doin' somethin'. Ye can't go leavin' the wee one here.*

I know, I know. But what can I do? he asked himself silently.

Ye ain't a good man, Faither Liam Dougherty.

I know that, too.

Ye drink too much. Ye steal. Ye covet riches. Ye lie.

Aye, I know all this.

Ah, Liam me boy, at least ye don't wench.

That be correct—I ain't a complete bad 'un.

True enough. After all, a man must have some standards by which he must live.

Having decided that breaking two out of three priestly vows was not a weighty matter upon which the salvation of his soul would depend—although his religious superior would have heartily disagreed—he made up his mind. Liam would have to steal the little girl away and take her to the blessed sisters, where she could be brought up as a good Christian girl. But first he must lull the old woman, for he had the unnerving feeling she might be a wee bit unhappy about this turn of events. Now, how could he disarm her? The fire flickered suddenly from a breeze, and he smiled slowly to himself as a plan formed in his mind.

"W-what be that?" the priest stammered, dropping his sword, and pointed beyond the hag's shoulder. He fell back, terror etched on his round face. "L-look. Save me, save me, L-Lord!" The priest dropped to his knees and covered his face with quaking hands. The old crone cackled and turned, prepared to see her Master, as she had before in her dreams. Angel, clearly puzzled, looked first at the priest, then at the old woman, then back at the cowering man. Ulrica squinted and peered into the dark.

"Why, there's nothing there, you fool!" she screeched. But Liam had grabbed his sword from the ground and now thunked her hard on the head with the flat of the blade. With a moan, her eyes rolling back into her head, she slumped to the ground. Swiftly Liam stood, sheathed his sword, grabbed Angel around the waist, and swung up into the saddle.

"Let me go, you beast!" the child wailed, beating at the

priest with clenched fists. "You have killed her! You have killed Old Woman! I hate you, you wicked man!"

"Now, quiet down, child." The Irishman gripped her hands, then shook her until her teeth rattled in her head. "She's not dead, merely stunned."

"Stunned?"

"Aye, in an hour or so she'll wake up an' be none the worse fer it. She might be havin' a wee small headache, but that be all, little one."

The flow of tears abated somewhat, and suspicion passed from her face. "If that's all that will happen to her. . . ."

"That be all," the priest reassured the little girl.

"Where then are we going, m'sieur?"

"I'll be takin' ye to a good home," he said, lying just a wee bit for there was no sense telling the poor mite all about the convent. Perhaps he should offer her a bribe, to lull her. Aye, that would be good. "Ye'll have a horse o' yer own. Although," he amended hastily, "not to eat, but rather to ride. Ye'll eat off fine china plates an' wear lovely clothes."

"Is that so, m'sieur? Well, I think I might be interested," she said in an adult tone. Snuggling close to the priest, Angel closed her gray eyes. In a matter of minutes he heard gentle snores and smiled tenderly at her in the moonlight. Wasn't she the precious one now? Wouldn't Jack be surprised when he—Mither of God! he thought frantically. *What am I goin' to tell Jack? It'll just have to be the truth.* He could not think of a good enough story, not one that would satisfy Jack, anyway. He sighed soulfully. For once the truth would prove to be the fair route. And, speaking of routes, he had best remember where he had planned to meet the other Irishman. Liam sighed again and continued riding through the black night.

Perched before Liam, the child gazed with rapt attention at the great city of Paris. Wagons and carts rumbled through the dirt-packed and cobblestoned streets, while the shrill cries of vendors and hawkers split the crisp morning air. Men in short cloaks, women in plain dresses and shawls with baskets over their arms, jostled past the cleric and the little girl, never giving them a second glance. The multistoried buildings alone bewildered and at first intimidated the child, who had never seen anything larger than a few rough farmhouses or the

miserable hut which had been her home and had never traveled further than two or three miles from the marsh. In time,
however, Angel grew accustomed to the loud noises and,
raising her head from where she had buried it against Liam's
chest, began to peer about with bright curious eyes. The noise
and bustle made her twist from side to side in Liam's grasp,
engendering muttered oaths from the man.

"Is it still will ye be sittin'! Like as not ye'll land in yon
gutter!"

Angel looked down at the crude trench running the length
of the unpaved street. Foul odors rose from it. She wrinkled
her fine nose in disgust. "That I would not like, for this place
smells very bad, very bad, indeed." Considering the vile
swamp from which Angel came, Liam thought that that was a
case of the pot calling the kettle black. "It is all so big, so
many people. Where do they all come from? Where are they
going? What's that? Who's that beautiful lady? Why does that
man have only one leg? Look, he has a patch on his eye! Why
is that goat all black? Are chickens worth less than pigs?

"How wonderful!" Angel exclaimed, clapping her hands
together. Her gray eyes danced with merriment. "This is such
an exciting place to be!"

Aye, some might say that, Liam grudgingly admitted to
himself. 'Twas the year of our Lord 1676. King Louis XIV,
the self-proclaimed Sun King, had sat upon the throne of
France for thirty-three years, and the nation was now reputed
to be one of the most powerful in the world. Even in the
common workman in the street, mused the Irish priest, there
seemed to be a pride, an élan, a French arrogance matched
nowhere else in the world.

Occasionally a gentleman, rich in saffron or burgundy satin
and velvet, with periwig daintily set upon his shorn head,
would ride disdainfully through the crowds, never deigning to
look down at the common throng of humanity pressing around
him. Or passing them would be an ornate sedan chair, its four
bearers running swiftly through the crowd.

"What is in the boxes?" questioned the child.

"Ye goose! Those be sedan chairs, an' they be no doubt
carryin' some highborn lady to a rendezvous."

"What's a rendezvous?"

"It's when a woman slips off from her lawful wedded
husband into the arms o' a lover."

"Oh," the little girl sniffed, "it is but a fancy word for rutting."

Stifling an unpriestly chuckle, Liam guided their mount down a narrow, crooked street. Wooden houses, covered with the soot and grime of centuries, leaned at precarious angles over the dirty streets. Overhead a window was flung open and they heard a cry. " 'Ware!" Liam quickly spurred the horse ahead and none too soon, for down where they had been riding came tumbling the noisome contents of a chamber pot. Angel wrinkled her nose and Liam, laughing, hugged her close.

They rode on, cutting from one street to another. Near the sun's zenith Father Liam halted Shannon before one of the sturdier-looking edifices, and Angel agilely leaped to the ground. She darted to the horse's head and bestowed a wet kiss upon his grizzled muzzle.

"*Merci*, Shannon. You are a good horse. And I do not think I will eat you. You brought us to Paris, where M'sieur Liam and I will do . . . What are we to do here, anyway, M'sieur Liam?"

The priest grunted as he swung stiffly from the saddle and shook out the folds of his black cassock. He straightened his black cloak about his shoulders, carefully concealing the sword at his hip, for priests did not normally carry weapons. Liam rubbed his aching spine and massaged the calves of his legs through the leather boots. "We go to this inn an' see if me companion Jack be within, or if he be hanged fer theft, or spitted fer cheatin', or hacked in twain by a troublesome husband."

Tossing Shannon's reins and a coin to a ragged and grimy-faced urchin who had slunk up to them, Father Liam grasped Angel firmly by the hand.

A stout man approached them from a doorway where he had been watching them. His head was covered with an elaborate curling wig and his wrinkled cheeks reddened with rouge, and his velvet coat and breeches were somewhat worn in places. He smiled at the child, who drew her black brows together in a frown.

"Enchanting," he murmured to Liam as he chucked the little girl lightly under the chin. Liam drew the girl close to him before Angel could bite the man's pudgy fingers.

"I will give you five pennies for her, m'sieur." The man

smiled, the powder on his face cracking into minute lines that reminded Liam of old china.

"No," the priest said firmly.

"A copper piece then, sir," the man said in an oily voice. "Surely she can be of little use to you, Father."

Liam shook his head and pulled the girl along. She turned to stare back at the stranger.

"A silver one!" he called.

Liam jerked the little girl toward the inn.

"Why did he wish to buy me, M'sieur Liam?" she asked, her eyes big with curiosity.

"Never mind, child," Liam replied crossly.

They entered the rustic inn, avoiding the drunken porter, who leered down at the silver-haired child. Inside, the noisy inn was dark, little natural light reaching through the dirty windows. The walls were paneled with dark-stained wood, wood that had blackened over the ages with the heavy smoke of candles and fires, and to which was now added the smoke of the tobacco leaf in long-stemmed clay pipes—a new fashion in England and Europe.

Liam pulled her hand and she smiled at him, then followed quickly. They climbed swiftly up three flights of uneven stairs sadly in need of repair, the little girl's legs twinkling in an effort to match Liam's long strides. He went down the hallway. The first door. The second. Third. Now turn left. Knock once. Pause for the count of three. Knock twice. Pause for the count of three. Knock three times. Pause and wait, and if he be there, and if this be the proper place . . .

The door, scraped and battered with the indentations of furious fists and boots and drawn weapons throughout the years, was thrown open, and framed in the low portal stood a courtier of amazing proportions and striking appearance. Set upon his shoulder-length red hair, which fell in outrageous natural waves, was a wide-brimmed, cornflower-blue hat. The white plume, large and fairly ostentatious, curled about his right shoulder. A frothing fall of the finest Mechlin lace supported his sharp chin. His coat and breeches were the same shade of blue as the hat but were cut of the finest brocade Liam had ever seen. A wide scarlet sash enveloped the man's waist, and at his narrow hip hung a sword sheathed in a scabbard decorated with the finest of paste diamonds and sapphires. In one hand he held a straight cane of ebony, trimmed alternately with delicate ribbons of cornflower-blue and crimson. About his neck hung a gilt chain and a filigree ball, and from the pomander arose the cloying scent of cloves. On his fingers were rings, paste diamonds and sapphires set in ornate gold bases. A small, round black patch at the corner of his mouth completed the very picture of a dandy.

"Behold Lord Shanny Fitzwilliam!" cried the man, sweeping the magnificent hat off with a flourish. He made a deep bow, and Angel stared with amazement, her mouth open.

"I behold a peacock and a fool," said Liam with a mocking bow in return, then swiftly dodged the blow aimed at him by the laughing fop.

"God's eye, man, I'd thought ye dead by some filthy Italian bastard these ten days past! Where in hell—".

But the sentence was never completed, for, infuriated by the attack upon her mentor, the silver-haired child had drawn back her foot and landed a solid kick with her sabot on the man's unprotected shin. He howled in deep pain and leaped back, one-legged, in dismay.

"Here now, what have we here?" He squatted and gazed, green eyes level with gray ones, at the furious little figure. "Where did ye find this precious agate?"

"I took her away from an old divil's hag, livin' out in a marsh outside o' Chartres," replied Liam. He glanced down the hallway, worried that the pander out on the street might have followed them inside. He drew the girl inside the room, then closed the door behind them and added in an undertone, "Ye can plainly see she be no peasant child."

"Aye, Liam," his foppish companion sighed, "but what are we to do with her now that ye've taken her away from the old hag? We can't be draggin' a child about Europe, not with the life we live. She'll just be gettin' hurt, or in the way. Perhaps ye should return her to her home."

A look of sheepishness passed over the cleric's face. He scratched at his ear and cleared his throat. "I'll be tellin' ye, Jack . . . I don't remember *where* the marsh be exactly, jes' that it be in that area."

A hearty sigh was released from the soldier of fortune. "Were ye drinkin' again, Faither Liam?"

"Only the tiniest amount. Jes' a wee tiny nip was all. It couldn't be hurtin' none, it bein' so cold that day I be searchin' fer ye."

"Did ye not remember ye were to meet me here, in Paris?"
With exasperation, Jack looked at the priest.

"Well, no, to be perfectly truthful, Jack, I didn't. I let
Shannon have his head, an' he led me straight here."

"The horse has more sense than ye, ye addlepated priest.
No wonder the bishop sent ye on a pilgrimage to Rome—aye,
but ye've yet to get there an' it's been nigh on to ten years
since ye left Dublin!" Jack laughed.

"Aye, I know, I know." The priest sighed and scratched
his belly. "I jes' get a little distracted, that be all. I'll be
findin' me way to Rome one o' these fine days, don't ye be
frettin' yerself none 'bout it, Jack."

"An' we've been ignorin' our problem here," the man
said. The little girl stood close to Liam's side and stared up at
the red-haired man. "An' what is it we're to be doin' with
her?"

"Well, I cannot return her," the priest said. "Even if I
could remember the place, 'twas an awful abode—hardly no
walls nor roof, not a fit decent home fer a wee child to be
livin' in. So tell me, Jack, what would you have me do?
Throw her out in the streets to fend on her own or leave her in
the care o' one o' yer poxy whores?" He frowned. "There be
a painted whoreman down in the street who took a right deep
interest in her. Offered me a silver piece fer her."

Jack ran an agitated hand through his tumble of hair,
dislodging the fancy hat, which fell, forgotten, to the dirty
floor. "Yer makin' me out to seem the ogre, ye be, but ye
know as soon as the wee thing begins to get a bit o' bosom
an' bottom on her we'll not be able to keep her safe. Those
randy whoreson mercenaries would be on her in an instant,"
he said, frowning.

"Aye," sighed Liam, fingering the black beads of his
rosary, "there's truth in that." He thought for a moment,
then said, "I had a wee idea while ridin' to Paris. I think we
should send her to a convent so that the good sisters may look
after the precious mite. She'll get a good home there, to be
sure. 'Twould be a hard life, mayhap, but she'd have enough
to eat an' decent clothin' 'pon her back."

Jack shuddered. "No," the man said firmly. "I'll not let
her go to any prayer-mumblin' cage. She's a wee little bird,
that one, with the look o' freedom 'bout her. 'Twould be

murder to send her to the nuns, fer her spirit an' song would
soon suffocate there.''

Unnoticed by the two men, the silver-haired child, bored
by the long-winded conversation, darted past them and gathered up the abandoned hat. She paused, the hat clutched in
her hands, and surveyed the room before her. A broken-down
bed, its torn sheets gray with age and use, squatted beneath a
window. The casement was brown with dust and the window
was open, stuck for all time. From the street below sounds of
hawkers, bleating animals, and curses floated into the room.
Propped against the opposite wall sat a shabby dresser with a
repaired pitcher and basin, the painted flowers on the procelain
having long ago faded, and beside the ramshackle piece of
furniture stood the cracked length of a mirror.

The girl's gaze was arrested by the mirror, and a small
frown of bewilderment formed between her black upswept
eyebrows. Cautiously, she approached the foreign object, and
so did the little creature within it. Then with a silvery laugh,
Angel darted up to the mirror and pressed her nose against the
cool glass. She touched it with a small finger, leaving a dark
smudge on the surface. Like water in a clear pond . . . hard
. . . and not wet at all. . . . This must be the glass that the
m'sieur had spoken of!

Deftly she perched the fine hat on her small head, holding
up one side so it would not fall over her eyes.

At her laugh, the men turned to watch Angel. As Jack
studied the piquant little figure preening before the mirror, a
feeling of . . . something held him. He stepped forward to
better study the face reflected in the glass. She glanced up at
him with dancing gray eyes and grinned, wrinkling her nose.

"I told ye, Jack, she's a darlin'. Now, how can we go
desertin' such an angel?''

The fleeting sense of familiarity, almost close enough to
grasp but so very dim after all the years of drinking and
wenching and fighting, slipped silently away, even as the
red-haired Irishman strove to capture it.

"Where ye be from, child?'' Jack asked gently.

"I live in the fog, m'sieur,'' she replied politely. Angel
raised her arms over her head and the hat fell, covering her
face. "Ooooooooooooohhh,'' she moaned through the heavy
material of the hat. "Ooohh, I am a baby of the swamp rat.''

The hat still obscuring her vision, Angel danced around the room, her sabots clunking upon the wooden floor.

The Irishman gazed with amusement at the girl. "Be that so, ye little divil?" He plucked the hat off her silver head and tossed it onto the unmade bed.

"Why did you take it away?" she cried.

"I don't want ye to be goin' an' hurtin' me fine hat. I paid many a stolen louis fer that." He faced the priest once again. "I have not much time, Faither Liam. We must be decidin'."

"Don't desert me!" she cried in a husky voice. She ran to Liam and threw her arms around his legs.

"There be a way, by God," Jack said slowly, "there be a way! Don't ye see it?" he cried, clutching the priest's shoulder. The other man's face remained blank. "We'll dress the wee one as a boy, an' none'll be the wiser!"

"And if she should grow and—?" Liam hesitated, then moved his hands suggestively over his chest.

"Well," said Jack, "we'll face that when we be comin' to it. What be yer name, colleen?"

"Angel, m'sieur."

"Now, what in hell's domain kind o' name be that? Here now, we'll name her . . ."

"Liam," suggested the priest.

"Jack. She's to be me child. After all," Jack replied defensively, "ye can't very well be sirin' a brat. An' we'll call her Jackie so there'll be no confusion."

"Now wait, Jack." A deep frown creased the priest's forehead. "Ye know it be 'gainst canon law, an' in some countries even 'gainst civil law, fer a woman to dress as a man."

Miffed and impatient with Liam for questioning his grand plan, Jack flung himself back onto the bed. "Well now, Faither Liam, ye be the one who plucked her up in the first place. I came up with a perfectly good scheme, an' now ye go an' turn coward on me. Fie on ye, Faither." He leaned forward, clasping his hands between his knees, voice softening persuasively. "An' who knows—she may even be useful to us. Why, dammit, man, if we'd had her in Milan we would have been away with the geegaws with no one bein' the wiser, instead o' us slinkin' off with our tails tucked 'tween our legs." His green eyes crinkled in a smile. "Besides, Faither, when is that ye have become so particular 'bout law, especially canon law?"

Liam Dougherty, looking heavenward, murmured a short
prayer. "Aye, it be true," he admitted. "It be little need I be
havin' fer the law. So. Ye win, Jack. Ye drive a hard
bargain. We'll be keepin' her an' she'll be our own sweet
boy. Well, I mean he, er, she, er . . . that be . . ." The
sentence foundered in a tangle of pronouns.

"There be the spirit!" Jack grinned. "I'll teach her swordplay an' horsemanship an' marksmanship, by God!"

"Aye, an' I'll teach her to read an' write an' figure."

"An' I'll teach her to gamble an' how to hold her drink,"
Jack said.

"I shall teach her her prayers," Liam intoned piously.

The ginger-haired man laughed sardonically. "Aye, that ye
will, Faither, an' Black Teresa will teach her—"

"Ye mean that big Spanish whore with the house near
Seville? What in heaven's fair name be she goin' to teach our
little angel here?"

"How to be a lady, ye fool," Jack O'Connell said in a
tolerant tone. "Teresa used to do a good dodge as a nobility
skirt a few years back. She knows all the fancy ways o' the
ladies. 'Course, no need to rush on that account. We can get
Teresa when Jackie be sixteen or so. Plenty o' time. Now tell
me, infant, how would ye be likin' to have me as yer ould
dad?"

Angel wrinkled her straight nose, her hands resting lightly
on her hips, and studied him from the top of his red head to
the soles of his feet. "You are not quite the father my real
papa is. He, after all, is the Lord of Hell. But he has done
nothing for me that I can see. . . . With you I will have a
horse."

Jack looked at Liam, who grinned and shrugged. "A wee
bribe to have her come with me."

"So . . . *oui*," she concluded blithely, "you may be my
father."

"What else do you wish, darlin', besides a horse?" Liam
asked, smiling.

"The big man's hat," she said simply.

"It be hats ye'll be havin' aplenty." Jack O'Connell beamed
at his newly acquired daughter. She grinned in response.

"Where to now, Jack?" the priest asked.

"A select card party at the home o' the chevalier de
Perrier, where only a fine piece o' nobility like meself be

invited.'' He reached behind and swept his hat onto his head.
The white plume drooped miserably in front of his eyes.

"You sat on it," the little girl calmly observed.

"Five louis!" Jack wailed. "Wasted!"

"Not completely," Liam said dryly. "Yer daughter gets a
toy."

"Aye," Jack sighed, relinquishing the ruined hat to the
little girl. She gleefully blew at the bedraggled feather and
then placed the hat on her head.

Liam swung her up, gently depositing her under the thin
blankets on the bed. "Ye be takin' a wee nap now, darlin',
fer I know ye be tired." He took the hat away from her and
set it on the windowsill. Jack's hands moved in a blur of
motion, cards appearing and vanishing, as if by magic. She
shrieked with laughter and happily clapped her hands.

"Did ye remember yer low men?" Liam asked with a
worried frown.

"Aye, I've got 'em." Jack put a hand into a pocket and
rattled something.

"What are 'low men'?" the little girl asked.

"False dice loaded so that they always roll low numbers,"
the red-haired man replied. "I'll teach ye 'bout that when yer
older," the Irishman said. "Ye sleep well, infant," he said,
his voice softening. Then, with a sudden sweeping motion, he
pulled Liam's sword from his waist. "Here, ye sleep with
this to one side o' ye, an' these"—the deck of playing cards
appeared in his hands again—"to the other. They're me
legacy to ye, Jackie me fine daughter, an' fer damn sure the
best ye'll ever have."

Chapter

Four

"OH SWEET JAYSUS!" a shrill voice cried. "Oh Mary, Mother of God, I'm done for! I'm bleedin'!" And out of her bedroom ran Jackie, thirteen years of age. The two men, startled by her cries in the light of the early morning, roused themselves from their drunken slumbers and clambered out of bed. They pulled on breeches hastily and dashed toward Jackie's room in the rented house.

They were met halfway by the silver-haired girl, distress plainly written on her pretty face. She hopped first on one foot, then on the other.

"Oh, help me!" she shrieked, wringing her hands in desperation, "before I die! Oh, whatever will I do?"

Liam and Jack, seeing the bloody streak on her nightshirt, looked at one another, then swiftly away and blushed deeply.

"To be sure she's 'come a woman," Jack said quickly.

"I'd not thought so soon," Liam said with a sigh.

"Aye, but the years have a wee sly way o' slippin' past. Remember that time the three o' us—'course she weren't more than seven at the time—gone to Baden? Ye must remember it!"

Memory flooded Liam's face. "Oh, aye, 'twas where ye—"

"Papa, Faither Liam! Don't talk when I'm dyin'! Help me!" the distraught girl pleaded, running her hands through her tousled hair. She shivered in the cold of the early morning and hugged her trembling body with her arms.

A red-faced Liam looked at Jack. "Er, uh, ye'd be havin' more experience here than me poor self, fer sure, Jack boy. Ye'd best be explainin' it. I'll be fer goin' back to bed. I cannot give you no aid here." The priest turned and retreated to the safety of his bed, and, once there with the covers pulled up to his chin, sighed a long sigh of relief at his narrow escape.

"Coward," Jack muttered under his breath. "Er . . . darlin'. . . ." Jackie was sobbing, and the pitiful sound went to the very depths of the Irishman's heart. He gently touched the girl's shoulder, and she jerked away, glaring at him out of tear-filled eyes. "I'll return anon, sweet."

Alone in the empty hallway and with tears running down her cheeks, Jackie huddled, feeling quite deserted. They didn't care that she was going to die. They were cruel and heartless. They didn't love her. These thoughts only served to bring on more weeping. What was wrong with her? She didn't *feel* bad!

Shortly Jack reappeared with several white handkerchiefs in his hand. "Aye, these be fer ye, me love." The girl reached for one and started to blow her nose in it, but Jack, his face the shade of his hair, stopped her. "Not fer yer nose, darlin'."

"If it's not for my bloody nose, then what in hell's name is it for?" she screamed, misery overcoming her completely.

The man coughed delicately. "Er, fer something else that be, er, bloody. . . ."

The silver-haired girl looked down at the spreading stain on her nightshirt. "You mean . . . ?" she began suspiciously, her gray eyes narrowing. Her mouth turned down at the corners in a most unhappy expression.

"Aye, darlin', that be what I mean." Jack looked down at his bare feet and sighed. "An' them bein' me best linen hankies."

She raised her hand to toss them at her foster father. "In that case, you can just take them back and—"

"Now, Jackie me love." Jack clasped her hand and stroked

it. The girl glared at him, unmoved by his soothing words.
"Ye take the hankies. The cost don't matter."

"But I'm dying," she said, her gray eyes sad. "Don't you
care?"

"No, sweet, yer not dyin' none. This be all, well, er, that
be to say . . . um . . . it be the way . . . ahem, natural
. . . darlin'," the man finished lamely, not meeting Jackie's
cool look.

"I don't think I like the sound of that," she said ominously. "When will you explain it to me, Papa?"

"I thought we might take ye to Black Teresa. It's time now
fer ye to be learnin' the ways o' womanhood." He patted her
on the shoulder and said, "Ye run along now, darlin'. I'll be
seein' ye later when we go fer breakfast."

She glanced darkly at the handkerchiefs in her hand and
muttered under her breath. At the door of the room, the girl
paused. "But what do I *do* with them?" she asked plaintively,
looking quite lost. Jack wanted to run to her and throw his
arms around his wee Jackie and tell her everything would be
all right. Only now it wouldn't be; it would be all different.

"Oh, darlin', sweet one, ye pin 'em to yer underclothes!"
She shuddered. "I think I'd rather be dyin'. At least I
could do *that* with dignity!"

Later in the day the trio set out on horseback for Seville,
where Black Teresa had her house. Jackie rode, sullen, and
spoke not a word more than necessary to the two men, who
seemed embarrassed to speak to her. If this be womanhood,
well—she sniffed disdainfully and tossed her glorious mane
of silver hair—she'd rather not be a woman, thank ye! She
glowered first at the priest, then at her adopted father, both of
whom avoided her angry eyes and spoke to one another in
low, hushed tones.

All her father had said was that this was simply the beginning . . . and that, Jackie thought miserably, had an ominous
ring to it.

They arrived, weary and saddlesore, a fortnight later at the
home of Black Teresa, Consuela Maria La Reina Francisca de
Vargas, who placed her hands on her ample hips and
laughed good-naturedly when Jack confidentially explained
the reason for their unexpected arrival. Glaring at the woman,
Jackie wanted to hate the dark-faced woman for laughing at

her but found she couldn't. Teresa was bluff, good-natured, generous, and, when the time was ripe, a tough woman to deal with.

Early the following morning the Spanish woman routed the girl out of bed. Then, under the astute tutelage of the retired whore, Jackie began the numerous lessons and refinements which would eventually lead to her becoming a lady of society.

Not an easy task, Liam thought, and not one that he particularly envied Teresa for. The woman met the girl's obstinacy directly when for the first time Jackie was faced with the operation of a fan. The two men, observers only at this informal finishing school, were lounging in chairs along one whitewashed wall.

Teresa, holding out a painted chicken-skin fan to the girl, requested that Jackie snap it open.

"No!" the child stubbornly refused. "I do not wish to learn these stupid things. I would rather be outside riding Briar. I don't want to be a woman."

"Briar ees a fine horse, but you know," Teresa said, smiling kindly, her brown eyes twinkling, "there ees some things that can be done outside, and some things which ees better suited for the inside. And when you are a very fine lady, you cannot always be outside doing thees things. No? *Si!* And eef you cannot do thees indoor things, why, all the men and the women weel laugh at you."

Jackie glowered.

"You see, you do not weesh to be thought stupeed—or laughed at. Therefore," the Spanish woman said, clasping the fan in her large palm, "you must become very accomplished at thees special things, and then you say, 'Eh, I am so much better than those silly people,' and you snap your fingers at them!"

"No," the silver-haired girl said again, her hands defiantly placed on her slim hips.

"Working with the fan," Teresa continued, flicking open the fan and fluttering it in front of her olive-colored face, "it ees a great art—a talent you should cultivate. You can learn to peep from behind it; you may completely retreat behind it. So! You can show your disapproval—and you may hide laughter. But, best of all, you may flirt!" She raised the

painted fan coquettishly until only her sloe eyes showed. Jack
grinned appreciatively. "It ees very versatile, leetle one."

"I will not learn it!"

"Why not?" Jack demanded, his eyebrows rising in surprise.

"I just won't!"

"Yer sayin' ye can't."

"No!" Her gray eyes snapped with anger. "I have better
things to do."

"Aye, I suspect ye might—easier things." He sighed and
inspected his nails. "The men in China—'tis said they use
fans. It takes quite an accomplished wrist, 'tis said, an' only a
few become wholly proficient with it. But," her foster father
continued, spreading his hands and shrugging, "I can see that
if ye think ye'd be clumsy, ye might not be wantin' to try.
After all, ye might look a fool. That I can understand, me
love, but 'tis disappointin'—what with me wantin' to make a
wee small wager. Of course, now. . . . You go an' do
somethin' easy, darlin', an' we'll just be fergettin' the wager."
He sighed and looked away, a disheartened expression on his
face.

"A wager?" Jackie inquired in a small voice.

"Aye, but if yer not interested, 'tis—"

"Well, I might be," the girl said with a great show of
unconcern in her voice. She studied her shoes, and Jack
smiled across the top of her silver head at the Spanish woman,
who returned the amused expression. "What's the wager?"
Jackie asked.

"I wager fifty pistoles ye can't learn to carry a fan, hold it,
snap it open—an' closed—an' move it gracefully, like the
fancy ladies do. Inside a week."

"A week!" she exclaimed.

"Well, if ye'd like longer—"

"A week it is!" she declared.

"Done!" her father said, and Jackie, her face shining,
raced across to him to solemnly shake hands on it.

The following afternoon she ran into the common room,
where Jack was resting from the heat, his booted feet crossed
at the ankles and propped up on the wide plank table. A mug
of ale, almost gone, stood at one elbow. His eyes were
closed, and for the time time that she could remember Jackie
saw lines of weariness around his eyes and on either side of

his mouth. A worried frown creased his forehead. It upset her and she didn't know what to do, so she chose to ignore it.

"Papa, Papa, look!"

His green eyes opened, and a fearful look crossed his handsome face. Then, seeing who it was, he smiled and brought his boots down on the floor with a clank of the spurs. In Jackie's right hand she held a folded fan. With a slight movement of her wrist it opened. The girl waved it delicately in front of her face, then positioned it so that only her gray eyes peeped mischievously over the rim. Then, with another flick, the fan was closed, and she ran to her father and whacked him hard on the chest with it. He staggered back, a mocking stance to his body, grabbed the fan, threw his arms around her, and hugged the young girl.

"Ye almost knocked me down on me butt, ye did!" He laughed and kissed the top of her head. "Aye, yer an imp, Jackie me love, me little angel! Here an' I go bettin' ye can't do it in a sennight an' yet up an' do it in a day!" He shook his head in wonderment.

The silver-haired girl wiggled out of his arms and held her palm out. "Pay up," she said, a pleased tone in her voice.

"All right, darlin', I know yer impatient fer yer wealth, but I'll be a few minutes."

Jack left the room and went in search of the good father.

"Liam."

"Aye?" The priest looked up at him from the goblet of wine held between his hands. His blue eyes were fogged over, and Jack sighed. Liam blinked rapidly. When the other man's face came into focus, the priest saw that special glint in those green eyes and knew, without words, what Jack wanted. In a few short moments he returned with a small gemstone in his unsteady hands. "This should be tidin' ye over, eh, Jack?"

"Aye, Faither Liam."

"What ye be needin' it fer?" the priest asked, curiosity in his slurred voice.

"To be payin' off a wee small debt," the other man said simply.

"Aye." The blond priest shook his head sadly. "Yer always in debt, me boy, always in debt. A sad state o' affairs it be."

For a moment a serious, troubled look crossed Jack's boyish

face, then it faded, and with an engaging grin he clapped his good friend on the back. "Aye, yer right. I'm always in debt. But I pay off in time."

Then followed long months of intensive instruction in the dance, the curtsy, riding sidesaddle, and always the cards—vingt-et-un, whist, casino, and, most importantly, how to stack the deck. It pleased her three tutors that she learned quickly and, after that isolated incident with the fan, avidly.

Finally, Teresa decided to give a small party. Her house was thrown wide open, and the warm, fragrant evening air drifted languidly into the room, casting a sensuous spell on all the party-goers.

When the stately strains of a minuet began, Jack led his daughter, elegant in a pink satin dress with a beige overskirt, out onto the floor. During the formal dance, neither smiled. Jackie swayed gracefully, an intense expression on her youthful face, her steps small and light. Back and forth they promenaded. The minuet, bourrée, passepied, gavotte—the silver-haired girl had learned them from her tutors and danced them all equally well that night.

When Jackie was sixteen she attended her first full-fledged ball in Seville. In a white dress with lace bows laddering the puffed sleeves, she was a vision of white and silver.

"A snow goddess," her father said, taking her petite hand and gently kissing it. He thought how pure she looked, and a pang went through him that someday this would all be changed.

She blushed, then tapped Jack lightly on the chest with her fan. Snapping the fan open and waving it, she curtsied low and then turned to be claimed by the dark-haired gallant to whom she had promised the next gavotte. And she left her father's side, a young woman at last.

A glass of deep hearty wine in his trembling hand, Father Dougherty looked at the young woman she had grown into in three short years. The priest remembered the many nights when, her pale face intent, the tip of her tongue sticking out of her mouth—it helped her to learn, she claimed—they sat before a fireplace and she laboriously read to him from a Greek primer. Then in quick succession had followed Latin and English and German, Spanish, Dutch, and Italian. She had mastered eight languages, including a thorough polishing of her own French. She spoke them all like a native, he

thought proudly. Aye, and that be more than most noble brats
could testify to. Then had come the long hours of practicing
with the quill pen.

Yes, thought Liam Dougherty proudly, though he had not
performed many good deeds in his life, his education of his
wee Jackie had been the best, his finest accomplishment. His
own education had expanded over the years of wandering
with Jack, and he had encouraged the girl to seek knowledge
wherever she could find it. She'd learned well her mathematics,
her poetry, her religion, her philosophy, her history, her
science.

'Twas a sorry thing she was not born a boy, Liam mused
sadly, for she would have made a right fine scholar.

Aye, but there was one thing they'd had no need of teach-
ing her, and that had been her acting ability, for she had
proved to be a natural-born actor. And right lucky for them,
too, that she be able to move with confidence and ease in the
role of either young girl or young boy.

In Vienna the summer ere she turned sixteen, the girl had
been disguised as a boy, and such a handsome lad she'd been!
Father Liam fondly remembered her lengthy promenades
through the carefully tended parks with the wealthy bejeweled
daughters of Austrian society in worshipful attendance. The
children had flirted and laughed, and ''he'' had sung sweet
love songs upon ''his'' guitar to the pretty maids. Some had
been moved to the point of tears by the sound of ''his'' pure
high sweet voice.

And who could resist so handsome a lad dressed in a
wide-brimmed hat of dove-gray bedecked with a white feather? The coat was of pearl-gray brocade, gold threads scattered
through it, the wide saffron satin-lined sleeves turned back
over Jackie's slender wrists. At her waist, tucked under the
wide saffron sash, were her gloves, elaborately embroidered
kid leather, a present from Liam a year ago Christmas.

'Twas surely a vision of delight to see her dressed as a boy,
he thought to himself, for he'd never seen such a darling lad.

And when the three had left the old city she had opened her
case, unwrapped the chamois, and out had poured dozens of
necklaces and rings like a torrent of pearly water.

Jack had let loose a great guffaw of hearty laughter and
clapped her hard on her straight back. Jackie, grinning, had
shrugged her shoulders, and then with an ironic tone in her

voice had said in her most offhanded manner, " 'Twas not half so hard to pick their pearls as 'twas to keep from being pawed."

The three, priest, soldier of fortune, and girl in disguise, had laughed at the foolishness of rich folk and then turned their newly acquired mounts westward. Through Munich, Venice, Milan, Geneva, and many other cities they had meandered, plucking the gems like eggs from under the very noses of their stupid pigeons.

When Jackie was sixteen years of age, the trio arrived in Paris once again.

Chapter
Five

EXCITED, HER STOMACH feeling as though it were tied in sailor's knots, Jackie paced the front room of their rented suite. Jack had engaged three rooms for them in an inn, not shabby, but by no means luxurious. He little expected anyone to pay them social calls, so it mattered not at all where the trio lived—as long as it was fairly accessible to the fetes, parties, and balls they were invited to attend.

As Jackie paced, she thought of their scheme for that evening. She had no qualms about its success, but it was the thought of going for the very first time to the French court which made her so nervous. She stopped before the curtained window and watched the light fade from the sky, then began her pacing once more. Her hands clasped behind her back, she measured off the dimensions of the room in an effort to relieve some of the tension.

Liam entered quietly from the room he shared with Jack. "No, Jackie!" he exclaimed when he saw her striding about the room. "Remember what Teresa taught ye—take smaller steps. They must be dainty paces. Don't stride, girl—yer not in breeches."

"I know, I know," the girl said, running a hand distractedly through her silken hair. "But no one's here, Faither, to notice. I need not be in character."

Liam eased his body into a chair. He stretched his feet out before him and pulled out of the recesses of his cassock a slim, amber-colored flask. Uncorking the bottle, he tipped his head back and drained some of the liquid. The priest stoppered the flask and wiped his mouth with the back of his hand. Looking up, he caught the girl's disapproving gaze on him and quickly slid the bottle out of sight. He belched softly.

"Aye, that's where yer arrow misses the spot, sweetlin'," he said at last in answer to her. "Ye must at all times be in character, always on yer guard. When we go out to cull an' ye must needs play a young society lady or a young cavalier, ye must create a character through an' through. An' ye must be that girl or boy at all times—with us, without us, in yer wakin' hours, in yer sleep. Never ferget that, darlin'."

"I won't," Jackie replied meekly, her silver head bowed humbly, but the mischievous twinkle in her soft eyes dispelled the mood. His sternness evaporated, and the man smiled.

" 'Tis time, don't ye think?" the priest asked. She nodded and then withdrew to her room to dress. First to go on were the linen drawers with the colored embroidery, hearts and roses and violets in pink and lavender silk. Next the corset. After a sufficient length of time, Liam entered, eyes discreetly averted, and cinched the corset in back for the girl, pulling hard at the laces. Jackie had little need for a corset other than to give her otherwise slim figure more shape for the dress. Around her narrow waist went the petticoats. Then over her head with a rustling sigh came the silk dress of shimmering rose, silver lace sewn across the tight, low-cut bodice and trimming the elbow-length sleeves. Around the full skirt were *prétintailles*, embroidered silver roses, and on her feet were cloth slippers of the same delicate tint of pink as the dress. Through her hair she wound long strands of pink pearls. Around her long white neck was set a single line of pearls, a shade lighter than the dress. The trio possessed a fortune in gems—most of them paste.

The young woman walked away from Liam, turned, and made a deep curtsy. "What say you?"

Tears filled his blue eyes, and for a moment he couldn't find his voice. Then Liam made an effort and recovered. "Yer lovely, darlin', as lovely as ever. More. Yer our own sweet rose." He gave her cheek a fatherly peck and squeezed her arm reassuringly.

Jackie turned her lovely head this way and that, admiring her profile and shape in the mirror. "I *am* lovely," she whispered, faint surprise in her voice. It was as though she saw herself as a girl for the very first time. "Oh, I'll break the hearts of all the lads, for sure." And the blond priest joined the girl in a round of hearty laughter.

When Jack knocked upon the door of her room a short while later, she rushed across the floor and flung wide the door. The Irishman's eyes widened with appreciation of her beauty, and he made a great bow, then clasped her slender hand in his and brushed a light kiss across the top.

"Marry, ye'll be the fairest lady there tonight, me love." He straightened, offering his arm. A wink of pink on the bed caught Liam's eye, and he hurried forward.

"Don't be forgettin' this, darlin'." Jackie paused and accepted the rose loo. "Must I go masked?" she asked Jack.

"Aye, I want yer beauty to shine, me love, but I do not want all the rakes to be oglin' ye—not completely, that be. Besides, 'tis to be a masked fete. Even the king, me dear, will be masked."

Jackie laughed, a silver tone, and squeezed his arm. "Very well."

"I'll join ye later," Liam said and nodded to the pair. The priest watched them as they left the room, she in her fair rose dress and silver trim, Jack in his apple-green breeches and coat with gold embroidery on the sleeves.

Aye, a lovely couple, Liam thought and then began his own preparations for attending the fete. He would slip in later, dressed as a somber courtier, and he would be there to collect the gems when Jack and Jackie began harvesting their crop of rubies, diamonds, pearls, and emeralds. He went stiffly down on to his knees and, light-colored head bowed, prayed for success. Tonight, though, he prayed longer than usual.

In the rented carriage, her adopted father seemed unusually pensive tonight, and that bothered Jackie not a little. "What's the matter?'' the girl asked. "Do you have a worry about this evening? Is there something I should know?''

The Irishman sighed, nervously fingering the gold embroidery along his wide cuffs. "Aye, I think I must have a worry or two. Me nerves be not what they be when I be a young lad. An', too, darlin', I always worry when we do a big cull. The small ones be no problem. But these . . . So much could be goin' wrong. I just don't know.'' He looked out the window again.

"You're not thinking of retiring, are you, Papa? Please say you aren't! What would we do? How would we live?'' Her hand shot out and grasped his wrist and, like a terrier with a bone, shook it.

Irony colored the Irishman's tone. "Retire, darlin'? An' lose me mind the first sennight? No, I thank ye not. I prefer an active life, perhaps even a dangerous one, it bein' I can't stay in one place fer long. Before long I feel the very bars o' the cage closin' round me.''

"What about your land in Ireland?''

"Well now, that be jes' another form o' that cage. An' a right cleverly disguised one it be, too. But I let me brother Tom have it. He be always one to be out stoopin' an' pickin' up dirt clods, siftin' an' crumblin' them through his fingers.'' He shook his head, and his green eyes glinted with amusement. "Aye. I never could find out what attraction he found in the soil. He thought the earth be far prettier than any maid he'd ever seen. Now me, I prefer a good bottle o' wine, a fine gal at me side, an' a lively song.''

"Oh, Papa!'' the young girl exclaimed. "You're never serious for a moment.''

"Life be too short—an' too sweet—to spend what little time ye have pullin' a long face. An' freedom be the most important thing in this old world, Jackie. That be why I kept ye rather than send ye to the good sisters, meanin' no bad 'gainst 'em. I just knew, when I saw ye all dirty an' fiery, with that blue hat 'pon yer pretty head, an' the way ye held yer chin up to me—well, I said, 'Jack me boy, ye can't cage this little birdie. 'Twould be too cruel an' she's got far too much spirit to be put in any convent cage.' '' He cleared his throat self-consciously. "Well now, old Jack has been runnin' off at the mouth again. Me faither always said 'twas one o' me better traits. Always wanted me to study an' be a barrister. But that be another cage."

The carriage slowed and gradually rolled to a stop. "We've arrived. Are ye ready, me darlin'?" Jack asked, confident of the girl's answer even before she spoke.

For a moment she was quiet and seriously studied his lined face, then Jackie winked and smiled reassuringly. "As ready, Papa, as ever I'll be!"

" 'Tis the spirit, me love!" He reached across and briefly hugged her, taking care not to crush her lovely dress.

No, Jackie thought to herself, *don't draw away, Papa*. His arms were a warm protective circle around her. *Hold me tight. I'm scared Papa. I'm frightened about tonight. Reassure me, Papa, oh, please do. Tell me that everything will be all right. Please.* But her feelings and fears went unvoiced, for she was a young woman now, not a silly mud-splattered child running wild. For an instant she thought of the old woman and wondered what she would think seeing her Angel dressed this way.

Jack paused to slip the green mask over his eyes and, once outside the coach, helped the girl down. Still holding on to her tiny hand, he turned her around for her first glimpse of Versailles, home of King Louis, *Le Roi Soleil*, of the house of Bourbon.

Nothing had prepared Jackie for the splendor that was Versailles, a palace which in the time of the Sun King's father, Louis XIII, had been merely a hunting lodge. Rather than to the palace itself, the girl's eye was drawn to the landscaping, the style of which had been brought to perfection by André Le Nôtre: the transformation of the wild into an organized, classical beauty. Jack and Jackie began walking down the *tapis vert*, the broad walk leading to the mile-long Grand Canal. But she hardly knew where her feet led her, for she stared about, hungrily taking in every detail: bowers, vases, brooks, fountains, waterspouts, colored stones, trellises, caves, grottoes, grotesques, and even organs played by running water.

Jack smiled at the girl's mixture of fascination and bemusement. "Wait 'til ye see the inside," he said, squeezing her hand playfully and leading her into the palace. She said not a word, merely gazed and drank in every sight as though she'd never before in her life seen beauty. Beauty she had seen, but nothing ever to compare with this! She found her

senses almost overrun by thickly carpeted floors, ornamental
candelabra, marble clocks inlaid with precious gems, crystal
chandeliers ablaze with blinding light, walls paneled or frescoed,
niches with marble busts executed in the classical style, walls
hung with rich tapestries.

Jackie stopped and closed her eyes, dizzy with the incompre-
hensible sight of so much dazzling splendor. Then, feeling a
gentle pressure upon her fingers, the silver-haired girl opened
her eyes to see her adopted father gazing at her with concern.
She cast him a reassuring look and walked on, her hand on
his arm.

At the rounded doorway to one room she came to a halt
and stared, then, quickly recovering, snapped open her fan
and briskly fanned herself. It was the Galerie des Glaces: a
spacious hall over three hundred feet long extending along the
garden front, with mirrors and marble and gold leaf and light
everywhere. The hall was so bright that she almost had to
turn away for a moment.

"Come along, darlin'," Jack whispered in her small ear.

"I've never seen anything like it, Papa!" the dazed girl
said. "How can they not be struck blind by all this beauty?"

He chuckled. "There be nothin' in heaven nor earth what
can compare to Versailles, me child. As fer them bein' struck
blind, why, they've seen it fer so long that it's lost all
meanin' to them. They can't see it. They can't appreciate it."
The Irishman guided her firmly along. "This way, darlin'."
He led her through a huge hall filled with talking and laughing and flirting courtiers and their ladies and the delicate
notes of court music, past row after row of tables covered
with linen cloths and lit with thousands of candles—tables
laden with delicacies far more numerous than Jackie could
ever have imagined. Rich creamy cheese cut into geometrical
shapes. Sugared almonds. Slivers of cooked fish in cream and
wine sauces. Breaded veal medallions smothered with capers.
Wild rice tossed with fresh mushrooms sautéed in wine.
Cherries in liqueur. Strawberries to dip in sugar. Marzipan
candy, cleverly fashioned into petite apples, lemons, grapes,
cherries and plums. Delicate pastry shells holding candied
cherries and apricots and apples. Apricot cream fingers. Chocolate candies cunningly molded into symbols of the sun to
flatter the Sun King. And to wash all this down was wine, but
wine served in a most unusual way. On each table rose

elaborate crystal fountains that bubbled musically, the liquid in them not water but white wine.

Fascinated, Jackie moved forward to watch the liquor froth. She smiled up at her adopted father. "Father Liam should certainly appreciate this!"

The red-haired Irishman grinned in answer, and the two continued down the corridors of Versailles.

At last the couple came to their destination, a room lined with immense oil paintings depicting glorious battlescenes from the reigns of Louis XIII and Louis XIV. The dining hall contained over sixty tables set for ten dinner guests each. Already the tables were half filled with chattering courtiers and their ladies, all dressed in vivid silks and satins and laces and plumes.

Jack and Jackie found their places far down the row of tables, closer in fact, to the last than the first. The young girl was plainly disappointed that they did not merit a higher table, but the Irishman could not quibble with the seating, counting himself lucky indeed to be at Versailles at all!

Given their extreme distance from the royal table, Jackie did not see the entrance of the king and his queen, but all the noble diners rose, then waited patiently until the royal couple had seated themselves and the monarch indicated that all might sit. The girl leaned over to Jack and whispered in a discouraged tone, "I can't even see him!"

He smiled indulgently. "You will later—durin' the ballet. The king himself shall dance. 'Tis said that he be a right fine dancer."

She raised a black eyebrow, but before she could comment, the first part of the supper was served. Along with stout bread and fine wines there were oranges, stuffed eels, calves' heads vinaigrette, beef tongues, partridges with cabbage, stuffed cucumbers, hot venison pies, broccoli in cheese sauce, and artichokes in drawn butter. Then in rapid succession came baked and broiled stuffed chickens, various stuffed birds, quail pie, kid with sorrel sauce, rabbits garnished with oranges, suckling pigs, and a cold pie of sparrows. The *issue de table*, or dessert course, followed: three kinds of jellies—white, clear, and amber; almonds and other nuts; cream cheeses; cakes of puff paste and rosewater.

Jackie, daintily restraining a mild belch with her white linen napkin and leaning slightly back in her chair, wondered with bewilderment how anyone could manage to eat this fare daily and still remain alert.

But the men, old and young seemed to be quite alert. After the meal they flocked around the amused girl like birds to a handful of bread crumbs. As they flirted with her Jackie smiled prettily and lowered her dark lashes over her dove-gray eyes becomingly.

"Ah, we see that one more fair rose has bloomed in our garden of delights." An unfamiliar voice, pleasant in timbre, spoke beyond the cluster of men. It was a commanding voice; it was a royal voice. The line of her male admirers broke, moved back, dropped to their knees, and murmured as one, "Your Majesty." Through the opening a man of medium height walked with a steady, elegant tread. He was dressed in subdued colors, his coat a dull gold and deep purple brocade. Jackie thought his mask the most interesting part of his dress. It was the color of the sun and fashioned into the shape of one—a stylized, smiling sun, with chubby cheeks and wide-open eyes, and pointed bursts along the sides and crown.

The girl dropped into her deepest curtsy. "Rise, young one." She did and, raising her head, looked into the clear eyes of the French king. "What is your name, child?"

"Mary Elizabeth Bridget Ashley, Your Royal Highness."

Jackie felt rather than saw his momentary frown, for, of course, his face was completely concealed by the sun mask. "Your father is"—he paused in thought, then spoke once more before she could answer—"Edward Jemmett Talbot Ashley, Earl of Tyrconnel."

"Why yes, sire." Flattered by the king's knowledge and not a little surprised that he should concern himself with these details, the girl moved her fan prettily, coyly peeping over the edge.

"We are pleased to have met such a beauty." He bowed to her and, his fawning entourage in attendance, moved away. When the king was out of sight, she inwardly released a large sigh.

"Ye did right fine," a familiar voice whispered in her ear, but when she turned, Jack was heading across the room. Jackie's group of male admirers, even larger now that the monarch had deigned to speak with her, oozed back to her. She spent the remainder of the time until the ballet began surveying the many pearls, diamonds, and other gemstones in great profusion. Yes, she and Jack—and Liam, who was standing by a fountain filled with wine—would walk away this evening with more than a few handfuls each. She had already secured four pins and three rings and only waited for Liam to come close to her so that she might hand him her loot.

The girl noticed Jack approach a young woman, her dark hair elaborately dressed. Then he was bowing over the woman's hand. Jackie, too far away to hear even the tone of the conversation, could tell from his stance, the graceful movement of his hands, the bold way he glanced at the beautiful brunette, that Jack had selected his next mistress. And, if she were willing enough—and she certainly wasn't a protesting maiden—Jack would have his new lady love before the night was over.

How often had she seen her adopted father follow this amorous pattern? It was so utterly predictable, the girl thought with amusement. Stifling a giggle, Jackie slipped her arm into that of an older man, the Marquis de la Rouchefort, her honored escort into the ballet.

The king, his well-known shapely legs in obvious display, was now clad in an elaborate costume of gold and white, and portrayed—who else—the sun god Apollo, who from his throne in Olympus would arbitrate the differences of the three immortals, Mars, Venus, and Vulcan. Jackie found the story insipid, and she hid a yawn of boredom behind her fan as she glanced sideways at her escort. The Marquis seemed enraptured by the ballet, or perhaps he was simply ogling the pretty legs of the women dancers. She repressed a cynical smile, then turned a charming smile upon the man. He returned the expression and leaned over toward her, as though he meant to steal a kiss from those tender, pure, and oh-so-luscious lips. The young woman blushed and gently pushed him away, demurely turning her head so that his lips brushed only her soft cheek. She then folded her hands serenely in her lap. In one of them, hidden by the expanse of the fan, was a brilliant-cut diamond from the lapel of his chocolate-colored velvet coat.

When the intricate ballet was finished and the king—having made his elaborate bows and been duly applauded—and his entourage had departed with all due magnificence, Jackie excused herself from the old man and quickly left the room. She found Jack standing next to one of the fountains of white wine. His handsome face was slightly flushed, and his hands were unsteady as he clasped a delicate Bohemian glass goblet, then raised it to his lips and drained the contents. Jackie frowned, for she little liked it when he drank. Liam did enough for the two—no, three—of them.

"How be ye doin', darlin'?" Jack asked, his voice slightly slurred. He smiled at the girl.

"Papa, you shouldn't drink during a job." Disapproval lay heavy in her young voice. She glanced around quickly, but no one stood nearby to overhear their whispered conversation.

He avoided her direct gray eyes and flushed to the roots of his red hair. "I know, darlin', I know. But things be goin' so well that I could not resist the temptation. To success," he said, raising the goblet again. "Ye heart should be gladdened to know that Liam's sober tonight."

She sighed. "If it's not one it's the other. You're both like children, and twice as much trouble!"

Momentarily Jack hung his head. "Aye, 'tis so," he admitted ruefully. He smiled at her, then looked beyond her shoulder. "I must needs go, darlin'. I see a lady who I must know better." She turned around and saw the pretty brunette with whom he had been talking and flirting earlier in the evening.

"Be careful, Papa," Jackie said earnestly, a sudden cold feeling knotting her stomach. "She has a married look about her."

His grin broadened. "Aye, she does, doesn't she? 'Twill make the chase all the merrier, me dear. Eh, me wee darlin'?" Bowing low to his silver-haired daughter, the Irishman moved unsteadily past her and went to hunt the newest apple of his eye. At that moment Liam joined her.

"Well, all seems well. Yer father said the king met ye," the priest said.

"Yes. He asked my name. And then said the name of my 'father.' " She glanced discreetly around to make sure that no one was watching, then opened her hand and dropped the diamond and other valuables into the priest's outstretched palm. In an instant the jewels in Liam's hand were gone.

"That makes me uneasy, it does. Our stories be safe, but aye"—the blond man shook his head and frowned—"it does bother me that he be askin' after ye. Ye don't want to be too much in the royal eye, darlin'."

"Oh pooh," she said. "The king was merely interested in

a very pretty face," she responded, a light tone to her voice.

"I doubt that be the case now that he be married to La Maintenon. They say he's given up mistresses altogether an' seems quite happy with her."

"How boring!" Jackie pouted, her gray eyes dancing with amusement.

"Ye wench! Yer as bad as yer father. When he saw the two o' ye he started dreamin' up schemes—such as how he was goin' to see that ye became Louis's next mistress!"

"Oh, how exciting!" The silver-haired girl clapped her hands together.

Liam scowled, and the glee in her died. "I won't have ye bein' any man's mistress, king or no, Jackie. They say dark things have happened at the court, rumors an' half-whispered tales o' witchcraft an' other foul darkness." The girl listened solemnly, giving her full attention to the intense priest. "An' people at court be jealous, Jackie, o' risin' new stars. No, Jackie, it be best if ye remain out o' the court life. I don't think it would be suitin' ye."

"I'm sorry, Faither Liam, I didn't realize." She touched his shoulder with her small hand.

"Of course ye didn't." He flashed her a reassuring smile. "Yer just a child—an' don't be fergettin' that!"

"Liam," she said, a serious tone to her voice.

"Aye?"

"Papa has been drinking heavily."

He gave a gusty sigh. "Well, perhaps we should be thinkin' o' leavin'." The man glanced around at the milling throng. "I think ye should be headin' out the door. I'll go talk to Jack, and I'll meet ye by the carriage."

The girl nodded and curtsied, then moved away quickly. Someone bumped into her, nearly knocking her down. "Excuse me," she murmured, then exclaimed softly in surprise, for the face that was staring back at her behind the brief black loo was her own! But there were differences. The eyebrows were silver, and the countenance, while still beautiful and firm, was a little older, with minute wrinkles at the corners of the pale eyes. A black satin *mouche*, cut in the shape of a tiny heart, had been applied to the corner of the generous mouth. From head to foot the woman wore black and white, a starkness that well suited her. The only color to relieve her dichromatic appearance was the red of the heavy necklace of rubies at her slender neck.

For a moment Jackie's greedy gaze was drawn to the beautiful red gems, then, feeling a curious prickling along her straight spine, she stared wordlessly at the stranger. The woman, too, remained silent. Jackie had the uncanny sensation that if she moved her hand to the left the right hand of the woman would move at the very same time, creating a feeling of peering into a mirror that was not quite accurate. Suddenly she felt she had to leave. She had to get away from this woman, this . . . apparition. The woman's red lips quirked into a cynical smile, almost as though she had correctly read Jackie's thoughts, and the young girl turned without ceremony and quickly plunged into the crowd. Soon she was across the room, far away from that disturbing mirror image. She left the room, refusing to turn back one last time, afraid to see the woman standing there.

Victorée de Marchaud L'Este du Plessis watched through narrowed pale eyes as the young girl left. *I should follow. I should find out who she is, what she is doing here,* the woman thought, but strangely she felt the languor of reluctance. Fear, too, kept her from pursuing that creature, that . . . by-blow? Of her father's? Oui, it *had* to be. She shivered, knowing that something unpleasant lurked in that direction, warning her not to follow. Victorée beckoned to a servant and indicated he should try to follow the girl, but in a few minutes he returned, reporting that he had lost sight of her and that she seemed to have departed. Still uneasy, Victorée joined her husband, the exceedingly dull duc L'Este du Plessis, to whom she had been married these past fifteen years. And try as she might, the image of that younger self, that mirror image, could not be exorcised from the Frenchwoman's mind.

When Liam met Jackie at the waiting coach, the young girl was silent and said nothing to him of her recent encounter. In silence the man and girl returned to their lodgings. Once there, they quickly packed their bags, and Liam dumped the jewels into a leather pouch he wore at his waist under his black cassock. Jackie changed her attire to that of a young man, sober clothing for her: brown and black velvet and broadcloth. Saddling their mounts and leading Jack's, the priest and the girl left the town.

*   *   *

Jack returned with the brunette, Fleur, to her lavish apartments within the palace. The couple was aggressively occupied when the carved door was kicked open, revealing a wild-faced man: her husband.

A horrible shriek rising from his throat, the man drew his sword and fell upon Jack before the Irishman could rise from the rumpled bed.

Jack lunged for his blade, then rounded on the woman, whose cries seemed to pierce the very heavens. "Oh, shut up!" he shouted at the hysterical woman. Miraculously, Jack parried the man's murderous thrust. The husband slipped momentarily, time enough for Jack to gain his breath, and he then saw a way to press his advantage. The Irishman lunged forward, but he had not counted on the treachery of the crazed husband. Parrying Jack's thrust, the man pulled from his boot a dagger, which he then drove deep into the Irishman's chest.

The woman flung herself at her husband, pulling him away. Wounded, Jack dressed, found his way out of the immense palace, stole a horse, and then made his way to the inn in Mantes-la-Jolil, the prearranged meeting place.

The knife wound was fatal. He was dying. Jack O'Connell, breathing raggedly, gazed down at the crimson gash in his chest, then looked at Liam, who sat beside the narrow bed.

"I don't have long, Faither Liam."

"Nonsense, Jack, ye've got plenty o' crusty years left in ye—why yer jes' five an' forty. 'Tis a scratch, that be all, Jack me friend." The priest turned his head away momentarily and wearily brushed a hand across his eyes. He had seen death many times in his life, in many forms, but now, now he refused to recognize that familiar shadow.

"No, Liam, I know what path me feet will be takin' now." The dying man's expression was earnest, pain-filled, and his breath rasped harshly. "Please, Liam, I'm askin' ye fer the last rites."

"No, man," the priest said, shaking his head. "I tell ye, ye'll be better. Ye jes' need a wee bit o' rest. Then we'll move on. To Bordeaux, this time. What do ye say 'bout that, Jack? Jack?"

But the red-haired man said nothing, having fallen into a

troubled slumber. The priest jumped to his feet and anxiously paced the small confines of the room. Outside wagons clattered by in the early hours of this morning of May 11, 1687. Through the unshuttered window a shaft of sunlight, motes of dust dancing in its funnel of light, fell on the scuffed boards of the warped floor. Jack lay on a cot against the far wall, away from the drafts of the open window. Liam had covered him with the two blankets they possessed and the priest's own cloak. Yet even in his troubled sleep the man's body trembled. Liam surveyed the dingy room and thought it accurately reflected the transitory nature of their lives. On a small rickety table sat a procelain pitcher and washbowl, a small steel mirror and a half-eaten sausage. Beneath the table were stored three satchels.

Where was that young wench anyway? the priest asked himself. She should have returned by now. She'd left hours ago to search for the missing Jack. The priest crossed the room to check on his ill friend. He was no better, but also no worse, Liam consoled himself. *He will not die. An' if yer so confident o' that*, he asked himself, *why then be ye so anxious fer the wee one to be back? Jes' in case*, one part of him cautioned. *He did ask fer her. He doesn't want to . . . No! But then*, said another part, more logical, *ye should give the*— "No!" Liam said aloud to the quiet room. "No. He will not die. He will recover. An' there be an end to it. No more."

The blond priest sat beside the bed on the solitary chair and told his beads and waited for Jackie. As the morning wore on, Jack's breathing became more labored, his color paler. Deep smudges like bruises appeared under his eyes. Aye, pale, thought Father Liam, so pale, but not as pale as *his* face had been when he'd first stepped off that scurvy boat from Ireland. It had been—how long now? Twenty years. Twenty years ago he had left Ireland, gone on a pilgrimage to Rome. A long-term journey suggested by his suffering superior in Dublin. One fine day Liam had been caught with his hand in the poor box. It had only been a wee loan. But the religious superior had not seen it that way at all, and then he had found the wine bottle, er, bottles. All sorts of unpleasant language had flown through the air then, and Faither Liam had covered his ears to keep out the terrible wrath of the man. "Off to Rome with ye," the Bishop had said, "an' I hope to God ye see the Holy Faither so that ye may beg fer fergiveness an' be blessed. It might be better, Faither Liam, if yer pilgrimage were not a hasty one." And so, dismissed from his post in his poor parish, given a few coins to help him make his way, he knew that the clerical door in Ireland had been shut forever in his face. On his way down to the docks he had visited the grave of his sainted mother and bade her farewell, knowing that he would never again return home. The journey from Ireland to England had passed uneventfully, but then had come the ride across the English channel—why, it had nearly been the death of him. What a miserable time! With the spring storms arriving and the churning choppy water, he'd been green-gilled the entire voyage. On his arrival upon French soil, he had wobbled, his frail stomach still heaving with the motion of the white-crested waves. He had staggered against a convenient post, only to hear a cheerful voice in French, tinged with an Irish brogue, exclaim: "Are ye in sore need, Faither? Perhaps I can be o' some service." A strong arm had slipped around his shoulders and helped him across the docks, down the steps to a lodging house. There the man had helped him up to a room. Liam had staggered across the dingy room to the bed and collapsed, a sick sodden heap, on it.

The red-haired man had smiled and said, "If there's nothin' else ye need, Faither, I'll be movin' along."

A sob had escaped Liam's lips. "I need me purse."

"Beggin' yer pardon, Faither?" the man, his green eyes neutral, had asked.

"Ye have me purse. I need me money. I have nothin' nor no one in the world. Please," he pleaded, turning a plaintive face toward the man, "don't steal it."

Jack O'Connell had studied the stricken priest, and some mercy crept into his brigand heart. On the whole, he avoided conscience where his pigeons were concerned, for it paid not at all to mix business with sorry feelings.

Gruffly, he said, "All right. To be sure, keep yer purse," and, pulling the small leather bag out of his shirt, he'd tossed in onto the bed. The priest had grabbed it with shaking hands and clasped it tightly. "Bless ye, me son." Jack had turned to leave. "Wait," the priest said.

"We be countrymen. I beg ye, where might I find a dinner? One that I would find—er, reasonable, if ye ken me meanin'. 'Course, I don't be wantin' it now—but fer when me guts settle down.''

Jack nodded sagely. "I have just the place in mind. 'Tis not far from here. We'll walk there; I'll show ye the place an' ye'll tell me news o' Ireland.''

And they had gone to the crowded inn, where somehow, Liam never really seeing how it happened, Jack had paid for a loaf of bread, a bottle of red wine, and a sausage but had returned to the priest's sparsely furnished room with two loaves, two bottles, and two sausages. Astonishment lit up the priest's pale face.

"Aye, that be a right clever thing," he said in an admiring tone.

Jack, surprised at not being condemned for his mild thievery, thought there might be more to this whey-faced priest than he'd first thought. " 'Twasn't hard," he said offhandedly. "If ye want, I'll teach ye."

Liam had blushed. "Well, would I like that. As ye can plainly see, I be not well-heeled.''

"Stay with me, me friend," the red-haired man had said, a smile on his handsome face, "an' ye'll be plump in the pocket always.''

And stay with Jack he had, for twenty years. Twenty years which had flown by so quickly. He'd still not gone to Rome to beg forgiveness of the pope. 'Course, 'twas not the same pope sitting in the Vatican as when he'd started his journey. Aye, three popes had passed through Rome, but Liam had never once been there. Aye, how he—But his memories were interrupted by the clatter of riding boots on the stairwell outside the room. The door flew open with a bang, and Jackie ran in.

"I've searched everywhere, Faither. He's nowhere to be found from here to Versailles. Whatever could—'' She stopped, seeing the figure on the bed. In her haste, her Flemish velvet cavalier's hat, with its plump ostrich plume, fell to the floor, and Liam was sadly reminded of a similar hat years ago when she'd first come to them. Dropping on her knees beside the rough cot, she stroked Jack's forehead. The girl examined his wound. It was bad. "What happened?" she demanded of Liam.

"A jealous husband," the priest said simply.

"Oh, you fool," she moaned, clasping the dying man's

hand tightly in her own. "Oh, Papa, don't die. Please don't die." Tears silently slipped out of her gray eyes.

Liam touched her shoulder softly. "Aye, child, he'll be all right. He be merely wounded. Jes' a flesh wound, ye'll see. Jack'll mend right enough soon."

The young girl stared up at him through her tears and wondered why the priest denied the obvious. She placed her hand again on Jack's forehead. It was hot and dry. Not at all like her father's skin, not young. Old. Dying now.

"Have you sent for a doctor?" she asked anxiously, glancing at the priest.

"No." The reply came fron the dying man, who opened his green eyes slowly and with extreme effort. She saw a gray film on them, and the girl involuntarily shivered. "It would do no good, me dear. Jes' stay with me here, like ye be. That be all I'm askin'." He moved his hand across the coverlet, and his daughter grasped it. Jack's head lolled to one side as he slid into unconsciousness.

A high keening rose from outside the room. The banshee, thought Liam remembering his past, come to wail for those o' the high Irish families, fer those about to . . . He rushed to the window, then turned back. Jackie had begun sobbing, rocking back and forth on her heels. With one final cry, the girl flung her arms around Jack's still form. The gash, though dressed with a linen bandage, had seeped through, and now the blood oozed onto her clothing. But she did not notice. The realization of Jack's death struck Liam, and he sank into the chair.

The priest rose and with a trembling hand touched Jack's motionless breast. *No!* His friend was dead. But he couldn't be. Dead. *An' I denied him the last rites while he lived. His final request. I denied him the release o' the shrivin' o' his soul, the known an' welcome absolution. I did.* Tears welled up in his blue eyes and slipped down his pale plump cheeks. *Oh, Jack, can ye ever forgive me? I didn't think ye'd die.* But what was done was done. He had waited. He had been a fool, he thought bitterly, and he had betrayed his friend.

"Oh sweet Jaysus," he cried out loud and, kneeling down beside the cot, began the ritual for the dead. As he murmured the comforting words of the Office of the Dead, tears ran, unnoticed, down his flushed cheeks.

It seemed hours later when he raised his head. Jackie stood

by the window, her rigid back to the room. The priest rose stiffly and went to the girl, placing a comforting hand on her shoulder.

He felt her body tremble ever so slightly, then it was under control.

"I'll fetch th-the gravedigger," she said at last, her gaze never straying from the street outside.

"Aye."

"I need money, Faither. Papa always said to come to you when my purse was low." She swung around, her eyes tear-stained, her upper lip quivering.

"Aye," he said slowly, not meeting her gray eyes, "yer faither be right. I have a wee bit set aside." And in the ritual he had performed so many times before for Jack, Liam took the frame from its hiding place and pried loose a gem, a marquis-shaped topaz the size of his thumbnail. The priest replaced the frame and dropped the stone in the girl's outstretched palm. "I warrant this'll more than cover a-anythin' ye need f-fer J-Jack. Lodgin's, too. We must live lean now, Jackie. We've got what we took last night, an' we can be livin' off that fer a while."

The silver-haired girl nodded, her fingers curling convulsively around the topaz. "I'll return anon, Faither."

Alone, Father Liam Dougherty took up his vigil beside his old friend.

"What now shall we do, me sweet?" Father Liam asked Jackie, his voice slurred, his plump face flushed.

She stared at him with wide-set eyes, a gray gaze that wrung his heart and served to calm him. In just this short time since Jack's death Liam's and Jackie's positions had changed. No longer was she the child, asking Liam for permission or advice. The roles had been reversed.

"Brussels," she said. "We have not yet visited there. I'll dress as a boy, Liam. You'll be a merchant in lace." As the silver-haired girl began explaining her plan, Father Liam thought, *Ye'd be right proud, Jack. She'll make a fine leader. She'll be all right now. Don't worry, me ould friend. Don't worry at all.*

Chapter

Six

THE STREETS OF London were dark this night. Some light passed through the windows of buildings lining the streets, but for the most part it was a rarefied, diffused light, doing little more than showing a pedestrian the faint shine of cobblestones or a mud puddle to be avoided. Or the light might be reflected off the buckles of the shoes of one's assailant. For the streets of London were a dangerous place to walk after the sun had set. When dusk arrived, the honest merchants, housewives, lords, and ladies returned to their homes and locked and bolted their doors, and the streets became the preying ground of the whores, the footpads, the thieves, the murderers, the roving bands. And honest folk out after that time were open invitations to disaster—just as Francis Arthur Randolph Blade, ninth duke of Avalon, was a temptation to those habitués of the London underworld.

Alone, and dressed in the brocades and silks and jewels bespeaking the presence of a man of wealth, he strode, careless of his surroundings. Indeed, it almost seemed that he did not know where he walked. Was it any wonder that the duke provided an ideal target?

As the man walked, he thought of the events of the day. Earlier, hardly before Avalon had risen from the breakfast table, the earl of Shrewsbury had come calling.

Avalon's personal manservant, Cornelius Snodgrass, had bustled into the dining room of Avalon's spacious town mansion and presented his master with a handwritten note upon a silver salver. The duke had pushed away the last of his beefsteak, drained his wine, and then directed the servant: "Send him in, Corney."

The man had bowed, left, and reappeared with a dark-haired man, his soft pleasant face set in sober lines.

"Charles," said Avalon, rising to his feet and offering his hand.

Charles Talbot, earl of Shrewsbury, shook his friend's hand and then sat in the chair indicated by the duke. He accepted a small glass of wine and then looked at Avalon, still not speaking.

"What's wrong?" The duke's eyebrows drew together in a frown.

"We . . . may have been discovered," the earl said quietly.

"What!" Avalon exclaimed.

"There is a prisoner . . . at the Tower. He's to be interrogated today by the king himself—on suspicion of treason, a plot to overthrow James."

Avalon leaped to his feet and paced around the room. "Who?" he began. "One of ours?"

"I don't know, Blade," the other man said heavily, sipping slowly at his wine. "That's the reason I've come so early. We need you to go to the Tower and find out who this man is. As well you know, we have few friends there, and hence little information on the prisoner."

"I'll go, of course, but why choose me?"

"You are yet on the fringes of our group," Shrewsbury replied. "Less suspect, although the king has noticed you for other reasons." Shrewsbury quirked a brief smile that touched only his lips, and Avalon acknowledged the irony with a nod of his head.

"Any news?" the duke inquired.

Shrewsbury shook his head. "No. It's been almost three weeks since Sydney left, and still no word on Prince William's decision." He sighed deeply. "If only James would realize what he is driving us to. . . ."

"Treason." The word hung in the air between the two men as Avalon mentally reviewed the events of the past month.

On the evening of June 30, 1688, at the town mansion of Charles Talbot, the earl of Shrewsbury, a small group of concerned men had drafted a letter to William of Orange, stadtholder of Holland. The son-in-law of the English monarch and a staunch Protestant, William had been invited to come to England to help defend the religious liberties of the English people. That very night one of their number, George Sydney, disguised as a common seaman, left London to deliver the letter to the Dutch leader. It was anticipated by the men who placed their signatures upon that letter—and thus committed a treasonous act for which all of them could be hanged if caught—that Prince William would agree to their request for aid. Yet only silence came from William, and now a prisoner was kept in the Tower, a prisoner who might well be the death of them all.

The prisoner, a Dissenter from the Church of England, was being interrogated at the order, and in the presence, of James II. When Avalon arrived at the Tower of London, the man still had not spoken.

His face impassive, James sat, a straight figure in a chair. Around him were the sycophants of the English court, come to amuse themselves at a torture.

"You are a member of a movement to overthrow us, is this not so?" the king questioned. Still the man refused to answer.

One of the jailers lifted the man's face and splashed water on it to revive him. At that moment Avalon clearly saw the Dissenter's face. It was no one of his group.

"Again," James said, nodding to the jailer. The burly man picked up the slender metal rod and began once more tapping the bottom of the prisoner's feet. Eventually, Avalon knew, the feet would swell and then—burst. The man screamed as the pressure increased. There was the sound of a muffled giggle from one of the painted courtiers.

"You wish to place our elder daughter upon the throne of England, do you not? Speak, you fool!" James turned an angry face toward the jailer. "Make him speak! We must hear from his lips of this treacherous plot."

"Yes, sire," the man said, and the beating began again.

Over and over the Dissenter screamed, yet he said nothing

to the monarch. Flowers of red appeared on the soles of the prisoner's feet and bloomed, their petals dripping down onto the floor. There was a rustle of appreciation around the prisoner, and Avalon glanced away. The screaming stopped abruptly.

"What is it?" the king demanded.

The jailor yanked the prisoner's head up. The eyes were rolled back in the head. "Dead," the man said. "His heart gave out."

Grim-faced and tight-lipped, the English monarch had risen and left the dungeon of the Tower, dismayed that the information he sought was still unknown.

Avalon had watched as the body was removed. Within minutes of the prisoner's death the dungeon was deserted. The echoes of the screams still in his ears, Avalon had glanced around the dungeon once more and left, wondering if the dead prisoner had family. When he reemerged from the Tower he had paused in the late afternoon light and breathed deeply. That man might have been one of his group. It could have easily been he. It still might, one part of him observed sardonically. Yes, William hadn't arrived yet; and yet—so many yets to this, he thought with dismay, too many, too many loose ends—some hope had been expressed the night before when, once more meeting at Shrewsbury's, the group had received word from Simon Martín, Avalon's closest friend and a Jew, concerning John Churchill. Churchill commanded the king's troops and heretofore had been a staunch ally of the Catholic king, but as the months went by it appeared that he was wavering in his support. The conspirators had decided that a message must be sent to William of Orange informing him of Churchill's vacillation. They hoped that this would decide William in their favor.

Blade was so deeply engrossed in these thoughts that it was several minutes before the sound of a frightened voice broke through his concentration. Startled out of his reverie, he looked about for the source of the disturbance. Directly ahead, illuminated dimly in the light of the moon and of a shuttered lantern set on the cobblestones, cowered a minister of the Church of England. A young brigand of medium height held the poor man by the throat and was slapping his face.

Quickly Avalon appraised the situation: the minister, returning from a sick bed or deathbed or perhaps on his way to one, had been set upon by the footpad, who was after money or, because of the recent religious troubles, perhaps out to harass the Anglican.

Drawing his sword from its pearl-encrusted scabbard, Avalon started forward, and then in the weak light something gleamed at the minister's belt. Something shiny and round. Beads. A black-beaded rosary. Anglican ministers did not carry papist beads: only Roman Catholic priests did. A slow smile curved Avalon's thin lips. *What do we have here*? he pondered. Catholics setting upon hapless travelers in revenge for the riots three weeks ago, or perhaps not one brigand but two. He glanced at the couple. The brigand was still slapping the defenseless minister, who struggled ineffectually against the assault. But was the footpad really hitting the minister? It seemed that way at first glance, but when Avalon studied it . . . . Very clever, indeed, he concluded. A proposed robbery, and it was no wonder the bandits expected their ruse to be successful, the duke thought ironically, surveying his clothing and gems. Well-dressed, obviously wealthy, alone, careless and inattentive. He would surprise these footpads, the duke of Avalon grimly resolved.

Avalon raised his sword and brandished it over his head. "Hold to, my good man," he called loudly. "I shall rescue you."

A strangled squawk was the minister's only reply. Liam, in his Anglican robes, hissed at Jackie. "Fer God's sake, Jackie, don't break me neck. I'm black an' blue, an' me windpipe feels half crushed!"

Instantly the disguised girl was chagrined. "I'm sorry," she whispered. Her hold around the bogus minister's neck loosened, but she pretended to strike him across the face once more. She was elated. Their plan would work: this stupid nobleman would rush to Liam's aid, and they would "amuse" him—Liam, grabbing the man's arm for support, would throw the man off balance instead, while Jackie at the same instant would fling a handful of snuff into their cull's eyes. He would be blinded long enough for them to knock him over the head, securely tie him, rummage through his pockets, steal what they could, and then be gone, disappearing down the streets in the cover of the night.

Avalon raced toward the couple, and Jackie, seeing him approach, scooped out the snuff to toss it into the victim's eyes. Swaying, Liam flexed his hand. He must make a sure, precise grab. Avalon reached them, and Liam, stumbling, grabbed at the man. But instead of helping the minister, the man seized him and roughly pushed him in front of the young brigand so that when the brigand tossed the snuff it settled into the minister's eyes, not those of their dupe.

"Aye, Jackie!" he cried, rubbing at his stinging eyes. Jackie, startled, rushed at the nobleman. Suddenly a well-formed leg was thrust into her path. Unable to check her momentum, the disguised girl tripped and fell, landing in a mud puddle.

Avalon bent and unshuttered the lantern. Then, his sword still out, he lazily regarded the pair. The bogus minister, tears falling from his outraged eyes, wandered about blindly, searching with his hand for his accomplice. "Jackie?" he called plaintively. "Jackie? Will ye answer me? Jackie!"

The young brigand crawled out of the mud puddle. His coat and breeches were ruined by the slime, and, his voice low with a barely restrained anger, he cursed Avalon in five languages. A rare privilege, Avalon thought wryly, to have such an educated bandit blister him in so diverse a manner.

The minister continued to wander about blankly, searching for his fellow brigand. Avalon, tired of watching him, lightly tapped him on the head with the broadside of his sword. With a slight moan, he slumped unconscious to the street.

Seeing her opportunity, Jackie jumped to her feet, ready to do battle. She raised her fists, prepared to knock the man down with a single mighty blow of his fists. Avalon laughed, placing the point of his sword to her throat. "I wouldn't try it, if I were you, boy. Stay put," he coolly ordered. "Put your hands down slowly. . . . All right. Now give me your weapon—and do that very slowly, for I am not at all amused."

She grimaced at the man's unintentional pun and with deliberate slowness reached down and pulled out a knife from the top of her boot, its blade gleaming wickedly.

"Toss it on the ground." She did, and Avalon picked up the weapon. "A very nasty blade for such a youth." He examined it and tucked it into his sash. "The other one, please."

"Other one, what?" she growled menacingly.

"Your other knife, please." He held out a hand palm up.

With a swift motion Jackie brought the second knife out,

letting it slide from its hiding place inside her sleeve, and slashed at his hand. Only it wasn't there. He had quickly stepped aside and deftly grabbed her wrist. He then bent it back until her fingers involuntarily released the second knife. It fell with a clatter. He jerked her around, so that her arm was at an awkward angle behind her back. The man pulled on the arm, and she gasped. He made a sound of disapproval and shook her roughly.

"Now your rope, please." With her free hand she reached inside her coat and pulled out the coiled length of rope, the rope she and Liam had intended using on their victim. "Sit," the man commanded, releasing her twisted arm.

Glaring at him, Jackie rubbed her shoulder but obeyed. He quickly tied her hands together tightly, then wound the plait around her ankles, between her pulled-up knees and back to her hands. She was effectively hobbled; even if she could rise to her feet, she would not be able to run off.

"I suppose you're proud of your handiwork," she sneered, irritated that this fop had wrecked their plan.

He laughed. "You are a most unpleasant fellow, boy. Tell me, what shall I do with you two?"

Jackie studied her opponent. He had long, curling dark hair. His blue eyes glinted with a sardonic expression, and there was a cleft in his strong chin. Broad-shouldered, narrow of waist, with a muscular leg, he gave the appearance of a natural athlete, of a man who rode and fenced and hunted, yet his clothes belied that. His shoes were red-heeled and far higher than any Jackie's father had worn. The man's broad-cloth coat was of a light puce, with black embroidered roses on the cuffs and coat skirt. His waistcoat striped pink and white, and his breeches, of mauve silk, were trimmed with black lace. The garters were maroon, as was his low-swept hat. The ostrich feather had been dyed pink.

Her lip curled in derision. What a fop! A peacock entirely. *Yet*, she thought, *with that determined chin there is a certain . . . air of masculinity, something attractive, almost compelling, about him and certainly dangerous*. A groan sounded next to her, and she knew Liam was waking.

The fop laughed at her. "Well, my fine bandit, you should indeed study your craft more. You are a most inferior footpad."

"I'll have your bloody head!" she yelled. She struggled against her bonds to rise and beat him for his insolence but only succeeded in losing her balance and tipping onto her side, her head half in the mud puddle. Her wig slipped slightly, and for the merest moment Avalon caught a sight of a tantalizing silver; then Jackie moved her head and the color was gone.

Shame and embarrassment mingled with anger made her discount her thoughts of only a few minutes before. How could she have begun to be interested in him? How could she think he was manly? He was nothing. An insect. Less! Only . . . only she didn't know what was less than an insect. In her frustration she spit at him.

Instead of reacting with anger, the man merely chuckled.

"Oh, Holy Mither o' God," Liam began wailing, wringing his hands together. Avalon supposed he really should tie the old man, but he suspected he wouldn't have the brains to run off and leave his young accomplice. Now *that* young man bore watching. "Oh, kind sir, please don't give us over to the watch! I beg ye! I'm a poor man, an' me son here, we thought only to find a wee amount o' money, fer we be starvin', we be, man, an' the wee little ones at home be all a-cryin', oh please, man, have mercy 'pon us!"

"Be still!" Jackie hissed. She glowered up at the nobleman. Slowly she pushed herself up off from the ground with her elbow and regained her sitting position. "When I free myself, when I remove this rope, you will pay for what you have done this night." Her voice was deliberate, calm, threatening. "You will regret having set foot out this evening. I shall remove you to a secluded spot, and once there I'll tie you up—"

"Oh, lordy, lordy, sir, don't send us to the prison," Liam whined. "I don't want to be goin'. Please, sir, I'll do anything ye—"

The boy interrupted. "And then when you can't move, I'll take out my sharp knife and I'll cut away your manhood, what little you have!" she spat.

"An' I be very accomplished at cleanin' boots, sir, an' play a right fine game o' chess, sir, an' am quite well-read, sir."

"When you beg for mercy I'll just laugh, then I'll kick your bloody body over with the toe of my boot, and I'll leave you there to rot!"

"Only please, kind sir, don't be sendin' the guard after us,

sir. We meant no harm, truly so, sir." The priest's voice, as
well as his round face, was earnest.

Listening to the two, the pretty boy threatening, the old
man pleading, Avalon realized the full absurdity of the situation. He gave a great bellow of laughter that only caused
Liam to cower, certain that they were done for, and Jackie to
passionately vow in her heart that she would kill him before
the night was over.

"I tell you what, little chicken," Avalon said mockingly,
his blue eyes snapping with amusement. He reached with his
fingers to chuck her under the chin. "I shall be kind to you
and not call the watch."

"Don't do us any favors. You can keep your kindness to
yourself and push it—"

"Jackie, Jackie," the priest said hastily, "leave 'lone."

She shot him a sullen look but closed her mouth.

"You, young boy, are a most impertinent puppy and must
learn good manners. You, old man, must learn to shut your
mouth."

"Puppy!" "Old man!" the pair cried simultaneously.
They glared indignantly at the mocking nobleman.

He chuckled. "But you must do something in return, if I am
not to call the watch."

"An' what be that, sir?" the priest asked cautiously.

"Let him call the watch!" the disguised girl said defiantly.
"I'll make no bargain with the likes of *him*!"

"Ah, lad, let's not be so hasty," Liam said quickly to his
young companion. "Let's hear what the good gentleman has
to say."

"You stand only to profit by it," the duke of Avalon said.
"I shall take you to my home, where I shall free you. You
will then explain who you are and what you were doing this
night." He looked at first one, then the other. "Agreed?"

"Well, sir, that don't sound like much o' a bargain," Liam
said, plainly puzzled.

"Your other alternative is prison," Avalon reminded him.

"Aye, sir, yer offer be right good, it be."

"It's a trap," the youth said sullenly.

"Don't be so sure o' it, me lad."

"I don't trust him. He has a murderous glint in those blue
eyes," the young girl said. But she allowed herself to be
overruled.

Avalon reached down and untied Jackie's feet, but kept her hands bound. She rose slowly, frowning at the man. Then he pushed Liam in front and, holding his sword in one hand and the rope binding the boy in the other, began walking. Liam picked up the lantern to light their way. They trudged through the streets without incident or conversation.

Finally they came to a large home, set back a few feet from the street. Seven marble steps led up to the immense bronze door, which was richly worked in bas-relief.

Liam let his eye rove over the figures, then froze. Jackie, directly behind the priest, bumped into him.

"What is it?" she demanded harshly.

"Look up there," he indicated the portal with his hand.

She studied it. Imps with pointed tails, scaly snakelike figures, hideous bloated monsters, beasts with one eye and one horn on their foreheads, figures with no legs or eyes or mouths: all manner of dreadful shapes lumbered and slithered and frolicked and crawled around the portal, creating a grotesque stone tapestry that seemed to breathe and come alive. She wrinkled her forehead. "What is it?"

"Do ye remember when ye be a wee tyke I told ye o' a terrible story of an English family cursed by the Lord an' what had no mercy, no fergiveness, nor any other kind o' decent human emotion?" The priest glanced fearfully at Avalon, who merely looked at him with interest. The girl nodded, her eyes growing wide.

"I heard tell," the priest continued, "that there be issue from that ill-met match o' that poor betrayed woman an' that evil man. The boy be raised by his tutors an' traveled far an' wide, learnin' all sorts o' strange things, studyin' the black arts, 'tis said. He conducts the most unspeakable dreadful practices, straight from the very depths o' hell. 'Tis rumored that this grown son be far worse than the father ever dared be." Trying to keep his hands from trembling, Liam laced his fingers in front of his stomach and, turning to the sober-faced nobleman, said, "That family's name be Blade. A knife in the side o' society if ever there be one. Are ye that son? Are ye that godless hell-raiser, man?"

The nobleman rapped loudly on the bronze door. It resonated deeply inside. He gave them both a mocking bow. "You, indeed, have the pleasure of my acquaintance. I am Blade, duke of Avalon."

The massive door swung open, and the flicker of flames could be seen. Beyond the opening Jackie saw a tall black-faced servant, clothed in ebony silk, with husky shoulders, waiting impassively. He moved not at all, and she shivered slightly with fear.

Blade beckoned with one hand for them to enter. "Come, old man and young boy, enter my home, if you will. Come through the gate of hell." The light emanating from the house's great hall spread a yellow tint on Blade's skin and seemed to make the widow's peak at his forehead even longer, more sinister.

Liam, gathering himself with visible effort, crossed himself and, murmuring a prayer, walked through the doorway. Blade followed, the rope that bound Jackie's wrists still in his hand. For a moment she hesitated, then the decision was made for her; the rope was jerked taut, and she was dragged through the doorway into the hellhole of "Satan" Blade, rakehell, libertine, roué, profligate, debauché, satyr, betrayer, seducer, alchemist, and necromancer. Jackie squared her shoulders, threw back her head defiantly, raised her pointed chin, and entered hell.

Chapter
Seven

HEARING THE RUMBLE of Blade's baritone voice outside the London town house, Simon Martín waited with ill-concealed impatience for the enormous bronze door to swing open and admit his tall friend. All afternoon Simon had paced the length of the front hall, unable to depart from his friend's house lest he miss the duke, for the intelligence Simon bore could wait no longer. Avalon must be informed this day.

A swordsmith of some renown, Simon was a quiet man of much intelligence and learning. He had a reasonable nature and a streak of practicality that belied the dreamer in his warm brown eyes.

Santu, Blade's black-liveried servant, a dusky-skinned man from the Dark Continent, heard his master's voice and glided across the room with only a sibilant whisper from his slippered feet. At last the door swung back as if by its own accord, but Simon had seen the swift and almost imperceptible motion of Santu's hand unlatching it.

In strode the master of the house, a drawn sword in his hand. But he was not alone, for behind him followed two companions and, viewing first the weapon and then the strangers in the firelight, Simon felt dismay rise in him. What deviltry was his friend up to now? He sighed, knowing that it would be best to endure his impatience in silence, for Blade would not and could not be pushed into a hasty explanation.

Simon studied the two derelicts. *Now where did Blade find these two pretty coves?*

"Ah, Simon." Blade, noticing for the first time the presence of his quiet friend, sheathed his sword and strolled across the room to briefly clasp the other man's hand. "What brings you here? I thought not to see you for another fortnight." Blade's blue eyes were curious and penetrating.

Simon nodded imperceptibly at the boy and the minister. "What I must say to you, Blade, no other ears must hear. Where might we talk privately?"

"Inside, my friend," the duke said, indicating an inner room. "But first I must interrogate these two."

Avalon turned back to the pair, who stood staring at the richness of the outer hallway. "Come." He snapped his fingers imperatively, and his was the voice of command, for without thinking the two thieves stepped forward to obey. Simon's eyes widened as he saw the ropes around the boy's slender wrists.

"Do you now go about capturing youths off the street, Blade?" he asked, his voice filled with incredulity.

Avalon chuckled. "So say the stories," he replied. He nodded to Santu, who moved to the boy's side and loosened the youth's bonds, then removed them.

The boy rubbed his wrists and glared at the duke. The old man consolingly patted his companion on the shoulder.

Santu now stepped past the group, gliding like a black ghost, and opened the door from the hallway to an inner salon. Avalon gestured for the two strangers to precede them, and Blade and Simon followed. Exclamations of surprise and pleasure marked the entry of the disreputable-looking pair, and Simon smiled to himself, remembering the first time he had seen this exquisitely turned-out room. It had been well over seven years now. He, a young apprentice swordsmith, had been dispatched by his master to the duke of Avalon. Arriving at the town house, Simon had paled at the sight of the demon-infested portal. He, too, had heard the tales of the Blade family. His tremulous knock had been answered by the impassive Santu, ageless then as now, who had led the nervous young man to this salon and opened a door into another world for Simon.

In the salon the plush carpeting was like a silver sea, the walls the blue of the sky as it trembles on the edge between dusk and night. Set upon graceful marble pedestals along the walls were statues of Egyptian gods and goddesses in human and animal form. Blade, seeing the young apprentice's curiosity, had quietly explained to the young Jew what each statue represented and had briefly related the story of each immortal. Above these statues, on the ceiling, sparkled specks of silver, so that if you squinted you thought you were seeing the stars in the heavens.

Facing Simon with a sardonic smile on his lips, the duke had said, "Here heaven and hell meet, Simon Martín. Are you man enough to face that?"

The young man's head had snapped around at that, and he had spoken quietly yet firmly. "As much a man as you, Your Grace. And I see now that you are no more a demon than I, although some would point their finger at me because of my religion."

"Here your religion does not matter. My only concern is the man." Crossing the room, the duke had held out his hand in friendship to the young Jew.

Hesitantly, Simon had clasped the man's hand in his own. Blade, studying him with those strangely intent blue eyes, had said, "Here today is born a friendship that will not end even in the grave."

His cheeks burning, Simon had turned his head away slightly, and the duke, seeing his embarrassment, had let fall his hand. From that moment Avalon had treated the Jew as a friend—and an equal—and, while it had not been easy these past seven years, Simon had achieved a social status that would not have been possible without his wealthy benefactor's influence. With the patronage of the duke had come increased business, so that at the end of his apprenticeship Simon Martín, opening his own sword shop, had found a large clientele eagerly waiting for his expertise.

With a start and a sense of chagrin, Simon realized that Blade was once more regarding him with amusement, even as the nobleman had on that day long ago. Determinedly, the swordsmith shook himself, bringing his mind back to the present—and to the problem of the boy and the man and the intelligence with which he must acquaint Blade before too long.

"A glass of wine?" Blade inquired. The swordsmith nodded, and Santu returned in a few moments with two cut-crystal goblets on a silver salver. Blade offered nothing to the two companions, who still stood gawking and scowling, respectively.

Avalon sat in a high-backed chair, one impeccably turned-out leg in front of him, and studied on the table in front of him a bowl of fruit—each piece carefully cut and skillfully crafted of green imperial jade. Simon rolled the stem of the glass between his fingers, displaying some of his impatience. *Damn Avalon for his sense of the dramatic*, thought Simon.

As the minutes ticked by, the boy and the old man grew progressively more uneasy. An expression of mulishness, offset somewhat by the awe in his gray eyes, transformed the youth's pretty face into a sullen mask. The old man quivered at the youth's side, fingering the smooth beads of a rosary. What the devil? Simon thought. A Protestant minister equipped with a rosary?

Unable to contain his curiosity any further, Simon whirled to his friend and demanded, "What goes on here, Blade? Who are these poor wretches?"

"Ah, Simon." Blade, arching one foot, stared pensively at the red heel of his shoe. "That I do not know, alas. I would hope that in the next few minutes they would feel obligated to enlighten us." He raised his blue eyes and stared intently at them.

"I shall not say a word!" the boy said defiantly. Then, with a savage cry, Jackie leaped across the room to where Blade sat and raised her hands to strangle the nobleman. Simon, stunned by the swiftness of the action, could only watch in utter silence and confusion at the unexpected attack. While the girl was quick on her feet, the English duke proved faster. As Jackie lunged at the man, Blade simply moved a leg in her direction. She tripped, sprawling face first onto the soft carpet. Her posterior in the air, she lay draped over the duke's leg, stunned. Unsuccessfully she tried to hold back the tears of shame and humiliation which gathered in her grey eyes and coursed down her face into the richness of the silver carpeting.

A silence filled the room. "For God's sake, Blade." Simon, his paralysis at last broken, rushed forward and gently helped her up from the ignoble position. Jackie hastily wiped her wet face on the soiled sleeve of her coat.

"Now we are prepared to ascertain the identity of my two would-be attackers." Gesturing with an impeccably manicured hand, Avalon forestalled Simon's expression of dismay. "Let me explain this evening's events for you. As I walked back from the Tower"—at this the Englishman's blue eyes locked with those of Simon for one steely moment, then flicked back to the boy and the bogus minister—"I saw what I presumed to be a minister beset by a footpad. But this fool had neglected to remove his papist beads, and I realized that it was a ruse, the true purpose to do me harm. I found it necessary to remove them from the scene of their anticipated crime to the house so that I might sit in judgment upon them. I promised that I would set the puppy free of his leash once we reached my domicile. I have done so. In return they were to acquaint me with their identities."

Jackie sneered at the duke.

"Perhaps I shall have Santu bind the boy once more."

"Do not abandon your promise," the young swordsmith pleaded. "If you demand that they behave as you expect, then you must treat them in a fitting manner. The boy is soiled and wet. No doubt they are hungry. Permit them to rest, and then interrogate them later. Besides," he added, his impatience pressing through, "I must needs talk with you, Blade. I beg you—send them away, and let us talk."

"You are too kindhearted by half," the man said mockingly, but he shrugged. "Still." He pulled a velvet cord, and the Nubian manservant appeared. "Santu, escort the boy and . . . minister to a room to warm themselves and to dine." He paused, then crossed to an enormous scrollwork desk. Blade opened it, and when he withdrew his hand a pistol resided in his palm. "Take this, Santu," Blade said, handing the gun to the servant. "You may find use of it if they should prove recalcitrant."

"Whatever can you be thinking of, Blade?" Simon asked as the servant directed Jackie and Liam from the salon. "Have you acquired yet another pet?"

The Englishman's reply was lost as the door shut behind them.

Santu indicated they were to ascend a curved stairway. Each step was muffled as their feet sank into the richly colored carpeting on the stairs. At the second-floor landing the servant pointed to the right with the pistol, and they obeyed the silent command. Soon they entered a door at the end of the hall. After lighting several candlesticks situated around the room, the servant then waited for their command.

"Ah, yes," the priest said, remembering the duke's words about a meal, "we be near to faintin' with hunger an' need a fair bite o' eatin'. We be startin' with a duck—"

"Bring us some ale and bread," Jackie burst in. "That is all we desire."

Santu nodded, closing the door. There was a rattling, and Jackie rushed across and pulled at the doorknob.

"It's locked!" she cried out. "How dare they? How dare *he*?" She whirled away, the very picture of outraged indignation, and stalked to the window.

"I suppose it be his prerogative," Liam said slowly. "It bein' his household—an seein' how 'twas us who be out to rob him."

Jackie brushed away their guilt with a quick hand. "We're not common thieves. We don't deserve to be locked up!"

Liam sighed heavily. "I think, darlin', we may be glad that it'll not be our necks that receive a stretchin'. Settle down an' enjoy yerself. At least we be gettin' a free meal out o' this, an' a warm room."

"Oh, all right," Jackie agreed reluctantly. Tight-lipped, she gazed around at the room in which they found themselves.

On either side of the door was a small table, a cane chair pulled underneath. Opposite the door was a recessed window with heavy maroon curtains drawn against the night. In the recess sat a large velvet armchair. An immense bed made of cherry wood took up almost the entire wall. A silk coverlet of maroon, apple-green, and Chinese blue in an intricate pattern of peacocks and phoenixes was spread across the bed, which, Jackie had to admit, beckoned seductively to her, for she realized now just how tired she was. Above the bed hung a set of four Chinese sketches. Curiosity outweighing hostility, Jackie advanced, staring at the pictures. Each one portrayed a delicate branch of a flowering tree—one for each season. Upon each branch was a richly plumed bird.

Overwhelmed with the simple beauty of the pictures, Jackie

raised a hand to touch one of the birds, then thought better. She mustn't deign to touch one of *his* possessions. Still, she had to admit to herself, the room showed excellent taste. Not *his,* though, she would wager. Shrugging, she joined Liam in front of the fireplace. She needed to warm her chilled body.

"Ye be a fair sight to see, Jackie love," Liam said with a chuckle. She grimaced. "Ye be mud from the tip o' yer nose to the toe o' yer boots. Mayhap if ye changed yer clothes ye might fare better in yer mood?"

"Oh, all right," the girl replied crossly. She lifted the heavy top of one of the chests. Inside, fragrant with the odor of cedar chips, were folded clean, starched cambric shirts, and several pairs of breeches. Liam, curious, opened the companion chest and peered into its depths. "Here be coats, Jackie me love, an' some waistcoats."

She frowned.

"I do not ken why he be havin' these clothes, darlin', but I warrant it don't do to be askin' too many questions o' that man."

Jackie shrugged as she stripped off her sodden clothing. Liam, with his back to her, waited patiently. She frowned again as she dropped the grimy shirt and breeches and used them to quickly rub the worst of the mud off her face and her boots. She brushed dirt off her brown wig, which she had adopted since coming to London, straightened it, and smoothed back some loose hairs. Then she put on the clothes she had selected from the chests.

At last Jackie called to Liam, and he faced her. "Lordy be!" the Irish priest exclaimed softly. She smiled and, turning, examined her image in the mirror above one chest. Reflected in the mirror's depths was an exquisite vision in fawn breeches fastened at the knees with gold buckles, a snowy white shirt with a lace front, and a chocolate-colored coat. Jackie tugged at one cuff of the shirt and brushed a hand over the breeches. It was expensive material, there could be no mistake about that, and the clothing was of excellent cut. Why would the duke maintain extra clothing here, and clothing, at that, which accommodated her small frame?

Jackie thought of the duke's foppish appearance, his dandyish actions, and remembered the other man's question concerning "pets" as they were led out of the salon. 'Twould take no straining of the mental processes, Jackie concluded cynically, to understand well enough why the duke maintained the clothing of young boys in a bedroom, and she resolved to harden her heart even more against the duke's depraved character.

"That other man not be too bad," Liam mused out loud.

"Well, we don't know what *he* would have done in the duke's place," the girl said acidly. "Perhaps he would have been worse!"

"Now, now, Jackie, simmer down," the priest said gently.

Both Liam and the girl started as someone knocked courteously at their door. They waited a moment and, when no one walked in, Jackie called, "Enter."

The door was unlocked, and Santu entered with a tray of food. Delicious odors wafted from it, and despite herself Jackie felt pangs of hunger overtaking her sense of outrage. It *had* been hours since she and the priest had last dined, and it hadn't been the best fare at that inn . . . .

"What did you learn at the Tower?" Simon asked Blade as soon as the doors to the salon were closed, for Avalon had ignored his question regarding the two failed footpads.

The duke, recalling the scene of torture at the Tower of London, rubbed a hand over his handsome face. His bantering mood was dropped, and when he spoke it was in a somber tone. " 'Twas not one of ours, thank God. But it was some poor wretch upon whom James had tossed his net of suspicions. The man, confessing nothing, died."

Simon drew in a deep breath. "But it could well have been one of us. May yet be one of us," he amended. He paused. "My information is twofold." Avalon arched a finely shaped eyebrow and waited. "First, Shrewsbury suspects that before the month is out, John Churchill will have made up his mind, if he is to throw in his lot with us. So he feels the message should be taken posthaste to William."

"Well, that's good news," Avalon replied, "inasmuch as we will have the king's army commander with us. What else do you have to report, Simon?"

"It is now impossible for you to go." Simon Martín paused and intently searched his friend's face. "The king's men are watching our group. You are followed, just as I am."

"God's blood!" Avalon swore, jumping to his feet. "What

now, Simon? Whom do we send? If we are all suspect, well
. . . what a pretty kettle of fry we find ourselves in, my
friend. Churchill finally crumbling in his backing of the king
and now—now, no way to reach—'' Avalon suddenly stopped.
He gazed at Simon, then at the ceiling. His handsome face
settled into an absorbed study, then blandness.

His friend's innocent mien was deceptive, Simon knew,
and hid a calculating mind. "What plots and intrigues have
you thought of, Blade?" the swordsmith asked warily.

The man only shook his head, smiling slightly. "Permit me
to first pursue my thoughts." He rang for Santu, who entered, bringing a tray with a light meal of bread, cheeses, and
fruit, and a large carafe of wine.

Minutes raced by as Avalon said nothing. He stared into
space and occasionally tapped a slim finger against his knee.
Simon, not knowing how else to occupy the time, sliced off a
chunk of the cheese, poured himself a glass of wine, and
began to eat.

Nearly thirty minutes had elapsed before Avalon returned
his attention to Simon. He smiled ruefully at his friend. "I
beg pardon, Simon, but I was lost in my thoughts."

" 'Tis fine," Simon replied solemnly. "I have dined while
you have thought."

Avalon chuckled. "And I have discovered our salvation—
perhaps." Pouring a glass of wine, he sipped the deep-colored
liquid. "We must find a messenger who is a stranger to the
king's men. Someone whom they have never seen . . . someone very much like my two guests."

"No, Blade!" Simon exclaimed. "Even if they could be
trusted," he said sternly, "the king's watchers have noted
their entry here, and would they not then be suspect themselves?"

The duke of Avalon's lips curved into an ironic smile.
"Now, Simon," he said lazily, "you know that London
denizens are aware of my pattern of living, and what would
be more familiar—nay, what would be more *expected*—than
the sight of a young boy departing my house in the early
morning hours?"

"Blade—" Simon began, but he was stopped with a sharp
gesture by his friend.

"You must agree with the logic. It *is* a familiar sight,
yes?"

"I'll concede that, but if you would only permit me to go on—" The swordsmith's voice was filled with exasperation.

"No, say nothing further—'Satan' Avalon has spoken. I shall send my hell-boy out tomorrow morning, and with him will go that decrepit oldster, whom no one in their right senses would ever suspect. And with them we shall send out a message for Prince William that the king's commander wavers in his support."

"A fine theory, Blade, but how will it be enforced? Once they have left, they will no doubt betray us, or at best simply do nothing at all."

"You, Simon, are not a student of human nature or you would have answered your own question, and then you'd not plague me." The smile on the duke of Avalon's face lightened the sting of his words. "They are thieves. They attempted to cull me this evening, and I have postponed summoning the watch. These bandits well know that they could end their days in prison if I spoke against them, or even dancing at the end of a rope. Do not discount their fear as a determining factor in their decision. I am sure they possess a healthy concern for their miserable hides. And I know of an even more persuasive element." He leaned forward, rubbing his thumb and forefinger in a slight circular movement. Despite himself, Simon grinned.

"Money, my dear Simon, always proves a sufficient incentive."

"Perhaps, but what is to prevent them from absconding with your money? Or worse, going to the authorities to claim a reward?"

"Ah, tonight you espouse the role of devil's advocate, or should I say Satan's? I shall award them a handsome sum— but only upon completion of their errand. I think natural greed shall triumph over any reluctance they might have. Too, they are not honest men. Why should they go to the authorities? Especially when their reward would, no doubt, be imprisonment."

Simon spread his hands in a gesture of defeat. Avalon stirred and jerked the bell cord. Santu entered, impassive and silent as ever, and waited for his master's command. "Bring down the guests. They will have eaten and rested by now, I warrant."

The manservant nodded and withdrew.

The "guests" in question were in reality sound asleep at that moment. Food and drink and the tension of the evening's escapade had taken their toll. Jackie had vowed as she listened to Liam's snores that she would stay awake and would avenge herself upon That Man. That Man would . . . but she never finished the thought, for she fell sound asleep.

Then, seemingly the next moment, Jackie grew aware of a firm hand gently prodding her. She glanced around in the gloom and saw the impassive Nubian servant standing beside the bed. He beckoned with one hand, indicating urgency.

She rolled over onto one elbow and poked at Liam.

"Ooo, er, um, whazit masser?" he mumbled.

"Faither Liam," she whispered. " 'Tis time to rise. The servant's come to fetch us."

"What?" The priest sat up slowly, rubbing his eyes, then peered at the silent manservant. "It be time to face the divil, me lad," he advised Jackie. They followed the servant out of the room and down the stairs.

Upon seeing them, now considerably cleaner, Avalon suppressed a smile and directed a stern countenance at the pair of rapscallions. "We have yet a few unsettled matters. Now, what are your names? What was your scheme this night?" Liam merely shuffled his feet and stared morosely, and somewhat guiltily, at his boots. Jackie remained silent.

"Very well, I shall call the watch." He moved to send for Santu, all the while watching the two footpads exchange furtive glances.

"No, don't, I beg o' ye fer the pityin' love o' sweet Jaysus," the Irish man said, taking a step forward. "We be poor people an' generally honest folk. Me moniker be Liam McKier, an' this be me nevvie, Jackie McKier. We ran 'gainst a bit o' hard luck an' thought to supplement our wee income a mite, if ye ken me meanin'." He smiled hopefully at the two men. Avalon drew his dark brows together in a frown.

Liam hastily resumed the tale he was weaving. "We meant to steal from ye, sir, there be no doubt 'bout that now. But we'd not have hurt ye, we be not murderers."

"Simply cutpurses and footpads."

The priest's face brightened. "Aye, sir, that be all."

In spite of himself, Simon laughed.

As though suddenly realizing what he had admitted, Liam

clasped both hands over his mouth. But the damage was done.

"You big fool!" hissed the boy. "Now you've gone and let the cat out. You have a mouth like a sieve!"

"Oh aye, Jackie, I be right sorry." He turned contrite eyes to the slight youth.

"Being sorry won't undo what you've done, Liam."

Liam snuffled miserably.

"You have been honest with me thus far," Avalon said. "And I did give my word that were you to provide me with certain explanations I would not call the watch." At this pronouncement, Liam's face brightened perceptibly. "However," the duke of Avalon continued pointedly, and Liam's face fell, "however, I find I must place one stricture upon this pact—you must carry a letter to Holland for me."

Liam's face creased with puzzlement. "That be it?"

"Yes."

" 'Tis a trick!"

"Oh, be hush, Jackie," the priest said.

"Why do you desire us to carry it?" the youth demanded.

"Because I cannot," Avalon replied, locking eyes with the youth.

"Why should we?"

"For this reason." Avalon pulled out a leather bag and shook it. From within sounded the metallic clank of coins. Liam's face creased into a smile. The duke loosened the drawstring at the neck of the bag and upended it. Gold coins rained down on the carpeting.

"Aye, 'tis a right good reason," Liam said, grinning with delighted avarice, as he scrambled for the money. But Jackie, snaking out a strong arm, grabbed the priest and restrained him from greedily scooping up the coins.

" 'Tis a trap."

"No, Jackie lad, yer wrong."

"I am right, Liam, and, if you used that head for thought rather than weighing down your shoulders, you would know I'm right."

"Oh, lad, don't be harsh with yer ould Liam." The Irishman's voice took on a pathetic note as he looked pleadingly at his youthful companion.

Jackie hardened her heart against his Irish wiles. "No, Liam, 'tis a trap. There's more here than meets the eye."

Avalon nodded slightly. "You are correct, boy. This letter must be carried secretly to The Hague. 'Tis a dangerous mission." He glanced across at his silent friend, who remained motionless. "I do understand," the dark-haired duke said, flicking lint off the sleeve of his coat, "if you fear for your skin. You might well be afraid of—"

"I'll not run, tail between my legs, from anything!" Jackie burst out. "I'll not have you talking as though we were cowards! We're not! We're braver than fifty nobles put together!"

"My," drawled the duke of Avalon, "I *am* impressed." Jackie glared at him with hatred in her gray eyes. "If it is not fear that holds you back, pray tell, what may be your reason?"

"Why should we do your dirty deeds?" she demanded.

Anger glinted for a moment in the duke's blue eyes, then receded. " 'Twould be no dirty deed I would have you undertake—on that you must accept my word as a gentleman. That is all that I shall say on the matter."

"The word of a jack—"

"Jackie boy," cautioned Liam, "leave 'lone."

She jutted her chin out and glared at the duke. Simon, thoughtfully stroking his chin, took the opportunity to study the lad again.

"You shall take this bag of gold now, before your journey," the duke went on. "When you return you shall receive five other bags of an equal amount of gold." Both Liam's and Jackie's eyes opened in astonishment. "Will that be sufficient for your traveling purposes?"

"How much be that?" asked Liam.

"One hundred guineas a bag—upon your return you'll have six hundred guineas."

"Mither preserve us," Liam said weakly, staggering to the nearest chair and sinking weakly into it. " 'Tis more money than I've seen together, well, in all me long life."

"And all we need do is deliver this letter to Holland?" the girl asked suspiciously.

"That is all," the duke answered blandly. "Plus return for your additional gold."

"Aye, Jackie," Liam said, looking at his young companion, "we'd be fools, fer certain, if we didn't accept."

"I think," the girl said slowly, studying the duke's handsome face, "we'd be fools if we did accept." She shrugged.

"Fool or not, we will take your damned letter . . . and your gold. Now, what of this letter?"

"That you shall receive in the morning," Avalon responded. He turned to Simon. "According to our plan, I think it best that you leave me now." The English nobleman smiled sardonically as he regarded the slight boy. "And leave me to my wicked devices."

At that pronouncement, Jackie's head rose, and she looked him squarely in the eye. Neither smiled as the adversaries faced one another, preparing for a battle of wills.

Simon left, after bidding his friend a good evening, and the trio remained in the salon in uneasy silence. At last Avalon poured three glasses of wine. With the cut-crystal goblet in his hand, he raised his glass and proposed a toast. "To Holland."

"Aye, to Holland," Liam said, tossing down the liquid and extending his glass for more.

"To Holland and . . . to success," Jackie replied slowly, never taking her eyes off the face of the man she vowed she would someday kill.

Chapter

Eight

EARLY THAT MORNING, while the light was still gray, they slipped out of the duke of Avalon's town house and returned to the inn where they had been staying. Jackie had seen no watchers, but the duke had cautioned that they probably should remain well in the shadows.

Once the two companions had collected their meager belongings and had their horses saddled, they were ready for the journey out of London.

Before they had left Avalon had warned them that, once on the road, they might be trailed. If so, he had said, they were to elude their pursuers as quickly as possible, and Jackie had replied tartly that she little needed advice on how to elude unwelcome followers from a town fop who hardly knew which end of a sword to hold without cutting himself.

His blue eyes mocking her earnest and angry retort, Avalon had dryly remarked that as the boy was a low scapegrace, he had no fear as to his ability in dodging trackers.

Liam, seeing the rising color in the girl's face, had decided to step in to prevent a potential altercation. The priest had restrained Jackie with a firm grip on her upper arm and with a brief shake of his head. She had bit her lower lip and her gray eyes had snapped with anger, but she had said nothing more to the duke, and his eyes had taken on a most humorous glint, which she took pains to ignore.

Avalon had admonished them once more to be careful, for such was the importance of the mission they were undertaking that if they were discovered their failure would mean the deaths, and unpleasant ones at that, of numerous people.

Liam had paled at the reminder of the danger to him and Jackie. The Irish priest tended to be more concerned about the welfare of his neck than he had in the old days with Jack. Then, too, he was concerned about Jackie.

The pair rode out of town on their way to Portsmouth.

"Jackie, me dear."

"Yes, Liam?" the disguised girl kept her eyes on the surrounding countryside.

"I be thinkin' that all that gold be more than we be ever to see the likes o' 'gain."

The girl nodded her head agreeably. Jackie, too, had indulged her fancy with dreams of their unexpected wealth.

Liam wet his lips nervously. What he would say in his next breath would not be easy, not with Jackie being the pepper mill she was. If only he could have a wee nip to fortify himself. Still. He took a deep breath and prepared himself.

"I be thinkin' we could be retirin' then, when we be given this money by the duke."

"Retiring!" Startled, the silver-haired girl gazed wide-eyed at her companion.

"Aye, me darlin'." He nodded his head sagely. "Ye know I not be gettin' any younger now. I be an ould man, as by some standards. An' ye be no yearlin' yerself, Jackie. Ye need to be thinkin' 'bout settlin' down. Mayhap we could be findin' a right fine sort o' young man fer ye an'—"

"No!" Jackie's reaction was explosive, and not totally unexpected. "I don't want to marry, Liam, and I'll not have you browbeating me into it!" Her gray eyes sparkled with anger, and he thought with a heartfelt pang how beautiful she was, and what a waste, a sheer foolish waste, to keep her all bundled up like a boy.

"Oh, darlin', just think o' it. Ye'd be the beautiful wife o' some fine an' dashin' an' handsome blade." The priest beamed.

A blade, Jackie echoed inwardly, and, unbidden, into her

mind came an image of taunting blue eyes, a mocking voice, and a strong chin. Confusion took over for a moment as she wondered that she should be thinking of *him*. And then reason replaced it, and she was able to thrust the sardonic image from her mind. Momentarily the girl closed her eyes and vowed that she would not shout at Liam. *It isn't his fault*, she told herself. *He's simply thinking of me*.

"No, Liam, I am sorry, but I do not care to discuss the matter again."

The priest sighed deeply. "Very well, me love." And wisdom came to Liam for one of the few times in his life, and he let go of the matter . . . for now.

"I don't be understandin' why we must needs ride to Portsmouth," Liam said, in an effort to change the subject. "We be at a port already in London. We needn't have put ourselves out any."

"Liam, apply your brain!" the girl said with some exasperation. "If someone were watching us or the docks, then they would know almost at once our destination and our plan. I told you before, Liam, that once we arrive at Portsmouth, we will set sail for France, and once there we'll ride north until we've reached Holland and The Hague."

"Do ye know where be The Hague?" he asked.

"No, but I'm sure we'll find it," she responded with a cheerful confidence.

"Jackie."

"Yes, Liam?"

"I've been meaning to ask ye somethin'."

"And what's that?"

"From time to time," he said, "I've noticed ye've taken somethin' out o' a pocket an' ye be turnin' it over in yer fingers." He paused. "What be it?"

She chuckled, reached into her pocket, and handed the object to Liam. He stared down at it. It was a tiny apple made of green jade.

Dismay filled him. "Oh, Jackie, ye didn't!"

"I did," the girl said cheerfully.

"Stole it from the duke of Avalon. No doubt he'll keep our money now," the priest said mournfully.

"I rather doubt it," the girl said. "Our mission is far too important for him to do that."

Liam sighed. "Well," he said, handing the jade back to

her, "it be sure that you take after Jack when it comes to havin' light fingers."

Jackie laughed and slipped the apple back in a pocket.

"Reading," Jackie said, surveying the weathered sign along the side of the road. "I thought you said you knew the way to Portsmouth," the girl accused, shifting sideways in her saddle to glare at her companion. Her horse snorted and pawed at the ground, and she absentmindedly patted his neck. In response the animal nickered softly.

Liam lacked even the good grace to blush. Instead he merely scratched his head and said, "I do know the way, Jackie. Leastways I did when I be a young man. I come by here once. 'Course, ye know, Jackie, that the roads be changin' all the time." He gazed pensively at the muddy track which lay before them. It wound through the landscape in a leisurely serpentine fashion. Liam breathed deeply of the heavy air, looked at the rolling hills in the distance, and, sighing, admitted he had no idea of their location.

Jackie looked around. The sun had passed its zenith some time ago on this third day of travel. She pulled a handkerchief, its once snowy folds now wilted and soiled, from her pocket and mopped her face and neck, wiping away the dust. She shifted her weight in the saddle to ease her discomfort, for they had been on the road long before the sun had risen that day.

One stop only had been made, to eat some cheese and bread and a hunk of salted meat, and to wash that uncertain meal down with tepid water. Jackie sighed and stared down at her boot, caked with dust. She slapped the leg of her breeches and the dust rose lazily, making her cough.

They would have many more miles to ride today. Best if she resigned herself to that. And now Liam was lost. At least, she thought, it didn't look as if it would rain, as it had for the past two days. Miserably cold and wet days those had been, and she had been left with a slight sniffle as a result. She hoped she hadn't taken a serious chill.

She shivered. "Where to now, Liam?"

"I don't be knowin', darlin'," the priest replied faintly.

"Straight ahead, I suppose." The girl sighed and straightened in her saddle. "Somehow, I suppose, I shall deliver us."

"Aye, just like Jack, ye be," the priest said, his face

wreathed in a smile of fond reminiscence. "Ye two with yer brains. Aye, it must be a right glorious thing to be so head-knobby."

She smiled and, reaching out, quickly grasped his hand in her slim one and gave it a brief squeeze. Then she directed her horse forward, and Liam followed.

After the two companions had ridden some miles farther on they spotted an inn off to one side of the road. "Ye could be askin' someone there where be the road to Portsmouth," Liam said hopefully, yearning for a large tankard of ale and some rest for his poor weary backside.

The girl groaned. "Liam, if we start asking questions, we'll simply draw attention to ourselves. And later it might be too easy to trace us."

As they rode past the inn, Liam sighed—for his missed ale and his darlin' girl. Jackie's own thoughts were turned to far different matters—in particular, the mystery of the sealed letter hidden in the hollow of her boot heel.

On the first day of their journey and when they were well out of sight of London, Jackie had paused and, much against the protests of the priest, drawn out the folded letter. She had stared at the parchment with the duke's seal upon it and then touched the wax with her fingertips.

"What be ye thinkin', darlin'?" Liam had asked nervous-ly, fearful that somehow she would get into trouble for what she was doing.

"Just wondering what it says, Liam. That's all."

"Now, don't be goin' an' openin' it, me darlin'," he cautioned. "They'd hang us fer sure!"

"Liam," she had said with some exasperation in her voice. "Credit me with some sense, please." The letter had gone back into the false heel; and once the heel had been put into place she had not again looked at it. Yet she remained curious about its contents. Perhaps they would find out when they reached their final destination. At first she had simply wanted the money and had decided they would leave as soon as they had left the letter in the hands of Prince William. Now Jackie wasn't so sure. The want of the money was certainly still there . . . but she was curious about all these politics and great matters which concerned the duke and his quiet friend.

She frowned as she looked into the distance, then straightened in the saddle and squinted. Over a slight rise in the earth rose horsemen and foot soldiers.

What could they be doing here, of all places? she wondered. Best to take no chances, the disgusted girl decided.

"Quick, Liam, make haste!"

Startled, the priest glanced behind them and then spurred his horse. "Oh, dear God, have mercy 'pon us!" he prayed. They spurred their horses, and the beasts leaped ahead as though the very devil were on their heels.

Her heart in her mouth, Jackie looked back over her shoulder as she and Liam raced across the barren, windswept plain. She groaned in despair. Four horse soldiers had broken away from the main party of men and were riding hell-bent for leather toward them!

"Faster!" she yelled to her companion, but the wind whipped away her words. She dug her spurs into her horse's flanks, and he jumped ahead of Liam's weary mount. Momentarily her horse stumbled, then regained its balance. Jackie frowned, her black upswept brows drawing together.

"Oh sweet Mary, Mither o' God," Liam prayed out loud, his lips moving with each word. "Preserve our miserable skins today. Oh, Lord, if Ye save us, I promise to reform an' never steal again." It was a promise that Liam had made many times before this latest escapade, and somehow he had always found himself ultimately breaking it. But never without good warrant, he reassured himself.

Slowly Liam's mount gained on the girl's, and Jackie realized that her horse was having trouble running.

"Over there!" she shouted at the priest, indicating with a jerk of her head the ring of stones, which stood like solitary sentinels on the plain. Liam nodded but never deviated from his intense prayer.

They reached the stone ring, and Jackie slid from her horse. She picked up the horse's hooves one by one and at last found a small round stone lodged in the soft substance of the frog. Her horse was lame; he would run no farther that day. She gritted her teeth in frustration and carefully pried the stone out with the tip of her dagger blade. She stroked the gray mount's flank reassuringly as he moved nervously.

"It isn't your fault," she sighed, and momentarily, weariness overtaking her, laid her face against the horse's neck.

Now what would they do? she wondered. Why were these soldiers giving pursuit? Could they have learned of the plan to deliver the letter to The Hague? Or had they been betrayed? By whom? Avalon's face drifted into her thoughts, but she steadfastly pushed it aside. There was no sense in thinking along those lines. But if the letter should be found and read, and these were the king's men. . . . She shivered, considering the consequences.

Panting, Liam leaned down. "What, child, can ye accomplish here? We should be ridin' fer our lives! Come on," he urged, "ere it be too late. Jackie, fer the love o' God! Come up here behind me!" He offered her a hand and waited, his face expectant.

"Hush!" the silver-haired girl admonished. Nibbling at the finger of a leather gauntlet, she surveyed the stones. Massive monoliths they were, some having fallen on their sides, some still standing, some with a third stone atop them, like a primitive arch. Could she turn this fortification to their defense? It would no doubt be hard for the horsemen to maneuver here, but still . . . there was little hope for a positive outcome for Liam or her.

"Jackie!" The priest's voice was frantic, the whites of his eyes shining. His horse, responding to its rider's fear, nervously sidestepped and pawed at the ground.

"Be reasonable, Liam. Your horse won't take both our weights. If you wish to save your skin, then ride on and leave me here. I must make my stand. You know that we cannot outride these soldiers. Our horses were tired when we first spotted them. We have no chance to flee, we must stay and face them. Or I must, and I shall." So saying, she turned away so that the priest would not see the unshed tears in her eyes, and slowly and calmly she drew her sword from its sheath.

The blond priest slid from the saddle to the ground and, putting a hand on her shoulder, turned her around to face him. "Did ye think that I value me own miserable hide so much that I'd run an' leave ye to be slaughtered like the Holy Lamb?" His voice was soft, the hurt darkening his blue eyes. "Oh, Jackie dear, do ye not know me better than that?"

Contritely the young girl hung her head and scuffed a boot across the ground. "I know you well, Liam, but I thought . . . perhaps ., . you'd want to save . . . Oh, Liam!" she cried, flinging her arms around his neck. "I'm so glad you're staying."

"Aye," he said, hugging her in return, "ye know that Jack would've never fergiven me! But now we must prepare fer our foes. Who'll no doubt be the very deaths o' us." He pulled out his pistol and brandished it. "Put aside yer sword, girl. We be needin' our pistols."

Jackie shook her head vigorously. "No. I'll make my stand with a sword in my hand." 'Twas the gentleman's way, as Jack had long ago instructed her. A pistol was fine in certain circumstances, Jack had explained, but a man should die with a true honest blade clasped in his hands. And, the girl thought fiercely, it would be no different for her!

Jack had taught her Italian techniques in swordplay, ensuring that what she lacked in force would be more than adequately compensated by her dexterity in wielding the blade. She had learned a few tricks but had never before needed to draw her sword in her own defense. In previous times the sword, clasped in her steady hand, had merely been a prop, part of the "encouragement" for the cull to hand over his valuables. But now her blade must strike true, strike hard, strike home.

The priest sighed and bowed his head. As stubborn as an Irish pig, he reflected, or her dear departed dad.

The riders came thundering toward the upright stones. "Hold there!" one man shouted.

A grim determination filled Jackie, and she clamped her lips together in a firm line. For answer, she raised her sword and readied herself for battle.

Liam would gladly lay down his life for his dear Jackie, but folly such as this surely be suicide, and that be a sin. The priest scratched his head thoughtfully, hitched up his breeches, and began loading his pistol. When the four riders came within close distance, the Irish priest leveled the gun and fired.

An explosion sounded next to Jackie's ear, and she whirled in surprise. Liam was sprawled on the ground beside one of the stone pillars. His pistol, gray smoke belching forth from the muzzle, lay ten feet away, and on his face was a most pained expression.

Sheepishly the priest shrugged. "I think the powder be a bit damp. An' the pistol, like its owner, be a might too old fer this sort o' thin'."

The hoofbeats thundered closer, and she prepared for battle. But now there were only three horsemen. She whirled, only to see the fourth soldier riding toward her back.

Surrounded! Damn them, the girl thought to herself, damn me and damn Liam for his misfiring pistol.

A soldier in front charged her, and Jackie slashed at him as he swept by. His horse shied from her blade, and she grinned savagely. She could not defeat them, that she knew, but 'twould be no shame in trying!

Now the four horsemen circled the girl and the priest, their mounts a respectable distance from Jackie's blade. Liam, his pistol beyond his reach, fumbled for his sword and drew it, his arm quavering from fright.

"Give up, boy," one soldier, a brown-haired man with a pleasant lean face, said.

"Never!" he spat.

As the soldier who had spoken to her trotted toward the girl, Jackie grabbed the reins of the man's horse. In an instant she was up in the saddle behind the soldier. Caught unaware, he could do little but gawk at her. Quickly she hit him on the side of his head with the flat of her sword and shoved him from the horse. She wheeled her new mount around and, yelling fiercely, rode toward the men like a demon out of the depths of hell.

Like hens in a chicken yard, the mounted soldiers scattered. The man on the ground had regained his senses and dove behind an altarlike stone to avoid being trampled by the horses.

Liam, thinking that perhaps he'd just be in the way and couldn't do much anyway to help Jackie, clutched his sword tightly and dove behind the same rock for safety.

The brown-haired soldier shot the priest an incredulous look. "What's that boy up to? Is he out of his mind?"

The priest sighed. "Aye, I think he be so." They peered around the stone to watch the battle's progress.

The three soldiers still on horseback encircled the fighting girl, who was shouting at them, haranguing them not to be cowards. Reluctantly one drew out a sword.

"No!" the man on foot shouted. Liam's head popped up from behind the altar stone, and he cried out. Startled, Jackie looked his way. She did not see the armed soldier turn the sword and bring it straight down on her head.

"Jackie!" Liam screamed. He rushed to his feet as she drooped over the horse's neck. "Murderers!" he yelled at the men. "Ye killed 'im! Ye killed me Jackie! Oh, Jackie love!" The only sound to be heard was that of Liam sobbing as he tenderly pulled Jackie's still form into his arms. He bent over her, and his tears spilled down his cheek onto her pale face. Oh Christ, he be losing her, as he'd lost his own Jack before. He did not think he could be bearing that.

"The boy's not dead," the soldier said gruffly, coming up to Liam and grabbing the reins of his horse. "He's merely stunned. He'll come 'round sooner or later."

Hope brightened Liam's face. "Ye be tellin' the truth? He be not dead?"

"No," the man said, "it's the truth. Now come, man." He nodded to a second soldier, who gathered the reins of Liam's horse. "Mount," he directed the priest. One of the soldiers reached across his saddle and, taking the girl from Liam's arms, draped her facedown across the front of his saddle.

For one panic-stricken moment the priest thought wildly of just turning tail and running as hard and as fast as he could, away from these men, away from sure imprisonment. But reason took over and pointed out to him that he was a man in his middle years, and no longer fleet of foot.

The soldier in command caught the priest's eye, and Liam, sighing with deep regret over his lost youth, wearily swung up into the saddle, and the four soldiers led the horses toward camp.

John Churchill sat in his tent that afternoon, writing to his wife, Sarah, of the army's inexorable move toward the town of Salisbury.

Warned by Louis XIV of France of a possible invasion of England by William of Orange, King James had summarily dismissed the notion that his son-in-law would come by force to the island kingdom. Churchill was not so convinced, and after the French monarch's warning, Lord Churchill had moved his men out of their bivouac toward Salisbury Plain. Invasion, if it were to come, would arrive on the southern shores of England.

Yet even as he penned the letter his emotions ran high and his loyalties warred within him. He served the king and would thus do his duty loyally; yet the king was a Catholic and, as such, threatened the peace of Protestant England. For days now these two sides had tugged Lord Churchill first one way, then another. If only, he thought, it could be resolved— one way or the other.

Lieutenant Ashley, a young officer, entered, snapping to attention as Churchill nodded briefly.

"The scouts have brought back a lad and an oldster, sir. The old man was most insistent that the boy was not to be searched. The youth sustained a knock on his head whilst he was being subdued, and Dr. Bishop is with him presently."

"Very well." Churchill leaned back in his chair and steepled his fingers. "Have the doctor examine and search the boy. Send him in when he is finished with his duties."

"Very well, sir." The aide-de-camp left, and Churchill returned to his letter. A son of a poor and obscure West Country gentleman, John Churchill, or "Jack," as his friends and family called him, was a self-made man, ambitious and always ready to advance his military career. And so, whatever decision he reached, it must be the right one. It could be his making . . . or his ruination.

Some minutes later the doctor eased himself into a chair and, leaning toward the writing desk, poured himself a drink. The physician swirled the contents of the glass and stared intently at the deep rose color. He sipped at it and sighed deeply. "Dammit, Jack, but what I don't think that's the best wine in the entire country."

Lord Churchill suppressed a smile, for he knew his friend's roundabout way of addressing an issue. He studied the man's features in the candlelight. Nature had been kind to the brilliant Bishop, the son of a prominent London physician, for he was a lean, elegant figure, fair of face and hair, and his hands were exquisitely formed—the hands of a surgeon. Somewhat of a dandy in personal life, the physician was immensely popular with the troops. Bishop had put aside a lucrative private practice to enter his country's service as an army doctor, and Churchill much admired him for that.

Dr. Bishop looked around the tent, then at the writing desk where Churchill sat patiently. Minutes passed, and Churchill found at length that he could wait no longer.

"Come, Edward," Churchill said, "time is a-wasting. What say you?"

"I have two items of interest to relate, Jack. Nay, three. First, the old man appears to be a Catholic priest in lay clothing." Bishop leaned back, waiting for the general's reaction. It was not long in coming.

"What!" Churchill stood, paced to the flap of the tent, then returned to the writing desk. He pushed aside the writing paper and inkwell, then sat and stared at his friend.

"I found a missal and a rosary on him," Bishop explained.

Churchill frowned. "Did he say why he was out on this road in disguise and why he fled when my soldiers approached?"

Bishop shook his head and took another sip of wine. "No, he wouldn't stop driveling on about some nonsense that he would lead a saintly life from now on. He seems to be terrified that we'll imprison him, or worse, murder him."

Churchill's eyebrows rose. "And the two other matters?" he asked.

Bishop chuckled appreciatively, his pale blue eyes sparkling with ill-contained humor. "Now, this was quite a surprise to me, as well might you imagine. The youth. . . ." He grinned, unable to continue.

"Yes?" Lord Churchill prompted.

"The youth is no lad, but, rather, a young girl."

"Dressed for safety's sake, I have no doubt," John Churchill replied with less surprise in his voice than Bishop had expected. "A woman my wife Sarah would undoubtedly admire."

"Indeed," the doctor said, perplexed at Churchill's calm acceptance of a matter that had stunned him. "Now for the third matter. 'Tis far more serious." He reached into his coat pocket and pulled from it a small sheet of parchment, folded into quarters, and sealed. Leaning across the desk, Bishop handed the paper to the general. "This I found in the girl's boot heel. No one else has seen it."

"Appreciated, Edward." He took the paper in his hands and stared at the seal.

Standing, the army doctor stretched. "Time I returned to my tent. I must check on my patient and see how she fares. Send for me if you should need me, Jack." Edward Bishop waited for Churchill to reply, but the military commander had broken the seal on the letter and was already engrossed in reading it, so Bishop shrugged and left.

When he finished, Churchill stared off into space for some time. He drummed his fingers on the desk top and thought at a furious rate. He paced, stopped before the tent's flap as though to call an aide, then appeared to think better of the idea. He returned to the desk and sat with a most absent air.

Finally, he held the parchment over the flame of the candle and watched as the paper ignited. It curled and blackened, and, as the flames crept back toward his hand, he dropped the letter onto the carpeting. Before the flames harmed the rug, he moved his boot across the burning letter. The ash, crumpled, left a smudge, nothing more.

He pulled his inkwell and paper toward him and pushed aside the letter to his wife. Churchill dipped the quill pen into the ink, paused for a moment with the pen over the paper, and then began writing in long graceful loops.

When Jackie awoke, a nauseating pounding in her head, she saw Liam, deeply absorbed in the study of his empty liquor flask, sitting nearby. His legs were stretched straight out, and the flask was lightly clasped in his trembling fingers. She painfully raised her head and looked blankly around. They were in a tent, and she lay on a camp cot.

"Liam," the girl whispered. His head came up, and the priest smiled wistfully. She knew instantly that Liam was once more drunk. Wherever did he find the source for his continual supply of liquor?

"Ah, me darlin', ye be awake at last." He rose tipsily and swayed, then sat down again as though his legs had gone out beneath him.

"Where are we?" asked Jackie.

"Me darlin', we be captured, we be," he said. "An' by the royal army, too, me dear. The royal army it be." He sighed deeply, scratching his side. "Ah me, ah me. . . ."

The silver-haired girl frowned. She pushed back the blanket covering her and swung her feet over to the ground. Momentarily everything around her turned black as the pain in her head increased. She blinked her eyes rapidly and rubbed at the sore spot.

She looked down; she was still in her clothing. Her black boots stood neatly alongside the cot. She reached over and began pulling them on.

"They be on to us, darlin'," Liam said quietly.

Jackie paused with one boot halfway on her foot and peered sharply at the priest. "What do you mean, Liam?"

"They be knowin' ye be a colleen. They be knowin' I be a priest." He sniffled. "All be lost, it be. All. Lost." He hiccuped. He fell onto his knees in front of her and began swaying back and forth, moaning all the while.

Jackie picked up the other boot and pushed aside the heel. Just as she had feared, the letter was gone. Now what were they to do? What would be done with them?

She pulled on her boot, then the second one and gave the suffering priest a disgusted look. The flap of the tent suddenly moved aside, and a man walked in.

With interest she studied him in the silence. He was almost impossibly handsome, with a broad high forehead, darkly curving eyebrows, and large and luminously blue eyes. His gaze was calm and bespoke a quiet authority. Beneath the straight nose the lips were firm and sensuous, the skin around the mouth and chin taut with leashed energy. He wore a long military coat, and his dark boots were polished to a high sheen.

"I believe this is yours." He pulled out a piece of parchment and held it out to her. "It was found in the heel of your boot."

The young girl felt the color recede from her face. Liam *was* right; they were done for. Oh God, what would happen? She gulped and tried unsuccessfully to talk.

He smiled, the lips slightly curving. "I know your mission, child. I shall not stand in your way. Here, secure this. Hide it now." The man moved toward her and handed the folded paper to the young girl. She took it and stared directly up at his blue eyes—friendly eyes—then away. There was a rustle of movement, and when she looked up the soldier was gone.

Liam was still moaning and praying out loud, and it seemed to the young girl he was growing louder and louder. The priest was oblivious to everything and apparently had not even noticed their visitor.

Jackie leaned over and gently punched the priest in the shoulder. "Liam, you can stop now."

"What?" He stared at her through watery eyes.

"I think we can leave."

His jaw dropped in astonishment.

She sat down again and, turning the heel of her boot,

inserted the piece of paper. Then she stopped and looked at the parchment. The seal was different. Should she tamper with it? she wondered for a fleeting moment. No, she would leave well enough alone, and when she met the Dutch prince she would explain that letters had been exchanged.

It was only after they had ridden out of sight of the army camp that she realized she had never once spoken to the soldier and that she did not even know his name. But Jackie had her belief as to his identity, and she realized just how lucky she and Liam were to have been allowed to leave unmolested.

Their mission would now go on unchecked, and soon they would be at The Hague—thanks to John Churchill, commander of the king of England's troops.

Chapter

Nine

THE FOLLOWING MORNING found the two companions walking up the plank of *L'Aimée*, a French merchant ship, destined for the French town of Calais across the English Channel.

As soon as his boot had touched the deck of the ship, Liam began groaning and moaning and clutching at his stomach, averring, "I be ill with the seasickness."

Concealing a smile, Jackie gently helped the priest below deck to their cabin. She eased him carefully into the bunk and, with a groan and a loud belch, he rolled slowly away from her, turning his face to the bulkhead. He shuddered and wept a little.

"Rest easy, Liam. I'll make this journey above deck."

"Oh, Jackie darlin', don't leave me to suffer by meself. Stay here with me." An uncontrolled sob choked him, and his body quivered.

She patted him briskly on his shoulder. "Now, now, Liam," the silver-haired girl replied soothingly, "I'll come around and see you. Have no fears upon that head."

For answer the miserable priest groaned, and a pitiful

whimper followed Jackie as she left the cabin and sought the fresh air of the ship's deck.

'Twas little wonder, she thought as she inhaled the invigorating odor of the sea, that Liam was sick when below all that could be smelled was the dubious combination of stale water, unwashed bodies, vomit, urine, and stale air. She shook her head wonderingly. Again she questioned her motives for carrying this message, this new message especially, of the Englishmen. Was it simply for the money that she played the messenger? Or was it because of the adventure it afforded her? Or was there a third reason? Blue eyes, sardonic and mocking, floated before her, and she closed her eyes to rid herself of their unwelcome presence. But the vision persisted, and even with her eyes closed she saw That Man's eyes.

Damn him, she thought, bringing her fist down on the railing. Then, whirling, she moved away from the railing and stalked across the deck.

She should check on Liam, the poor man, below deck. She climbed down the ladder and knocked on the door of the cabin. A moan sounded from within. Quickly the girl entered to find Liam curled on the bunk, his face still to the wall. She leaned across and checked him. The priest was sound asleep, and lovingly held in one hand was a flask.

She smiled ironically to herself. At least he had found some comfort on this trip.

From Calais the two companions rode through Dunkirk, following the coastline, and Ostend, then inland to Antwerp, Breda, Dordrecht, Rotterdam, and finally back toward the coast for their ultimate destination.

At the end of a fortnight of traveling they reached The Hague. What a surprise the Dutch city was to them as Jackie and Liam rode through the streets.

The houses here were airy, well-proportioned, and spotlessly clean, as were the streets, for while refuse and sewage often lay in the streets in England, the Dutch burghers spent much time and money cleansing and beautifying their towns and streets.

After asking for directions to the prince of Orange's city residence, Jackie and Liam rode quickly to the Binnenhof, the stadtholder's official residence. Once there, Jackie jumped off her horse and knocked upon the door. Liam watched as the door swung opened and Jackie conversed with a somber-faced man. In a few minutes the girl returned and mounted her horse.

"What be it, darlin'?" Liam asked with some concern in his voice. "Be we in the right country?"

"Oh, there's no doubt of that, Liam," the girl replied wearily, " 'tis simply that the prince is not in The Hague but at Honselaersdijk."

"Where be that?"

"The man said not more than ten miles from The Hague." She rubbed her hand across her face and sighed.

Liam, looking at the girl, felt a pang of sorrow go through him. Her face was lined, and there were smudges of dirt on her cheeks. They'd not rested more than five hours at any one time in the last few weeks. He rubbed his backside and straightened his spine slowly. He could feel the effects, too, and would like nothing more than a clean soft bed and no horse under him.

They rode for some miles in silence, then Jackie spoke. "I pray that we may be granted an audience with the Dutch stadtholder."

"Ye mean we came all this distance an' like to be killed, an' we may not be seein' the man?" Liam's face, as well as his voice, reflected his incredulity.

"Oh, there's no doubt that we'll see him eventually," she replied. "But the duke said it would be difficult. The man works all the time. Sometimes even through the night."

"Right busy he must be," Liam said with awe. "How'll it be that we see him?"

"The duke gave me a password to use."

"He be clever, that one," Liam said.

Jackie merely growled, and the priest lapsed into silence.

Over a sand dune they rode, and then in front of them was Honselaersdijk, with forests at its rear. The road led to a brick gate and across a short bridge. The house was light-colored, with numerous windows. The park around the residence was large and freely adorned with statuary. Flower gardens abounded.

"That not be like many palaces we be seein'," Liam said quietly.

"No, 'tis very unlike Versailles," the girl agreed. "It's as different, I'll warrant, as the man we'll find inside. Ready?"

He nodded and directed his horse to follow hers. Once their mounts had been taken, Jackie and Liam secured the attention of a retainer. Jackie talked with the man a few minutes, then he bowed and left, and they stood in a great hall, with intricate tiles on the floor and gold-and-crimson drapes at the spacious windows. The windows were open, and a fresh breeze, carried off the sea, drifted in to them. Jackie shifted her weight from one foot to the other and watched the dust motes laze and twirl in the golden light of the autumn afternoon. She felt deliciously comfortable, despite her weariness.

"Hsst!" Liam said, and the girl looked up to see the Dutch man returning.

"Come."

Led by the silent man, the two companions passed through lengthy corridors lined with windows, through which could be seen the green shapes of an autumn garden. Green draperies shot with gold threads hung in soft folds but were pulled back to allow the entrance of the warming sunshine. Gold-and-rust patterned tiles made up the hallway floors, and the walls opposite the windows were hung with delicate oil paintings of flowers.

It's obvious, she thought, *that the prince's passion for flowers doesn't end in the garden*.

At last they reached the end of a hallway and entered a room ablaze with sunlight streaming through two walls of windows. The retainer crossed to the far wall and knocked upon a lacquered door, decorated with pictures of birds and flowers. Liam and Jackie followed him, then stopped and waited.

"*Binnen*."

The man opened the door, ushering in the two weary travelers. They found themselves in a small audience chamber hung with cloths of gold in which crimson and green were woven. Across the ceiling raced Duval's winged Mercury. Below, the floor was tiled in gold and green and crimson, forming an immense geometric design. Along one wall were windows and a door leading out to the manicured gardens.

The retainer bowed. He spoke rapidly in Dutch, a language with which Jackie was quite familiar. "The men of whom I spoke, Your Royal Highness. They possess the password."

William Henry, by the grace of God, prince of Orange; count of Nassau; count of Katzenellenbogen, Viaden, Dietz, Lingen, Meurs, Buren, and Leerdam; marquis of Ter Veere and Vlissinger; lord and baron of Breda, of the town of Grave and the lands of Diest, Primbergen, Herstel, Cranendonck, Warmeston, Asley, Moseray, St. Vity, Doesberg, Polanen, Willemstadt, Niervaart, Isselstein, Steenbergen, St. Martinsdijk, Geertruidenberg, the Higher and Lower Swaluwe, and Naaldwijk; hereditary burgrave of Antwerp and Besançon, hereditary stadtholder and governor of Holland, Zeeland, Gelderland, Utrecht, and Overijssel; and captain- and admiral-general of the United Netherlands, looked up from the ebony desk where he sat writing.

He was brown-haired and had a Roman, eagle nose. His hazel eyes were bright and sparkling, and his forehead was large. The prince, like many of the courtiers whom they had passed in the corridors of the palace, was dressed in dark colors. His hands were tiny and neatly kept. At present the Dutch stadtholder was frowning, so that twin creases appeared between his smooth eyebrows, and the corners of his thin, pinched mouth were pulled down.

Behind him, waiting patiently, stood a young blond man, with a sullen expression on his handsome face. He was tall and rather well-built in the shoulders, somewhat stocky in figure, and would no doubt in later years run to fat. Unlike the man in front of him, he was dressed in clothes that seemed almost festive—a dark blue coat trimmed with silver and breeches of velvet of a buff the color of sand.

The prince raised his hand. "You may leave now, Michael."

"Very good, Your Royal Highness." The young man strolled from behind the desk, bowed to the prince, and departed, but not before first giving Jackie a studied half-lidded look. She was too tired to wonder at that. The retainer followed the young man, closing the chamber's door, and the two travelers in their stained clothes were left alone with the prince.

The prince carefully studied their tired faces and soiled clothing. "So," he said in French, the language of the Dutch court, "you are here from England. From whom?" His words were slow in coming, but precise when he spoke.

"The duke of Avalon sent us, Your Royal Highness," Jackie replied. Liam thought it best to have quick-witted and quick-tongued Jackie do all the talking.

"You must needs have been in a hurry to reach Holland," the prince said, indicating the condition of their clothes with a nod of his head. "Now that you are here, you do not remember your social graces.'' His tone was slightly ironic.

Jackie, the color rushing to her face, suddenly remembered that neither she nor the silent Liam had removed their hats in the royal presence, nor had they bowed. Oh, no, the girl thought with dismay, to have come this far only to insult royalty. Best, she decided, to brazen it out.

''Your Royal Highness must forgive us. Our mission has lived with us every second of three weeks, and if we forget to bow or to show reverence, it is not that we are disrespectful. It is simply that we are weary and that we have not yet been discharged from our mission.''

For a long moment Prince William stared at her, then a slight smile curved his thin lips. ''Spoken well, lad. What is your name?''

She introduced herself and her companion and briefly related to the man their experiences along the road. She opened her boot heel and pulled out the concealed message. The girl handed it to William, who did not immediately look at it.

The Dutch prince's eyes narrowed. ''You say that the man who talked with you appeared to be a commander?''

''Yes, Your Royal Highness.''

William broke the seal on the letter and then unfolded it. Both Liam and Jackie waited in uncomfortable silence as the small man read it. He read it a second time, and then at last he looked up at them.

''Do you know what is in this letter?'' He indicated the parchment.

Jackie shook her head. ''I knew only, Your Royal Highness, that a letter had been exchanged. But I did not seek to tamper with it.''

''Wise, wise,'' William murmured. ''This letter is from the king's commander, John Churchill. He is the man who captured you. I shall read it to you.

'' 'Sir,' '' William read in his curiously slow voice.

'' 'My honor I take leave to put into Your Royal Highness's hands, in which I think it safe. If you think there is anything else that I ought to do, you have but to command me, and I shall pay an entire obedience to it, being resolved to die in that religion that it has pleased God to give you both the will and power to protect.' ''

Having finished, the prince folded the letter once more.

"I don't understand," Liam said in a mournful voice. "What be the significance?"

"The significance, sir," said William, rising and coming around in front of the ebony desk, "is that John Churchill, commander of King James's troops, has made his decision. And now," the small man said, staring thoughtfully out of a window at the graceful garden, all in bloom with various-colored autumn flowers, "because of this, I have leave to invade England."

"Oh, me darlin,' I know we be in danger. We stuck out our necks this time, Jackie. Oh Holy Mither o' God." Liam began to weep and finger his rosary. Jackie sighed and, trying to ignore the priest's distraught outburst, looked around at their new accommodations, to which they had been shown after the prince's dismissal.

Their suite consisted of two bedrooms and an adjoining sitting room, which was decorated with traditional Dutch folk motifs in blues, greens, and white. She approved of the taste of the Dutch so far—clean, simple, honest, unpretentious. And comfortable, she thought, as she sank down onto her bed. Liam knelt below the open window and fervently prayed.

"Liam, please," the girl said, yawning, "I'm too tired for doom and gloom." She pulled off her boots, and swung her feet onto the lemon-colored coverlet, then lay back and closed her eyes. She heaved a great sigh of relief that this portion of the journey, the most pressing and potentially dangerous, had been completed. Why ever did Liam think they were done for? What nonsensical ideas he had sometimes. Didn't he realize that they were safe? She yawned again.

"Jackie, I feel it in me bones," the priest said, getting to his feet with some difficulty. "We should leave ere it be too late. Do ye not be in agreement, Jackie? Jackie? Jackie, me girl." He looked at the girl and sighed, for she was fast asleep, her long dark curling eyelashes resting on her cheeks and making her look again so like the wee agate he had found on that French road so long ago. He smiled fondly at the remembrance. "Angel," he whispered and softly touched her cheek. She murmured in her sleep but did not wake.

But nothing good, Liam reflected, his thoughts shifting, could be coming of this. He looked out the window and saw beyond the sand dunes the rolling waves of the sea. He felt it in his bones. Troubled times would be coming, and his Jackie would be involved in them. He gently touched her forehead with his lips. She stirred slightly, lost in some pleasant dream, for there was a secret smile on her rosy lips.

He must protect her so that she would not get hurt. Aye, he would see to that . . . would ould Liam.

The prince had indicated to them that they should return to his audience chamber once they had had a good night's rest. In the late evening, when no one stirred, Jackie bathed for the first time in weeks, and as the lukewarm water sloshed across her arms and legs and stomach, she sighed and closed her eyes. What a comfort this was.

Jackie ran a soapy hand across a silkily wet arm and shivered. If ever she was rich, she would have baths as often as she pleased, two and three times a day, and she would have a score of servants whose only duty was to keep her bathwater hot. Or perhaps she would have this modern convenience of running water. When she was rich.

If ever, she thought ironically. *How can I be rich when I spend my life constantly searching for money? I'm a fool*, she told herself in a rush of bitterness. *Why, Liam and I'll be nothing more—ever—than poor footpads. Nothing more.*

Unless. She sat bolt upright in the marble bath, the water sluicing from her satiny skin. 'Twas true that the prince desired their presence again. *Why*, she said to herself, *it must be to reward us.*

A sly smile touched her lips. She scrubbed her leg and surveyed her skin critically.

The prince had said he would invade England. If he did, he had a fair chance of winning, and if he did win, she could be at his side, as a faithful follower.

And faithful followers were granted generous rewards.

If he did not win, she could easily and quietly go over to the other side, the Catholic one, to serve there, for, after all, she was one of the faithful.

Yet, if she could secure an appointed position at the Dutch court . . . with Prince William. . . . After all, she *had* met him. . . .

Here lay the path of her future, here she could become *someone*, even advance. She would never be considered aristocratic, no matter what title she received from the prince, but she could gain position and wealth, and in those two factors was to be found safety—for her and for Liam.

Well, the girl thought, as she briskly rose from the bath and began drying her body, she would simply have to make herself indispensable to the man.

But how, was the puzzling problem.

Early the next morning Jackie selected her clothing with care. A dove-gray coat with a silver sash, white breeches, black leather shoes with silver buckles, and a black hat with a long curling white plume completed her outfit as a sober-sided young man. Her gloves, though, were extravagant. Made of white kidskin, they were sewn with hundreds of tiny seed pearls in elaborate floral patterns.

Satisfied with her appearance, the girl then crossed the sitting room to knock on Liam's door.

"I be comin', I be comin'," she heard his breathy voice cry, and she wondered for an instant if he had been drinking so early. Once the priest came to the door, her worst doubts were confirmed. His face reddened from early-morning tippling, Liam beamed a generous smile at her, then hiccuped. She gave him a frown of disapproval, then, shrugging, clasped his shoulder.

"Come, Liam."

"I be comin'," he repeated and duly followed her.

Once more they were ushered into the beautiful audience chamber, and once more the Dutch stadtholder awaited them. But this time he was alone, and the blond young man was nowhere to be seen. The three greeted one another, and then silence fell as the small Dutchman regarded the two travelers.

At last William broke the silence. "You two must have your reward for this mission." He motioned to a footman, who turned and left the room, then returned in a moment with another man, who carried a flat box. The second man approached the prince's ebony desk, bowed, and placed the box upon the desk's surface. The lid was opened, and gold gleamed.

"This is yours," William said, watching their faces closely.

"Why, thank ye, thank ye kindly, Yer Royal Highness," Liam said effusively.

"Thank you," Jackie said simply, "but to serve you is reward enough."

William nodded that they might leave, and the two com-

panions bowed. As they walked toward the door of the audience chamber, the prince spoke again. "Master Jackie, come
riding with me this afternoon."

She turned and bowed low. "Very good, Your Royal
Highness."

Again the prince nodded toward them, and the pair withdrew. Once outside Liam looked at the girl speculatively and
broadly winked.

"Ye be charmin' the breeches right off o' the likes o'
him."

"Liam!" She gave him a horrified look, then chuckled
richly. "Well, I cannot say that I would wish him to be so
charmed that his breeches would fall off, but I do wish he
would secure a position for me."

As they slowly walked down the corridor, Liam stared
thoughtfully at the tiled floor. "What be in that stirrin' head
o' yers, Jackie?"

"Only this, Liam: that if you wish to retire from the road,
we need to find us a supporter and a way to live—honestly.
And I believe the prince is the key to our lives of reform."

When the sun had passed its zenith, Jackie strode out to the
stables and ordered a horse saddled. She bowed when she
saw the small prince. He directed his horse toward her and
nodded his head.

"You are prompt, Master Jackie."

"I endeavor, Your Royal Highness."

As she hoisted herself into the saddle and moved the reins,
the chestnut-haired man looked sideways at her. "If you do
not mind, we shall have a riding companion."

"Not at all, sir."

Approaching them came the blond youth she had seen in
the audience chamber the day before. He bowed low from the
saddle to the prince, then nodded briefly at the girl.

"Ah, Michael," greeted the prince, "now we are ready."

They directed their horses out of the stable yard, along the
cobbled way, past the palace. As she slowly rode through the
yard, she glanced around. It was a comfortable place, and she
could well understand why it was the prince's and his wife
Mary's favorite residence.

Soon they had left the grounds of the royal residence
behind and were headed toward the sand dunes. Once he was

on the beach William kicked his gray in the flanks, and the horse broke into a gallop. Down the length of sand he raced, his chestnut hair streaming in the wind.

The young blond man spurred his horse, and the mount jumped forward, galloping. Not to be left behind, Jackie urged her horse ahead, and soon she and the young man were riding neck and neck. She glanced over at him, and there was a look of determination on his face. She kicked her mount, and the boy did likewise.

It was a race between them, Jackie thought grimly to herself, not just a race between their horses. A race for what stakes? She glanced at the boy's face again and saw that his eyes were fixed ahead on the distant prince. Were the stakes the prince's affections? Was this Michael then a favorite of the Dutch prince, and did he fear usurpation by her?

Good, the girl told herself. That was precisely what she desired—a strong place in the heart of the prince and his household.

Far ahead of them up the beach the prince had stopped and was even now watching the race between the two young people.

Jackie crouched down on the horse's neck and patted him. She placed her mouth close to his ear, which flicked back, and soothingly coaxed him for more speed.

To her side the boy raised his crop for the first time. It fell, and his horse leaped ahead of hers.

"Faster," she urged, and somehow her mount complied. Her horse's nose was at the bay's flank, then by the boy's leg, then at the other horse's neck. Now his ears, his muzzle, and for a paralyzing moment they were neck and neck, both horses straining, their eyes rolling, their riders hoarse from calling commands, and then her dapple inched ahead, and they flashed by the prince, who smiled and roundly applauded.

Slowly she brought her dapple to a trot, then to a walk and allowed him to cool off. She directed the horse to the boy and held out her hand. "A good race," she called cheerfully.

In response the boy scowled at her and turned his head away.

"Come, come, Michael." the Dutch prince said coaxingly. The boy turned back to Jackie, and she saw his lower lip protruding petulantly. Reluctantly Michael held out his hand.

"You're right, of course. It was a good race. And fair," he

added, after the prince caught his eye and made a small gesture.

"Thank you." She smiled at him, then at the prince.

"I have forgotten my manners," the prince said. "You two do not know each other."

"Michael Random, earl of Malvern," the young man said, bowing from the saddle.

"Master Jackie McKier," the girl replied and did likewise. It could be a trick of her imagination, but she thought she saw that he frowned slightly when he realized no title was attached to her name.

"Now come," the prince said, "I wish both of you to attend me. You, Michael, continue in your duties, and you, Master Jackie, will be an aide-de-camp."

"Thank you, Your Royal Highness."

"I think," the prince said slowly, as he looked out at the sea as though he could see the island kingdom in the far distance, "that in the future I shall need many aides."

"In any manner that I may serve you, I shall," the girl said gallantly, and yet the words were sincere, for as she grew to know the man, her respect for him increased.

He gazed at her, a solemn expression on his thin face that made him look extremely sad. "I believe your words, boy. All I ask is that you do not fail me."

The prince turned his horse around. "Come now, we have ridden enough. I have work to do, and you must acquaint yourself with the court." He urged his horse back along the beach, and Michael Random and Jackie followed.

Aide-de-camp to the prince of Orange, the Dutch stadtholder? Better and better, Jackie told herself. Yet she should be wary of this young earl. Somehow she would need to win him over. She glanced at his sullen profile. At the moment, her task seemed well nigh impossible.

But, Jackie thought, squaring her shoulders cheerfully and smiling at the blond man, nothing be impossible if you're of good faith, as Liam always told her. When the boy did not respond to her smile she knew she would need more than the usual amount of good faith.

In the months of preparation for the prince's invasion of England, Jackie and Liam became involved in the social life of the Dutch palace. The prince and princess commonly kept open house at Honselaersdijk, and on autumn afternoons visitors from The Hague would often drive out to wait upon Their Highnesses. Evenings were spent dancing or card-playing or strolling on the grounds.

Jackie and Liam were introduced to the quiet and retiring Princess Mary, and she and Liam took an instant liking to one another. She insisted that Liam join her retinue and, before long, he was spending many evenings with the Englishwoman, reading to her and talking to her.

They attended Protestant religious services with the royal couple, and Jackie could hear Liam muttering frantic prayers under his breath. No doubt to assuage the Catholic saints, Jackie thought wryly to herself.

Before the prince was to set out, a state dinner was ordered. It was the first time that Jackie had seen the residence other than in its everyday guise. In surprise her gray eyes opened wide.

Here now were all the proper things: whiskered Swiss halberdiers in blue cloaks and flat caps lining the courtyard; lackeys in green; gilt-laced liveried servants holding candelabra on the stairs; pages of honor in blue satin, crimson, and gold; fantastic confections served on brass plates.

Jackie entered the state dining room, which was adorned with Pieter de Greber's pastorals and Rubens's "Ceres, Bacchus, and Venus." Table after linen-clad table was sumptuously covered with every sort of delicacy. Her trained eye roved over the repast, and she admitted to herself that all that had been at Versailles was to be found here. Yet somehow it was different. Healthier, perhaps, more open, more honest. More what, she did not know.

Jackie watched the velvet- and silk-clad ladies and lords move through the room to find their places at the dining tables and was reminded of another dinner in another palace just one short year ago. So much had happened to her since then, it truly seemed another lifetime.

Sadly the silver-haired girl thought of Jack and sighed, a feeling of constriction in her chest. She rubbed a hand across her eyes, then breathed deeply. 'Twould not do at all to be found sniveling before the dinner. She brushed her fingers across her lace cuffs, straightened her wine velvet coat, and strode purposefully forward to find her place. She knew that they would eat richly tonight, and rather suspected it would be many weeks before she did so again.

Jackie was correct, for not long after, on October 16, 1688, Prince William, stadtholder of Holland, commended his wife Mary into the care of the States General. He then bade her farewell and told the princess that if anything should happen to him she was to marry again.

She unhappily acquiesced, not daring to consider a future without her beloved husband. Tears filled her dark eyes as she parted from him, and tears filled the bleary blue eyes of Liam as he parted from the company of the princess.

"You'll see her soon," Jackie reassured him.

"Mayhap," the priest sniffed and wiped at his eyes with his sleeve. "More likely we'll be killed." He choked back more tears.

Comfortingly the girl patted him on the back, then helped him aboard the ship, where he went immediately below deck and took to his bunk.

On October 20 they sailed, and the Dutch armada set forth—fifty warships, five hundred transports, five hundred cavalry, eleven thousand infantry.

Jackie's good spirits, buoyed by the appointment to the Dutch court, kept her from noticing the inclement weather under which they took sail for England. Liam, his stomach sensitive to every roll, thrust, and lurch of the vessel, was made only too aware of the poor sailing conditions by the strong winds driving the fleet back. It was feared by William's adherents that the enterprise might have to be abandoned, but crew members reported that the damage was slight. Once the damage was repaired, it was simply a matter of waiting for the wind to veer to the east.

On November 1, 1688, the "Protestant wind" began to blow, and the large armada edged once more out into the North Sea. A great cheer went up from the crew and passengers, and among the cheerers was Jackie, who felt curiously elated that they were finally on their way to England.

She little questioned her motives now and paid no attention to nagging thoughts that came to her in her sleep. Thoughts of a certain duke back in London, of her religion clashing with that of the prince of Orange, of her new honest living that involved lying about her old dishonest ways. The girl only knew that she was happy and content, and as Liam did not press her on her beliefs, she felt quite confident. Things were certainly looking up for them—that she knew. And, without a doubt, she knew they would be rich in a few years, and she would buy Liam a house and have a marble bath put in, with hot and cold running water, and she would never, never have to take to the road again.

Yet somehow this idyllic dream was less than totally satisfactory, and whenever she tried to pin the reason down, she could only see mocking blue eyes in her mind's eye.

He was a devil, she thought as she took a turn on the deck the following day. Well did he deserve his nickname of "Satan," for it was no decent thing but a hellish one that he should haunt her dreams the way he did. In vain did the silver-haired girl try to put the image of the English duke from her thoughts and return to the business at hand.

The "Protestant wind" played a crucial part in determining the focal point of the Glorious Revolution. It dictated William's landing place. The east wind carried the armada through the Straits of Dover and down the English channel. Keeping well clear of Portsmouth with its large Catholic garrison, which information had been gleaned from Jackie, the armada headed further west. While it had been easy for two grubby travelers to slip past the unwary noses of the troops at the English port, an armada would hardly go unnoticed.

On November 5, 1688, one day after William's thirty-eighth birthday, the fleet landed near Brixham in Torbay, an inlet of the channel on the Dorsetshire coast.

The date was significant, Jackie studiously informed Liam, for November 5 was the anniversary of the Gunpowder Plot, in which the Catholic, Guy Fawkes, had tried to blow up the houses of Parliament with kegs of gunpowder in the cellar. Of course, she said, that had been long ago, in the reign of King James I. To William this was another day in which there would be deliverance for the English people from the popish perils.

Within a short time the army was organized, and with William at its head it marched off to Exeter, where it entered on November 9 with full pomp and ceremony.

King James ordered Churchill at Salisbury to meet this foreign threat provided by his son-in-law, and the Catholic monarch soon joined the army there. But the royal master found his troops so lukewarm in their support of him that he could not trust them to give battle, and he ordered a retreat on November 23.

"So, boy," said a vaguely familiar voice, with a curious emphasis on "boy," "we are met again." Jackie felt a hand firmly placed on her shoulder. Turning, she faced the man who had captured both her and Liam on Salisbury Plain.

"Sir." She swept her hat off and bowed low, making an elegant leg. "Your servant, General Churchill."

A smile touched his lips. "You have found your voice this night, child."

"Yes," the girl said, "for tonight I shall raise my voice in victory."

Churchill's strong face took on a thoughtful look. "Aye, victory tonight," he mused. "And where is the prince, boy?"

"Here, sir." And Jackie led John Churchill, commander of the king's army, to Prince William. She heard a soft exclamation as she pushed aside the flap of the tent and then, as the flap closed, she heard nothing else.

That night, an evening most significant to the cause of Prince William and the Protestants, Churchill and two colonels, along with four hundred of the men under them, defected to Prince William.

The king's army still remained substantially larger than William's, but the monarch's nerve had gone with the defection of his army's commander, and he believed, perhaps rightfully so, that he could trust nobody. On November 28 he accepted the recommendation of an assembly of Tory notables that he should negotiate.

William's advance then became a regal progress. As they moved toward London, an increasing excitement grew within the girl. Was it over seeing London and claiming the last of their gold, or was it because of a certain pair of blue eyes? What nonsense, she told herself sternly, thrusting the idea from her mind.

Jackie found herself, when not needed by the prince, more and more in the company of Churchill, who willingly used her as a messenger.

"You've served well once in this capacity," he remarked dryly. "So shall you serve again."

"Of course, sir," she replied easily.

Lord Churchill found a good mount for the girl and sent her

on her first mission. She was to ride as quickly as possible and with as little notice as she could manage to check the situation in London.

That night she visited with Prince William, and before she left his side he pressed a small ring into her hand. She gazed down at it, a gold ring with five tiny rubies set around a pearl.

"It's beautiful, Your Royal Highness," the girl whispered, touched that he should wish to give her a present.

" 'Tis nothing," the Dutch prince said, waving it aside, and yet she saw in his brown eyes that he was pleased. She slipped the ring on her finger and found it was a perfect fit for her slim finger.

"A ring"—he cleared his throat self-consciously—"that I have had since my youth. It was my father's, and I desire it to be yours."

"Oh no," Jackie protested, "I could not take it if it was your father's. Here, please." She started to remove it. All who served William knew that his young father, Willem II, had been killed in battle just six months before the prince's birth and that the Dutch prince had felt the loss severely, throughout his life.

"No, no, I insist," William said, his somber face breaking into a slow smile. "I have no son. It is one of the sorrows of my life." Briefly his eyebrows drew together in a frown, and then the expression was gone. "But had I one, I would have wished for one such as you." He clasped the girl on her shoulder and, turning, left his tent.

Red-faced, the girl stared down at the ring and nervously twisted it on her hand. She felt terrible. He was not supposed to regard her as a son. She wasn't even a boy! Somewhere deep inside her a mocking voice laughed at this turnaround in her deception. She was flattered. . . . She was awed. . . . She was humbled. . . . But still. . . .

Liar, one small part of her whispered.

The following morning, December 7, Jackie set off for London, and later in the afternoon the prince of Orange received James's commissioners at Hungerford. The Catholic lords were distinctly uneasy in the Protestant camp, and the sight of familiar faces, former allies such as John Churchill, did little to ease their discomfort.

For the moment, however, William of Orange chose not to make his terms known. "Tomorrow," he said to the Catholic aristocrats, and the men were shown to their temporary quarters.

The following day the Dutch prince stated his terms. They included dismissal of all Catholic officers and the revocation of all proclamations against William and his adherents; James was to pay William's army; James, William, and their armies were to remain at an equal distance from London, and both James and William would attend the next session of Parliament. The prince was prepared to leave James on the throne but with greatly reduced powers.

William's terms were met with consternation. "No," James's representatives said emphatically, and as one.

William simply let a half-smile play about his lips. "That is all I ask, gentlemen, and I will not concede. I suggest you take these terms to your master and listen to what he has to say."

The men agreed, and the following day they were on their way to London to bring the prince of Orange's terms to the king.

London, after the invasion of Prince William and his army, was quiet, although a current of uneasiness ran under the everyday activity of the town. The city watched and waited. Jackie had been in London but a few days when the commissioners arrived with the prince of Orange's terms. The men had gone straight to Whitehall, where they were closeted with the king.

In the last day or so gossip and speculation had swept through the streets, and it seemed wherever Jackie went, street or tavern, people spoke of the matter.

The prince is even now marching on London with an army of a hundred thousand men.

The prince is forcing the king to abdicate his throne.

The prince will save London.

The prince will destroy London.

Just that afternoon she had seen a fistfight between two men, one Roman Catholic, the other Protestant. Neither knew the cause of the fight, only that they were of two opposing religions.

Now, as the day's light faded behind the brick buildings, a

wind swept through the streets. Far off in the distance the girl heard what sounded like the murmurings of bees among flowers. Curious, she nudged her mount forward to investigate, and the murmuring became louder and louder until at last she could distinguish the sound.

Human voices. The voices of men uplifted in chants and shouts. And the sound was moving in her direction.

Nervously, the girl cocked her head, listening. The sound was growing closer. Could it be in the next street? She looked past the roofs of the buildings. To the east was a red glow.

Fire.

Suddenly the calm street became a scene of chaos. Bricks and boards were hurled through windows; men and women alike screamed as the thrusting mob converged upon them. Jackie found herself the only rider in the midst of a sea of walking men. One man reached up to grab her reins, and she whipped his hand away.

Slowly her horse cut through the rioting crowd. She spurred it forward, seeking an exit to the street. Then she saw four men back another in a corner between two shops. She paused. The man in the corner was weaponless, and the four attackers all bore swords in their hands.

A fire lit up one of the shops, and in the flickering light Jackie could see his face. It was the man who had been with the duke of Avalon that night, Simon Martín.

Quickly Jackie urged her nervous mount past the milling people, shouting at them when they got in her way. She reached the quartet and Simon looked up, astonishment on his face when he recognized Jackie.

"Come quickly," she cried, holding out her hand. In an instant he grasped it and swung up in the saddle before his attackers could act. Then she whirled the horse around and plunged back into the crowd, whipping at those who tried to stop her.

She rode until they were long gone from the street, yet all through London could be heard the sound of shouting and chanting, of lewd and rough songs, and the red glow of fires could be seen lighting the night sky.

When he had his breath, Simon, his arms about her waist to keep his balance, said, "I thank you for saving my life."

He felt the ripple of her coat's material as she shrugged. "I couldn't let you be killed."

"Again, thanks." He paused. "What brings you to London? I had thought you would not be returning. Do you know where the prince's army is?"

"I've come on the business of the prince of Orange's army to scout London, and well it was that I came. I shall have much to report." The girl glanced over her shoulder at the Jewish swordsmith. "The prince is, or was, in Hungerford. I know not now whether he is moving on London. But tell me, Master Martín, how came you to be attacked?"

In his turn, Simon shrugged. "The crowd has become completely unruly, and they attack those unlike themselves."

"Ones such as you," the girl said. "A Jew."

"Yes." The man fell silent for a moment. "But how is it that you, a Catholic, come to stay with William's army? I would think your support would lie with James."

Again Simon felt the ripple of cloth and sensed a certain amount of uncomfortableness with his question. "Money," she murmured, and he wondered if that were, indeed, the entire truth.

"If you are able, put me down in Avalon's street."

The girl nodded, and they rode the rest of the distance in silence. At last they turned onto a familiar street. It was quiet, unlike the scene of the rioting far from that area. Jackie halted the horse, and Simon slid to the ground.

"Come in," he offered, "and have a drink."

"No," she said simply. "I must return to the prince before dawn."

"Very well." Simon Martín faced her and held out his hand as one equal to another. Quickly she grasped it, then released the man's hand. "Again, thank you."

He turned and walked up the seven steps to the door, so familiar, so hated to the girl. Not waiting for the immense bronze door to open, she turned her horse and headed down the street, ready to return to the army camp.

"Not only are there riots against the Catholics, Your Royal Highness," Jackie reported to William, "but King James has fled London. The queen and the 'warming-pan baby' have already been sent to France, and I heard that he would follow them there."

She finished her report and looked at the prince, then at Lord Churchill. William thoughtfully sipped at a glass of schnapps.

"It would seem," Churchill spoke slowly, "that the riots were sparked by James's departure."

"Indeed," William murmured.

"Your Royal Highness," a young piping voice called, and a boy dressed as a messenger rushed into the prince's tent before anyone could stop him. "Here!" He thrust a sealed paper into the hands of the startled Dutch prince. William broke the seal, and unfolded the letter, and slowly read it.

"What does it say?" Churchill asked, watching the prince's intense face.

William looked up, a faint smile on his thin lips. "It is from the authorities in London. They think it wise to invite me to enter the city. They are persuaded that my presence might quell the demonstrations."

The prince raised his glass. "To London." And he smiled fully.

Before William could take advantage of the invitation, however, King James was back in London, or so William's spies in the city reported. After Jackie had returned, the Dutchman had dispatched a handful of men to spread throughout the city and to return periodically to report on the events occurring in London. James, it seems, had been stopped by some well-meaning Kentish fishermen, who had returned the Catholic king to Whitehall before the prince could order him to stay where he was.

William conferred with his advisers, and in the end it was agreed that James should be allowed to escape. This would be the least embarrassing alternative, and it would avoid a direct confrontation between the prince and the Catholic king.

Dutch troops were sent to Whitehall with instructions to escort James to the coast. He left London on December 18, finally sailing to France on the twenty-third; he would never again see England.

And on December 19, 1688, William, prince of Orange and stadtholder of Holland, entered the city of London with his troops; with Churchill, the defector; and with Liam and Jackie, the equivocators.

"Here is the remainder of your . . . reward," said the duke of Avalon, tossing the five bags of gold one by one into Liam's outstretched hands. Simon Martín, standing to one

side of the fireplace, merely watched, yet frowned at Avalon's cynical expression.

Upon Liam's and Jackie's entry into London with the
Dutch prince, the two companions had quickly departed the
retinue, albeit temporarily, to go to the duke's town house in
order to claim their well-earned reward.

Liam, enjoying visions of the comfort and ease in which he
would live the rest of his life thanks to their newfound
wealth, fingered the bags, then began to stuff them inside his
coat. Best to take the money now, he thought apprehensively,
lest the duke change his mind.

"Wait, Liam," Jackie said, touching his arm. "Perhaps
we should count the gold to ensure that it is all there." She
spoke in a low tone that nonetheless carried to the handsome
duke. "We would not wish to be cheated."

Avalon smiled indolently, and his blue eyes glittered with
ill-concealed amusement.

Liam eyed the aristocrat nervously. "Jackie boy, I think
that we don't be needin' to count the gold. I be sure that we
can take the good duke's word fer it."

She sniffed. "Have you forgotten this man's family, Liam?
Brazen as a Blade, you always said. How can we trust him?"

"Jackie, fer God's sake!" Liam hissed, sneaking sidelong
glances toward the seemingly impervious duke.

"No," the girl persisted, a sneer crossing her fair face. "I
shall pursue the matter . . . with this cur."

"Boy," Avalon warned, his hand straying to his side.
Luckily for both Jackie and the priest he wore no sword. His
hand closed on air, and for a moment the duke seemed to
tremble on the edge of some terrible emotional cliff.

Seeing his friend's distress, Simon stepped forward, placing a hand on Avalon's sleeve. "Come, Blade, do them no
harm. You cannot hold them to blame for doubting you . . .
not with your hellhound reputation."

Blade shrugged, and a rueful smile touched his lips. The
hand relaxed. "Alas, Simon, you are all too right. As always,
my friend." He faced his two minions. "Count your gold,
and if you should find the sum short, acquaint me with your
findings and I shall make remedy." His blue eyes cool and
distant, he made a brief bow and left the salon.

Jackie dumped the bags of gold out onto the table, and
Liam began counting the gold guineas, gently fingering each

coin as though doubting its reality. "Ten, twenty, thirty . . . fifty. . . ." The girl watched as the stacks grew higher.

Simon continued to study the girl as she stood to one side of the priest. He could not tear his eyes from her. As if she suddenly remembered the swordsmith's presence, she turned and faced him. Under his close scrutiny she blushed, the crimson spreading upward from the base of her slender neck. Jackie dropped her eyes demurely.

Simon smiled a gentle smile. To be sure, what a pretty lad this was, he thought, and then moved his hand to his chest, for it suddenly felt tight.

The priest, who had blithely forgotten the presence of the quiet, watchful man, spoke, momentarily interrupting the counting of his money. "Jackie, g—" he began, then stopped guiltily as she poked him hard in the ribs.

"Shush, you old fool!"

Seeing Simon staring thoughtfully at him, the Irish priest displayed an engaging grin meant to disarm the swordsmith. In truth, it only served to increase his suspicions.

"Jackie boy," Liam began again, then fumbled to a halt, his original thought now having fled from his brain. He stared down at the gold stacks, flashed a weak smile at Simon, and resumed counting out loud, fervently wished for a wee nip of something.

"Seventy-five . . . ninety. . . ."

"Well, now, . . . boy," Simon said with a twist to the last word.

The silver-haired girl looked up sharply. Had he caught Liam's slip of tongue? Who could not? she thought angrily. Liam could be such a fool at times. If he knew of her true sex, what would the man do? Terror seized her, and it was all she could do to keep from grabbing Liam by the hand and running from the room. But it was no use running away from the matter. That was Liam's way, not hers. And she must face the situation like a man . . . like a woman?

She took a deep breath. "Sir?" she inquired calmly.

"Come with me a minute, child." Gesturing with his hand, Simon led the girl from the salon into a smaller room, a room lined on three walls with books from floor to high ceiling. Liam, aware of his blunder, did not look up as they left the room, preferring to seem completely absorbed.

Above the fireplace, which took up the library's fourth

wall, hung a large oil portrait of a dark-haired woman in a gauze gown of an earlier fashion. From the intense blue of her eyes and their direct gaze and the slight cleft in her chin, the silver-haired girl knew that this must be one of the duke's ancestors, perhaps even his mother. But how strange, she thought, as she remembered the story of the Blades as told to her by Liam. She would have thought he'd not have any portrait of her hung in the house if he were such a devil's spawn, and yet here was this painting. . . .

She shrugged, then turned her attention to the collection of books. Mesmerized, she gazed at the endless volumes. Moving to one wall, she lightly touched a tome bound in velvet, its gold spine encrusted with diamonds.

Simon Martin regarded her with some amusement, for the reaction of this "boy" to the library, one of four in the house, once more paralleled his own seven years ago. He, too, had never seen so many books, so much knowledge, gathered in one spot.

"Sit, child."

She did, but her eyes never strayed from the volumes. What could be contained in these wonderful books? She ached to open one and to read its wisdom. Then Jackie's brow wrinkled as she thought that they might contain devilish learning.

"It is impressive, is it not?" Simon waved a hand, indicating the room. "And there are three other libraries of equal size in this house. These libraries represent many years of travel for Blade."

The name of her enemy seeming to penetrate Jackie's daze, she snapped her attention back to the man. "Devilish learning," she muttered.

He glanced at the books and refrained from smiling at her, for while she spoke against the books, he could see her intense interest. "No, child, not learning of the devil, but rather learning for enlightenment, learning for the sake of knowledge."

She stuck her lower lip out, refusing to be placated by the Jew's reasonable words and tone.

"Can I not persuade you that Blade is not evil?"

"No!" she declared adamantly. "If he's called 'Satan' then he must somehow have well earned the name. He is utterly despicable, a man of high birth but low manners, a man who—"

Simon coughed. "Gently, boy." Again he gave the word a strange twist. "You do speak ill of my good friend. Yet that is not the reason I called you in here. There is something I must say to you."

The silver-haired girl felt a chill of fear creep through her. She waited, lacing her fingers together in her lap and trying to keep them from trembling.

Simon, still standing, paced along one wall of books. He stopped and faced her. "I find it difficult to form the proper words, child."

She raised her chin and looked straight at him. "Fling convention away, sir, and simply speak your mind."

"Ah, to be so young and impatient again." Sighing, he sat at the reading table, across from the girl. "I do say this, child, though you will little like my words." He took a deep breath, then: "I know your sex."

Inwardly she groaned, but she did not lose all hope, for perhaps she could brazen it out. Convince him otherwise. Oh, that fool of a priest and his ever-moving mouth and sievelike brain!

She plunged in. "Why, sir, 'tis no secret, my sex. 'Tis obvious to any who has two eyes and a wit in his head."

"No, Jackie," the man said gently, "do not attempt to turn my thoughts. Master McKier did loose the cat from the bag. I could not overlook his slip. I know now that you are a girl dressed as a boy." He watched Jackie as her gray eyes dropped to her folded hands. "I know not your reasons, nor do I particularly wish to know. Suffice it to say, that is your business, not mine."

"You'll not tell *him*, will you?" Jackie said with a jerk of her head toward the other end of the house, indicating Avalon.

"I should inform him," Simon replied, although somewhat reluctantly.

"No, please, do not, I beg you!" She fell to her knees in front of the Jewish swordsmith and looked beseechingly up into his face.

All he saw was youthful guile and those beautiful gray eyes, like the silver of the sea in winter. He could watch them, those silver pools, and drown himself, going ever deeper and deeper, farther down . . . down. . . . With a jerk he pulled himself back and looked away.

"Please, sir," the girl pleaded. "The duke would turn me

in to the authorities. Perhaps I would go to prison for flouting religious law. I would lose my place with Prince William. The duke would have no tolerance for a girl in male clothing. 'Twould simply amuse him to discover this and to use it against me.'' She looked up into his warm brown eyes. ''This is my last hope to care for Liam and for me to live decently. If you betray me, I will have to go back to the road, and perhaps one day I will end up at Tyburn, swinging by my neck at the end of a rope.''

''There are other occupations for a woman,'' the man said reasonably.

She drew herself up proudly and threw her head back, her eyes dark with anger. She stared at Simon coldly. ''I may not be honest, sir, but I would never stoop so low as to become a woman of the streets.''

Instantly his face colored. ''No, no,'' Simon hastened to reply, ''that was not what I meant.''

''What then, sir, did you mean? What can I do? I have been trained for nothing else—nothing less, nothing more. Sir, I beg you!'' Her gray eyes were distressed. ''I fear the man and what he may do. Do not tell him.''

Simon, much against his will, felt his heart warm to the words of the plaintive girl. She was right. Blade would not tolerate the situation. He had earlier humiliated the girl, had shown anger toward her. He would wish to see her further exposed. He would try to ruin her. No, Blade need not know the truth of the matter. Yet . . . perhaps . . .

''Besides''—the girl hesitated for just a moment—''I *did* save your life during the riots.'' She took Simon's hand in her own two cool ones and gazed up at him. ''Please, sir. Besides, what can it avail you to uncover me? But if you do not, I shall be able to make an honest living and to reform myself.'' Unshed tears clung to her long curling lashes.

Her sad expression melted the last of Simon's resistance. ''Very well, child. Your secret shall remain safe with me.''

''Thank you, sir,'' she said. ''You shall have no occasion to regret your decision. I swear that.'' For a brief moment Jackie laid her soft cheek against his hand, and he felt a tremor pass through his body.

Rising to her feet, Jackie bowed low to him, then left the library. Simon dropped his head into his hands, the memory of the silver eyes haunting him. Taunting, too, in their grateful kindness. But that was the key—the kindness. That was all there was. He knew her not, not even if Jackie were her true name, but somehow it didn't matter.

He wondered at her life that she was forced to go on the road. He wished to see her again, to be with her, to talk with her.

Fool, one part of him chided, *in so short a time you cannot have lost your heart. Especially to one so different. She is . . . . Indeed, what is she? No one. A thief. A rogue. A chit on the road to Newgate, or worse yet, to the noose on the tree at Tyburn.*

She'll end her days in misery, and so shall you, Simon, another part of him said. *Leave 'lone. You are a Jew. She is not. That should end it. You cannot—*

No! he cried out. *Hush!*

But it is true, the other part pursued cruelly. *You know it is.*

And he had no answer to that.

When Jackie came out of the library, she found Liam still counting and wondered if he might not have interrupted his counting to put his ear to the door. But she decided that was unfair of her. Or was it?

"Five hundred an' ninety-eight, ninety-nine, an' six hundred." He surveyed the numerous stacks, and the gold clinked as he began to push the coins back into the bags. Jackie stepped across to help the priest.

"Let us leave now, Liam."

"Aye, darlin'." He glanced up at her face, then toward the door. "The sooner we be puttin' this house far behind us the better I'll be feelin'."

When they had the gold secreted away inside their clothing, Jackie and Liam picked up their satchels and departed the room. They did not again meet with the master of the house. Santu quietly showed them to the front entrance and let them out.

As they walked down the street, the young girl felt as though something was boring into her back. She knew she was being watched. And she knew the watcher was in that house of hell. Determined not to glance back, Jackie continued her progress. Liam, at her side, had fallen silent and seemed to be lost in his own thoughts.

She frowned. She knew whose eyes they were, too, that

were watching her. Blue, bored eyes, they would be. Hateful eyes. Eyes that she would someday have the immense pleasure of putting out, she thought with ghoulish relish.

The thought of those despised eyes grew and grew, until, no longer able to restrain herself, she snapped her head back to stare toward Avalon's town house.

All that she saw was the quick movement of a curtain as it was released in the window in the house's second story.

Triumphantly the girl smiled and linked her arm through that of the priest.

Chapter

⇒ Ten ⇐

"Ah, do come in, Simon."

The duke of Avalon glanced up momentarily from the charcoal brazier that he had been feeding with black briquettes and wiped his sooty fingers on the linen towel by his side. Straightening the brown leather apron protecting his clothes, he extended his hand to the young swordsmith, who shook it firmly.

Simon surveyed the spacious laboratory, contained within the bowels of Avalon's London town house—or to be more precise, Simon thought, the cellar—and smiled to himself. It rarely failed to awe—and amuse—him when he penetrated Avalon's scientific domain.

Enclosed cabinets ran the entire length of two sides of the chambers. Every surface in the room was crowded with glass jars, beakers, chunks of rock and, of course, papers. Charts illustrating the effects and uses of the four elements, wind, air, fire and earth, maps of the heaven, drafted by the duke himself, decorated the walls above the counters. From the ceiling hung numerous iron-mesh baskets with mysterious contents, although Simon thought one appeared to contain nothing more sinister than a handful of purple onions.

At the far end of the room a door led onto a balcony, overlooking a sunken garden. It was on the balcony that Avalon's large telescope, the mirrors painstakingly ground by hand in his own laboratory, had been mounted so that he might, if the winds of London had proved kind and swept away the concealing layer of smoke, view the starry skies with this advanced instrument.

Simon wrinkled his nose. "What is that horrible odor, Blade? Brimstone? It smells as though the defenses of hell have been breached!"

The duke chuckled. "No, 'tis not so exotic by half, Simon. Simply a failed experiment."

"Better that it is the failure and not the success."

Avalon chuckled again and, rising from the workbench, stretched. He pulled the leather guards from his sleeves and untied the apron, then tossed it on the bench.

"I do not have half the time necessary for my work down here," he said, shaking his head. "Come." He indicated one of the chairs. "It's time to break for now." When they had seated themselves and he had propped his feet up on the brick athanor, Avalon reached over to the small table and picked up a letter.

"Have you seen this, Simon? Good news from Schoenberg in—" Catching sight of the expression on the other man's face, Blade stopped. He sighed. "Ah, but you did not come her to hear the results of my German friend's experiments, did you?" Not waiting for an answer, he said smoothly, "But tell me now, what brings you, Simon?"

" 'Tis no urgent matter, really, Blade, but Shrewsbury desires a meeting with you at your earliest convenience. He is presently at Whitehall. Tonight or tomorrow morning, he said it mattered not."

Blade stroked his chin absently. "I think it might be better if I go this evening."

"Very well," Simon replied. He surveyed the smoking remnants of Avalon's latest project. "Have you discovered the philosopher's stone yet, Blade?" he asked, a flippant tone to his voice. The instant the words were out of his mouth he regretted them.

Blade's dark brows drew together. "I thought better of

you, Simon," he rumbled, rising to his feet, the true image of indignation.

"Come, Blade," Simon said in a placating tone. "Do sit down again. I meant no ill, as you well know. I simply meant to inquire into the nature of your work. As you know, I am curious about it, and I admit I do admire your scientific studies."

"Very well," the duke said, allowing his scientific feathers to be smoothed. Just as he was preparing to reseat himself, a quiet bell began chiming. Simon looked around for the source of the noise.

"The termination of a lengthy experiment," Blade explained, walking across the floor to a small oven. He pulled on leather gauntlets, opened the oven door, and, grasping the cauldron within, removed it from the heat. He then took a long glass pole and began poking at the substance within the pot.

Simon sighed, knowing that his friend would now be lost to the world for hours. He shook his head mentally, watching the tall aristocrat work with the multitude of substances.

Avalon had come by his scientific inquisitiveness naturally, for both his father and his mother had been absorbed in the rigorous and formidable process of obtaining gold from lead with the aid of the philosopher's stone. It had been one such experiment that had proved fatal to Blade's mother, and Simon belatedly realized that mentioning the philosopher's stone to Blade was hardly tactful.

The duke, Simon thought, proved a contradiction in many aspects. And that, too, had its origins in the lives of the man's parents.

Handsome blue-eyed Richard Francis Blade, eighth duke of Avalon, had met Sybilla Hastings, daughter of a wealthy squire, when both were riding one day. Richard Francis, a young man given to frequent laughter despite his early orphaned state, met with Sybilla more and more in the woods. As the months went by they maintained a secret correspondence.

Within the span of a few months Richard Francis had wooed the young woman and won her heart, and he gathered his courage to approach her family. When he did, he was summarily turned down. Sybilla's father had wished his daughter—too serious by nature, he felt, and by society's standards, which frowned upon well-educated women—to make a more socially advantageous match. Richard Francis did not lack social standing; he simply cared little for the social aspect of his title, and because of this as well as his extensive travels and varied interests, was labeled an eccentric by the less-informed residents of the district.

The title and money would be quite welcome, Squire Hastings remarked to his eldest son, but the nature of the man was not at all to his liking and would, he doubted not, bring heartbreak to both families if they were linked. The Squire firmly put his foot down, forbidding Sybilla to marry her titled swain.

Not possessed of a particularly submissive nature, a fact of which her father was painfully aware, Sybilla disobeyed her parent's stricture and, creeping out a second-floor window, ran to her beloved. Within an hour they were in the ducal carriage, with a maid and a manservant, on the road to Gretna Green in Scotland to be wed.

When Thomas Hastings discovered his daughter's absence, he and Sybilla's two brothers immediately set out for Richard Francis's estate, only to discover that the master had left hours earlier for a destination unknown to the servants. But Sir Thomas had known instinctively where the couple had fled.

Richard Francis had pressed his horses to their fullest that night in an effort to outride the pursuing trio. Yet he knew that soon the three horsemen would overtake them, so he decided to trick them. He turned back on the road, and, by roundabout driving, arrived in London in three days. The couple then secured passage on a boat sailing to France. There at Calais they had obtained a special license and been married at last.

Her family returned home without their renegade daughter, and months later a letter from her father was forwarded to the young duchess informing her of the severance of family ties. Even her name had been stricken from the family Bible. This upset Sybilla, so her husband took her to Spain, then to Germany, Russia, Greece, India, and China. It was in China, where they lived for one year, that she announced her pregnancy.

Richard Francis insisted upon returning home to England immediately, but Sybilla vetoed the idea, insisting that they should remain in the Orient to pursue their studies of Chinese science. He agreed, and a few months after the birth of their son Sybilla had gone down to the laboratory in their rented home early one morning to check on an experiment. Unknown to husband and wife, a small pocket of gas had formed in the enclosed room, and when Sybilla entered a spark from her candle set it off. She was killed instantly.

After her death Richard Francis had lost his laughing, easygoing ways. For two years more he had traveled, then returned to England with his young son and a black servant named Santu. Inside six months the father was dead from a broken neck after a fall from a spirited mount.

It was Cornelius Snodgrass's opinion that the present duke's father's death had been more deliberate than accidental. The plump manservant had proved to be the primary source of Simon's information concerning the duke's family background, for Blade never offered a single word about his family.

After his father's demise, young Blade had been raised by various estate servants and Santu. When he attained the age of seven, Blade left with Santu on a worldwide tour, at the express written instructions of Richard Francis. They had returned when the young man was seventeen, and it was then that he had resumed his position politically and socially as a courtier and a nobleman, one that he had held for the past thirteen years.

Avalon's life had been a most unusual one, Simon thought, giving rise to many speculative stories, from the rumor of demonic allegiance to that of depraved dilettantism, and earning him the not-so-affectionate nickname of "Satan." Blade, amused by the imaginative fabrications, did nothing to dispel the rumors. In truth, his friend thought, the duke seemed genuinely delighted as the tales expanded in each retelling.

The London town house, purchased just a decade ago, had been outfitted with the relics of Avalon's journeys and had proved a haven to many, Simon Martín among them. Simon would always remember his anxiety and even his fear when he had first met the young duke, only a few years his senior. Yet he, too, had ended by becoming one of the duke's "pets."

Simon chuckled, considering the popular view of Avalon's practices. It was true that on occasion the duke sought out young boys, orphans more often than not, cold and hungry, to bring back through the gate of hell. But not to warm his bed, as was commonly held.

Simon chuckled again. Yet no pet had been as spirited as the boy the duke had found that dark night more than half a year ago. Simon shifted in his chair, recalling the events of that evening, when Avalon had brought home the disguised girl and the old man.

He remembered the enchanting face of Jackie. *She is not for you, Simon,* the swordsmith said to himself firmly. *Forget her.*

And forget her he had tried valiantly to do in the intervening weeks, but sadly to no avail. There could never be an alliance between them. Why did he fool himself into even imagining it?

"Why so pensive?" Blade asked, intruding on the swordsmith's thoughts. He wiped his hands on a cloth and stared down at his friend.

With a start Simon realized that close to an hour had elapsed while he had been lost in his maze of thoughts.

"What grim thoughts have possessed you? Come now, I've finished my work here," the duke said. "Allow me to change, and I shall be with you anon, good friend."

Simon followed Blade out of the laboratory and up the long flight of stairs to the duke's bedroom suite. In the outer chamber Simon picked up a delicate lacquered box with inlaid seed pearls. On it was painted a tableau depicting a moonlit forest in which a beautiful girl danced with her image in the lake.

Blade strolled out of his dressing room, pulling his crumpled cravat from his neck. "Do you like it?" he asked, nodding to the black box in the other man's hands.

"Yes. Where did you find it?"

"In Russia. For hundreds of years the peasants have made them. Artful, is it not?" the duke asked as he began the process of tying and looping the intricate folds of a new neckpiece.

"Oh, yes. I have not seen a box so beautiful by half," Simon said, tracing the painting with one fingertip.

"It's yours then," Blade said, staring intently at his snowy white cravat in the mirror and poking at a fold to arch it correctly.

"No, Blade, I could not," Simon protested.

"You could, and I insist," the duke said in a tone of finality, and the swordsmith knew that there would be no further discussion of the matter. Instead, Simon nodded his head in thanks and slipped the box into his pocket.

The manservant Snodgrass entered, with a discreet cough, to hold his master's coat, and Blade slowly inched into it. At last it was secure, and Corney ran a suit brush over the duke's outfit.

Avalon stepped back to admire his image in the mirror. His coat was fashioned of a bronze velvet, decorated at the cuffs and along the edging with countless seed pearls. He wore cream-colored breeches, and his waistcoat was a gold satin, embroidered elaborately with silver thread. In the folds of his cravat he had secured a stickpin with a pearl head the size of his thumbnail. Corney handed Avalon his walking stick of wood polished a deep red-brown and decorated with black bows.

Quite the peacock, Blade told himself with a quick quirk of the lips as he saluted his image. He allowed his servant to apply a small patch to the plane of one cheek but forbade any cosmetics. Not tonight, he thought, tired of the extremes of court appearance.

"I am prepared, Simon. Shall we go?" Avalon, picking up his hat with its long trailing plume, set it upon his dark curls, bowed to the other man, and departed.

Shrewsbury leaned over the desk and shook hands with the duke. "I am pleased you have come so soon, Blade. Do sit." He indicated two embroidered chairs, where Avalon and Simon established themselves. "I have good news for you." The dark-haired man smiled at the other nobleman.

"Oh?" Blade, from long experience, maintained a neutral expression and tone of voice.

"I have talked with Prince William at great length, and, as you know, he is considering the various rewards to give to those who helped in the Glorious Revolution. He has asked that you consider a position in the new government. William wishes to appoint you second gentleman of the bedchamber. The Convention has convened already, and it should not be long before a decision is made concerning the new head of state."

Avalon nodded his head. "Tell His Royal Highness that I am flattered by his kind gesture, but I find I must decline."

Charles Talbot chuckled and laced his fingers together. "I

told the prince that you would prove reluctant.''

"Let it be said that I have played my part in the Revolution," the duke of Avalon said, "and that was reward enough."

But Shrewsbury was not prepared to drop the matter so easily. Obviously he and the prince had covered the possibility of Blade's refusal. "The prince has asked that I acquaint you with the other factors in the prince's gesture. In other words, you would also be awarded a title and the land incumbent upon it." He paused, waiting for Blade's answer. When the duke said nothing, Shrewsbury continued. "You would be the new earl of Greystone, the title having fallen to the Crown some years ago with the death of old Ashton MacConnell. The accompanying lands, which prove extremely sizable, would bring in a large revenue."

"I have one title already," Avalon replied somewhat lazily. "I find it more than sufficient for my needs and my income. I desire no further headaches. Thank His Royal Highness for his kindness, but that is my last word upon the matter. Now, I believe I have friends I must meet for dinner."

Avalon rose and bowed to the young earl of Shrewsbury, who watched the two men take their leave. The duke was, Shrewsbury concluded, his own man and would be bought by no one, not even a prince.

"Some would think it foolhardy what you refused in there," Simon Martín remarked, with a nod to the closed door of Shrewsbury's office.

Avalon smiled. "Would that 'some' include you, old friend?"

Simon, lacing his fingers behind his back, walked alongside the duke. "No," he replied slowly. "I would not include myself there. I would not call your action foolish, for you have the station and money that you desire. You do not seek more."

"Ah, but I do, my good friend," Avalon replied.

"What else do you desire?" Simon asked, puzzled.

"A wife," said the duke, bursting into a gust of hearty laughter. Simon chuckled at his friend's good spirits.

They rounded a corner and stopped abruptly to avoid colliding into Michael Random, who was lounging insolently by a window. Simon frowned, for he little cared for the blond courtier who had accompanied Prince William on his progress to London. He had often seen the young man about Whitehall but had spoken with him but once during the month-long residence of the royal party at the London palace. And that single incident had not created a favorable opinion of the young man.

The boy condescended to Simon because of his religion and, because he was himself largely ignorant, scorned Simon's vast knowledge. The earl of Malvern, Simon admitted, lived only for pleasure, and sordid pleasure at that. It was whispered at court that the boy had lovers among both men and women. What William found to recommend the boy he could not understand.

The stocky man sketched a mocking bow. His stance was slightly shaky, and the two men could readily see that Random had been drinking heavily for some time. "Your Grace," he said, indicating the duke. "Master Martín," he acknowledged, then dismissed the swordsmith with a curt nod.

It seemed apparent to Simon that the young earl desired a chance to speak with Avalon alone. "I shall take my leave now, Blade," he said.

"Wait, Simon," the tall man called as his friend walked off. "Meet me for dinner later."

Simon's face broke into a smile. "Very well. Until later, Blade."

"Lord Malvern," Avalon murmured, impatient that Lord Malvern should say what he must and leave it at that.

"So, Your Grace," said the younger in a mocking tone, "you have gained your reward at last."

"I know not of what you speak, my lord." Blade attempted to move past the young man. "Now, good eve to you."

Random's hand reached out and touched Blade's shoulder, and the duke frowned at the intimate contact. "Oh, come, come, Your Grace." The fingers traced the line of embroidery on the bronze coat. "You cannot be as naïve as you would appear. After all, I've heard the stories, too."

True puzzlement appeared on Avalon's face. "Sir, kindly elucidate."

"Your reward," Random breathed, the distance between the men growing narrower.

Blade stood transfixed, merely staring at the other man. The earl was obviously in his cups. It was the only excuse Blade could find for Random's abominable behavior. He had no conceivable idea what Random was talking about. Better then to ignore him.

Avalon pushed past Lord Malvern without bidding him farewell and continued down the hall.

Not to be rebuffed so easily, the earl was determined to pursue the matter. His hands on his hips, he surveyed the broad back of the duke. "At last, Blade," the young man called after the departing duke, his voice strident, "you have an administration that well suits you."

Avalon stopped, fingering his cane and garnering his control at the boy's rudeness. When his face had been pulled into a deliberately bland expression, he turned slowly and faced the blond boy. "What precisely, sir," the duke said, twisting the last word into a sneer, "are you attempting—and poorly, I might add—to say?"

Random flushed, then threw back his blond head. "Why merely, Your Grace, that your preference for little boys is common knowledge."

"Yes?" said the duke impatiently.

"Well, the prince can, I have no doubt, match you in that perversity." Random leered at the duke.

For the briefest moment Blade did not react as he attempted to control his emotions, then a red rage, clouding his vision, seized him.

"What did you say?" the duke demanded, advancing on the earl of Malvern, who backed away a few feet.

"Merely," said the young man, "that the position you surely have been offered for your 'part' in the 'Glorious' Revolution has been gentleman of the bedchamber, perhaps even that of royal bedwarmer." He smiled—a sneering expression that twisted his features. "Perhaps now you may share the same 'pets.' "

Unbidden into the duke's mind came the vision of two wide-set gray eyes and a pert mouth, and quiet rage filled him. He cared little what this or anyone else said of him, but he would defend the prince against any remarks made by witless toadies such as this one. Too, the boy deserved to have manners beaten into him. Blade's lips tightened and, taking a step forward, he raised his cane.

Michael Random dodged, yet it was too late for the first of many blows that rained down upon his back and shoulders.

"You insolent toad," Blade hissed as he thrashed the boy.

Random ducked and caught a blow along the ridge of his spine. He cried out in fear and pain and tried to move away, but the alcohol he had been consuming since early morning had slowed his reflexes. This game had gone far beyond his expectations. He had simply meant to tease the handsome man, perhaps coax him into a little flirtation.

The rage enveloping Blade knew no bounds. He ground his teeth and prepared to deliver a blow that would knock the impertinent youngster unconscious.

Suddenly his arm was caught in a steel grip. Growling deep in his throat, Avalon whirled, breaking the hold on his arm, and met the direct gray eyes of Jackie. Momentarily he was taken aback to see the young rascal, then he quickly recovered. "Leave 'lone, lad," he said.

"Pray, sir," she admonished quietly, "remember where you are, and who you are. I could hear your argument down the length of the corridor."

"Go away," Blade said through gritted teeth and turned back to finish thrashing the earl, but Random had fled, seeing his opportunity for escape in the intervention of Jackie.

Frustrated that his prey had run off, Blade rounded on Jackie. Damn the child for his interference! He would teach him a lesson, too. Jackie faced the duke, unflinching, as he held aloft the wooden cane.

"Do you plan also to beat me? I, too, am weaponless and, as you well know, cannot raise my arm against a noble," Jackie said, her gray eyes never leaving Avalon's face.

Blade breathed deeply several times and slowly lowered the walking stick. His rage receded, and a calmness enveloped him. "No, I shall do you no harm." He rubbed his hand wearily over his face and stared at the boy. "Why did you see fit to interfere?" He knew the boy had misunderstood, and he wished him to know the truth of the matter, but he was damned if he would explain.

"Your Grace, 'twas hardly interference," Jackie said, turning away slightly, disturbed by Blade's behavior yet knowing she should not be surprised. " 'Twas the decent step to take, lest you beat to death an unarmed man. I do not know the particulars of your quarrel, but this was hardly the time nor the place to air your differences."

"It was not as it appeared," the duke said slowly.

"I know only what my two eyes saw," Jackie replied.

"Aye, so you say."

"And what does that mean?"

"Only that it proved convenient for you to step in at that moment, and that Lord Malvern—and should I not term him your 'accomplice'—might escape?" Sarcasm lay heavily in the duke's voice, and he had once more regained his lazily cynical composure.

Jackie glared at the duke of Avalon. Anger filled the young girl, and she was unable to find her voice. Her vow to murder the nobleman someday established itself anew in her mind, for she realized that in the month since she had returned to London thoughts of the despised duke had filled her head.

Why had she bothered to stop the man from his foolhardy action? She should have left and thus allowed him to beat to death his unarmed opponent. Then she would have had the rewarding knowledge that the duke of Avalon would be at last brought to justice. Yet, Jackie thought, that would have denied her the satisfaction of being the engine of his destruction, for she was convinced that one day it would be her own blade which would find its cold way into his black heart. Still. . . .

"Pray excuse me, sir," the girl said, bowing mockingly before the tall man, "but I must needs follow my 'accomplice,' as you term him. Good eve."

Her jaw set squarely, she marched past him, not looking back. Accomplice indeed! She mentally added this to the list of wrongs done her by the foul nobleman.

Fie on the boy! the duke thought stormily. 'Twas a simple guttersnipe that had proved to be a headache, and no more. And yet . . . those snapping gray eyes . . . the soft curve to the cheek.

Avalon! an inner voice commanded. *'Enough! You'll soon find yourself believing the stories of your 'pets' if you should be so foolish as to pursue this train of thought.*

It was indeed enough, Avalon decided angrily, for he was totally convinced of the complicity of Lord Malvern and Master Jackie and knew beyond a shadow of a doubt that the two were illicit lovers. There was no evidence to support this conclusion, but that mattered little. For some reason, where Jackie was concerned the duke's logic tended to evaporate like the chemicals in his basement laboratory.

Loudly he damned them both to perdition, but somehow his curses proved less than satisfying.

The news of the duke of Avalon's apparently unwarranted attack upon Lord Malvern soon spread like a wildfire through a court hungry for any tidbit of scandalous gossip. Eventually the duke's error of judgment became not only the tantalizing *on dit* for the salacious satisfaction of the courtiers and their ladies, but it also reached the ears of the prince of Orange.

Prince William found that he was little pleased with the news of the duke's latest indiscretion, notwithstanding the man's devilish reputation. And it was with a heavy heart that he sent for Avalon several days after the incident.

"Your Royal Highness," Blade said, bowing low before the prince in the man's writing closet in Whitehall. Despite the frequent use of the palace audience chamber, William while still in his tenuous position preferred the intimacy and informality of a smaller chamber for such an interview.

The Dutch prince nodded his head but did not say anything for a long moment. Then he sighed deeply, the sigh turning into a hacking cough. His health, while never good, had suffered excessively during his brief residence in London. The cold damp mists rising off the Thames, which flowed alongside Whitehall, were the source of his congestion, compounded by the layer of smoke in the city. Each day, it seemed, his condition worsened, and it was feared that he might not live to see the end of the year. Nevertheless, Prince William bore his weakening physical condition well, refusing to give in to it and preferring to continue to work as hard as he had ever done.

"I have heard bad news, Avalon, very bad news. Is this so?"

A slight smile played at the duke's lips as he replied. "It depends on what Your Royal Highness has heard." These days he could not pass through the corridors of Whitehall without the toadies, trucklers, fawners, and lickspittles of the court drawing back, a sea of sycophantism parting for—what? Avalon asked himself. A ship of lepers would fare better than he had these past few days. Conversation ended with his entrance into a room, and his departure was followed by a wave of whispering. And the number of his social invitations had dropped alarmingly. Well, at least, he thought wryly, it would give him more time for his work in the laboratory if he did not have to attend so many routs and fetes.

William drummed his fingertips impatiently. "Do not act with me. I have no time today to fence with words."

" 'Play,' " Avalon gently corrected the Prince's awkward English.

Anger flashed momentarily through the mild hazel eyes, then receded, for he was not a man of turbulent emotions. "Even it is so, Avalon. You have not pleased me."

"I am aware of that, sir."

"You have beaten a man of my retinue for no apparent reason." The prince leveled serious eyes at the duke. "What do you have to say?"

The fluid tongues of Lord Malvern and that boy had not been idle these past days, Blade observed to himself. And yet it angered him that the prince should believe those puppies over a proven man like himself, one who comported himself with honor and dignity. Until a few nights ago, an inner voice pointed out.

True, he replied. And true, also, that his reputation as "Satan" Blade had only been reinforced by Random's beating. 'Twas said he had a devil of a temper, and he had done nothing to dispel that estimation. He should have known better; he *did* know better, and yet his anger had commanded his entire being, clouding his good judgment. 'Twould be folly to discuss with the prince the topic that had led to his attack on the young earl, even though it had been in protection of the prince's honor. If Avalon were to speak his mind and tell the prince the cause of the altercation, William would no doubt think the duke was being petty and shifting the blame to the other man, who, being absent, could hardly defend himself. Too, Random commanded a better position for the ear of the prince than he, who had turned down the prince's offer of a title, who walked his path in life with no other man. And he had no doubt whatsoever that William, an honorable man, would feel himself duty-bound to respond to the ill treatment of one of his "boys."

"I have nothing to say in my defense, Your Royal Highness," Avalon said at length. "I can only add that it shall not reoccur."

"I should hope not!" the prince exclaimed, an astonished expression on his pinched face. He coughed once more, then said, "Once was quite enough! This cannot go unchastised, Avalon."

"I realize that, sir."

"I have thought long, and I do not wish to punish you. But I must, for this sort of behavior among my courtiers cannot be tolerated." The prince stood and paced alongside his desk. In a moment he turned back to the duke and said, "You must leave the court for now. Depart for your country estates, remaining there until you are called back. By then the incident will have been forgotten, and the vultures will have found some other man's liver to tear out."

Smiling slightly, amused at the prince's classical reference, Blade bowed his dark head. "As you wish, Your Royal Highness." He bowed from the waist, was dismissed, and left the prince to his dark thoughts.

William frowned at the troublesome thought of Avalon and Random, for he liked both men and did not care to see them in conflict. Lord Malvern, a most attentive young man, had been in his retinue for over a year now, and he flattered himself that he knew the blond man well. There was little cause for William to doubt Lord Malvern's word on the incident, for the boy had never before lied to him. When these rumors had first reached the princely ears, Random had been sent for, and William had sternly requested an explanation. The blond youth had been reluctant, as might be expected, to tell the tale, but William had slowly and patiently extracted the painful story from him. The earl could offer no explanation for the duke's behavior. William suspected, based on the duke's nefarious reputation, that Avalon had made an unwelcome advance to the boy, who had proved averse to the man's attentions, and that Random's decline of the offer had provoked Avalon's unreasoning rage and then the shocking attack. All because, William thought sadly, the man had simply been spurned.

He respected the duke of Avalon, but the man who allowed no hand of royal friendship to be stretched out to him bore watching. Prince William knew it did not pay to have too individualistic a man who commanded a high title and respect in a monarch's realm.

There was a slight rustling sound before him. William looked up from his brown study and eased his facial muscles into a rare smile.

"Sit down, Michael, and we shall talk."

Grinning engagingly, the earl of Malvern did so.

Upon returning to his town house, Blade found Simon Martín once more waiting for his return.

" 'Tis becoming a custom with you, Simon, to kick your heels in my hall," Avalon said, a sardonic tone to his voice. He strolled into the salon to pour himself a drink and Simon followed.

The swordsmith flushed. "I came around earlier to ask you to dinner, then found you had been summoned by the prince. How did you fare?" His expressive face and voice conveyed an earnest and honest anxiousness about the duke's plight that Avalon found singularly comforting.

"Banishment," Avalon replied airily. "I am to travel to my estate in the country and wait until the heat has died down in this furnace of gossip."

"Blade," Simon began.

"No, no," the duke said, raising a hand to stop the man from speaking further. "There's nothing to be said. I have metamorphosed into Abaddon, lower even than Lucifer himself. Abaddon Avalon," he remarked thoughtfully. "I rather fancy the sound of that."

Despite himself and the gravity of the matter, Simon chuckled, and the duke turned a mocking eye to his friend.

"I suspect," Simon said, in an amused tone, "that you rather enjoy the adverse attention given you, 'Satan,' and the notoriety this tale adds to your already infernal reputation."

Avalon opened his mouth to offer up an indignant protest but stopped when he caught his friend's eye and, instead, began to chuckle. " 'Tis true," he admitted with a smile, "I mind it not as much as I make out to. Still," he continued, a serious note in his voice, "I must go."

"When?"

"Tomorrow, I suspect, for the feeling conveyed by the prince was that all due haste upon my part would be significantly appreciated. And," he added mockingly, "I cannot disobey the wish of the prince."

"Is there anything that I might do for you?" Simon asked.

"Nay, Simon. Satan rules alone in hell. I shall see you upon my return—at some uncertain future date. I shall come back at the bidding of the prince." He walked out into the hall and began climbing the stairs, then paused, one hand resting lightly on the wooden balustrade.

"There is something that you might consider doing for me," the duke said slowly.

"Yes?" Simon asked. "You know that I shall do that which you request."

"Then play the spy for me," Avalon said grimly.

"Spy?" Simon echoed, surprise on his face. Of all the requests that his friend might have made, this one was the least expected. "On whom?"

"That puppy Jackie McKier," Avalon said, his face an unreadable mask. "I wish to know his whereabouts and his companions. Write to me, Simon. That is all I ask of you."

Simon, knowing Jackie's true identity, wished he could explain to his friend that there need not be this unreasonable enmity toward the youth, but he had vowed silence to Jackie, and he could not go back on his word. And, too, he knew that at this particular moment such an admission would only serve to further infuriate the volatile duke. Instead Simon nodded his head, saying, "I shall write you, Blade, and abide by your wishes."

"Excellent," was all the duke said, and his face now held a most unpleasant expression. Avalon knew he would soon have the information he needed to destroy the puppy, this creature who sought to undermine his position. And it would be a day to avidly welcome!

Chapter
Eleven

THE LIFE OF the courtier dancing attendance upon the Dutch prince, Jackie had discovered to her chagrin, proved not to be as exciting an adventure as she had previously anticipated. In fact, if she were to be truthful with herself, it was downright boring.

To be sure, the English court maintained many activities, even though no monarch ruled the country as yet. Along with the young men of the court, Jackie often attended the horse races among the aristocrats. She played cards and chess with Liam and Simon Martín, who inexplicably often sought out her company during the week. Once, without Liam's knowledge, she slipped away with young Dickon, page to the prince, and saw her first cockfight, Jack never having allowed her to attend one. 'Twas her last such spectacle, too, for the sight of such cruel "sport" and useless bloodletting utterly repelled and sickened the girl, so that thereafter when the lad approached with a similar invitation she was sure to be busy.

But it did seem, from the court gossip and backstairs talk that Jackie avidly listened to, that the entire tone of the court of the prince and princess was different from the previous courts of Charles II and James II. The courtiers spoke some-what regretfully of the licentiousness of the previous two monarchs. Prince William had even rebuked a young man who swore in his presence, saying that the court should set a good example to the nation.

The days, despite the many entertainments and Jackie's numerous activities and new duties at Whitehall, seemed to pass in yawning monotony, and she idly wondered whether she hadn't died and gone to hell. Perhaps, she told herself listlessly, she should dance, for there was no opportunity lacking for that activity. At the moment she was thinking these thoughts, in fact, a masquerade was underway, its theme Mount Olympus.

A courtier swept by and bowed in her direction, and she frowned. It had not been easy, either, these past few weeks, dodging the libidinous overtures of ladies and gentlemen alike at the court. The women would have her as a young boy lover, whom they no doubt felt they would instruct in the ways of love, and certain men pressed their suit as well. Some kept stables of young boys around them. It was true that the young men did seem to improve their station in this manner, but it was certainly not a manner which she would have chosen. Jackie thought it odd that in spite of the stories she had heard of the duke of Avalon's pets, she had never heard his name in connection with an entire stable of them.

She sighed deeply as she watched the dancers—Pans and satyrs with their nymphs, shepherds and shepherdesses, a pantheon of gods and goddesses stepping in graceful dignity to the strains of the music.

Tonight . . . tonight she wished she were out of male dress and in that of a young nymph's. How much fun they seemed to be having. The girls laughed with their escorts, teased, flirted . . . and did not live a lie, as she did. Now that she had chosen that lie, she did not see how she could ever leave it behind. It would forever follow her, no matter where she might go. But, oh, tonight, how Jackie longed to be simply herself. To flirt . . . to tease . . . to gaze at mocking blue eyes? She frowned at the thought.

"Pray, what can the matter be, boy?" asked an amused voice.

Startled, she looked up into the blue eyes of John Churchill.

"My lord," the girl said, sweeping her hat of Flemish velvet off and bowing low.

"Why do you not dance this evening, Master Jackie?" Churchill asked.

" 'Twould not be seemly, for I am ill fit to tread light this evening, or to be a willing dance partner. I fear I suffer from the melancholy, sir."

"I see." Churchill's luminous blue eyes danced with ill-concealed amusement. " 'Twould seem you need a change in your life."

"Oh?" the girl asked excitedly, her mood lifting. "You wish me in your army?" Her face was lit with pleasure, and the man could hardly bear to disappoint the girl.

"Well, no," the army commander said slowly, watching the glow fade from Jackie's face. "But I do have an offer which might prove, if not as adventuresome as my army, an intriguing interlude."

"Yes?" she inquired politely.

"My wife, Sarah, has begged me to convey her greetings and to ask if you cannot dine with us on the morrow. She has heard much of the young boy who acted so bravely and gallantly by taking my message to Prince William. Will you come, boy?" he asked kindly.

"I would be honored, sir," the girl answered truthfully, pleased that the commander of the royal army and his wife had displayed an interest in her. "When shall I come?"

"Seven," Churchill replied. "Until then, boy, do not be so stricken. I am sure matters shall not long remain dull and that you will find sufficient excitement for your youthful appetite."

He watched Jackie move off and smiled to himself. He had kept to himself the interesting fact that this youth was in reality a girl. It amused him greatly that the court was so completely hoodwinked, and he would like to help her continue her masquerade so that she might further tweak the court's nose. But Sarah should know. Sarah would be amused and appreciate the joke, as well. Churchill chuckled richly and left to tell his wife of their guest's acceptance.

"Aha, Liam! Can you image whom I visit tonight?" Pausing with a sly expression on her face, she whispered with a wink, "And from whom I shall receive a free meal?"

Liam, his face ruddy with good health and too much spiritous liquid, beamed at Jackie as she stood, hands on her hips. She pulled the wig from her head, and her real hair fell in long silken ringlets below her shoulders.

"No, Jackie, love, I cannot imagine who it be that you be spongin' off now," the priest said, a merry glint in his blue eyes. "Tell me, child, who ye be visitin', fer it must be admitted that I be fair to dyin' o' anxiousness."

She spared him a withering look. "The Churchills," the girl exclaimed. Liam frowned, and the girl hesitated, for this was hardly the reaction she had expected.

"There's no need to worry, Liam. The prince may not like him personally, but he respects Churchill's capability. If I am a protégée of both the prince and John Churchill, then Jackie McKier cannot go wrong!"

Liam still looked doubtful and muttered darkly about playing with fire, but he shrugged, then hugged the girl tightly to him and rumpled her silver locks. She put her head on his shoulder, and for a long moment neither moved nor said a word.

"Come in, Master Jackie!" Sarah Churchill exclaimed as the maidservant showed the young girl into the Churchills' drawing room. As was customary with the more prominent members of the court, John Churchill and his wife had procured apartments so that he might remain close to the royal offices.

Jackie swept off her hat of burgundy velvet and bowed to the sprightly woman opposite her. Then she surreptitiously studied her hostess.

Sarah Jennings Churchill possessed straw-blond hair that sprung thickly from a broad forehead, brilliant coloring, and a masterful glance that made the girl momentarily uncomfortable with its perception. Lady Churchill was attired in a simple seal-brown gown with an embroidered bodice and gauze sleeves that fell just below her elbows. Fawn-colored slippers sheathed her feet, and Jackie marveled at the coordination of the colors, which served to heighten the woman's blond looks.

Lady Churchill, like her husband, had known an early life of genteel poverty, and it was this experience which had molded her into a shrewd, hard-minded businesswoman. And her husband's success in the army was due as much to Sarah's constant coaching and advice as it was to John Churchill's talent.

"John was detained by the prince and will be but a moment," the woman explained, seating herself upon an oak-backed settee. Patting the striped cloth, she indicated that Jackie should sit beside her, saying, "I am pleased that you could come this evening. My husband has spoken much of you."

The girl blushed.

"Do not be modest. 'Twas brave of you, child."

Inwardly Jackie cringed, a wave of guilt washing over her, for she had not taken the message voluntarily. Why must these people at court make such a fuss over her and her actions?

The door to the drawing room opened, and John Churchill stood there. His blue eyes met those of his wife, and he smiled.

"My love," he murmured, crossing over to the woman to kiss the cheek she offered.

"Our guest is arrived, John."

"I see that." He beamed at Jackie, who had risen to her feet and bowed to the man. "You are a prompt boy." He indicated with a wave of his hand that she should sit back down, and she complied.

"I endeavor, sir."

"John, we are prepared to sit down. Hurry and change," his wife admonished.

He ducked his head guiltily and left the drawing room.

"The prince sent for him late this afternoon, and I thought for a while that he would not be able to come." Lady Churchill rose and gestured for Jackie to follow her. They entered a cozy dining room, painted and wallpapered in varying tones of vermilion and gold. The long table, of a highly burnished wood, gleamed with the crystal and china set upon it.

"You must sit here," Sarah said, pointing to a romanesque chair close to the head. At that moment Churchill, who had hastily attired himself in a handsome coat of brown cloth, entered and bowed first to his wife, then to Jackie.

"We do not have all our servants here," Lady Churchill explained as the meal progressed and they were served by one impassive footman. "We have but small apartments here whilst we remain unsettled."

Jackie nodded as she hungrily attacked the meal before her:

fresh asparagus with a cream sauce, a saddle of mutton, beefsteak, green peas with carrots, a meringue, and wine aplenty.

"I have a surprise for you, Sarah," Lord Churchill said after the meal, breaking the silence that had fallen as the trio sipped at the small glasses of cherry cordial he had poured.

"Oh?" she asked, one fine eyebrow raised in inquiry.

He smiled, a dimple showing in one cheek. " 'Twill be a revelation, I've no doubt, for our young guest as well."

Jackie looked up from her drink with interest. She had indeed always enjoyed surprises and could not imagine the nature of this one.

Churchill rose and took a turn around the room, then leaned against the mantel of the fireplace and surveyed his wife with a slight smile on his lips.

"Well, John?" his wife asked impatiently.

He chuckled and turned to face Jackie. "It concerns our young friend."

Despite Churchill's good humor, Jackie felt the first tentative fingers of fear trail along her spine. She gulped at her cordial and waited, her heart hammering against her rib cage. Perhaps she should now make her excuses and leave quickly, before—

"Jackie, my dear, is no boy."

"What!" Lady Churchill exclaimed, staring wide-eyed at first her husband, then at Jackie. For the merest moment, too, Jackie sat wide-eyed, astonishment overpowering her vocal capacity. Then her mind working lightning fast, she resolved to attempt to brazen herself out of this awkward—and potentially dangerous—position.

"Sir!" she thundered in her most outraged tone and jumped to her feet, her hand straying to her side as though a weapon hung there. "You have gravely injured me. Have you taken leave of your senses, sir?"

Instead of seriously considering this denouncement, as Jackie had expected, Lord Churchill simply began laughing. The gales of laughter whipped through him so hard that he found it necessary to wipe at his eyes with his hand.

"John, what is the meaning of this?" Sarah demanded, wondering why her husband should make this seemingly inappropriate comment. She was vaguely concerned that perhaps he suffered from some fever of the brain.

"Sir!" Jackie called again in a vain attempt to command Churchill's attention. Oh, Lord, what was she to do now!

But the man, still convulsed with laughter, would not answer either his wife or Jackie. Sarah frowned, obviously angry at her husband's uncaring attitude and impatient that he would not explain himself. Jackie could feel the walls of the room closing around her. If he told others of her secret, she would have to leave the court. The foundations of her safe and secure domain began crumbling, and she railed inwardly at the man. It would be back to the road for her and Liam. It was not fair that she'd had so little time in this new honest life!

At last Churchill recovered his control and, staggering across to a wing chair opposite his wife, he dropped in to it. Sarah pressed her lips together and waited.

"My dearest heart," he said, looking at her lovingly, "Master Jackie is a *girl*. 'Tis a well-worn disguise that our young friend has adopted, and it has fooled most—nay, all at court. Of course, the girl will deny it. Would you not also?"

"Verily," Sarah Churchill reluctantly agreed, then turned to Jackie, who stared at the pattern of the carpeting on the floor. "It is true, Jackie, what my husband alleges?"

Jackie reluctantly raised her eyes to look from one Churchill face to the other, and then found it was not in her heart to mistrust them. Had not Jack counseled her to always follow her feelings, for he had said they would always lead her right, while her head would lead her down the wrong path. She sighed deeply and brushed a fold of her burgundy breeches. " 'Tis true," she finally admitted. "I am a girl."

"How delightful!" Sarah cried, clapping her hands together.

The girl stared at the woman as though she had taken leave of her senses, for she certainly hadn't expected this reaction from Lady Churchill.

She was totally confused. If they meant to unmask her, why were they playing this elaborate game? They must be certainly be after something of hers, if not a confession then perhaps monetary remuneration. Yet surely they knew she had no wealth to speak of.

Sarah studied the girl's heart-shaped face, then said, "John, I do believe we have upset the child."

"Is this so?" the man asked kindly, gazing at Jackie's

distraught face. She nodded mutely. " 'Twas not done to tease you, child."

"No?" she inquired, lifting her chin defiantly.

"No, Jackie, you must believe us. The reason I revealed your identity was that once my wife dressed as a boy."

"She did?" Jackie gave the Churchills a cautious glance.

"Aye, 'twas so," Sarah supplied. "I was but fifteen at the time, and in a play in the court of good King Charles."

"I saw her and fell immediately in love," Churchill said. "She was a most sprightly, quick-witted lad, much as you are, child."

Jackie shot him a suspicious look. "Is that how you penetrated my disguise?"

Churchill shook his head. "No. How could I be so astute? 'Twas not an imperfect disguise, Jackie. But when you were brought into the camp after you were knocked on the head, my physician checked you to ascertain that no great damage had been rendered. That is when. . . ." Churchill stopped, a flush rising in his face.

Jackie colored in answer and looked away.

Sarah smiled at the discomfort of both her husband and the girl.

The girl looked at her. "But you were not truly disguised as a boy for any length of time," Jackie pointed out. " 'Twas simply for a play."

"Yes, so it was, and yet I sympathize with your concern when you were unmasked by John," Lady Churchill replied. "For some time after we first met I continued dressing as a lad and, eluding my chaperons, I met clandestinely—and yet publicly—with John." The blond woman laughed suddenly, recalling the pleasant memory. " 'Twas a marvelous time in my life, and there are moments when I wish I could return to it." There was a hint of sadness in her voice, and her vivacious face assumed a thoughtful expression. She turned to the girl and asked, "Has anyone ever seen through your disguise? I confess that I was totally fooled."

"No, no one has pierced it," Jackie replied slowly, although the face of Simon Martin came into her mind as she answered the other woman. Yet she had exacted a vow of silence from him, and surely he would keep it. But perhaps she should tell the Churchills that this man knew. . . . No, not yet.

"Then you are safe," Sarah Churchill said, "for my husband and I shall say nothing of your true nature. You must now explain what has prompted you to adopt such a mode of attire."

"I am a Roman Catholic," she admitted, prepared for their reaction. If they disapproved, the Churchills did not allow it to show on their faces. "We thought it best to dress me as a boy . . . because of the times, you know."

"Yes," Sarah said. "Is Master McKier, your uncle, also Catholic?"

"Yes, he is a priest," she said.

This was met with some surprise by the couple. " 'Tis good he conceals both," Sarah commented.

"Aye," Jackie replied slowly, "for it is a dangerous time to be a Roman Catholic. It is not so long after the riots." She shuddered, remembering the turmoil of the streets that night.

"You seem well at home in those clothes, Jackie," the blond woman said. "Tell us all about your life."

The disguised girl doubted that the Churchills would be pleased if she related all the details, honest and less than honest, of her life. So, determined to omit the less savory aspects, she launched into a doctored account of her life.

Both Churchills listened with avid interest as Jackie related the story of how twelve years earlier Jack and Father Liam had taken in the grubby, mud-stained orphan they found in France. The girl told them of Black Teresa, who had trained her in the ways of the woman of the world, and who she said was a retired lady's maid, for she well knew that the Churchills would be most scandalized to know that the girl had learned her social graces from a retired whore. She alluded only briefly to the death of Jack, saying simply that he had been killed in a duel. As for her travels with the priest throughout Europe, Jackie merely said that her adopted father had left them some money which they used.

Lady Churchill could sense the suppressed agitation in the girl, noted Jackie's clenched hands, the nervous movement of her dove-gray eyes. She perceived that Jackie needed to talk to someone of the same sex. Yet if John were to remain, the girl would not speak her mind freely.

"Shoo, John. Go away!" his wife said suddenly and impatiently, a sharp tone in her voice. The man, surprised, merely stared at the blond woman. "I have matters which I intend to discuss with young Jackie, and I do not think I, or she, or even you, wish you to be present for that!''

''Ahem, no,'' he admitted hastily. He rose and bowed to both women. ''Good evening, Jackie. I shall take my leave of you now. 'Night, my dear,'' he said, leaning over to kiss his wife gently on the cheek.

Sarah Churchill waited impatiently as her husband left the room, firmly closing the door behind him. At last she faced Jackie and flashed a reassuring smile at the girl. ''He is a dear, you know, but such a dreary nuisance at times, as are all men.'' She laughed, a rich merry sound, at the astonished look on the silver-haired girl's face. ''Do I sound as though I loathe them? I do not, but at times—how weary one can grow!—they are like little boys and do need much leading about by the hand. I declare that my children are far less trouble than John.'' She rose and rang for a servant. ''Now we shall have further refreshments and then discuss what I see lurking in the depths of those innocent gray eyes, Jackie.''

Once the servant had brought the tea service and left with instructions not to bother her mistress further that night, Sarah poured tea and waited for Jackie to make the opening gambit.

But it seemed Sarah's expectations would come to naught, for Jackie volunteered nothing of herself, preferring to remain silent and stare down at the bone-china teacup clasped in her hands. She was shy around this strong woman, who seemed so indomitable, so sure of herself, so headstrong. Jackie had known only such women as Black Teresa and later the silly lighthearted girls from whom many a lovely jewel had been stolen. She simply did not know what to say, where to begin, how to be open with this woman, so she kept her eyes lowered, her hands tightly gripping the cup, as if the warmth of the tea were heating her body.

'Twas a shame in many respects, Lady Churchill thought, that this girl was above the age of her eldest son, for this was the type of woman his mother would have happily chosen for his wife. There remained, too, the serious matter of money, and the girl possessed no great fortune, despite the money her foster father had apparently bequeathed to her. 'Twas not the most serious obstacle, for Sarah herself had possessed little money in her youth and had yet steadily risen in social scale since that time. However, the girl would certainly find money to be useful. What to do? Sarah thought. How could she help this girl? And then. . . .

"You must marry!" Sarah declared so abruptly that the startled girl nearly dropped her teacup. Recovering herself, she looked blankly at the other woman. " 'Tis the only way," Sarah said, smiling at her uneasy guest.

"What do you mean, 'the only way'?" Jackie asked, her suspicions aroused.

Lady Churchill was pleased that her abrupt words had acted as a prod to the silent Jackie.

"Why, you cannot mean to stay dressed as a boy all your life," Sarah averred with surprise.

"Well, no, yes, I mean . . . I do not know at this time," Jackie replied with some confusion. She appeared to be sunk deep in thought, and only with a supreme effort could she recover her wits enough to continue speaking. "Father Liam, too, has urged me to marry. But I know not along what path my feet shall guide me," she said sadly, sighing somewhat dramatically.

"Come, child, you cannot remain a bandit all your life," the other woman said pleasantly.

"Bandit?" Jackie echoed, her gray eyes widening.

"Aye, is that not your profession?"

"Well, hardly!" the girl hastily exclaimed. " 'Tis that we are—are soldiers of fortune. Swords and pistols for hire."

"I see," Sarah replied, wisely dropping the matter. "Yet you cannot always remain a soldier of fortune."

"Why not?"

"Why, child, you could be hurt or possibly killed. 'Twould be a most unpleasant and disagreeable end for you. Would you not agree, Jackie?"

Jack's face came into her mind, his laughing eyes closed, his boyish face twisted with pain. Jack, his lifeblood draining from the fatal wound. Jack, who'd thrown the dice once too often and had lost.

"Oh, aye," the girl said soberly, "for I have no desire to end my days dead in a gutter. But what else am I to do? This is my life—the only life I have known. I have no fortune, no family, no protector."

"Young women can be protected in many ways," Sarah said slyly.

"Oh?" Jackie asked innocently.

"There are always men who wish the pleasant company of a beautiful and talented woman. Men such as these would pay much to ensure a woman's independence."

Jackie rose stiffly to her feet and coldly surveyed her hostess. "I think you misjudge me, Lady Churchill," she said harshly. "For I would never consider that alternative. 'Tis a less than honorable life, that. I have no quarrel with the poor women who must needs choose that path, but I elect not to be the trifle of some man who would cast me off when he grew tired. Not all the money in England shall change my mind!"

"Bravo!" Lady Churchill cried, clapping her hands in approval. "Bravo, my dear. Those were the very words I wished to hear from you!"

Abruptly, the young girl sat down and stared at the woman. Her head whirled with confusion. How baffling these Churchills were to her! "I fear I do not understand," she ventured.

"I simply wished to determine the nature of your disposition," Sarah said calmly. "You are not a lazy girl, nor one given to exploiting her physical charms to make her way in the world. Of course," the woman continued, "one must use the beauty one was given. You simply cannot ignore it, but I am pleased that you do not misapply it for money."

"If I did, madam," Jackie said dryly, recovering her composure somewhat, "I would hardly be dressed as a boy. I have been told that I am a pretty boy, but my mirror tells me that I make a more than passable girl."

"So you would," Lady Churchill said, leaning back to study the girl. " 'Tis a pity about that brown." She tapped her fingers along the arm of the settee. "Is that your own hair, child?" When Jackie shook her head, Sarah commanded, "Remove the wig at once so that I might see your real hair."

Reluctantly Jackie obeyed. Down tumbled lock after lock of silver, which glinted with an elfin air in the candlelight.

Sarah gasped at the silver mass that framed Jackie's heart-shaped face and accentuated her black wing-swept eyebrows. "I had not expected such a glorious color! Oh, child, if you were to dress as a woman, all the court would be in love with you at a moment's glance."

Lady Churchill thought for several minutes. Jackie sipped her tea and watched the woman's face undergo various transformations. At last it settled into a most cunning and self-pleased expression.

"Do you know, I have an idea."

"Oh?" Jackie asked cautiously, wary of the machinations of the agile Churchill mind. The man and woman seemed so similar in their thinking that it was most surprising that Lady Churchill was not a general as well!

"Why yes, 'tis assured that you cannot now change your sex—'twould be most unseemly. But nothing prevents you from appearing now and then as a girl. Perhaps at a masquerade or some such. What do you think of that?" She watched as the excitement grew on Jackie's face. "We could say that you were a cousin of mine from the country. The only ones who would know would be my husband, your priest, and the two of us. I would give you introductions, and while you were in the guise of my young cousin you would stay here with us to create an air of reality about your new identity. You would not be missed as a boy at court, for you could claim you were staying with friends in the country. Do say you will try it, Jackie!" She beamed an excited smile at the girl. "Do agree!"

"I shall!" the girl exclaimed, a merry look on her face. " 'Twill be such a lark! I shall slay the men-beasts by the dozen. They shall lie gasping at my feet." Suddenly a cunning light entered her gray eyes, and she smiled with deep satisfaction.

Oh, yes, she could break hearts, that she did not doubt for a single moment. And there was one heart in particular that she would truly desire to rend to pieces. If she could not kill that mocking, blue-eyed devil with her sword or pistol, she would do such damage that would prove irreparable. She would force him to his knees, make him grovel, destroy him, demand his heart, and then she would spurn him . . . and all that would remain of him would be a shell of the sardonic man he had once been.

Seeing her protégée's unholy mien, Sarah Churchill wondered at the girl's intensity. She had no doubt that she would soon discover the source of the girl's sly look. Sarah smiled with glee as she imagined her husband's face when she informed him of her marvelous scheme. Or better yet, she decided with sudden craftiness, perhaps she would say nothing to John, merely allowing him to find out for himself in good time.

The blond woman laughed at the thought, and Jackie joined in, both women immersed in their devilish plans.

It was half past two in the morning when Liam unlocked the door and staggered into the dim room. If he had been sober, perhaps he would have been surprised to see that Jackie was still awake.

"How be yer fancy dinner?" Liam asked as he slowly sank into a green-and yellow-striped chair. He groaned as his bottom met the seat cushion, then stretched his legs carefully in front of him, his arms comfortably placed along the chair's wide arms.

"They are a delight, the Churchills." She paused. She had thought to tell Liam of her plans with Lady Churchill, but now that she saw him she was not so sure. Should she say that the Churchills knew her true sex? No, the girl concluded, for Liam would fall into a fit of the worries and be anxious to move on so that they would not be further unmasked. And at present she preferred not to leave England. At least for a while, she hurriedly assured herself.

"An'?" he prompted.

"We talked of this and that, politics and the court and fashion."

"Ah," Liam breathed.

"But what of your evening, Liam?" the girl asked.

The priest's face took on a sly expression, and he grinned.

"What does that mean?" his companion asked, somewhat warily.

"I be havin' good news fer us—fer ye, especially."

"Good news?"

"Ye remember that ye be tellin' me o' that scrape that the duke o' Avalon be gettin' himself into?" She nodded. "Well, it do seem that the prince be not at all pleased with the duke's action—most unruly an' undisciplined, I might be addin'!" He smiled again.

"Well?" she prompted, fairly impatiently now.

"Well, the upshot o' the whole matter be"—Liam paused, trying to milk all the dramatics out of the affair that he could—"that the prince be callin' him in—that be the Duke." He ignored Jackie's exasperated look toward heaven and continued his tale. "An' then the prince be sayin' to him—"

Liam, leaning forward, whispered, "that be he," and the following words were lost to Jackie.

"Liam, don't mumble so!" she cried. "What did the prince say to that stupid pig of a duke?"

"He said that he—that be the duke, o' course—be banished from court!" He ended his narrative on a triumphant note, looking immensely pleased with himself.

Banished! Her greatest enemy on this earth had been sent packing from the court in disgrace. She was furious. How dare that oaf provoke the prince and spoil her plans? How was she to flirt madly with the duke and cruelly break his heart if he were not to be at court?

She stamped her foot in anger, rose, and paced around the room.

Liam blinked with surprise. He had been more than happy that "Satan" Blade had been sent into exile. The less Liam saw of that man the better he felt. But Jackie wasn't acting properlike; she should be laughing with delight, not frowning!

"Do ye not think that be good tidin's I bring ye?" he ventured at last, still confused.

The girl drew her black brows together in a scowl. "Yes, Liam, 'tis a good thing," she replied in an absentminded manner. "I must rise early in the morning. I shall leave you now." She kissed his round cheek and then in a moment was gone.

Most perlexing, Liam thought as he slowly rose to his feet and stretched, then scratched his side. Listening for any sounds from Jackie's room, he tiptoed over to the wall and paused, his heart hammering. All he heard was the squeaking of the bed's leather straps and a wee mousie in the corner.

Well, at least she be abed, he thought slyly, pouring himself a furtive glass of wine. He tossed the drink down, then poured himself another, and soon it did not matter one bit to him that her response was not as it should have been.

Chapter

Twelve

"MY LOVE," MICHAEL RANDOM said, kissing his current ladylove upon her white neck. The bewigged woman shrugged away from his caress and continued, her concentration unbroken, penning a letter. The light of the candles sparked the large emerald ring on her finger with a green fire as her hand moved back and forth across the page.

Rebuffed but not greatly concerned, Random strolled away from her, idly wandering the length of the sitting room. Heavy persimmon brocade curtains, embroidered with gold thread and depicting the four seasons, were drawn against the blackness of the evening. The yellow light in the room was provided by the blaze of a roaring fire in the black marble fireplace and by the dozens of candles set in the crystal chandeliers. Extravagant in its rich shades of damask and crimson, the room sported a simple elegance in its furniture. The carpeting was of Armenian crafting and had been transported down from the Caucasus Mountains on the back of a mule.

The room was but a small part of the London town house which the woman had purchased upon her recent arrival in

London. The air was laden with a spicy scent, redolent of musk and cinnamon, and the colors of each room in the house were shades of black, red, and gold. Her country house, on the estate her agents had purchased before she arrived in the country, also displayed the same penchant for the three colors, and even the woman's clothing expressed her obsession.

That evening she was attired in a black gown of crushed velvet. Embroidered damask roses decorated the underskirt, while the overskirt was of fine black net lace sewn liberally with tiny jet beads that twinkled in the light. The tight-laced bodice, so low as to prove an almost inadequate restraint to the swelling ripeness of her breasts, was threaded through with a diamond-encrusted ribbon. Scallops secured with diamond roses edged the hem of her full skirt. Her wig was as black as a raven's wing and adorned with diamond-and-jet pins. Around the lovely white throat she wore a "dog collar" of beaten gold inset with bloodred rubies. The stones cast a rosy light upon her throat and snowy bosom, and Random felt the demanding ache of lust stir within him.

Studying her, Random thought the flash of green fire upon her lithe hand was the only other color he had seen her adopt, and she seemed quite fond of the ring, for she would occasionally stop what she was doing to caress the baguette-cut emerald.

He shrugged and picked up a small figurine. Its tiny body was pudgy, and a bow and quiver of arrows was clutched in its fat hands.

"Put it down," said Victorée de Saint-Martin L'Este du Plessis. "You are such a child, *mon petit,* always into something." The woman shook her head.

The young man smiled, his smooth face easily accommodating the ingratiating expression. "True, Your Grace." His voice was laced with heavy mockery. "At this very moment I know what I would most enjoy being in." His plump fingers rhythmically stroked the gold figurine, and his knowing blue eyes bore into her.

She laughed shortly. "Do not be lewd, my pet, it does not well suit you. Desire should be delicate. Better you should play the outraged infant." Victorée applied herself once more to the letter, one which faced an impending deadline. It was always difficult for her to concentrate on her important work when Michel was present, and it was no different with this letter. He was forever interrupting her, just like an *enfant*. And he *was* a child—just barely twenty, compared to her four and thirty. Young, she thought, so very young, but extremely knowledgeable in the arts of Eros. Unlike poor Étienne Jules, who was less an artisan than a technician. Her husband, in his seventies, was a man well past the prime of life.

Life had not been particularly easy these past seventeen years for Victorée de Marchaud de Saint-Martin. Discontented a short time after her marriage at the age of seventeen to the senescent but politically important and then still potent French duke, the silver-haired woman had sought pleasure and diversion elsewhere.

Trembling on the edge of ripe womanhood, the beautiful Victorée did not search for long. France possessed many gallant sons willing to while away the hours with the lovely Victorée and to console her in her marital unhappiness. Many men had been brought to her bed, and these tender interludes had simply been convenient arrangements for the body, for pleasure only.

Perhaps, she thought idly, had the duke been able to provide her with a child . . . but the years had proven fruitless for them—an irony when she thought of the two pregnancies terminated before her early marriage and the soon-killed issue of her only completed pregnancy. Had the times been different, she might well have brought a ready-made family to the home of her husband.

Random crossed to stand behind her and trailed his skilled fingers down the soft nape of her neck. Victorée quivered, feeling the telltale prickling in her stomach and inner thighs as the young man continued his rhythmic stroking. The Frenchwoman arched her back with delight, and Michael's hands moved across her bare shoulder blades and then around in front to cup the smooth orbs of her perfect breasts. One hand slid insidiously inside her low bodice, and she stirred as his warm hand touched her flesh. The heat of his hand seemed to scorch her cool skin, and she licked her dry lips. Playfully he tweaked one nipple, feeling it harden with her desire, and then his other hand joined its mate. He bent, kissing her ear.

"Ah, Michel, you do not know how much I wish to go to bed with you at this moment." Her voice was low and throaty as his hands firmly fondled her breasts.

"Then do," he whispered.

"It is not as easy as that." The Frenchwoman regretfully retrieved the young man's hands from the interior of her bodice and placed them against each other, like hands in prayer. The silver-haired woman kissed his fingers one by one, then gently nipped them. Random moaned and pressed himself against the woman.

"But no, not now, *mon cher*," the Frenchwoman said with a smile on her luscious painted lips. "I have work to do. But when I am finished. . . ." Her voice trailed away, and her eyelids narrowed with anticipation.

Random jerked his hands away from her grasp. "You are always working, Victorée," he said, pouting. "You don't spend enough time with me." He moved in front of the intricately carved writing desk and archly smiled at her. "Perhaps if you do not take care I'll find another, more willing love."

She laughed throatily, and Michael's lower lip protruded.

"*Ma foi!* You are *très adorable, mon cher*. Such kissable lips, so full and pouting. You would do well as a woman." She smiled as an unreadable expression crossed his handsome face. "Ah, *touché, n'est-ce pas?*" She sighed, picking up the quill pen once more. "I work, *mon cher*, so that we can be together."

"I don't understand." His sullen face betrayed his lack of wit.

"Do not force me to explain anything, Michel. It grows most tedious. Come to me later."

Still pouting and virtually dismissed, the young man made a leg to the woman and left, the door closing behind him with a little more force than was absolutely necessary.

Victorée shrugged and continued writing. *Imbécile*. He was simply a pawn in the hands of the chess master at Versailles. *As we all are*, she thought ironically. She glanced down at the letter and reread her words.

"With the convening of this Convention, the English are faced with five possibilities, sire.

"The first is to recall James from your court, but only a small Jacobite minority has supported this. The English lords feel that James has deserted his followers twice, and they fear in their stolid English hearts that he could do it a third time.

"The second possibility is that the prince of Orange be made sole ruler, and the little man himself has favored this idea. Of course, his Dutch advisers see nothing wrong with it, but the English wisely refuse to seriously consider this alternative. After all, it is Mary by law, and not her husband, who is James's heir, and it would appear that the convention members wish to preserve at least some semblance of continuity and legality after the 'Glorious Revolution.'

"The third alternative is posited on James's alleged inability to continue his kingly duties. Proponents of this plan argue that his desertion and general behavior have shown him unfit to be a ruler—so that Mary should rule as regent on his behalf. Absurd! Parallels are dutifully drawn to regencies on behalf of lunatic kings in Sweden and Portugal, but many of the Convention's members little like the comparison or the implication that the king is insane.

"The fourth solution is simple. Mary should be sole ruler, and this, of course, would be best for your plan, Your Highness, but neither William nor Mary will agree to this, so it has been summarily dismissed.

"The fifth solution is that the crown should be offered jointly to the prince and princess. The legal basis, I find, is decidedly shaky for this solution, and I think the English barrister mind tries hard to make the facts fit the solution.

"My sources at court reveal to me that the fate of England should be decided this very month. I shall write you as soon as a decision is reached."

She looked up and smiled, recalling the days before she left France. "Do not," the French king had said to her, "fail me. You know that what happens in England is crucial for my plans for Europe. You will be my so-lovely messenger and will send me all the news as soon as you have heard it." And he had chucked her hard under the chin, then ordered that wine be brought for a toast to the beautiful woman and her important mission. For it had not been lovers alone who had approached the voluptuous albino woman in the early years of her boring marriage. Louis had sought a spy whom no one would suspect and yet who would move in high social circles— hence the French aristocrat. Despite the court gossip, they had not become lovers in the intervening years, Louis having had his fill of mistresses and the troubles they produced. But there had developed between them a firm working relationship, a wary friendship, and a mutual respect for each other's wills.

Life was easy at the English court, and her search for amusement had ended with the discovery one evening at a rout of the young earl, Michael Koenraad Random, the son of a Dutch noblewoman and an English lord. Her selection of the petulant blond boy was not as casual a choice as it might have seemed at first glance, for the youth was a favorite of Prince William, and, as such, shared the confidences of the Dutch leader.

She did not know if the boy also shared the bed of the Dutch prince, for on this matter the boy was strangely silent, preferring only to smile at her when she questioned him.

No matter. The fool did not realize he was a puppet, for from this unwitting boy, eager to please his older lover, she daily learned of the activities of the Dutch prince. There was not a step that Prince William made that was not reported to the French spy and then, in turn, relayed to Louis XIV.

Victorée dusted the letter with sand, and when the ink was dry she delicately blew the grains away and then folded the letter into thirds. She sealed the communication and tugged at the bellpull to summon a servant.

"Send Carel in," the Frenchwoman directed when the servant entered. Her pale eyes strayed to the flame of the candle on her writing desk. She studied the aureole of light and waited.

Carel was, in a way, a bequest from her late papa. Dear old Papa, she thought wryly, her pale eyes glimmering with reminiscence. Raoul de Marchaud had passed into an energetic old age, until one evening when he carelessly dined with his daughter. She had watched with amusement as he feebly called out to her when the first leadenness of paralysis crept through his taut body. In the end only his dark eyes could move. What a tragedy, everyone at the French court had murmured, and how kind his daughter was to take the old invalid into her own house. He had lived on for many, many years until Victorée had grown tired of taunting the sufferer.

Poor Papa had fallen one day from his cane chair, striking his forehead upon the corner of a marble-topped table. How long he had lain there, unable to move or call, yet feeling his lifeblood draining from the gash on his forehead, only the good God knew, said the physician in attendance. A tragic affair, he had murmured, kindly patting the arm of the bereaved daughter.

Victorée had duly gone into mourning the requisite length of time, and the day that the year was up, she had directed all the black crepe to be stripped from the house. And, within a week, Victorée du Plessis had held one of the most brilliant, most lavishly accoutred social affairs of the decade. In its licentiousness, hysterical gaiety, frenetic gambling, and excess of fine liquor and rich foods, it had earned a place second only to Louis XIV's fetes.

And, she thought, stroking the hilt of an emerald-encrusted dagger that always traveled with her, her subsequent life would not have been at all possible without the devious old hag in the swamp. The ancient crone was exceedingly wise in the ways of herbs—herbs to make a man love a woman, herbs to rid a woman of an unwanted babe, herbs to take away the sensation and strength of a body.

The click of the door broke her reverie, and she looked up as the pitiful creature shuffled into the room and waited patiently for his mistress to command him.

The years had not been kind to the giant, the Frenchwoman thought as she looked at his grizzled hair and stared into eyes the color of scum on a stagnant pond. She repressed an unconscious shiver. Still, he maintained his strength and had proved indispensable on many occasions. He tugged at his black coat with its gold buttons and red cord design, the livery of Victorée's own personal servants.

"Here." Victorée handed the sealed letter to the henchman, who stared blankly at it. "Conceal it, Carel. Then go as quickly as you can to the king, and give him my sweet regards. Do not go by direct route."

The hulk of a man made mewing sounds and attempted to stroke his mistress's arm. "Get away!" she snapped, shoving his meaty hand from her. "Leave—and wait for an answer, you fool."

She waited a few minutes, then glided to a window and, pushing aside the brocade curtain, stared out the diamond-paned window. Like fireflies, lights could be seen flickering in the dark streets of London on this night in February, 1689. She heard the clatter of a horse's hooves on cobblestones and knew that Carel had departed on his mission to King Louis XIV of France.

Victorée left the window and carefully unbuttoned her dress. With a sly rustle the dress slid to the floor in a heap. The maid could pick it up on the morrow. The Frenchwoman did not wish the silly girl bustling about now. Now . . . now was to be given to pleasure.

Victorée swept into a crimson and black bedchamber. Above the tall bed, embedded in the ceiling, was mirror after mirror.

The Frenchwoman slowly peeled off her petticoat of black silk decorated with tiny bows, then let her hair down. She ran her hands through her silky silver hair and stretched, a particularly sensuous, catlike movement. She stood completely nude in front of an ebony wardrobe and trailed her hand past the various dressing gowns as she deliberated on what to wear for Michel and their evening of love.

"Do not mantle your beauty," a low voice said behind her. She started, then half-turned and smiled at the young man. "The girdle of Venus," Michael Random whispered, his hands encircling her lithe waist and slipping down to caress her firm hips. She sighed, leaning back against his chest, the starched frills of his cravat slightly scratching her bare skin. Victorée rubbed her back against the material and shivered at the sensation it produced.

"You possess an exquisite sense of timing, Michel."

He laughed, lifted her up in his arms, then dropped her onto the bed. She opened her mouth to protest, but in an instant the stocky blond man was on her, covering first her mouth with his, then moving to the white globes of her breasts, then to her hips. She moaned and entwined her fingers in his hair, pulling his face closer to her warm body.

Random withdrew from the bed and quickly pulled off his clothes, flinging them in his haste to one side. She chuckled with appreciation as she watched his member enlarge with lust.

"The little man," she said, her eyelashes lowered over her pale eyes, "becomes a big man. Come," she said, crooking one finger to the blond earl, "come to me, little man."

"Gladly, bitch." With a movement that sent a shudder through the bed Random flung himself onto her. She fought him, her hands becoming talons and raking the tender skin of his back. She nipped at his shoulder and drew blood, which she licked away with her tongue. Capturing her heart-shaped face in his hands, he pressed his lips down on hers, forcing her mouth open.

Her sharp teeth gnawed at his tongue, and he cried out with pain. She chuckled and, clasping her hands in the small of his back, pulled him even closer to her.

She withdrew his lips from his and smiled at him, licking her kiss-inflamed lips. He gazed at her hungrily, and she laughed. Roughly Random thrust his hand between her legs, forcing them apart. She clamped her legs together. "I have your little explorer," she said in a low tone. "What would you do, *mon cher*?" Her eyes widened, and her chest rose and fell more rapidly. "Ah, yes, sweetling, *that* you must do by all means." She reached out with one hand and stroked his flanks and his belly. Then she reached under and gave him a sharp tug.

"Uggh!" He grunted with pain. Laughing, she rolled out of his reach. "Victorée!" he called. She laughed again from the other end of the bed and, flinging her head back, looked up into the lust-darkened eyes of dozens of Victorées. He looked up, too, and grinned.

Random lunged forward and thrust himself onto her. He grabbed her hands and forced them over her head and with one of his legs forced her own apart.

She looked mockingly up into his blue eyes. "Are you the conqueror come to take me, *mon cher*?"

For answer he only grunted, intent on the business at hand.

She raised one leg and hit him in the back of the head with her foot. She laughed as his eyes crossed momentarily.

"Bitch!" he muttered and ran his hands down her sides. He trailed one hand across her stomach and down to the white junction of her thighs.

"I'll take you yet, my dear," the young man gritted, as he savagely thrust into her waiting body. She laughed as she felt the penetration, and her legs gripped his. Their bodies rose and fell rhythmically as Random called out for release. But she continued to laugh at her young lover, and he was determined to teach her a lesson. He continued thrusting deeper inside her, and she laughed still more.

"Victorée!" he cried out in his frustration, tears coming to his blue eyes.

"No, *mon cher*, you must beg me," she said huskily, licking her lips.

"Beg you?" he cried. "For what?"

"For me to give you the satisfaction you demand."

"No!"

She chuckled, and with a great movement he buried himself in her flesh, becoming lost in the hot whiteness, and some time later he heard distant screams and realized they were his. He opened his eyes and stared down into hers, so light, so alien, and drove his manhood deeper inside her body, and he heard her crying out to him. Tide after tide of turbulent emotion washed through the young man, and at length he pulled himself from her, propping his body up on his elbows so that he might look at her. She lay there, her lips curving slightly in satisfaction. He rolled over on his back and fell heavily asleep.

Some time later the Frenchwoman rolled onto her side and ran a long finger down his side. The young man stirred.

With a laugh, the Frenchwoman, her eyelids heavy with passion, suddenly sat astride him. "*Cosa ben fatta è fatta due volte,*" she murmured.

The blond earl of Malvern pouted. "You know my Italian is poor, Victorée."

" 'A thing well done is twice done,' " the silver-haired woman quoted as she covered Random's soft face with kisses and traced the lines of his stocky body with her capable hands.

For simple answer, the young man's arms snaked around her, pulling her tight against his bare chest, and he kissed her deeply.

"Good day, Master Martín," the girl said, bowing to Simon.

"Good day, Master Jackie," he replied. "Are you prepared for our chess game?"

"As always, sir." The board had been set up in the suite she shared with Liam, and Simon sat in one chair and stared thoughtfully at the stone figures.

Jackie brought a bottle and two glasses to the table and then sat, stretching her booted legs in front of her. She stared at the swordsmith, then tapped her foot.

"I have a question to pose to you," she said softly.

"Yes?" he answered, not looking up.

"Do you spy on me for the duke of Avalon?" Her shrewd gray eyes never left his face, which turned in her direction.

That warm open face, unable to conceal dishonesty, turned extremely red, and Simon sputtered as he sought a reasonable answer.

"No, no," Jackie said, waving aside all the man's protests. "You have well answered my question, Master Martín. 'Twas as I thought."

"I—I would not have you think ill of the duke for that," Simon managed, at last, to say.

She laughed, a chilling sound in the silence of the room. "No? And how should I regard it? 'Tis certainly not a friendly action. Does he wish me to be one of his 'pets'? Ah, perhaps that is the reason he sends you to spy on me. You watch me, and you report my actions and my behavior to him, and then he plans to come to me sometime to make me one of his darlings. How now shall you explain that this is impossible without revealing my true sex?" Her eyes glittered as she watched him.

"No, Master Jackie, I do not watch you for that reason."

"Ah," she said slyly, "he has boys aplenty."

Simon sighed at the futility of explaining. Jackie went on, " 'Tis common knowledge at the court that when the duke retired to his country estate in disgrace, he took to solace himself a young boy of the streets."

It was true, Simon thought, that the duke had taken a boy with him, but for quite different reasons than this girl thought. As Avalon was going out the evening before his departure, he had found a boy in the street outside his town house. The child, no more than ten years of age, slept the uneasy slumber of the starving, and his fair face was pinched from suffering.

Avalon had stopped, picked up the child, and brought him into the town house, ordering Santu to prepare a bath and meal at once. When the lad had been fed, Corney had brought the trembling child to Avalon. The boy had stared at him wide-eyed but silent. Avalon had demanded the boy's name, and the child had tremblingly told him. As Simon watched, the duke skillfully drew from the boy the story of his life.

It was a common enough one, Simon thought, and one that Avalon and he had heard many times from these imps of

"Satan." The boy's family, having grown too large to support all the children, had brought him to the rich section of London, and there his parents had left him, hoping that the boy would either die or soon be found by a nobleman and taken in. The boy had been lucky. Others were not so fortunate, Simon thought, and were taken in by other aristocrats with less than wholesome appetites.

"It's too early," the duke said, "to see if the boy bespeaks some promise, but I shall take him anyway to the country with me. I am sure that I can find a home for him there."

"Perhaps with one of your servants or cottagers," Simon suggested.

"True," the duke murmured. The child's long lashes had dropped, and he had signaled Corney to put the child to bed.

Simon wondered now what would become of the boy. In his last letter to his friend, the duke of Avalon had written that the boy grew stronger and healthier in the country and that his skin was no longer a deadly white color. Would this child enter the service of a household when he was older, as others before him had done? Or might he, if he showed exceptional promise, be taken in as a companion to the son of a household and tutored the same as the noble's son and given the same advantages?

Simon hoped the boy would follow the latter path. He sighed, thinking of those few boys who had spurned the duke's generosity. Those who had exhibited no promise, who had tried to steal from the duke—those unfortunate lads were given a few coins and sent on their way. But, the swordsmith knew, there had been few of those boys. Most had preferred to take the opportunity offered by "Satan" Blade.

It was odd, Simon thought, that Blade had never mentioned making a "pet" of Jackie McKier. It was as though from the first the two spirits, both indomitable, had clashed beyond reconciliation. Yet it was a good thing that Blade had not attempted to reform Jackie, for it could have spelled her betrayal.

He was not sure how Avalon would react if he knew the girl's identity. No doubt with anger. Yet Avalon's pride was often overbearing, and it would do him no harm to be led by the nose by this snippet of a girl. When the duke ultimately discovered Jackie's true sex, and of that Simon had some certainty, he wished to be well away from his friend.

What misunderstanding these two aroused in each other's breasts. He could not tell Avalon the girl's true nature, nor could he tell her of Avalon's. Long ago Avalon had sworn him to secrecy, much as the girl had done. 'Twas little wonder, Simon mused with some humor, that he said little— he shared many confidences and all who gave them swore him to silence.

"Enough of this," the swordsmith said at length, well aware that the girl had been studying him. "Shall we return to the matter at hand, namely, our chess game?"

"Very well, Master Martín. I wish, though, that you would call me by my first name. 'Twould be far simpler."

"If you will call me Simon," he said, smiling at the girl.

"Done." And both clasped hands briefly.

"I have a new gambit for you," Jackie said.

"Good," the brown-haired man answered, pushing all thoughts of his friend from his head. For the moment, he would simply enjoy the charming presence of this delightful girl.

Jackie saw Michael Random coming down the hallway toward her and realized that it was far too late to turn and leave, for he had already seen her. It was not that she particularly disliked the young blond man, but of all the men at court he flirted the most openly with her in her boy's disguise. Of all her ardent suitors of both sexes the blond earl was proving the most persistent, somehow failing to comprehend the meaning of an outright "no."

He bowed to her, and she bowed in response. "Good eve to you, Master Jackie."

"Lord Malvern," she acknowledged.

"I have come seeking you for one purpose alone," he said with a smile.

"And that is?" she asked.

"To ask you to dinner to thank you for saving me from the duke of Avalon."

"I thank you, Lord Malvern," the girl replied easily, "but I am already spoken for with Simon Martín."

"That Jew?" he asked flatly.

"The very same," Jackie said, realizing there was no advantage to getting angry over the man's tone.

He smiled, but it did not reach his blue eyes. "Very well, Master McKier." And he turned and walked off.

She watched him for a few moments, then turning, nearly bumped into Simon Martín. "Oh!" the girl exclaimed, surprised to see him, for she had not heard his approach. "I came to find you. How long have you been standing there?"

"Long enough to overhear that rather brief conversation," he replied.

She colored with some embarrassment. "It is very hard for you here, isn't it?" she asked the man with some curiosity.

He glanced sideways at his companion as they began walking down the corridor. "Because of my religion, do you mean?"

"Yes," the girl said.

"It is far easier now than before at the court of James. The prince is tolerant of all faiths, Christian and non-Christian. He has said that conscience is God's province, in which man should not interfere. He has Roman Catholic allies, officers, servants, and friends."

"Yet the Catholic officers in the English army were dismissed under the prince's terms."

"Yes," the Jewish swordsmith said, "for the English expected it of the prince. I do not think they would have accepted him so readily otherwise." Simon chuckled. "It is amusing that he has even been accused of being a papist by some of his enemies."

The two walked outside to the stables and ordered horses saddled, and they continued their conversation.

"What of the Jews?" the girl asked as their horses were brought out and they mounted.

"Ah, yes, the Jews. Well, William has in the past proved tolerant toward us. You know that Jews were expelled from England in 1290 and were not allowed back in the country until 1655."

"But you were born in England?"

"Yes, just a short year after that. Before that," he said, anticipating her question, "my family lived in Holland, and before *that*, in Spain and Portugal."

"Has it been hard being a swordsmith here, a Jewish one?" she wanted to know.

"At first it was, but I have my . . . patron, if you will," he said, with a twinkle in his brown eyes, "and business has been good since he took me under his wing."

"Who's your patron?" She leaned forward and patted her mount's neck as the horse moved forward.

"The duke of Avalon," he replied.

Jackie wrinkled her nose as if she had just smelled an unpleasant odor, and Simon chuckled at her reaction. "Come now, child, he cannot be as bad as you would imagine, or I would not be his friend."

"Just remember," the girl said darkly, "that his nickname is 'Satan.' "

"That I cannot forget."

She glanced down at her boot, then at the face of her riding companion. "Is he not disturbed by your religion?" she asked.

"No, not at all. In fact, he finds me more interesting, or so he claims," the man said with a smile.

"Why is that?"

"You are a thousand questions today, child. Ah," he said, glancing ahead and then pulling on the reins of his horse. "We have come to our destination."

Jackie looked at the building. Squat and heavy-beamed, the tavern sported a freshly painted sign in pink and gold. On the wood a saucy sow gamboled through a bag of coins.

She raised her eyebrows. " 'The Pig and the Penny,' " she read.

He shrugged, his face slightly red. "It has good food," the man offered by way of explanation. She laughed, and they dismounted, handing the reins to two little stable boys who had scampered out to take their horses. Simon waited for the girl to enter the inn first, then followed behind.

They found a secluded booth by one wall, and Simon gestured for the serving girl to come over. He made his recommendation on the food, and soon after they were served a hearty meal of meat stew, beefsteak, and golden pears.

While Simon ate his dinner the girl stared at him and chewed her steak thoughtfully. "I thought the Jews ate differently."

"We do not all follow the old laws. My family has broken with many of the dietary laws, as well as those of dress." She glanced at his pale gold coat, white cravat, cream-colored waistcoat, and ivory breeches. He reached for a hunk of bread to butter. "My family is Marrano. Which means," he said, as he saw the look of confusion on her face, "Jews who were forced to become Christians while they lived in Spain, in order to escape the persecution of the Inquisition. Yet secretly they remained Jews."

"Oh." The girl sat for some minutes, quietly reflecting on what he had said, then looked at Simon. "You never answered my question about *him*."

"Ah, yes. Why does he have a particular interest in me?" Simon paused and sipped his wine. "Because I am a Jew, I am well educated, and the duke likes people of learning about him."

"I've had a good education!" the girl blurted out without thinking, then immediately looked stricken.

Simon, however, chose to ignore her startled comment and poured himself another glass of wine. Her face red with embarrassment, Jackie stared at her plate.

"The duke," his friend said after a few minutes of silence, "has perhaps more volumes in his home than any twenty or thirty other nobles combined."

The silver-haired girl stirred her fork through the steak's juices. Why had she blurted out that stupid statement? Was she trying to prove something? If, so, what, and to whom? She felt perfectly mortified now and hoped that she could somehow make amends.

"It is no great matter, child," Simon said at length. "I understand why you said what you did." She raised grateful gray eyes to him and tremulously smiled, and in that moment Simon thought that the duke of Avalon was a very great fool for antagonizing this beautiful girl. "Are you finished?"

"Yes." She tossed some coins down on the table, as did Simon, took one last swig of her cup, and rose. The girl stretched, and as she did so she noticed that one of the men in the dim light of the tavern looked familiar.

As they walked outside to reclaim their horses from the stable boys, the girl puzzled over that familiarity. She swung around to stare back at the tavern, then shook her head.

"Why do you frown?" Simon asked gently.

"I thought I saw someone I knew," she replied quietly.

"Michael Random," the swordsmith supplied.

"Yes!" Astonishment lit her fair face. "Then it was not my imagination, after all?"

"No," the man said, his face growing concerned. "It is not your imagination, nor, I think, is it a coincidence. I believe"—he paused and swung around to face the girl—"you have been followed!"

Her expression was filled with dismay, and a cold shiver ran down her spine.

Chapter

Thirteen

THE SOMBER TONE set at court little dampened Lady Churchill's enthusiasm as she schemed to debut Jackie attired in feminine clothing.

The Convention met daily, but Sarah worried little now about politics, for she was sure of the eventual outcome. She had no doubt that William and Mary would be crowned as double monarchs, and that simply would be that. She need not concern herself with matters that could not be altered.

"I do believe it's the loveliest gown I've ever had," Jackie said in a hushed tone, pivoting before the mirror for the final fitting of the gown Sarah Churchill had commissioned for the ball. "I *know* it is." She lowered her lashes and stared in the mirror at the glimmer of misty white.

"It will do," Sarah replied critically. " 'Tis the girl inside who'll make the gown shine."

"Do you think so, Sarah?" Jackie asked eagerly, her heart-shaped face glowing with happiness. After their initial meeting and the establishment of their friendship, Lady Churchill had declared that Jackie simply could not continue calling her by her title and had insisted that she call her by her

Christian name. Too, the woman had shrewdly pointed out, it would appear more natural when Jackie assumed the role of her cousin.

"Hurry now, out of the dress. And be sure not to crumple it," the older woman cautioned. "You must go and rest for this evening."

"I'll be all right," Jackie said in a bright voice, and Sarah, seeing how excited she was at the prospect of appearing as her true sex, thought she was right.

Lady Churchill was busy at her writing desk when the door to the room opened. Footsteps fell hushed across the carpeted floor, and warm lips pressed against her cheek.

"John," she said, leaning back against her husband. "My cousin has come."

"Oh? Which cousin is that, my dear?" Churchill asked, for his wife's family was large with distant relatives of one sort or another. She waited until a servant deposited a tray with its contents on a table. John Churchill poured a glass of wine for his wife and handed it to her, then poured one for himself. He raised his glass to the blond woman and then sipped at the liquid.

Sarah, who had come to sit beside her husband, closely examined the depths of the dark liquid. " 'Tis my cousin, Jasmine."

Churchill frowned in concentration. "I am afraid I do not remember a Jasmine, my dear."

"She is very distant," his wife replied, "and quite young."

Churchill paused with the crystal glass to his lips and stared thoughtfully at his wife. She sat with a most innocent expression on her face, and her bright eyes would not meet his. He well knew Sarah and suspected that some mischief was afoot.

"Sarah," the man began in a cautionary tone.

She looked at him, her lovely eyes innocent. "Yes, Jack?"

He knew by her use of his nickname that indeed something was being kept from him. "What goes on here?"

"Why nothing, John! I declare that I do not know why you are always so suspicious. You are the most mistrusting man!"

"I know you better than myself, dear heart," he said with a smile, leaning across to kiss her. "That is why I mistrust." He paused. "When may I see your cousin, Sarah?"

"Tonight, ere we attend the ball. She is at present resting.'' Again her demeanor assumed too great a mildness, but he could find no suitable remark, so he decided to drop the matter. 'Twould not do to provoke an argument with his volatile wife before the ball.

"Very well." He lifted his glass. "To tonight, then, my dear."

"To tonight," she agreed, raising her glass and gently tapping his. And to success, she thought slyly as she swallowed the sweet wine.

"Blade!" Simon exclaimed as the man was shown into the room. Pleasure creasing his face, the swordsmith rose and stretched out his hand.

The duke nodded and shook his friend's hand briefly.

"Do sit down. How long have you been in London?" Simon asked. He rang for a servant to bring drinks while Avalon sat in a striped chair.

"Since last Monday. I know," he said quickly, catching the expression on the other man's face. "I did not contact you because William asked me to arrive quietly."

"Yes, but surely, you could have let me know," Simon said, unable to keep the hurt from his voice.

"I—" The duke stopped, and Simon noticed a slight red in the other man's cheeks.

"I understand," the swordsmith replied quickly, for now he did. Even though they were friends, had been for the past seven years, Avalon had been embarrassed by his dismissal from court and the subsequent recalling by the prince of Orange.

"I hear that the Convention is no closer in its decision," Avalon said in order to change the subject.

"No," Simon replied. "I do not know how long the Convention believes the country can be without a ruler. Do the members not understand that it is crucial at this time for England to be united?"

The handsome aristocrat shrugged and took another sip of wine. "Perhaps they do not. They are, after all," he said with a curl of his lip, "politicians."

Simon chuckled. "More wine?"

"No," said the dark-haired man, rising to his feet. "I must go now, Simon. I thank you for the drink." He placed his goblet on the table and shook Simon's hand once more. As he turned to leave the pale brown and green drawing room, Simon spoke again.

"Shall I see you tonight at the ball?"

Avalon whirled. "Why, yes," he said, his eyebrows raised in surprise. "Do you also attend, Simon?"

The man nodded assent. "The prince has specifically asked for my presence there."

"Ah," the duke said, smiling, "your path becomes less obstructed, Simon. This cannot hurt your business."

"No, it certainly can't. I have also received a contract from Churchill and the prince—for the army!"

"Congratulations, Simon! That will help you far more than anything I could do."

"But," Simon pointed out, "you were the first. You opened the door."

"So I did," the aristocrat said quietly. He paused. "Have you seen that boy of late?"

"Jackie, you mean? No, I understand that he has gone into the country for a week or so. To visit friends or some such."

The duke's face was bland. "Ah . . . . Again, thank you for the wine, Simon. And I shall see you tonight."

He left Simon's house and strolled leisurely down the street. Today he disdained the use of horse or carriage, for he sought the exercise provided by walking. 'Twas a good day for being outside. The sun was shining, and the air was fresh . . . as fresh as it could be in the city, thought Blade cynically. He paused at a street corner as a carriage pulled by four black horses rolled past.

Idly he glanced at the window of the carriage, and a pair of pale eyes met his, then the carriage was past, rumbling down the street. For one shocked moment the duke thought he had seen that rascal, Jackie McKier; then, remembering the boy was in the country, he realized the pale eyes had belonged to a woman. Frowning, Blade tried to recall to mind the face he had seen.

Ah, yes, it was the Frenchwoman, Victorée L'Este du Plessis, who had arrived at the English court just prior to his banishment by William. She was a beautiful woman, whose acquaintance he'd not had time to make. Due to intervening circumstances, he thought ruefully.

But perhaps tonight, he thought, smiling wickedly, they might meet, and who knew, they might indulge in swordplay.

* * *

"Good God!" Churchill exclaimed when he saw Sarah's "cousin." "Sarah, my dear, you cannot think to—" He stopped.

Jackie blushed at his astonished reaction, then turned apprehensive eyes to Lady Churchill, who made a sharp gesture of reassurance to the girl.

"I may think to do many a thing, my dear," she responded somewhat archly, "and I shall do this."

"No, Sarah," he said firmly.

"Yes, John."

Jackie glanced unhappily at the man. Oh, he could not think to spoil their fun now. Or could he? It wouldn't be fair! But, she thought grimly, Jack had always been quick to point out that life itself wasn't fair. Still, he had always winked at her when he said it.

But their plans mustn't go awry—not when the ball was just hours away.

Some of the silver-haired girl's disappointment must have been reflected on her face, for John gave her a quick glance, then looked away.

"It is unseemly," he countered, desperately attempting not to lose ground with his argumentative wife.

"And why is that? Were you not the man who pointed out her true sex to me? Why should she not take advantage of her beauty upon occasion? Answer me that, John! Should she continue to dress as a boy? Would not most consider it unseemly for her to be disguised?"

"This could be dangerous," he pointed out.

"She stands in far less danger attending a court ball than acting as a mercenary soldier. Do you not agree?" Sarah asked, her eyes narrowing. "She is an innocent," she continued, "but quite able to take care of herself. Have no fears on that head, John. Worry not. All things will right themselves in time. You well know that, sir!"

Churchill smiled ruefully. "That I do know well. And you will pull your plan off without a hitch. That, too, I know. Very well, I concede to this misbegotten scheme." He turned to Jackie, who scanned his face with anxious eyes. She gave him a tremulous smile. "Go with luck, child, and enjoy yourself."

"Thank you, sir," Jackie said shyly, dropping a polite curtsy.

Sarah burst into laughter and, grabbing the young girl's hand, pulled her from the room in order to prepare her for the ball.

"You are a most outrageous flirt," the Frenchwoman said, tapping the man on the wrist with her painted fan. She smiled archly at him, her eyelids heavy, and Blade refrained from the smile of the triumphant, for he knew that he would soon bed her. She seemed fair hot for a romp in the hay, and he was not averse to having this pale-eyed vixen.

He stroked her hand as she moved closer to him. The duke could feel the warmth of her body emanating through the heavy dark satin and silk she wore, and her scent was of musk and cinnamon.

"You are beautiful," he whispered, touching her hand to his lips, caressing it, and she laughed in response.

"You are very handsome, sir," Victorée du Plessis replied, knowing that she would soon have her prize. All evening she had sought this beautiful man. This stag had not had a chance since the accomplished huntress first saw him—since that afternoon, in fact, when their eyes had met as she swept by in her carriage. She had known then that their destinies were intertwined.

Avalon touched the silk of her ebony gown with his stroking fingertips and, in spite of herself, she shivered. She pushed back a lock of the black wig which had fallen over her shoulder, and he smiled at her.

How much more . . . tantalizing he was, the Frenchwoman mused, than that plump boy. She peered up at the tall man, and pale eyes met with blue and locked into a stare that spoke more freely than words.

He brushed his lips across her hand again, and she stepped closer to him, so that she knew he was so very aware of her body heat. There will be so much more heat tonight, the woman thought as she flicked with her fingernail one of the gold buttons on the duke's rust velvet coat.

"I am pleased your banishment was short," she whispered.

"So am I," he admitted, a rueful tone to his voice. A fortnight into his exile, a letter from the prince of Orange had arrived asking that he return to court within a week. Not questioning why, he had done so, gladly leaving behind his country estate. Avalon enjoyed the country, but only in moderation.

There was a whispered stir, a rustling among the party-goers behind them. Blade paused in the action of kissing the woman's hand again and quickly glanced up. He started to bend over her wrist again, for the occurrence had simply been the entrance of John and Sarah Churchill, when something—or rather someone—attracted his total attention. Blade allowed the Frenchwoman's wrist to drop. She shot him a hurt look, but he did not notice her petulant expression.

What commanded the duke of Avalon's attention and that of every man in the room was the sight of the exquisite creature who waited slightly behind the Churchills.

She was a young girl, dressed entirely in white. The gown was of a soft white satin with an overskirt of white tulle. The skirt was closely gathered in small pleats at the waist, each pleat laddered with delicate silver crepe bows, and hung in loose folds to the floor. Open in front, it showed a petticoat of virginal silk edged in delicate silver rosebuds. Silver embroidery and seed pearls also adorned the petticoat. Embroidered silver roses with pearl leaves were sewn on the bodice. Row upon row of silver Brussels lace hung from the elbow-length sleeves, so that the material was draped softly over her lovely forearms. Her small feet were shod in silver embroidered slippers and seemed impossibly narrow.

And what a glorious color the vision's hair was! It cascaded in abundant silver curls that framed her enchanting face. A narrow ribbon of white rosebuds was woven throughout her hair, and silk gloves sheathed her tiny and delicate hands. The only jewelry she sported were delicate pearl drop earrings and a simple, single strand of pearls at her swanlike throat.

Her face was heart-shaped and finely proportioned. The cheekbones were high and slanted, and her eyebrows, dark in color, rose like fine raven's wings, drawing attention to her large dove-gray eyes. Her movements were graceful, and her air dainty and well-bred. She wore an expression that combined vitality and youthful curiosity without appearing indelicate or wanton. It was obvious from where Blade stood that she was the daughter of a fine and noble family; that much he could see from the exquisite way she held her head and carried herself.

The Frenchwoman followed the duke's line of vision and stared, thunderstruck. There could be no mistake—this was the girl she saw at Versailles almost two years ago. Victorée frowned. What was she doing here? And why was she with the Churchills? She shivered, seeing the resemblance . . . the mirror image, and she drew her light brows together in concentration.

Forgetting his position with the Frenchwoman, Blade pushed forward to greet the new arrival. Victorée glared at his retreating back, impatiently tapping her foot.

But the duke of Avalon had not been the only man to see the girl, and by the time he reached her the enchanting vision was surrounded by a crowd of admiring courtiers.

Jackie looked out over the blur of faces, her gray eyes searching for one face alone, and when she found it, her pert lips curved into a smile.

Smiling triumphantly, Sarah turned to her husband and raised her eyebrows as if to say, "As usual, I am correct."

Lord Churchill answered her with a rueful smile, then tucked her hand under his arm and led her out onto the floor. The chamber orchestra struck up a gavotte, and the new arrival was soon beseiged with requests for her hand for the dance.

But the exhilarated Jackie had not missed the awestruck expression on the face of the man she loathed. So, her plans was thus far working well.

She smiled favorably at him, and Avalon pushed past the other men to claim Jackie's hand. She curtsied low, and he bowed long over her hand, gently brushing it with his lips.

The tall duke led her in the spirited dance and then claimed her for the following dance, a minuet.

"What is your name, mistress?" he asked.

"Jasmine Jennings, sir," she replied quietly. She wished to combine the perfect amount of boldness and maidenly demureness, so she raised her eyes to his handsome face and smiled. 'Twas a small encouragement of sorts. His hand tightened on hers, and she felt a devilish, triumphant delight course through her.

"I am a distant cousin of Lady Churchill's."

" 'Tis a shame that you have not been presented to the court, little one," Avalon said, his blue eyes frankly admiring her pointed face. Jackie felt the color rush to her cheeks, and she was frankly puzzled, for she had not willed this maidenly blush.

"My parents have but recently died, and 'twould not have been appropriate for me to be presented. Ere that, sir, I was too young to come to court."

"'Tis true," the man murmured, his blue eyes never leaving her heart-shaped face.

"I—I do not know your name, sir," she said, and he told her with a slight smile on his lips.

"Perhaps you would care for some refreshment?" he asked as the music ended. She nodded her head, and he escorted her from the floor. But this now presented a problem to the duke of Avalon. If he left young Jasmine unattended while he sought refreshments, she would no doubt be claimed by another court gallant before he returned to her side. The only safe alternative was to shepherd her to the punch table with him.

She smiled secretly, knowing the predicament in which he found himself, and she immensely enjoyed his obvious discomfort. Jackie was only too happy to add to the duke's problems.

Avalon handed the girl her punch glass, and she calmly sipped the sweet liquid. She would have preferred a good stiff beaker of ale.

The duke was preparing to speak to Jasmine once again, when a smiling man, of medium height and pink-faced, stepped up to her to claim her hand.

"Beg pardon, Your Grace," the man breathed happily. With a small smile on her pink lips, she handed her half-filled glass to Avalon and left with the man.

He glared at the two glasses, then deposited them with a bang upon the refreshment table. His jealousy mounting by the moment, Avalon watched as they danced first one dance, then another. He advanced on the couple, only to have them move away.

He gritted his teeth, thinking unpleasant things about the young man. He advanced once more, but by now she had been claimed by another man, and they moved far out of his reach. Each time he approached to dance with the girl, the little minx seemed to be in the arms of a different court gallant.

Not to be outdone, he glanced around for the Frenchwoman.

She was dancing with another man. Up to that moment, all thoughts of the pale-eyed Victorée had been pushed from his mind.

"You are not gaining against the headwind this evening," a calm voice said beside him.

"No, Simon," Avalon replied shortly.

"Who is she?" the swordsmith asked, nodding toward the laughing girl, who had shot a glance at the two men.

Blade never took his eyes off the dancing girl. "Jasmine Jennings. A distant relative of Lady Churchill. From the country," he said tersely. "Her parents are dead."

"You are quite enchanted with her," Simon observed in his usual quiet manner. He had also noticed the look on the Frenchwoman's face when Avalon abandoned her for the young girl in white, and he thought that for all his friend's great learning he knew little of women.

Avalon whirled on his friend but stopped when he saw Simon's large eyes placidly watching him, and the unthinking response that had leaped to his mind died. For, he thought glumly, Simon was correct. He *was* enchanted with her. Bewitched and beguiled. In short, for the first time in his many years in the role of heart's rogue, Avalon felt the heart-tuggings of love. And he did not suffer his affliction well.

"I am sorry, Blade," Simon said quietly. Smiling grimly to himself, he strode off, walking with a deliberate pace. He timed his actions well, and soon he was dancing with the lovely sensation of the evening.

Jackie's dove-gray eyes widened slightly as she recognized Simon, and instinctively she glanced past his shoulder.

"He is on the other side of the room, mooning for you, child," the man said. "You are a cruel mistress."

"Fie, sir," she demurred, dropping her eyes coyly.

"Cupid has smitten him."

"Indeed? I have heard that he is given to breaking hearts himself. 'Tis said that he's called 'Satan' because of it."

"A heart does not remain broken for always," Simon responded.

"You sound, sir, as though you speak from experience," the girl replied in a laughing tone. "Has your heart been broken?"

"No," he said softly, "nor will I allow it. . . ."

Startled, Jackie's eyes flew to his grave face. She made as though to speak, but the man shook his head.

"I—I do beg pardon," she stammered at last, unable to meet his brown eyes.

" 'Tis of little matter," Simon said. "Friends we shall remain, . . . Jasmine, or perhaps I shall become your brother. I do think you need one."

Jackie said nothing to the swordsmith, for she did not know how to answer him. Her joyous and triumphant evening had, in the span of a heartbeat, turned to ashes in her mouth. Whatever would she, could she, do?

"I must, however, not beg one request of you, child."

"What is that, sir?" Her large luminous eyes were filled with concern.

"That you leave him alone. This game is no longer amusing."

"But, sir, as you pointed out," the girl said, "he shall not die of a broken heart. 'Men have died from time to time, and worms have eaten them, but not for love,' " she quoted.

"You play with words, Jackie, or rather 'Jasmine' tonight. That is all." He frowned at her, and she could feel the guilt growing inside her.

"He does not recognize me?" she asked with sudden apprehension.

"No, child, for he does not expect 'Jackie' to be a girl. Surely by now you should know that men only see that which they choose to see."

And yet, Simon thought, his friend was a fool for not seeing clearly.

"Ah, you have met her," Blade said, as he quickly claimed Jackie's hand for the next gavotte. The silver-haired girl fanned herself rapidly and peeked at the duke over the lace-decorated fan.

"Yes," Simon said quickly.

"She is a pearl, is she not?" the man asked, his eyes never leaving his face.

"She is indeed above worth," Simon replied gravely and, it seemed to Jackie, with irony. Bowing, he departed from the floor and disappeared into the crowd of courtiers, gallants, and their ladies.

" 'Tis strange," the duke said, his eyes narrowed, as he watched his friend's departure.

"What is, Your Grace?" the girl asked innocently, tapping her escort upon the wrist with her closed fan to remind him of her presence. He turned at the slight pressure on his arm.

" 'Tis naught," he said, making a deliberate effort to collect himself. "Would you care for some fresh air? I find that it has grown exceedingly hot inside, and the color is fast fading from your cheeks."

She smiled her assent at the tall nobleman, and he quickly guided her across the stuffy ballroom to a French window. They moved out onto a balcony, set a few feet above the level of the grounds. A low stone balustrade ran the perimeter of the terrace, and to the left marble steps led to the grounds. At the top the steps were stone lions on either side, whose ferocious snarls had been caught forever in the stone. Lanterns were hung in trees on the grounds of the palace, giving the scene before the young girl a fairyland appearance. Beyond the broad smooth lawns she could see the golden lights reflected in the waters of the Thames, which flowed past Whitehall.

For a moment she closed her eyes, listening to the faint sounds—of the whispering river, of distant shouts of the watermen on the river and the gentle lapping of oars, of the music from within the room, of the rapid breathing of the man by her side.

A cool breeze drifted across the terrace. She shivered and opened her eyes to see him regarding her with a most quizzical expression.

"I should not have brought you outside," he said, the sound of his voice breaking the stillness. " 'Twas most inconsiderate of me."

"No, in faith, sir, 'twas not. I—I—" Her voice faltered, and she looked away. Jackie drew in a deep breath and then faced him with a cheerful mien. " 'Twas nothing, Your Grace."

Avalon stepped closer to her, clasping her slim hand between his and cradling it protectively.

"Jasmine, I must speak to you."

"You have known me only a short time, Your Grace."

He gazed down at her solemnly; her large gray eyes gazed back at him. "I believe we have been acquainted with one another far longer than this evening."

Panic rose inside her like a trapped butterfly beating its wings. Jackie wondered breathlessly if, despite Simon's assurances, the nobleman had connected the appearance of

Jasmine Jennings with the disappearance of Jackie McKier.
But that fear was dispelled in the next instant.

"I beg you to allow me to call upon you tomorrow
afternoon."

"Pray, sir," she said with a laugh. "You have barely
spoken with me. You know me not."

"Words are not necessary, Jasmine," he said, his handsome face unsmiling.

"Sir, it is not seemly," she demurred, dropping her eyelids, so that her long curling black lashes caressed the high
planes of her cheeks.

His breath caught in his throat. He desired so to clasp her
in his arms.

"We must return inside." Jackie disengaged her hand and
brushed by him, but he suddenly caught her by the arm, his
grip firm and sure.

"No!" the girl said, protesting, suddenly fearing him.
What if he tried to overpower her? He was, after all, nicknamed "Satan." No, she would remain calm, and she would
do as Jack had once told her. "Hit a man there, me love, an'
ye be able to run the length o' the world after he recovered."

His grip loosened, and he stepped closer to her. She arched
her head back so that she might see him, and above her were
those mocking blue eyes . . . but now they were kind. He
slid his arms around her, then stopped, an ironic smile touching his lips.

"No. Not yet," he murmured and, moving away, stared
across the smoothness of the lawns.

She shivered, and yet heat rushed over her. How she ached
to feel his arms around her again . . . yet . . . yet. . . . No,
she would destroy him. . . . He would destroy her. . . .
No! She put a hand to her head, and her fingers trembled.

With a sigh, he said, "I shall return you to the bosom of
your family now."

He escorted her to Sarah Churchill, bowed, and said, "I
am sorry to have monopolized your cousin, Lady Churchill,
but I was showing her the stars. Pray forgive me."

"I quite understand, Your Grace," Lady Churchill replied,
a tinge of amusement underlying her voice. "I understand
you are something of an astrologer."

"Astronomer," he corrected. "I must take my leave now.
Ladies. Churchill." He bowed to Sarah and Jackie, then to

Churchill. Soon he had pushed his way back into the crowd painted and bejeweled courtiers and their ladies.

"You have proved to have as much success as I'd hoped!" Sarah exclaimed, her eyes sparkling. She smiled triumphantly at her husband.

"Yes," the girl said, still watching the crowd. One aristocrat bowed to her and asked for her hand in the next dance. Jackie declined, pleading a headache. It was not a lie.

"And have acquired a mighty admirer," Churchill replied quietly, surveying the subdued "Jasmine."

"I have no doubt in my mind whatsoever," Sarah said, already formulating plans, "that he will come calling."

"He said he wished to visit tomorrow afternoon," Jackie said in a distant voice.

The Churchills exchanged significant glances, the wife well pleased with the success of her protégée and happily anticipating the future, the husband hesitant and concerned for that same future.

The duke of Avalon came to the Churchills' apartments on the following afternoon, and in his hands was a bouquet of white roses mingled with baby's breath and greens.

"How kind, Your Grace!" the girl exclaimed when she saw the flowers. At once Sarah rang for a servant to bring a vase so that the roses might remain fresh.

The duke, handsome in a gold brocade coat and plum breeches, took the girl's hand in his long-fingered one and brushed his lips across the top. Above his bowed head, Jackie met the eye of the older woman, and a smile curved her pert lips.

"Come sit, Your Grace," Sarah Churchill said easily and patted the cushion beside her as she sat down on the settee. He sat down, as did the girl.

"What word have you, Blade, from the Convention?" the woman asked.

He turned his blue eyes on her and shrugged elegantly. "None, I am afraid. It would seem that England is to slip into a morass of somnolence while these politicians debate and defer and delay."

"Do they not realize that England's enemies amass while this debate continues?" "Jasmine" asked.

Blade's eyebrows shot up in surprise, for, of all the women

he knew at court, only a handful, Sarah among them, professed interest in politics. That this young country girl did also was to her advantage. He was well pleased that she was apparently not completely caught up in the social circle at court.

"Yes," Blade replied, "I believe they are aware, but they appear to have the lawyer's mind and wish to produce a maze of detail."

" 'Woe unto you, lawyers! for ye have taken away the key of knowledge,' " the girl quoted. "The Bible. St. Luke," she said quickly in answer to the duke's questioning expression.

"It would seem," he said, smiling to her, "you are well educated."

Sarah, who preferred to remain silent, rang for a servant to bring refreshments.

"Yes," the girl replied, recalling an earlier conversation of a similar nature with the duke's good friend Simon, "I am well-read."

"Oh yes," Sarah interjected, her luminescent eyes large, "Jasmine's" parents had always thought it wise to educate their girls as well as their boys."

"Of what topics do you have some knowledge?" Blade asked with interest.

The servant brought a decanter, three glasses, and a plate of orange sugar cakes. Sarah dismissed the man, then sat back, enjoying herself immensely.

The silver-haired girl smiled, thinking that he was, indeed, going to be very surprised. "Mathematics, poetry, religion, philosophy, history, science, penmanship, reading, riding, driving a coach, and eight languages," she listed. His eyes grew wider as she enumerated her skills. Her gray eyes twinkling with humor, she named the languages which she could speak: "Latin, German, Spanish, Dutch, Italian, Greek, French, and English."

The handsome duke looked to Sarah Churchill for confirmation, and the blond woman nodded. "Very impressive," he drawled. "What science have you been taught?"

"Not as much as others," the girl admitted. "I have studied Aristotle's *History of Animals*, Pliny's *The Natural History of Metals*, and some Bacon."

"Roger or Francis?" he asked.

"Both."

"Then you do not have a grounding in astronomy," he said. He lifted the glass to his lips. "Are you interested, Mistress Jennings?"

She nodded. "Oh yes. I have read some Copernicus and Galileo, but I would dearly love to learn more." She dropped her eyes, her long lashes curving downward, and he hastily sipped his wine.

"Good, for I have copies of many of their papers, as well as Pascal. If you would care to come to my home . . . You, too, Sarah," Avalon added hastily when she caught his eye with a slight movement of her hand, "you would be able to peruse them."

"I would enjoy that, Your Grace," the girl said truthfully. "I understand that you are an alchemist. Do you have Paracelsus's essay, 'How to Make Gold and Silver'?"

A brief smile quirked the duke's handsome lips. "Yes, but I am afraid that I must disappoint you, for I am no alchemist. Others would pin that badge upon me. I am an astronomer and work with a telescope to view the distant stars and planets."

"I do wish to see the stars!" the girl exclaimed. "Oh, Sarah, may we go?"

Sarah smiled indulgently. "Of course. Whenever it is convenient for you, Blade, we shall come."

"I shall send a note around tomorrow afternoon, and perhaps the two of you could join me for dinner, and then afterward we could view the stars. Would that be suitable?" He cocked an eye at the blond woman, who nodded. "Perfect, then." He rose, brushing a hand across the legs of his breeches. "I fear I must go."

He turned and, bending, kissed Jackie's hand, then turned to the older woman and kissed hers.

"Thank you for allowing me to visit," the duke said.

"Come back soon," Sarah said with a smile as she rang for a servant to show him out. He nodded toward Jackie, who returned the nod, and soon the two women were alone in the drawing room.

"Well," said Sarah, sitting down again and sipping at another glass of wine, "I do believe that was a most successful social visit. He stayed far longer than the proper thirty minutes. I do believe," she said, surveying the girl closely, "that the duke of Avalon has developed a *tendre* for you, Jackie!"

"Oh," said the silver-haired girl, smiling slyly, "I do hope so!"

Avalon's note arrived midmorning, and before Sarah could take it from the servant girl Jackie grabbed the note and eagerly tore it open.

"It's confirmed," she breathed and looked up to meet the amused eyes of Sarah Churchill. Blushing, the girl dropped her head and handed the note to the woman, who scanned it.

"Yes," the woman said in an amused tone, "I see that. Dress carefully, Jackie. I think the duke may well be very interested in you."

A deeper color rose in the girl's cheeks, and she started to answer but fumbled to a halt.

"I did not know you loved him," Sarah said.

"But I don't!" the girl exclaimed. "I hate him, Sarah."

"You have a most peculiar way of showing it then."

"You don't realize, Sarah, what he did to me while I was dressed as Jackie," the girl explained. "I cannot 'love' him. I cannot even like him."

"Umm," the woman replied noncommittally. "Still, dress well."

"I will."

With huge eyes Jackie stared about the laboratory. She moved to one of the cabinets and silently read the chart hanging over it. She turned and found Avalon's blue eyes on her. She met his gaze directly, and a faint smile touched his lips. Without thinking, she returned the smile. Then mentally she castigated herself as he held out his arm to escort her to the telescope.

She scowled, looking away from the tall duke. He was her enemy. He had hurt her, had hurt Liam. And, in turn, she would hurt him. That was her plan. But, somehow, it didn't seem to be working.

Sarah followed after them, and Avalon presented the telescope to the two women. For long minutes Jackie stared through the lens at the cold and faint stars. She was strongly aware of him, close by her side.

"Well, now," Sarah said briskly, "I would like to see the

stars, too!'' Blushing, Jackie stepped away from the telescope, and Avalon showed Sarah how the telescope worked.
She glanced into the lens, then at the two silent people. "I've
seen enough," she announced. " 'Tis time for us to leave
Your Grace.''

"So soon?" he asked, seeming disappointed.

"Yes," she said. "We have much to do on the morrow.
Jasmine is to go on a picnic to the country in the afternoon.''
Avalon frowned. "Then we are to dine with Lord Fawns-
worth.''

"That puppy?''

Sarah hid a smile. "The very same, I am sure. Jasmine.
Jasmine!'' The girl glanced at her. "Come, drag yourself
from the stars.'' The woman turned to Avalon. "We thank
you for the dinner. It was quite delicious, as usual, Blade.
Give my compliments to Santu.''

He inclined his head, then turned to Jackie. "May I see
you tomorrow?''

Before Jackie could say a word, Sarah said briskly, "You
may try, Blade, but our door is constantly opening with all of
Jasmine's suitors.''

"Suitors?''

"Yes. She has at least seven or eight.'' And, with that,
Sarah took her young charge by the arm, and they departed
the duke of Avalon's town house.

"You're up to something," the girl accused her friend,
once their carriage had pulled away from the town house.

"Oh heavens, no," Sarah said in a most innocent tone.

"You aren't trying to matchmake, are you?" Jackie asked
suspiciously.

There was no reply in the darkness of the carriage.

"I told you that I hated him.''

Silence.

"I do.''

Silence.

"I really do.''

Silence.

Jackie glumly stared out the window of the carriage as it
wound its way through the streets of London. Why, it had
been just a year since Liam and she had arrived in the English
city and had met the duke. And been humiliated by him.

She was going to kill him. She had vowed that.

Or, failing to kill him, she would dishonor him.

Or, failing that, she would break his heart.

Or, failing that, she would break her own.

"I thought I might find you here," said a quiet voice. Startled, Jackie looked up to see the duke of Avalon standing beside one of the rose bushes in Lady Churchill's garden. She glanced down at the roses in her basket, then back at the man.

"And why were you so confident of finding me here?" she asked.

He moved closer to her. "Because you are as fair as a rose."

Her expression was one of scorn. "Spare me, sir, your honeyed sentiment."

" 'Tis true, Mistress Jennings." Blade caught her by her arm, and she glared at his hand. "Don't go."

"I am unchaperoned."

"It doesn't matter."

"It does to me!"

He pulled her into his arms, and the basket dropped, forgotten. Avalon stared down into her warm eyes, then frowned as an unwanted face drifted across his mind.

"What is the matter?" the girl asked with some concern in her voice.

" 'Tis nothing," he said. He clasped her tighter.

"This is most unseemly, Your Grace."

He grinned wolfishly. "Yes, it is." He bent his head toward her.

"Pray, sir, do not move any closer, for I would not wish you to be hurt."

The man stopped. "Hurt?"

"Yes." Jackie smiled sweetly up at him. "I still have my rose clippers in my hand."

"Oh." He released the girl and quickly stepped back. Indeed, she did hold the clippers in her hand. "You would not have stabbed me, surely."

She smiled, then glanced down at the clippers. She could have hurt him and said later it was an accident, or even that she had been defending herself against him. But she had not.

Suddenly she dropped the clippers and, turning, ran from the garden.

"Jasmine!" Avalon called, startled at the girl's unexpected

action. "Wait!" But she ran into the building, leaving the duke alone in the garden.

Damn, he thought to himself. He was acting like a fool. No, he wasn't acting. He *was* a fool. A stupid fool. A senseless fool.

A love-stricken fool, a sly voice pointed out to him. And he feared it was all too true.

"Well," said Sarah, "the duke has been paying numerous calls upon you, Jasmine."

"Umm," the girl said, not looking up from her book. "The duke of Essex?" she inquired.

"That old fool? Hardly!" the blond woman exclaimed.

"What duke can you possibly mean, then?"

"Don't play the innocent with me, Jackie. 'Twill not do," the woman said sharply.

Jackie looked up. "I am sorry, Sarah. I meant nothing by it."

"Why are you so difficult with Blade?" she gazed at the girl, whose face went pale at the mention of Avalon's name.

"D-difficult? I'm not difficult. It's just that I have other beaux, and I wish to see them. I cannot devote all my energies to one man alone."

"I see." Sarah stared at the girl's pointed face. "You *are* in love."

The girl jumped to her feet and paced around the sitting room. "You keep saying that, and I keep telling you it's not true!" Her words were as agitated as her actions. "You must listen to me, Sarah. You must! I don't love him! I really don't! I hate him. I hate him so much, I just want to destroy him!"

Sarah watched calmly, waiting for Jackie's tirade to stop. The girl paused, then raised her hands to her face.

"What am I to do?" Her shoulders shook with silent sobs. Quietly the woman rose and enveloped the girl in a motherly hug. "What am I to do?" Jackie repeated.

"You must do what your heart directs," the woman said.

"My heart doesn't know what it wants anymore," the girl said miserably.

"Come and sit down. Have a cup of tea. Then we must think."

The girl obeyed Sarah and sat down on the settee. "I really

thought I hated him. I had turned my heart against him. I saw him as 'Satan' Blade. And yet—yet, for some reason, I can't maintain the anger, nor the hatred.''

Sarah Churchill nodded sagely. "It's love."

"Well, it's a miserable emotion," the girl responded, gloomily sipping her tea.

"There's only one solution," the woman announced. The silver-haired girl raised an eyebrow. "Tell him you love him."

"No!" In her agitation, Jackie dropped her cup on the table, and tea spread across the polished surface. "No. I can't do that. It would humiliate me."

A look of confusion crossed Sarah's face. "To declare your love? I don't understand."

"If I should indicate that I care for him, he would simply cut my heart to ribbons."

"But that's what you wanted to do to his," the woman pointed out.

"That's different," the girl replied.

"Oh, I see."

"He hurt me first."

"Oh."

Jackie looked away.

"Well," Sarah said briskly, "at least he promised to send a note around tomorrow, as he could not come today. You'll have a few more hours to think by yourself."

"I've already thought enough," the girl said, "and my thoughts remain the same."

Sarah simply smiled and looked out the window.

Avalon did not send a note to "Jasmine" and Sarah that day, nor did he call upon them the day after that. She did not lack for other callers in those two days. The cavaliers came with flowers, and sweets, with invitations for walks and rides. "Jasmine" accepted as many as she could, and she enjoyed herself, welcoming the attentions and the compliments and the flattery. But always at the back of her mind was that the duke of Avalon had failed to keep his word, had stood her up. And this did little to soften her opinion of the man.

On the third day, Jackie thanked her hostess warmly for her generous hospitality. Sarah began to speak of Avalon, but the girl forestalled the older woman.

"I must go now, for I fear that Liam will worry, and 'tis not right to do that to the old man. He thinks I stay with friends. And I must return, or I'll outstay my welcome."

"Nonsense," the woman said. "I would have you stay with us longer, for I have not yet found a husband for you."

"Nor are you likely to find me one," Jackie said dryly. "I thank you for your efforts, Sarah, but 'twould appear that I am not destined for the married life."

"Pooh, girl," the older woman said with a laugh, "leave those thoughts to others. You have had proposals of marriage. But there was always something wrong with the men, you said." She eyed the girl, "Still, you are but a child—a beautiful one, and there will be time enough later."

"Perhaps," Jackie said, shrugging. "Nonetheless, I must take my leave—reluctantly, I might add, for I have enjoyed myself." She grinned impishly.

"We must do this again!" Sarah cried, clapping her hands.

"I think not," Jackie began but stopped when she saw the expression on the woman's face.

"The court buzzes with the news of the latest sensation!" Sarah Churchill declared. "They demand to see 'Jasmine Jennings' again. I have explained that she returned home, owing to family matters."

Jackie did not respond.

"Come, come, girl," the older woman said in a wheedling tone, "you must return"— she paused dramatically, and Jackie rolled her eyes, thinking of Liam's feeble attempts at the dramatic—"for the king has asked to see this fairylike vision," Sarah concluded triumphantly, a smug expression upon her face.

"What!" Jackie cried. " 'Tis impossible!" She paced about the room distractedly.

" 'Tis not," Sarah said. "Jasmine shall return inside a month, and I shall arrange for her—you—to attend the prince and princess."

"Sarah, think!" the silver-haired girl exclaimed. "What of Jackie?"

Sarah glanced sharply at her. "What of Jackie, you ask?" The girl nodded mutely. "Well, I imagine that eventually Jackie will have to leave the court, and Jasmine will simply stay with us."

The girl wrung her hands. "I am not yet prepared for that,

Sarah. Please do not ask it of me. Jackie is . . . well, Jackie *is* me, and I cannot give him up so easily. Too many problems arise. What of Liam? How shall I explain this to him?''

''You said once that he would have you put aside your boy's clothing, be a woman, and marry,'' Sarah shrewdly pointed out.

''B-but,'' fumbled Jackie, caught in the net of her own words, '' 'twould not be safe to bring Jasmine back until Jackie was prepared to leave for good. Else some sharp-eyed cavalier might make the connection between the two, and that could prove disastrous.''

Sarah smiled wickedly to herself, idly wondering if that imagined ''sharp-eyed cavalier'' possessed a name and a face belonging to reality. She doubted it not at all.

''Well, child, very well,'' the woman said at length. ''Finish your packing now, and then we shall see to the future.''

The girl had not been gone from the house half an hour when a servant came in, announcing a guest.

Sarah Churchill, taking off her gold-rimmed glasses, looked up from her writing desk.

''Your Grace!'' she cried as the duke of Avalon strode in and bowed over her hand.

''Ma'am,'' he murmured. ''I promised Mistress Jennings that I would send a note, but I decided to come in person, instead, albeit somewhat late.''

''I should say so,'' Sarah exclaimed tartly.

''Where is your young cousin?'' he asked, looking around.

''Jasmine has left. She gave you up for lost.''

''Left?'' the man echoed, surprise on his handsome face.

''Aye, left. Did you think she would sit and dangle her heels whilst she awaited your pleasure?''

Blade started to answer but could find no words in his astonishment. At last he sufficiently recovered his voice. ''But I was not delayed above three days.''

''Aye,'' Sarah said knowingly, ''and sent no word to her, either, that you were delayed. Jasmine had callers aplenty—flowers and gifts, too, from all manner of men who fancied their hearts beset by her charms. But not a single word did she receive from you, Your Grace, heartless rogue that you are!'' Her eyes snapped with anger that was more make-believe than real. Still, she was irritated with his shabby behavior toward her protégée. For one thing, it had spoiled her plans for "Jasmine." Too, Sarah knew that the duke's failure to follow through on his invitation had hurt the silver-haired girl far more than she would ever admit.

"It would appear that you simply wished to trifle with my cousin and had no serious nor honorable intentions, sir."

"No honorable intentions? Is that what you truly believe, madam—as well as that mealymouthed cousin of yours? Well, Lady Churchill," he said, leaning close to Sarah, "I care this little for that silly missish female!" And he snapped his fingers by the woman's ear. She jumped and stared at him.

"Good day to you, madam." He bowed and left, the door slamming behind him.

For a long moment Sarah did nothing, then she rose and crossed to the settee and slowly sank down on it. Putting her hands to her face, she began to laugh. She could not stop, and when her husband arrived, Churchill rushed across the room to her, thinking her in some sort of distress.

To his astonishment he discovered she was laughing. John sought the reason for her amusement, but all she would say, between gasps, was that her plans had advanced even more steadily than she had hoped.

"Ah, Jackie, there you are!" cried Dickon, the page who had befriended her upon her arrival at the English court. "You should have seen her!" the boy rhapsodized.

"Seen whom?" Jackie inquired casually, an innocent expression on her piquant face.

"The fair vision which has swept the entire court off its feet. The beautiful Jasmine Jennings. She is the country cousin of Lady Churchill," he explained. "Why, half the cavaliers have turned poet to express their divine love for this new star in the heavens. I have penned one." Dickon looked shyly at his friend. "Would you care to read it?"

Jackie smiled warmly. "Of course, foolish Dickon. You well know that I would wish to see it."

Dickon reached into an inner pocket and pulled from it a most crumpled piece of parchment. He carefully unfolded it and, trembling, handed it to her, explaining as he did so, "I carry it close to my heart."

She took the page in her hands and quickly read the words penned upon it. The poem was filled with comparisons. Jasmine's eyes were like twin stars; her voice was like the nightingale's in the eve, or alternately, like that of the lark in the spring; her grace was that of a doe; her beauty that of a Helen, a Juliet, a Venus. Her lips were pink seashells; her throat the color of swansdown; her hands like two doves.

Thickly sentimental, yet it was a poem from the boy's heart. Jackie realized with a start that Dickon had probably only seen Jasmine Jennings from a distance and thus was writing from largely secondhand experience, from information he had gleaned from the conversation of others who had stood closer to this new wonder at court. But it was sincere.

Tears filled her eyes as she handed Dickon the poem. He carefully folded it up and placed it inside his waistcoat. "Do you like it?" he asked anxiously, scanning his friend's face for approval.

She nodded mutely.

"Do you think Jasmine—I mean," he said, coloring, "Mistress Jennings would like it at all?"

"I think"—she paused, her voice breaking—"that Mistress Jennings would think it the most beautiful poem she had ever read."

Dickon's face broke into a broad smile, and he hugged himself. "Oh, Jackie, I am glad you think so." His face grew serious. "I must go. I have a message to deliver." He hurried off, then turned back once. "Jackie, I do wish you had seen her!" Then he turned a corner and disappeared.

Frowning, Jackie pulled her thoughts together. 'Twas unjust that Jasmine could inspire such devotion in boys such as Dickon, and other men of the court as well! Did she not have stack after stack of billets-doux, tied in pretty pink and blue ribbons, from the gallants who poured out their hearts to her upon paper, their blood being the very ink with which they wrote?

And damn that nobleman, that nemesis! How dare he stand her up! He had promised to come calling and then had not. Others had come; others had clamored. He had *promised,* and that promise had quickly been broken. He simply could not be trusted. And Simon Martin had almost convinced her to be sympathetic toward the duke of Avalon. But she could be proud of herself. She had resisted, but she not capitulated.

Now she knew better; she simply would harden her heart again, and 'twould be the end of it.

Wouldn't it?

Chapter

Fourteen

"Now, FAIR HIPPOLYTA, our nuptial hour draws on apace; four happy days bring in another moon."

The black-clad Frenchwoman listened with only half an ear to the opening of the play, for she had caught sight of the boy once again. He wove lithely past the watching court members, a goblet in his hand. Reaching the dais where Prince William and Princess Mary sat apart from the others, the boy bowed, presenting the small chestnut-haired man with the goblet, then laughed quietly as the Dutch prince said something to him.

Seating himself at the feet of the prince, the boy watched the comedic play unfold. The players were members of the court, chosen by the prince's master of ceremonies, and were attired in elaborate pastoral costumes.

A cold feeling running the length of her supple spine, Victorée studied the young boy's features. Black brows that shot up at angles, giving the face a perpetual expression of surprise; the clear white skin; the high cheekbones; the face. . . . The Frenchwoman shuddered.

"Love looks not with the eyes, but with the mind, and therefore is wing'd Cupid painted blind." The audience murmured in appreciation, and the boy touched the arm of the prince, who leaned down to speak to him.

There was no doubt about it. The boy must be related to her. A natural son of her late papa? She thought not, for after the death of his faithless wife, he had never again touched a woman. So . . . how . . . who?

She she sat in the ballroom, in the midst of the gaily dressed men and women who were celebrating the impending coronation of William and Mary, a most horrible thought occurred to Victorée. She remembered the nightmare vision at Versailles. She had never known who . . . or what that person was. This child, though, was . . . was. . . . But that was impossible! she declared to herself. *Absurde!* But perhaps? Her slim hand fluttered to her breast, and she felt the heat of the room envelop her. She rubbed a hand nervously down the side of her raven-wing skirt, edged in silver thread. With great difficulty she rose and moved unobtrusively to the refreshment tables.

She quickly drained one glass of champagne and then called for another. After her third glass of the bubbly liquid she felt better. But that idea—it must be nonsense! Yet she was compelled to find the solution to this enigma. She could not dismiss it.

She watched the remainder of the comedy, her mind ill at ease. Soon Puck had scampered from the stage, and the entire court was applauding, after first looking to see if the prince had enjoyed the play. Apparently he had, for he was smiling and clapping. He appeared deep in animated conversation with the brown-haired boy.

Victorée edged closer to the dais. Between the Frenchwoman and the intimate group lay an open space of ten feet or more. She could gain no more proximity without drawing attention to herself, so she would attempt to eavesdrop from her peripheral position. It was imperative that she find out more about this boy.

A man, dignified in appearance, brushed by her and murmured his apologies. The Frenchwoman smiled, then whispered to him, brushing his brocaded sleeve with the edge of her folded fan. "One moment, monsieur."

"Of course, mademoiselle."

"I beg you, sir," Victorée said, displaying her prettiest

smile, "but who is that young boy with the prince, the one with brown hair?"

The man turned in that direction and eyed the boy through a quizzing glass attached to a black riband. "Ah," he chuckled. "Striking, is he not? A great favorite with the prince, I believe."

She drew her silver eyebrows together in a puzzled frown.

"That one I think," the man stated, nodding toward the young boy, "seeks a high place at court—as do many hundreds of other 'true spirits' who seemed to have helped us in the revolution. Perhaps," the man mused, "he has already found his place," and he winked at her.

"I see, sir. Thank you for your intelligence." She dropped a curtsy to him; he bowed and moved on toward the tables along the side of the room.

Victorée resumed her watch. She frowned as she recalled another similar face, that of the girl in a rose and silver ball gown at Versailles. How long ago had it been? Almost two years. A face so similar that it could have been the twin of this boy, or . . . or . . . she continued grimly, it could be that very boy. The face, too, could be that of Jasmine Jennings, the girl in white. Yet the gentleman's innuendo confused her, for if the child were a girl and the prince had brought the "boy" to bed, would something have not been rumored throughout the court? She had heard no such tale. Odd, the Frenchwoman thought, that Random had never mentioned his competition . . . unless, of course, the child, male or female, posed no threat to the earl of Malvern.

But what was the creature—boy or girl? 'Twas true that Philippe d'Orleans, the younger brother of Louis XIV of France, sometimes dressed and made himself up as a girl, and as such flirted with the men at the French court. Might this not be a similar case, for she recalled the face of the girl called Jasmine Jennings. The cousin of Sarah Churchill, was she not?

I should have spoken with Mademoiselle Jennings, the woman angrily chided herself, *just as I should not have allowed the girl at Versailles to slip away*. 'Twas a clumsy mistake, and one that the Frenchwoman would not soon forgive herself for making.

The Dutch prince reached over, touched the boy on his shoulder, and pointed toward one of the courtiers. He said something to the lad, and the boy laughed, a clear musical sound which Victorée could clearly hear.

The child's eyes shifted, and Victorée's pale eyes met the dove-gray ones of the boy. For the merest instant a current of tension passed between them, and then the child turned away, breaking the contact. There had been recognition in those eyes.

There could be little mistake now. Victorée's heart hammered beneath her ribs as she walked along the path of logic and arrived at the only possible explanation.

No, there was only one child, a girl, who was of the age of this one—the grown-up infant of her sixteenth year . . . the baby she had borne in the country at her father's cruel insistence and which Ulrica had been paid to kill. But apparently the old woman had not. For some reason, it would appear, the child had been saved. *Bitch,* thought Victorée, *you shall pay for your foolhardy treachery, old woman.*

Trembling, she could stomach no more of the fete, and, making the appropriate excuses, she left quickly. She must think.

From his comfortable vantage point at the refreshment tables, where he was able to supply himself with a never-ending, never-empty glass of champagne, Liam groggily watched the ebony-clad woman leave the ballroom.

She be a beauty, he thought, but not as pretty as his Jackie. The priest had first noticed her interest in the disguised girl, for he was ever watchful of his Jackie, even when he was in his cups, as now. He had smiled, thinking the woman in black's interest to be the obvious inquisitiveness that men and women alike of the noble class displayed when they saw the young girl. But after a few minutes he realized that her concern went beyond that level, was of a far more serious nature.

He scratched his head. Now, why be that woman so familiar-looking? Liam sighed. If only Jack be here to help him with his old failing memory. Jack be the one with a good mind for faces, he be. Jack.

Jack. The color draining from his face, he grasped another glass and tossed the contents down his throat. He paused, his hand trembling, then filled his glass again from the fountain of liquor. That woman. . . . Quickly he fumbled inside his coat and, throwing all caution to the winds, withdrew the missal. Carefully he turned the pages, and there it was: the miniature from so long ago. The face was the same as that of the woman at the English court. He put the missal back, his hands trembling from the effort.

It could not be . . . or could it? It must be a coincidence. Liam rubbed a hand over his face and closed his eyes, concentrating. Yes, it had to be. He glanced over at Jackie, and he felt an abrupt need to sit down. No wonder the woman had been interested in the disguised girl.

Aye, Jack and he be dolts that they never saw the resemblance between the little girl they had found that day and the woman in the miniature that Jack had stolen. The events of those days so long ago assembled in his brain and marched across his consciousness. Jack had bedded a French wench in Paris, at that fancy hôtel, and the girl must have come into the family way. 'Twould seem likely that she had gone into the country to have her child in privacy, to avoid embarrassing her family. And, somehow, that child had been raised by the devilish hag in the marsh. Should he tell his own Jackie of her lineage? That she was Jack's true daughter and not his foster child, that her mother was this Frenchwoman?

No, Liam thought, it would not be proper for him to be telling her now. Not yet. He would wait . . . until when? That he did not know. He quickly gulped down another glass of wine and tried to calm his shaking hands.

"Only a few more days and we shall once more have a king and queen," the dark-haired man said and poured more wine in his glass. He sloshed the contents around for a while, then stopped as his eye drifted outside again.

"Yes," Simon said, feeling a restraint between them and unable to explain its nature. "Your mind seems distant today, Blade. Is there anything amiss?" Simon's brown eyes were filled with concern.

The duke leaned back in his chair, shifting his weight. How could he explain to his friend that he had problems and that they all dealt with a very private aspect of his life? He had penned several letters to Jasmine Jennings, but as yet had received no reply. He had indicated to Sarah Churchill that he cared not a fig for her cousin, but 'twas a lie. He knew it, and she knew it. Why didn't the girl answer him? It would take but a moment of her time. Surely she was no longer angry with him. When he had asked Lady Churchill when London might expect to be graced with Mistress Jennings's presence, the blond woman, refusing to meet his eye, had been singularly vague on the matter.

And then he had this infernal attraction to Jackie McKier, that irritating boy who now seemed to stay well out of his way. 'Twas for the best, the duke grumbled to himself, for he had no wish to fence verbally with the lad. Yet he had seen the boy sometimes watching him, when the lad thought he wasn't looking.

Avalon glanced across at Simon, who was studying him with a worried look on his face. With some effort the duke affected an unconcerned manner. "Come, Simon, do not pull a long face with me. All things shall right themselves, given enough time."

The brown-haired man shook his head slowly. "Will you not trust in me, Blade? You know that I would never betray your confidence." His dark eyes searched the other man's face.

No, no, not after walking alone so long. No one shares my soul, the duke thought, and perhaps that was part of the problem. He could confide in no one. Pride and training and discipline prevented him from speaking openly. Even to a friend.

"No, Simon, it is nothing." He smiled what he intended to be a reassuring smile at the swordsmith, then rose gracefully to his feet. "Come. I have a new astronomy paper sent to me by an acquaintance in Holland. I think you will find it of interest."

Victorée had not yet heard from King Louis, and his silence made her uneasy. Adding to this uncertain feeling was the new dilemma of the girl/boy Jackie. What was she to do? Victorée wondered as she reclined upon her bed in the London town house. *The girl must have somehow traced me. How?* She gave it hard thought, and the answer that crept into her mind had the face of a crone. Ulrica. She was the link between Victorée's present and her past. But that link could be broken. The old woman would pay dearly for the betrayal of her mistress.

The voluptuous woman rose and gave a sharp tug at the bellpull. When her maid responded, she told the girl to send Carel in to her.

Shuffling in, Carel waited for his mistress's command. She surveyed him with disgust. "You did well, Carel, this last time, when you delivered my letter to the king."

He grinned, revealing broken teeth. His breath whistled through the gaps most unpleasantly, and for a moment she looked away. He was such a disgusting creature. Sometimes she wondered why she still tolerated his existence, except that upon occasion he did prove useful.

"But I am hurt."

He shuffled forward as if to touch her. Victorée wanted nothing more than to recoil, but she suffered the damaged man to place a beefy hand upon her shoulder. He whimpered.

"No, you cannot see the damage, nor the pain, Carel. But it is here." Taking his hand, she placed it upon her bosom. "The agony is within me."

Carel, panting, gave Victorée's breast a rough squeeze. She gasped from the pain but said nothing to him. He licked his cracked lips and, throwing his arms around the woman, pulled her harshly to his barrellike chest. He bruised her soft mouth with his rough lips. Victorée struggled, but it made no impression on the brutish man. His panting came more quickly now, and small flecks of saliva appeared on his lips.

Victorée thought rapidly. If she did nothing, he would no doubt rape her. Yet if she struggled he might hurt her more by beating her first. A thought occurred to her, and she smiled. It was repugnant, but she had little choice.

"Carel, Carel," she murmured, "I have desired you for so long. When you followed me when I was a child and tried so foolishly to run away, oh how I wanted your great weight upon me."

With a quick fluid movement, surprising in someone of his bulk, Carel picked her up and gently deposited her on the silk sheets of the bed.

The mute bent and pushed her silk and lace dressing gown up with both hands. Then, frustrated by the bunching of the material, he grasped the gown at the neck and ripped it downward. In a moment the material had been peeled back as though it were a second skin, and the Frenchwoman lay, revealed, on the bed. Carel, licking his lips, studied her body from the hollow of her white throat, down past the firm breasts, over the slight rounding of stomach, to the white thighs below. He traced a hand slowly down the length of her body, then back up to cup one breast with his hand.

She told herself that she was the mistress of the situation, but underneath Victorée felt fear.

Carel grinned, an awful expression on the ruin of his face. He tugged at the buttons on his breeches. A low sound emerged from his throat, and the Frenchwoman, quivering, had the sinking sensation that the noise was a laugh.

Frustrated by the uncooperativeness of the fastenings on his breeches, Carel growled and threw himself onto the bed. For a moment Victorée felt as though she were in the midst of an earthquake, and then the shaking of the bed subsided, although the velvet curtains still trembled from the force. She glanced up at the mirrors overhead and almost laughed out loud at the groteque scene reflected there.

She firmly put her hands on his shoulders and said adamantly, "No, Carel, I cannot."

The Slav grunted his surprise, released her, and stared into her pale eyes. Her gaze never faltered. The giant ran a hand between her marble-white legs, but she grasped it and removed it.

"No," Victorée said again. "I could not rest easy, knowing that the person responsible for my pain is still loose." She sighed deeply. "And do you know who it is that causes me such sorrow, Carel?"

Dumbly he shook his head and watched, fascinated, as she gracefully swung her legs over the side of the bed and stood. Quickly she paced back and forth in the darkened room. His eyes never left her nude form.

"It is Ulrica."

Carel made a sound low in his throat.

"She has harmed me, Carel. She has betrayed me. She has tried to destroy me."

Suddenly Carel sat up on the bed, which creaked ominously under his weight. On the ceiling a dozen hulking brutes moved.

"Would you allow this, Carel?" Victorée went onto her knees in front of the man. He shook his shaggy head. "I knew that you would not. You see why I cannot . . . be with you. You know now why I am distressed." She watched through her long pale eyelashes as he nodded his head in dumb agreement. "Oh, but Carel, what am I to do?"

"Errk, errk," the man said, pointing to himself and thumping his chest with one balled fist.

Victorée's pale eyes widened. "You, Carel? You would do something for me?" He nodded eagerly and mewed. "But what could you do?"

Grinning wolfishly, Carel thrust out his hands as though they encircled a throat and made a twisting motion.

"You would kill Ulrica for me?" his mistress asked. Carel nodded, and Victorée allowed warm tears to fall upon the rough material of his breeches. He slowly traced one of the wet circles with a blunt finger and then stared at the fingertip. He touched her damp cheek.

"But, Carel, be careful. You would not wish to be caught," Victorée said softly. Carel firmly shook his head and with harsh gestures indicated that all would be taken care of. She hid a smile. He clumsily patted her soft shoulder and then ran a finger down her bosom to her thigh. He looked a question.

"You would go at once?" she asked. Carel nodded. "I would so appreciate it, Carel. You are so kind." His mistress enfolded his hand in hers and kissed the palm. "And when you return, ah, then, dear Carel, you shall be rewarded." Victorée smiled as she placed his hand at the warm junction of her thighs.

Carel, licking his lips, grinned in anticipation.

And Victorée smiled up into the overhead mirrors, for the henchman she planned to send would deal as effectively with Carel as Carel would with Ulrica.

Chapter

Fifteen

VICTORÉE STRETCHED LANGUIDLY, like a well-fed feline, then rolled onto her stomach. She pushed up on one elbow and stared at the sleeping man. Bending down, she playfully nipped his neck. Groaning, Random turned over on his side.

The Frenchwoman rose and walked, nude, to the window. She pushed aside the heavy curtains and opened the casement, then leaned her arms on the sill and looked out at the street in front of her London town house. Nothing stirred in the gloom of predawn. She crossed over to the bellpull and gave it a sharp tug. She was looking out the window again when the maid entered.

Griselle demurely kept her eyes on the floor. "Yes, madame?" The girl bobbed a low curtsy.

"Send in a breakfast for two, Griselle. Something light."

"Yes, madame." The maid once more curtsied, then left the plush bedchamber.

Victorée closed the window, then selected a crimson-colored velvet robe trimmed with ermine, belted it at her slim waist, and crawled back into the bed. Smiling, the albino woman winked at her image overhead and, arching one finger, trailed it down the length of Random's back.

"Come now, Michel, it is time to rise." Victorée smiled wickedly.

The young earl stretched and yawned, then leaned over and kissed the cheek the silver-haired woman demurely offered.

"Food?" he asked, rubbing his face.

"Coming," Victorée replied.

"But not as quickly as I," Random said, laughing, as he pushed her back down on the bed.

Some time later they emerged from the tangle of satin bedclothes at the sound of a discreet tap at the door.

"Enter," the Frenchwoman commanded. The young maid entered with a large tray. Random ogled the girl, who ignored his salacious stare. She curtsied, deposited the tray on the bed, then left, closing the door firmly behind her.

Victorée finished her repast first, and, leaning back against several pillows, studied the young man. How best should she approach him? She had now fed two appetites. Surely he should be in a good humor by now.

"Michel," she murmured.

"Yes?" he asked, his mouth full of the warm bread.

The Frenchwoman leaned over and kissed his bulging cheek. "You are such a *chér*. I could eat you at this very moment, *mon coeur*."

"Not now!" he protested. "I haven't finished my breakfast."

She pouted slightly. "Very well. I shall wait."

A silence fell between the two lovers as the young earl speedily finished the remainder of his meal. Finally, he pushed away the tray and turned his attention to the woman.

"Now we shall enjoy our dessert." Random dropped kisses on her mouth as his hand snaked inside her elegant robe. She shivered at the touch of his cool hand on her flesh as he stroked her breast.

"Ah, Michel, it is no use." Reluctantly she pulled his hand away from her breast and patted it.

He clenched his hand convulsively into a fist, his lips pressed together in anger. "What is it, Victorée? You were only too ready for love a short time ago."

She sighed, put her fingertips to her temples, and shivered, a long convulsive action that somehow managed to open the front of her dressing robe so that he might see her firm breasts.

"My darling," Random said, enfolding the woman's shaking body in his arms. "What is wrong?"

"I thought I should not have to tell you," Victorée said, hiding her face against his bare chest. Uncontrolled sobs rocked the woman. Stroking her long silver hair, Random attempted to still her crying. "There, there, my love, shhhh." He wondered what she had to say, and for a fleeting moment of panic he feared that she might say she was with child.

Nothing seemed to stem the flow of Victorée's tragic tears. The earl of Malvern kissed the top of her silver hair, stroked her satiny back, and hugged her even tighter. Finally, it appeared she was spent, for with a little gasp and a hiccup the tears stopped, and she breathed deeply.

Victorée pushed the boy away. "It is no concern of yours, Michel. I should not trouble you."

Then it wasn't a child. Good. "Victorée, no," the boy crooned. " 'Tis little trouble, I assure you. Confide in me, my love. Your secret shall remain safe with me. You know that I would wish to aid you in any manner possible. Anything you ask."

She sniffed, delicately wiping the tears on her cheek with the edge of a sheet. "Very well," the albino woman replied huskily. She cleared her throat rather self-consciously, then sighed deeply. She did not meet his eyes but instead stared off into the distance, the corners of her mouth turned down in a most tragic manner.

"I have seen a specter from my past, *mon cher*."

"Ah. . . . But surely that is not all that troubles you, my sweet one." He took her hand in his, gently kissing her fingertips one by one.

"No. No, it is not." She paused.

"And?" the blond youth prompted, interest kindling in his blue eyes. Perhaps, he thought, licking his lips, she would relate some juicy tidbit, a nice morsel of gossip.

"It is a boy," she said at last.

"Oh?" His eyebrows rose.

"*Oui*. A young boy, like yourself, Michel. But there the resemblance ends. He is a terrible *tyran*. He is evil. I—I am so distressed to see him here." Momentarily she covered her face with her hands, then she recovered.

"Which boy is it?" Lord Malvern asked eagerly.

"The boy with the older man. No doubt his lover, *n'est-ce pas*? He has gray eyes—the one who calls himself 'Jackie.' "

A gloating satisfaction filled Random at the name of the

unknown youth from Victorée's past. A simpering sycophant, the blond earl told himself with a derisive curl of his thin lips, unaware of the irony in his dislike. He had met the boy's likes before—lads desirous of securing any position in the court, even that of the royal bedwarmer, all to advance their careers. He was uncertain if Jackie were indeed a lover of Prince William, but why else would the youth remain with the sickly old man?

"Tell me about this terrible boy, this Jackie," the young earl murmured softly, stroking the Frenchwoman's silver hair. "It is all right. You know that I shall not whisper a word of what you tell me to a soul."

"Very well." Victorée leaned back against Random, snuggling close to him as his arm snaked around her. She closed her eyes and began her narrative.

"It happened but a year ago. Étienne Jules, my husband, had traveled to Versailles to attend the king. Absent for several months, he then sent word that he would be further delayed in his return. So I was left alone on our estates. I tried to fill my days with riding and walking and reading, but even those activities pale after a few short days.

"At that time we had a boy who had been hired as a page. An intelligent child and the son of a merchant, he was ambitious to further his position in life." She paused at a seemingly painful part of her recollection, then, drawing a deep breath, continued. "He was bright, flattering, good company. What could one expect, *mon cher*? How could I fail to be charmed? I began thinking myself in love with this *petit enfant*.

"Oh, how I grew to love that rascal! I thought of him morning and night. He invaded my dreams, my thoughts, . . . my desires. My hunger for him increased by the hour. He encouraged my affection, too, by reading to me, running my littlest errand with a glad heart, by being the most charming *enfant* alive. I adored the ground upon which he trod. Finally, I could contain myself no longer. My hunger overwhelmed my sense of propriety. I sent for him, and he came . . . alone to my chamber."

She shivered at the memory that existed only in her fertile imagination.

"He was not the joyous *enfant* then. *Non*. He became a beast. He tore my clothing, abused me. He threw me upon the bed and would have done his worst, but my maid, alerted by my screams, ran in with a pistol. She tried to shoot him but missed. It was enough. The shot scared the *vilain*, and he grabbed his clothes and dove out the open window. After that we did not see him again. I had no idea where he went. And now . . . now I see him again . . . and I fear what he may say. I am afraid that he will lie about that day, about our relationship, and that he will inform my husband.''

"Could you not leave the court, depart England?" Random asked.

"Oh no!" the Frenchwoman cried. "The damage has been done. If I were to leave, I believe he would simply follow me to France, and then I would truly be undone!"

The silver-haired woman looked at him. She cradled his hand in hers, then placed it against her soft cheek. "There is more, *mon cher*."

"Oh?" he asked with renewed interest. This morning was proving to be of excessive interest.

"*Oui*." She quickly rose from the bed and glided across the floor to the wardrobe, the light touching her silver hair. She opened the door and stooped to pick up a high-heeled shoe. When she returned to the bed, drawing the bedclothes tightly around her trembling form once more, she held a piece of parchment in her hand.

"Here." Her voice was faint. She lay back on the pillows and gazed up at the mirrors, watching him as he unfolded the paper and quickly scanned it.

Random's blond eyebrows rose in astonishment. "I see," he replied slowly, "why 'tis an immediate matter of concern."

"*Oui*," Victorée said, not looking at the young earl directly. "He wrote that letter—well, it must have been soon after I first saw him at court. The older man delivered it. He did not wait for an answer. That villain claims that he will tell my husband that he is my natural son." She burst into outraged tears. "Of course, it is not true! It cannot be, for *I* would have been just a child myself! How unfair is his accusation! Oh, I am so miserable, Michel!" The distraught woman threw herself down on the bed, and her sobbing increased.

Absently, Random caressed the woman's shaking back and made soothing sounds. He studied the note in his other hand and pondered its contents. He was not totally prepared to accept his mistress's story at face value. Yet a certain amount of truth might well be involved in the fabrication.\ To what extent it was true was the intriguing question.

"You know, my dear, that I would do anything for you," the earl said. "You have but to say the word."

Victorée smiled into the rich coverlet of the bed, where her expression could not be seen by her lover. "You are so kind," she said shakily.

"Not at all." His fingers maintained the rhythmic stroking of her light-colored hair.

"Then . . . but it is too—No, I cannot ask it of you."

"Ask what?" Random pursued.

Facing him, she earnestly searched his face. "I fear not for my reputation, but for my life!"

"What!" the man cried. This was certainly a new development!

"Yes. It is so, *mon cher*. I think that he might attempt to harm me, for I know his humble origins. He will fear that I might obtain an audience with Prince William and inform him of his disreputable background. It is true, Michel, that I have much to lose, but now he has even more. I think he seeks a high position at the royal court!"

Random rose abruptly and paced like a caged animal around the opulent room. His face was a study in absorption.

Finally the earl of Malvern stopped his pacing and faced his mistress. "Yes, that boy seeks much. I had not told you, my love," Michael Random said as he climbed back into the tall bed, "but I saw the boy at The Hague before the invasion."

"What!" Her astonishment was indeed genuine.

Random drew his brows together in a frown that relieved the chubby petulance of his face. "Yes. I was with the prince when two riders were announced. They had traveled hard from England and had supplied the password, signifying they were messengers of Lord Shrewsbury's group."

"The ones who asked the prince to come to England?" she asked.

"Yes," the blond earl replied, "the very same group. Imagine our surprise when in strolled this—this callow youth and old man! Yet the boy presented Prince William with a letter. That much I know. And," he added with a significant glance at his mistress, "the letter was from the commander of King James's troops himself!"

She gasped. "That would appear to be a selfless mission.

But he could not have taken the message out of altruism alone."

"No," Random said, giving the word an ironic twist. "I am sure he was compensated quite handsomely by the group in England. I know that he was rewarded by the prince."

"We must do something to help the prince against this boy. Surely he will try some harm," Victorée said; her pale eyes wide. "What can be his game? *Ma foi*, I am afraid." She shivered.

"It is certain that he is up to some mischief," Random said, a serious note in his voice.

"But what is the solution? How shall we deliver ourselves of this threat?" the woman inquired.

Random leaned back against the headboard of the bed, locked his fingers behind his blond head, and smiled into the distance. "Allow me to manage that, my dear."

"Hullo, there!" cried the young blond man.

Jackie looked up as she hurried down the corridor on her errand. She returned the greeting and continued on her way.

"I thank you again for stepping in that day . . . the duke of Avalon attacked me," the young man said.

"You're welcome," she replied somewhat stiffly at the mention of the duke. "No doubt he would have thrashed you within an inch of your life."

"No doubt." Random smiled ironically.

"I doubt it not that he attacked you with little provocation. The man is most unruly," Jackie said.

"But," Random said, stopping abruptly, "I know that you are busy, so I shall allow you to go your way. Perhaps on another occasion we may visit with each other."

"When I am finished I shall not again be needed this day. My duties are rather light," Jackie offered.

"Ah, then we could have a drink together later?" Random asked. "Or perhaps a supper, as we never did dine together."

Her gray eyes swept over his face. "I must ask you a question, Lord Malvern."

"Yes, child?"

The girl smiled to herself, for she was not that much younger than he, certainly not more than three years. "It concerns that day you asked me to supper." He raised an eyebrow. She took a deep breath and plunged in. "Did you follow me that night? I—I thought I saw you at the tavern.''

He smiled, his expression one of sunny benevolence. "Of course, I did, child.''

"Oh." She was completely taken aback by this seemingly artless confession. "Well, why? If I may ask,'' she added hastily.

Random smiled again at Jackie. "Of course, Master Jackie, for I have nothing to hide. I followed you because I would enjoy knowing you better, and I was disappointed that my plans had fallen through and that you were already spoken for. That's all.''

So simple, she thought, and she and Simon had attached such sinister significance to it. How silly they both were.

"Well?'' he asked. "Drinks or dining, Master Jackie?''

"Agreed, sir.''

"I have an appointment, but that may be broken without a second thought,'' he said, winking slyly. She responded with a grin.

"I shall meet you here in an hour's time,'' Jackie said. "Now I must go, or I'll be late. Good day to you, sir!'' She made an elegant leg to the earl of Malvern and walked off quickly down the corridor.

Pausing at a gilt-edged mirror, she smoothed her cream velvet coat decorated with gold braid and seed pearls and straightened the wide folded cuffs, flicking a piece of lint from her sleeve. She pivoted slowly so that she might examine fully her striking outfit, admiring the debonair appearance she presented to the world.

"I shall take that message, little peacock,'' drawled a languid voice, irritatingly familiar.

Startled at the interruption and somewhat embarrassed, Jackie looked past her reflection in the mirror.

He stood there, casually eyeing her through a quizzing glass attached to a black riband around his neck. His lips quirked into a thin smile as he let the glass dangle. Beside him stood Simon Martín.

"Quite, quite exquisite,'' the duke of Avalon murmured.

Jackie felt the heat rise in her cheeks. Heat from the shame of having been caught being the narcissist and heat from the anger at once more seeing her nemesis. How arrogant of him to demand *her* message, the message she had been charged by Prince William to deliver to Lord Shrewsbury.

"No," she said, "the message is not for *you*." Her tone was definitely condescending, and she cared not a fig.

He chuckled, which only served to feed the young girl's fury. "You must labor under a great misapprehension, child, if you believe it is *your* message." He reached toward her, and she backed away from him, her hand clutching the paper behind her back.

"Blade," Simon warned.

But Avalon seemed not to hear his friend. Quickly he reached out with a long arm and grabbed the paper from her.

"Return that to me at once or—or I'll . . . . I'll. . . ." She stopped, anger overcoming speech.

"You shall what, poppet?" Avalon asked mockingly. "Will you trip over my leg again? Or fall into a mud puddle?" He viewed the irate girl through his quizzing glass again, ironic amusement etched on his handsome face.

Simon put out a hand to the duke to stay him, but the duke waved him away.

Without thinking of the consequences, Jackie drove her fist toward his chin. Still chuckling at his own joke, the duke did not see her quick motion and was totally unprepared for the blow that jolted his chin, slamming his head back with a snap. The unexpected action stunned him into momentary inaction. Then he regained his balance and lunged at Jackie. Luckily for the girl Simon's hands closed tightly around the duke's arm.

"For God's sake, Blade, let there be no brawl. Remember your position, and who you are."

Avalon glared down at the impudent boy, who had retrieved the folded paper and was smiling smugly. Simon's grip on the duke relaxed.

He would teach the young puppy a lesson now. He would beat the child within an inch of his life until he screamed for mercy. Avalon lunged at Jackie, grabbing the tail of her coat. Simon quickly moved after the duke.

Jackie quickly spun out of the reach of the irate man. She skipped to one side, made a deep mocking bow, and then quickly left the corridor without waiting to see the duke's reaction.

When she returned to the palace an hour later from her

errand she was still in a happy mood. Humming an old Irish air that Liam had taught her, she strolled down the corridor where she had met Random earlier to find the earl of Malvern already waiting.

"Your servant, sir," she chirped brightly, sweeping off her plumed hat and bowing low.

"Yours," Random replied amiably.

"Now, sir, where to? Dinner or ale?" Jackie asked.

"I thought," Random said, "that we would first take a turn around the garden to invigorate our appetites. I think dinner would be welcome then."

He crossed the hallway and opened a French door leading out into the cold exterior. Jackie shivered, wishing she had worn a heavier coat or a cloak. " 'Tis a bleak place here in the winter, Lord Malvern," she said.

"Yes, so it is. But then most places are, Master Jackie."

"Unless you visit the southern countries during the winter," the girl said. She thought of Spain that first year, the year she had become a woman, and of the beautiful bright colors of the country, of the warm sunshine, of Jack and Liam.

"You've been there?" the blond man inquired.

"Oh, I have traveled to Spain and Italy," she answered in a casual tone of voice. "They are beautiful countries, and in their southern reaches very warm at this time of year. Very intriguing, too, sir."

"As you are, Jackie," Random said with a smile. "I may call you that, may I not?" The earl moved in front of her and stared down at her.

Momentarily confused, Jackie stared down at her shoes.

Gently Random placed a finger under her chin and lifted it. "Your eyes are far too lovely to hide. Never look down, little one."

Her eyes widened. She felt a tremor pass through her body, and she chided herself for her weakness.

"You are cold," he said, releasing her chin and rubbing his gloved hands together. "Let us go in now and seek our dinner. I admit to desiring a warm pint. Eh, Jackie?"

She nodded silent agreement and strode back with him toward the palace.

"And then you shall relate to me your travels in Spain and Italy, far-off places that I have never seen. How would you

like that, child?'' Random asked as they walked toward the
royal residence, their footsteps echoing along the path laid
with crushed white stone.

"I would enjoy—'' Momentarily she glanced up, then
stopped, for at a window on the palace's second floor she saw
a familiar face. Jackie recollected herself and continued walking, without giving Avalon the satisfaction of seeing her
anger or even appearing to notice him. But what, she thought,
was he doing at that window? Spying on her? She could not
keep from her mind the pleasure of how she had trounced him
earlier in the day. She chuckled silently.

"You were saying, Jackie?'' the earl of Malvern asked,
curious about her sudden lapse into silence.

"Oh yes, I would more than enjoy that discussion.'' And
she vowed she would, too, for this blond earl was an infi-
nitely more preferable companion than that mocking fop in
his fine jewels and satins and brocades and his silly quizzing
glass, Francis Arthur Randolph Blade, duke of Avalon.

She would show him!

It must be some sort of a joke, the Frenchwoman thought,
looking once more at the terse note in her hand. Some
horrible joke. Surely he could not be serious. She sank weakly
into a chair.

Five short words, and that was all.

"You will kill William. Louis.''

Why did he require that *she* do it? Victorée dropped the
note, and it fluttered to the floor. Ever since the special
courier had arrived a scant thirty minutes before she had been
reading and rereading the note, hoping that somehow she had
misunderstood her master.

But she had not. She rose unsteadily and moved to the
window of her bedchamber and stared out into the street, not
seeing the carriages or horses passing by.

With all the various people at the English court, the
Frenchwoman had no doubt that there were other spies for
Louis XIV of France. Surely, one of them would be in a
better position?

Over the months Victorée had become comfortable with
her life, and it was proving a pleasure to be sought after. She
attended the routs, fetes, balls, and soirees and dutifully
reported the gossip she heard. She had reported on the deci-

sion of the Convention. Louis had known, before anyone else had, that William and Mary were to be crowned joint monarchs.

And this was how she was repaid.

It was *regicide*.

And if she were to be caught— But no, she would not think of that.

Very well, Victorée told herself, she had been given a task by the French king. She would have to do it. And yet the French king could not expect her to murder the prince completely by herself. Could he?

But whose aid could she enlist? Carel was no doubt dead by this time, and no one else among her henchmen could be trusted for this important job.

Victorée L'Este du Plessis walked back across the room and lay down on the bed, then stared up at the mirrored ceiling. Her silver hair hung loose and fell in long ringlets across her shoulders and breasts. She twined a curl around her finger and stroked the silky hair.

She closed her eyes. She was a spy, not an assassin. No, Victorée thought, she must remain calm. She forced herself to think over the events of the past month.

On February 13 William and Mary had received the Lords and Commons in the banqueting house at Whitehall, where the two had been asked to accept the crown. William had replied: ''We thankfully accept what you have offered us,'' and the two promised to rule according to the law and to be guided by Parliament. They were then proclaimed king and queen.

Louis knew all this, for he had received her letters, and so it would seem that the absolute monarch of France had seen no alternative. The death of William would leave England once more rudderless and confused and with his wife, Mary, on the throne as sole ruler. Dependent upon William's judgment and morally unable to reconcile her gain of the throne with the dethronement of her father, Mary would prove pliable in the hands of certain French agents, who would be carefully placed in positions of importance at the court. As queen she would do nothing—could do nothing—to impede Louis's invasion of first, Holland, then the Lower Countries and Germany. Once these nations had been subdued it would be but a short step across the channel, and James would be back on his throne.

But James would owe his crown to the Sun King, and then at last, through his royal pawn, Louis would control this troublesome island.

She closed her eyes.

And two faces came into her mind.

Random and Jackie.

She would enlist Random's aid in this matter—no doubt he would sell out his precious prince, now king, she thought, for the right amount of money, and perhaps a title; and, as far as that girl/boy was concerned, since she was destined to be taken care of sometime, why not first allow her to be useful?

Victorée smiled, immensely pleased with herself.

Chapter

⋙• *Sixteen* •⋘

THE CORONATION TOOK place in venerable Westminster Abbey on April 11, 1689, amid the shouts of "God save the king" and "God save the queen."

As she dressed for the coronation ball that was to be held later that night, Jackie smiled, remembering the day's events. The king's and queen's procession; the herb woman with her six maids preceding the royal couple and strewing rose petals and sweet-smelling flowers and herbs along the walk; the flash of sunlight on the royal regalia; the communion service; the chanting voice of the archbishop of Canterbury; William in his white linen shirt, his dark head bowed in prayer.

When Jackie finished dressing she promenaded in front of the mirror. She smiled, for she would cut quite a dashing figure. Silver thread embellished her Paris-green silk coat. At her chin frothed a lacy cravat secured by a stickpin set with a tear-shaped emerald in a cluster of tiny diamonds. Gaily colored ribbon loops lavishly decorated her silver silk breeches. She had donned a large French wig of dark auburn hair, the irregular curls framing her heart-shaped face and falling in masses about her shoulders. Silver-and green-striped bows secured the lovelock. The girl pulled on her gloves, then picked up a large cambric handkerchief. She smiled fondly as she remembered another handkerchief long ago.

She left her room and knocked on the door of the priest's bedchamber. In a few moments he appeared, attired in rust-accented velvet, with cream-colored ribbons on his sleeves and a diamond-shaped black *mouche* upon the curve of his cheek.

"You look magnificent!" Jackie cried.

Liam simply stared; for the briefest moment he thought he saw his friend Jack again. The green outfit . . . the red curls . . . that certain look.

He'd been a fool—Jack, too—never to have seen the resemblance between the young girl and the Irishman. No wonder the girl had been so much like Jack. . . . And they had thought it had simply been training. Momentarily Liam's eyes filled with tears as he stared at the beautifully attired girl.

"Cat have your tongue, Liam?" the girl cried merrily. "Did you not hear what I said?"

Liam snorted. "I be hearin' ye. Aye, an' I be a fool tonight, lookin' to be a fop an' all."

She took his arm and fondly kissed his plump cheek. "Nonsense. Liam, you are quite respectable, not at all an 'exquisite.' "

"Oh?" the priest said in an uncertain tone.

The silver-haired girl chortled with amusement. "You *want* to be outrageous tonight, Liam. Own up to it now!"

"Aye," the Irishman sighed. "I be tired o' wearin' all that dark an' dreary clothin'. I thought it might be excitin' to wear somethin' right fashionable. Well, I be ready. Let us go." And the priest led the way down the stairs. Passing other courtiers, they bowed politely to them and continued on their way.

When they reached the audience chamber, Jackie hesitated, surveying the peacocklike dancers.

"Me darlin', I see they be servin' a wee bit o' nourishment now, an' bein' as I be so famished . . ." the priest said, his astute eye focused on the various wines at the refreshment table.

"Go on with you, Liam," Jackie said. She watched as he wove his way carefully through the dancers, intent on his liquid goal.

The dancers swirled, then stopped, as did the music. There was a scattering of applause. Into the ballroom had come the newly crowned monarchs, William III and Mary II. They proceeded with stately precision, the robes of state draped across their shoulders. In silence they trod regally, until one hurrah went up. Then the air was filled with applause and cheering for the new king and queen.

William's face, which had been set in deep lines that gave him a most sober look, softened at the encouraging sound and smiled.

His wife, jewels glittering in her dark hair, turned her head and smiled at her beloved husband. He responded with a quick quirk of his thin lips and their fingers, intertwined, clasped tighter.

Jackie, watching the slow procession, felt a lump rise in her throat and tears come to her eyes. 'Twas surely grand, and she and Liam had had a part in the forging of the new government. It was of little importance to her that her part had been strictly involuntary. That didn't matter now.

The king and queen reached the royal dais, on which were set the thrones. When they had seated themselves, various government ministers and courtiers took up their stations around the monarchs. The small chestnut-haired man leaned forward and made a gesture indicating that the festivities should once more resume. The orchestra began playing a minuet, and the dancers moved into formation.

It was a shame, a deep shame, the girl thought, that tonight of all nights she could not have dressed as Jasmine Jennings. For one wild minute she thought of running back to Sarah and telling her she would change into the garb of the girl, but she restrained herself. No, she was here as Jackie McKier, and Jackie McKier she would stay for tonight. And she would enjoy herself immensely, whether as Jasmine or Jackie.

A hand fell upon her shoulder, jarring her out of her thoughts, and Jackie whirled. "My lord," she said, bowing to the earl of Malvern, who was attired in a heavily jeweled outfit of cream, gold, and rose.

The blond man nodded his head in greeting. "You are not dancing this evening, Jackie. You will break many a heart tonight. Have you not seen the coy glances sent your way by the young—and not-so-young—ladies of the court?"

A slight smile played around her lips. "Aye, I have seen

those glances, looks that pierce the heart far deeper than any
arrow a man might loose.''

Random threw back his head and laughed. ''Truly you are
a charm, boy.''

''Nay, sir, n-not a charm,'' she faltered as the duke of
Avalon, brushing by her, touched her sleeve and coldly apologized. Scarlet flooded her face, and she bit her lips to keep
back the tart response that sprang unbidden to her mind.

Random's sharp blue eyes did not miss this small incident,
and he pursed his lips in thought. It was an interesting
quarter, this enmity which seemed to exist between the boy
and the duke. He wondered how it had begun. Perhaps the
duke had approached Jackie, and the lad had refused. God
knows, the boy had rejected *his* offer! Could this dislike
between the two be played upon for his benefit? He smiled
grimly to himself. Of that he had little doubt.

'' 'Tis an important man now, the duke of Avalon,'' Random offered casually.

''Aye, he be full of *self*-importance,'' Jackie said with
bitterness and a slight Irish lilt in her voice, which the earl
found most enchanting.

Michael raised his eyebrows in apparent surprise. ''You
seem to bear little love for the handsome duke.''

''Love? For him? Ha!'' She turned her head sharply and
watched as the duke bowed over the hand of a petite dark-
haired woman, put her arm through his, and led her out to
join the other dancers.

''I would assume, Jackie, that he has caused you some
ill.'' Random's voice, so smooth and unctuous, was the very
soul of consideration.

''Caused ill? That he has certainly done.'' Her lips curled
in a barely restrained snarl, and her gray eyes blazed furiously, but they never left the dancing figure of the duke.

''Perhaps if you were to speak of it, it would aid you.
But''—he made a quick gesture—''I would understand if you
did not wish to open yourself.''

''No, 'tis something of which I cannot speak—yet. Perhaps
later.'' Jackie shrugged. ''Let us speak of something more
entertaining.''

Random chuckled. ''In truth, then, I shall not speak of the
rumors I have heard. For I see you are well able to care for
yourself and do know the cut of this man's cloth.''

"Rumors?" Jackie asked with renewed interest, although she attempted, without much success, to hide it under a mask of unconcern.

"Aye," the blond man said smoothly. "Rumor, although there is some debate as to how fabricated these stories may be. Yet it's my belief that they are indeed true, and that the duke himself spread the word that they are false. After all, is he not nicknamed 'Satan,' and is the Devil not the father of all lies?" The blond earl paused, saying, "Shall we take some refreshment? I declare that it is hotter than a steam bath in here tonight, and I am in sore need of something cooling."

Agreeably the girl nodded and allowed herself to be led across the grand ballroom to the refreshment stand, well away from her original companion. Random had no desire for them to meet with Liam.

Wine was procured from a crystal "tree," whose sap was clear or red liquid. Jackie stared hungrily at table after table laden with every sort of delicacy imaginable. Dishes of lamb, veal, duckling, hens, and sauces for the main dishes and vegetables. Sweets of every color, size, description, and flavor. But the *pièce de résistance* held a place of honor on the center table. It was a fifteen-layer cake, each layer growing progressively smaller until on the top layer stood two hand-painted ceramic figurines of the newly crowned king and queen in their royal garb. Random nudged her and handed her a glass of wine, which she slowly sipped.

"Aye, 'tis warm in here," she admitted. "I had not noticed before."

The young earl drained his glass and filled another for Jackie when hers was empty. She held up her hand and started to protest but stopped when Random spoke again.

"A toast to the royal couple," he said with a smile.

She raised her glass and drained it, as did Random. He gave her another glass, saying, "I am sure you have heard the story of Avalon's family."

Jackie tossed the liquid down her throat and held out her glass for more. She was feeling reckless this evening. "I heard the story as a child—all about 'Satan' and the Blade family."

" 'Tis a sad tale, Jackie," Random said, sighing. "One pities his mother, the poor woman. May she rest in peace." He turned his blue eyes heavenward. "At least, boy, we can be truly thankful that she is now removed from her misfortunes.''

Jackie murmured a small amen, but her mind returned to the portrait that hung in the duke's downstairs library. Almost assuredly it was the duke of Avalon's mother in the oil portrait, and Jackie did not think she looked like a cowed, heartbroken woman. In fact, the woman looked pleased with herself. She pushed away the paradox to listen to the earl of Malvern.

"But," the blond man sighed, " 'tis a shame that we cannot say the same of those who come within the duke's orbit.''

"Oh?" Jackie asked, draining another glass of liquor. She gazed around at the heavily laden tables and admired the pretty colors. One bottle arrested her attention. She pointed a slightly trembling finger at another decanter. "I should think I could.'' She stopped, a pained expression on her heart-shaped face. "I think I should, I could, er, would." She gritted her teeth and enunciated slowly. "I should think I would like to try that . . . if I could,'' she finished quickly.

Hiding a smile of amusement, Random made a small bow and retrieved her glass before it fell from her numb fingers. "Consider it done, lad." He handed the empty glasses to a lackey, who replaced them with crystal goblets filled to the brim with a deep rose-colored liquid.

Random sipped at the drink and gently ran his tongue along the rim of the glass. It was so easy, this ploy, as it would seem the boy had no head for liquor. It was almost too easy, Random thought. Here was no sport.

"What 'bout the duke's orbit?" Jackie slurred. She stared at the earl, willing his pale face to stop its cheerful bobbing independent of his neck and shoulders. She really shouldn't be drinking all this liquor. "Here," she said, thrusting her glass toward Random. He misunderstood and had it filled once more. "Damn," she muttered, staring down at the wine. Well, she couldn't let it go to waste, and besides, the fog was pleasant.

"Well?" she demanded. "What 'bout the guke's orbit?"

He hid a smile and sighed, as if debating on what he should tell Jackie. Finally, it seemed as though he reached a decision. "Well, I should not tell you this, Jackie."

"Tell me, tell me!" the girl urged, holding out her empty

glass. Once it was refilled, Random resumed his tale. " 'Tis said that the duke prefers his sport young."

"Young?" Her head moved from left to right slowly, as if the man before her kept shifting position.

"Aye, and male. Of course, you would no doubt have already known this," the earl of Malvern replied smoothly.

"Aye, I know it well, for he would have tried the very same on me." It wasn't precisely the truth, but it wasn't completely a lie, either. For she had little doubt in her mind that had Liam not afforded her some protection, she would have suffered greatly at the hands of this infamous aristocrat. Of course, Simon would have helped her, too. He was good and kind, was Simon. Good old Simon, she thought. Poor man to have the duke of Avalon as a friend. Perhaps, she told herself, the swordsmith should gravely consider obtaining new friends, ones that did not possess diabolical reputations.

"My poor lad," Random crooned sympathetically, one hand stroking Jackie's sleeve. She stared down at his fingers as they traced a circle. "You were lucky though, boy, to have escaped that hell. You have seen the portal, or heard of it?"

She nodded her head, and it was hard to tell which question she was answering.

"Demons and worse, things that should remain unmentioned, slither around the frame of the door." Random shuddered delicately and took a sip of his drink.

"And he's got animal gods in his house!" the tipsy girl blurted out.

Michael's eyes widened in surprise. "What is this, child?"

"I saw them with my own three, er, two eyes," she said. "Statues. Of misshapen cats and birds and other beasts, and one statue was simply beyond description. I did not know what it was, but 'twas horrible. A creature from hell, I would have no doubt whatsoever."

Astonishment lit Random's face. So the boy had been in the duke's town house. Yet when and why? Could it have been before the child carried the message to William at The Hague? If so, the earl wondered, how had the boy been selected as messenger? How had Avalon and Jackie met?

"He is a practitioner of the deepest and blackest arts, you know," Michael whispered in horrified accents. " 'Tis said he works long in his hellish cellar, a most un-Christian place, on . . . experiments." He gave the last word a singular twist, and Jackie shivered in spite of herself. "Some say he does so to make gold from lead; others say 'tis more fiendish than that. He leaned close, looking from side to side, and said in a very low voice, " 'Tis said that his dark practices involve human sacrifice ."

Jackie's eyes widened in surprise and horror, and she gasped, then held out her empty goblet, as if in need of fortifying herself against this demonic knowledge. She had known that all those books contained wicked learning. "I did not know thas. That," she corrected. Her voice was husky, a horrified—and yet faintly delighted, he realized—whisper. "Whas else?" she prompted.

"The boys he brings to his town house are orphans."

"I be an orphan," she said, nodding somewhat stupidly.

Random's eyes narrowed at this guileless admission, but he did not choose to reply to it. Heathenish, he is, they say," the young earl continued, handing her a full goblet. "Most unnatural rites and practices—he worships the Devil. After all, why do you think he has the nickname 'Satan'?"

Because he's a devil, she thought foggily. A devil. A Satan. Lucifer. Her father. No, not for real, she told herself. Father Liam had said many times that her father was a person, not a devil. She wasn't—

"I be an imp," she said in mournful accents. Her dove-gray eyes filled with tears, and moisture glistened on the ends of her curling black lashes. She sniffed. "I—I—" She gulped rapidly. "I don't—I feel ill. Flesh air," she gasped, shuddering and setting down her half-filled glass.

Quickly Random set his own glass down and guided her through the crowded room. They were not given a second glance, for it was a common enough sight at the court to see a friend helping another out into the fresh air, away from the closeness of the crowded and overheated room.

For Random, too, this was no novel experience, but only one in a long series of planned excursions. Further and further they traveled from the royal festivities until they came to a small dark room far from the crowd. Random propped Jackie against an outer wall and lit a candle, one of several he had stocked. The room had but one window, a small shuttered aperture set high in the wall. The door could be locked from inside and was constructed of heavy unadorned wood. It apparently was used as a storeroom, for along one wall sat a neglected settee which had seen better days. Several chairs crouched in haphazard patterns around the room. A large cabinet sat along the wall opposite the settee, and one door hung open, its latch apparently broken.

The blond earl staggered with his burden across the room, raising a small cloud of dust. He helped the stricken girl onto the sofa. She coughed and looked around, bleary-eyed.

" 'Tisn't outshide," she observed.

"No, 'tis not." Random patted the girl's hand, then returned to the door and locked it. He lit another tallow candle and placed it in a wall bracket opposite the first candle. The two candles gave the room more light but still maintained the dark, mysterious atmosphere he desired.

He walked to the inebriated girl and looked down at her. She raised her head to stare up at him, but her head fell back on the settee.

"Watch it," he cautioned, placing his hand around her neck.

"Thank you," she replied seriously, a silly look on her heart-shaped face. Momentarily her vision blurred, and she blinked rapidly. "You sly fox," she said, shaking a finger at him.

The young earl's eyebrows rose in mock surprise. "I?"

"Yesh. You are a fly sock. I mean a flox sy. No, no, I mean, I mean—" She stopped in utter confusion.

"I know what you are saying," he said gently, sitting beside her, "but I cannot understand how you come to say that. Would you not consider that to be quite uncharitable? After all, I have only your best wishes at heart." For emphasis, Random placed his hand on her knee, and she felt its pulsing warmth through the material of her breeches.

"Shy flux." She chuckled, allowing her head to loll onto his shoulder, for it had suddenly grown too heavy to hold upright. "Shee, sheeee." Her shoulders shook from barely restrained laughter.

Random, too, chuckled, but for a different reason. He snaked his arm around her lithe waist and pinched her. She giggled in response.

"Tickish. Licktish. Whasever."

"Master Jackie, I find you . . . exceedingly desirable."

She giggled again. "Sho on."

"You are a bright lad, full of promise," Random breathed.

"Did you know that? You are so full of laughter and good
spirits. I quite forget any ill feelings I might have had, for
when I see you laugh, I, too, wish to laugh."

Jackie broke into a peal of laughter that lasted for several
minutes. The blond man stared at her in some puzzlement.
What he had said had not been amusing.

"Tell you shomthin'," she said, grasping the collar of his
coat and pulling his face close to hers. She giggled, then
belched softly. Sighing, he turned his head.

"No, no," she said, thinking better of what had appeared
to be an absolutely marvelous idea one moment before. "No,
don't wanna tell."

"So be it, boy."

She giggled again, and Random pulled her into his arms.
He kissed the corner of one eye, then her cheek.

"You lice boys?" she asked with a hiccup.

"When they are as handsome and exquisite as you, child."
He pinched her pointed chin and smiled at her.

"Heh, heh," she chuckled. "Kish me again."

The young earl pressed his lips to her cheek, and she
wiggled closer. "Nose. Rights 'way. Nose cheeks."

He moved his mouth down to her pink lips. His lips closed
on hers, capturing them even as they tried to draw away.

"No," he murmured and again pressed his mouth to hers.
She squeaked in protest and tried to wriggle out of his grasp,
but he would not allow her to elude him.

Lightly Random ran his tongue around her lips, and she
cried out in surprise. With a supreme effort Jackie broke
away from the man and half-turned from him.

She put her hands to her head. Why was Random kissing
her? He should not. She should not. And why, oh why, did
she feel the way she did? If she could think properly, but all
that wine . . . She had imbibed so much. . . . She knew she
wasn't sober . . . and she didn't mind.

"Jackie," Random coaxed, trailing a finger down the ridge
of her spine. She shivered but did not turn back to the man.

This would not do, Random told himself firmly, and put
his arms around her torso, drawing her back toward him.

"Jackie," he murmured again, nibbling at her ear. "You
are the most handsome boy I have ever seen. Your beauty can
drive a man to tears."

"Yesh?" she asked, rather pleased at his admission. Let

him find that out! she thought irrationally, he who thought she was good for nothing except tripping and pushing into mud puddles. *Someone* liked her! Someone didn't laugh at her! Someone didn't sniff and sneer and snarl at her! She rubbed her nose. Who needed the duke, anyway? He was an irreligious pervert, was he.

One hand slipped inside her coat and moved carefully. She wriggled. The blond man turned her around and began to unbutton her coat.

"Oh no!" Jackie cried. "No, I beg you!"

"Come," Random replied smoothly, kissing her again on the lips, "we have traveled thus far on the road to love, and we cannot turn back now."

"Road?" she asked, a horrible suspicion growing in her foggy mind. "Love?"

"Yes," Michael said, nuzzling her white neck as he withdrew the girl's snowy-white cravat and let it fall to the floor.

It was so odd, these feelings that slipped through her body now and made her feel sort of watery inside. She shivered, even though she was not cold. She could not have moved even had she wanted to, and of that she was not sure. She should protest. Really she should. Yet it was nice . . . comfortable here with Lord Malvern . . . and his kisses . . . And she felt good. She had never felt this way before. Never.

He had stripped off his breeches, and her gray eyes widened. 'Twas one thing to see the male horses and bulls along the road; 'twas quite another to see a male of her own species.

Kneeling, Random began tugging at her boots. Finally they came off, and then he stripped off her outer shirt, carefully straightening it so it would not get badly wrinkled.

There was something she should tell him, Jackie thought, but she could not recall what it was. She reclined on the settee and sighed. 'Twas so comfortable.

What an odd binding under the boy's shirt, Random thought. Had he been injured? Curious, Random ran his fingers under the edge of the binding until he found an end. He pulled it out and began unraveling this mystery. When the blond man at last drew the cloth away, he was not at all prepared for what he saw.

Good God! It was a woman! This boy was a female! He sat back on his heels, laughing.

"Whazzit?" she asked, pushing herself up on one elbow and viewing him quizzically. "Well?"

Random had plied "him" with drink and come to this room for one thing—and had found altogether quite another! But it mattered little, for he liked both. Clad only in his linen shirt, he stood and smiled down at the still-tipsy girl. Then, with a growl of satisfaction, he flung himself onto the settee and Jackie, and she cried out as he ran rough hands over her.

The earl of Malvern pressed his mouth down on hers. He forced it open, ramming his tongue into her virgin mouth and licking at her teeth. She squirmed beneath him.

Random dropped kisses on her face, then moved to her neck and proceeded swiftly down to her firm young breasts. She cried out, gripping his hair. Random grunted with pain, but it deterred him not at all from his inevitable path.

He began his siege, and the fortifications of her secure castle fell to him, the invader. Jackie cried out as Random's manhood penetrated her, in body and mind.

It's wrong! one part of her cried, and Jackie whimpered out loud. She had only wished to play, not to . . . not this! *No, no, go back,* she cried to herself. *No further! No more!*

"No, no, no!" the girl sobbed out loud.

For answer, Random only rammed deeper into the girl, his breath whistling through clenched teeth. She twisted first one way, then the other, trying to escape the violator and the pain. But it was impossible. Harder and deeper he thrust, animal sounds wildly escaping from his throat.

She was resisting him! He would not countenance it. She would give in, she would submit to him, this little shy one. He would force her, take her, use her. And she would be his. He cried out as he climaxed within the young girl.

Slowly her sobs quieted as he lay, spent, on her small frame. He ran a hand down her sweat-drenched side, and she shuddered. She grimaced as he kissed her closed eyes.

Burning shame flooded her, and she could have wished for death at that very instant. She hadn't wanted to do this; he had tricked her. And that knowledge made it no more acceptable. Tears formed under her closed eyelids and slipped down her cheeks.

Random, propped up on his elbows, was little surprised by her unhappy reaction, for it was fairly typical among young virgins of either sex to be upset afterward. And certainly he'd had many occasions to observe firsthand young innocents in distress. He smiled with malicious remembrance.

The earl of Malvern stroked Jackie's hair. He wondered what her hair color actually was, for he knew that this sodden auburn mass was a wig. Always before she had been brown-haired. Random tugged at the wig, pulling the inside combs out of her real hair. The girl offered no resistance and seemed almost dead, so still was she. When he had pulled the wig from her head and tossed it aside Random was treated to the second surprise of the evening.

Her hair was silver. Not blond, but silver—just like Victorée's.

The young man sat bolt upright, and in response Jackie curled up on her side, miserably tucked her head in her bent arms, and sobbed.

The feeble light of the two candles, burning low, shone on her hair, giving it a moonlit effect. Random touched the silver and, biting his lip, thought furiously.

He turned Jackie's face toward the light so that he could better study the young girl's features. The winglike eyebrows, the heart-shaped face—thinner, of course, on this child—the high cheekbones.

Random released her face, and, her eyes still shut, she huddled miserably on the aged settee. He rose and paced the length of the room, clouds of dust rising and swirling with each footstep.

He should have seen the resemblance long before this. How had he not? But then, he hadn't been looking for it.

He was no fool. It was no boy here who threatened Victorée's peace of mind with blackmail. He chuckled at having caught his mistress in such a blatant lie. No, here was—dare he think it—a relative, very close. Very, he thought with wicked glee. A daughter. A natural one at that. 'Twas little wonder that Victorée had wished him to rid her of this pest. And what a complicated story the woman had fabricated.

The blond earl chuckled as he thought of the expression that would appear upon Victorée's face when he informed her of his new intelligence, and he rubbed his hands in gloating anticipation, for he had little doubt that she would "purchase" his information.

On the other hand, he thought, what if he should announce to the entire court that this "boy" was an impostor—was, indeed, a girl. King William would be outraged, and he would have every right indeed, Michael told himself piously, for the girl had deceived him from the very beginning. The king would be so incensed that he would no doubt strip her of all rank and send her posthaste from the court.

And that would be one less rival for Random in the king's heart.

He smiled, imagining, too, the expression on the duke of Avalon's face when he discovered that one of the boys he had tried to make a "pet" wasn't male.

Oh, but there was little reward in taking that path. No, the route he chose would have money along it.

Michael Random quickly dressed, smoothing as best he could the wrinkles from his clothing. He leaned over and nuzzled the upset girl's cheek. She flinched and kept her eyes shut.

"Rest well, my dear," he murmured. He strode across the room, then turned back to look at her. "Don't worry, Jackie. I shan't tell a soul about your secret. I find it far more amusing to keep everyone else ignorant of the truth." He chuckled, then unbarred the door and left the secluded store-room in search of the Frenchwoman.

It did not take him as long as he had anticipated to find his older mistress. Attired in a black gown that nearly revealed the entire whiteness of her breasts, Victorée L'Este du Plessis was ensconced in a velvet petit-point chair, fanning herself again the heat of the grand room. Random noted with amusement that she was "holding court," for around her were various courtiers. She raised one hand, and a brown-haired nobleman went off to fetch her a glass of wine. The others waited patiently for her command.

Michael, a slight smile on his lips, bowed deeply and waited.

She glanced at him coolly and inclined her head. "Yes, Lord Malvern?" she inquired languidly.

"I would beg a time when you and I may discuss a very important development." His tone was somewhat conspiratorial, and, Victorée, her eyes narrowing, studied the young earl's deceptively bland face, attempting to decipher his cryptic remark.

"Very well, sir, in an hour's time," she replied evenly.

The earl of Malvern nodded and bowed. Moving across to

one of the refreshment tables, he accepted a glass of wine given him by one of the lackeys. Confidence rising in him, he became jaunty and happily joined the court festivities. He well knew that Jackie would say nothing of this night's experience, for if she did it would only give her away. Random little understood why she chose to hide her pretty female form behind the clothing of a boy, but he assumed the girl must possess a reason of some import.

Random chuckled, immensely pleased with himself, and sipped at the wine. It would appear that his situation in life was indeed improving.

After many long minutes of emptiness, of darkness and misery, pain and anguish, Jackie slowly pulled herself up off the old settee and began dressing, her hands numb. She pushed back her disarrayed hair and eased the wig back onto her sore head.

She could blame no one but herself. She had been foolish. Worse than foolish—stupid. She should have realized what was going on when he pressed the drinks on her. After all, weeks earlier he had been pursuing her. She should have known . . . but she had not. She had been reckless in her attitude, in her cockiness.

She stood stiffly and massaged her inner thigh. He had bruised her tender flesh with his uncaring weight. Dirty and stupid—the words echoed in her brain. Used. Vomit rose in her throat, and she retched and retched until her stomach was empty. She wiped her mouth with the back of her hand and looked dully around, a sour taste in her mouth.

Suddenly, she stiffened. He knew she was a girl, and although he had said he wouldn't betray her, how did she know that he would not go back on his word? What was his word worth, after tonight? Perhaps she should leave the court at once . . . this very moment. . . . She should tell Liam. No. No. Tears formed in her eyes. Perhaps she should just go to bed and sleep and forget.

She sniffled, rubbing at her face with her hand. Her eyes were sore and red from crying, and she knew she must look—and smell—a sight. To what avail had she cried? It had made her feel no better; it had simply wrung her out.

All her emotions were gone. . . . They had dribbled out onto the ground, like the blood that was now dried on the skin of her inner thigh. All gone. Her virginity was gone. She choked, and a loud sob escaped her violated lips.

Damaged. Ruined. Despoiled. Tears slid down her cheeks as she blew out the candles, and with her hat tucked under one arm, she hobbled down the corridor. She carefully made her way back to the ballroom, whence she could hear the sounds of festivities. She stopped, and each sound was like the jab of a knife in her. She could not go in there, not the way she looked, the way she smelled, the way she felt now. She heard a sound nearby, a faint laugh, and shuddered. A man brushed by her, murmuring an apology. His eyes swept across her form, but she averted her face so that the duke of Avalon would not see her.

No fool despite Jackie's opinion of him, Avalon recognized her at once and stopped, studying her somewhat bedraggled appearance. He clucked his tongue in admonition, for he had seen Jackie leave with Random, a man possessing a bad reputation among the young. Blade hesitated, wondering if he should say anything to the youth. But he remembered the boy's hostile reaction to him and to any kindness he proffered. Shrugging mentally, the duke decided to remain silent. No doubt the boy was no innocent and knew well what he had involved himself in.

Jackie saw the duke's lips curve in a smile, and she felt anger, inasmuch as she was able to feel any emotion. She turned and pushed brusquely past him, then limped down the hall and up the stairs toward her quarters, away from the laughing voices, the music, the gaiety, that man.

Once inside her room she went to the dresser and washed her face and hands, then rinsed out her mouth. Some of the sourness was gone, yet she hardly felt better.

She dropped onto the bed without pausing to remove her boots. She lay on her back, one leg dangling over the edge of the bed, and stared up at a crack in the ceiling. She would just lie here for a while. She was no longer upset. No, she was past that. She felt . . . nothing.

What did her young lover want? the Frenchwoman wondered as she rose to leave the ballroom. She deftly made her excuses to the coterie of courtiers around her and moved through the crowd. Outside the overheated room she paused for a breath of fresh air and rapidly fanned herself. Once she had recovered, Victorée began looking for the young earl.

The Frenchwoman did not search long, for she found Random in an adjacent salon. She made her entrance, waited, yet the young man said nothing. "Well?" she demanded. "What can this important matter be, *mon cher*?"

"Ah, Victorée, do sit down," Random said expansively. With a broad gesture he indicated an ornately carved chair with a velvet back and cushion. The woman gracefully sat and waited, folding her hands in her lap.

What sort of cat-and-mouse game was he involved in? she wondered with some curiosity. As usual, he could not be straightforward on the matter. Little devious minds must play their little devious games, Victorée thought. Long minutes passed, but he still did not say anything.

"I met with Master Jackie this evening," the blond earl said at last. "The boy who bedeviled you, my dear."

She leaned forward eagerly, her hands clenching. "*Oui?*"

"He is quite intriguing," Random offered casually.

"Is that all you have to say, Michel?" Victorée asked crossly.

"No," he said, smiling. "I have rather a lot to say, but I am carefully selecting my words and organizing my thoughts." He grinned suddenly and unexpectedly. "You see, I lured Master Jackie away from the coronation ball and—seduced him!"

"What!" Her face froze in astonishment.

Michael grinned wolfishly. "Yes, it was a lengthy process, but the benefits, I can assure you, were well worth the wait." He cocked an eyebrow at the pale-eyed woman. "I lured Jackie to a deserted storeroom, and can you imagine my surprise when I stripped him of his clothes?" He watched her face as several emotions struggled for supremacy in her.

"It was a hoax from beginning to end, your story," the earl said. "You knew that Master Jackie was your by-blow, and so you spun this tale for me, hoping in the endeavor that I would never discover the truth and that I would rid you of this tiresome nuisance. Hoping that somehow I would talk with him and then challenge him for some niggling reason. Then I would duel with the child and conveniently kill him. Is that not so?" he asked casually.

The Frenchwoman seemed to have difficulty in finding her voice, then finally she said, "*Oui*, it is so."

"Really, my dear," he said in a chiding tone, "could you not have thought of a simpler plan?"

"I was not yet desperate, Michel," the woman replied quietly.

"Ah, yes. And if one of your henchmen killed the boy it might easily be traced to you. If I should kill the boy, well, these duels often result in death. Now," he said expansively, "we shall discuss the terms of our compromise."

"Blackmail, *n'est-ce pas*?"

"Call it that if you will. I would prefer to term it an 'investment.' "

" 'Investment' or blackmail—it is the same to me, Michel." Her voice was weary. "What do you wish?"

His fair eyebrows arched. "What it is it that you have to offer me, Victorée?"

The Frenchwoman thought rapidly, considering the alternatives. If she confided in him she must ultimately have him eliminated. Well, she was growing tired of his sulks.

"Very well, Michel, I shall make my offer. If you aid me in what I must do, the king shall reward you greatly."

"The king?" he asked cautiously.

"Louis XIV, of course." She leaned forward and lowered her voice to a whisper. "He plots to overthrow William and Mary and to restore the rightful king, James, to the throne. If Louis should succeed, he would offer much recompense to his faithful followers."

"For your part in this, what do you receive?" Random asked.

"A dead husband, without any questions asked, a very extensive estate in the south of France, and greater freedom. Any woman such as I would jump at this opportunity. Do you not agree, *mon cher*?"

"Aye, I do," the young earl said. "But what have you to offer me? And how shall James be restored to the throne?" Now, from which monarch could he receive more—Louis for helping bring James to the English throne or William for telling him of this plot?

"Such simple answers for such basic questions," the Frenchwoman said slowly. "Your reward would be yours for the asking." She smiled at his dubious expression. "If you sought wealth, *mon cher*, it would be yours. If you sought a higher title, that would be granted. If you wished both, I am sure that it could be arranged. Louis is a most generous master.

"As for ridding England of this Dutch blight, that would prove so simple, *mon cher*. Assassinate him. That is all. Kill William, and his weak wife would not stay long on the throne. She would concede to her father, for she harbors guilty feelings even now that she and her Protestant husband have deposed him. In the ensuing confusion after William's death, King James would land and march to London, taking up the reins of government once more. He has avid supporters here. Louis's army would lend support, as would the French navy. The Catholic king will find many more supporters in England once he has arrived."

"As simple as that?" Random asked, somewhat skeptical but taken aback by her knowledge.

Victorée shook her head. "No abrupt change of government is ever simple, but it is the most convenient way that we know presently. Any other plan would prove too cumbersome and time-consuming." She was amused that it had taken so little to divert him from the subject of that tiresome child.

"I would just have to help you . . . assassinate William?" Random asked slowly.

"*Oui*. Come now, *mon cher*, own up to it. You are not so fond of the crookback as you avow."

She was right, of course. He stayed with William for the power, wealth, and position that he might receive, but as yet no title had been forthcoming, and what if he were to gain those three great desires more rapidly with someone else? Could anyone blame him?

Random took her hand in his and kissed each fingertip gently.

"I am with you, my dear. I shall want a large estate with excellent revenues, and a high title, perhaps that of a duke. Yes, I would like that. And then"—he smiled slyly, so that they would completely understand each other—"I shall not expose 'Master' Jackie as your child."

"Excellent, Michel," the woman said, smiling triumphantly.

Father Liam Dougherty staggered up the stairs, lurched down the hallway, and collided with the immovable opposition of the door. He fumbled with his key, all the while humming off-key under his breath. Finally he entered the sitting room, then crossed to his own bedchamber.

He stumbled from his bedroom into the sitting room and lit a candle, then unsteadily crossed the floor. He tapped on the door of her room.

"Jackie love, be ye awake?"

There was a muffled sound and a creak of the bed, but she did not reply. The priest scratched his head, for he had the distinct feeling in his old Irish bones that she was in there wide awake. He tried the doorknob and found it unlocked. As he entered his eyes adjusted to the dimness of the moonlit chamber, and he made out Jackie's form on the bed.

Some sixth sense warned him that all was not as it should be. His heart hammered under his ribs, and he thought of that night with Jack. *No*, he thought. *No*.

Sobering quickly, Liam quickly crossed to the girl's bed and stared down at Jackie's face in the moonlight. Tears had left trails down her cheeks, and her face was pinched and unhappy. There were dark smudges under her eyes. Sitting on the edge of the bed, Liam took her cold hand in his and gently stroked it. He gave it a fatherly squeeze.

Her eyes fluttered open, and he saw that they were red from crying. *Mary, Mither o' God*, he exclaimed to himself with growing concern.

"Jackie girl, what be the matter?" His voice was just a whisper, but it sounded loud and harsh in the stillness of the room.

She started to answer, then a sob caught in her throat. Liam placed his arms around her and gently stroked her hair. One part of him idly noticed that she had not even bothered to remove her wig. He carefully took it from her head, tossed it aside, then ruffled her silver hair.

"What be it, Jackie? Ye can tell yer ould Liam, ye can. Trust me, darlin'. Come now, sweet girl, tell me what it be."

"It's too terrible to tell," the girl said in a muffled voice.

"Nothin' be too terrible to tell, not to me, me love," the priest said soothingly. "Come now. Sit up, dry yer tears, an' tell me what it be that be plaguin' me wee dear one."

She did obey to the point of sitting up and wiping her tears with her shirttail. Jackie sniffed several times, opened her mouth as though to speak, then closed it.

The two sat in the moonlit darkness, and Liam waited patiently, recalling the times long ago he had waited in a dark booth to hear the confessions of his parishioners. *Aye, but that be a lifetime ago,* he thought wearily.

"Have ye been hurt, Jackie?" the priest asked gently.

She nodded her head, then shook it in confusion. "Yes. No. Yes," she said finally.

"An' who would it be that be harmin' ye?" he asked in a grave voice.

"That nobleman," she said listlessly.

"The duke of Avalon?" Liam asked immediately, cold fire igniting in him. His stomach knotted at the mention of that devilish man.

"Good God, no! The other one. Michael Random. He is an aide-de-camp to the king."

"An' how might he have hurt ye, love?"

The girl sniffled and passed a sleeved arm across her nose. "He fed me drink after drink, then lured me away to this horrible room, a-and he s-seduced me and I don't be a virgin anymore and, Liam, I hurt so m-much!" She flung her arms around him and buried her face in his chest. "I didn't want it to be this way. It wasn't nice. Not at all. Why would anyone want to do it? Why would my father? I don't understand, Liam, I don't," she uttered in a childlike voice.

Liam's grip on the distraught girl tightened. There was a time, many years ago, when he would have made a different reply. But the intervening years had taught Father Liam Dougherty a tolerance, if not an overall wisdom, that his religion would have condemned.

Fighting the pain within him, Father Liam stroked the girl's silver hair and rocked her as though she were a small child again. She clutched at the material of his coat.

"Jackie dear, ye cannot go an' let this experience destroy all the love ye have in yer heart," he said softly. "Ye cannot. 'Tis no shame that be killin' ye. Ye must go on livin'. Ye be havin' a bad time, but ye be wiser now, too. Ye must not allow it to hurt ye. Be that not so?"

The girl nodded her head slowly against him. His grip around her tightened even more.

"Yer next experience, in marriage, will be better, that I be knowin', Jackie. When yer in love, it be makin' a world o' difference. Can ye believe that, darlin'?" He felt the slight assent and continued. "Ye must not allow this to take unnatural control o' yer mind. Ye must not, me dear." He continued stroking her hair.

"Ah, Jackie love, I don't want ye to be hurtin' inside. Come now, don't be thinkin' 'bout all the bad. 'Tis night, an' things always look their worst then. We'll see 'bout it in the mornin'." He continued to hold her close until he heard her rhythmic breathing.

Carefully the priest lowered the sleeping girl back onto the bed. His eyes sad, he gazed down at her exhausted face and pulled a blanket over her form. He rose and slowly straightened his back, feeling now very old.

Father Liam quietly left Jackie's bedchamber and reentered his. Then he did something that he did not often do anymore: he dropped to his knees and began to pray to his Maker. He asked for strength, for will, for perseverance.

After an hour of prayer, Liam got stiffly to his feet, his face set in hard lines. He pulled an object from his saddlebags, checked it, then slipped it into his coat.

Grimly pressing his lips together, Liam left their apartments, the cold comfort of the pistol next to his breast.

He would find the man who had hurt his Jackie in body and spirit, and he would take care of that monster.

He would kill the ravisher, no matter what it took.

Chapter

❦ Seventeen ❦

A WEEK PASSED, and another, and another, and the physical pain diminished. So did the mental pain, if she would admit it to herself. Yet she avoided the contact of all at court, and once she was discharged of her duties for the king each day, she would return to her room and sit on the bed and stare out the window.

She mustn't sit in the darkness and brood, she told herself one day. She got up, walked across the room, opened the door, and walked out. And she discovered it was not as hard as she had imagined.

She found the Irish priest reading a book in his bedroom. He glanced up at her briefly, then back down at the pages of the book. His face was set in unhappy lines, and a tear ran down his cheek.

Consternation grew in Jackie as she watched more tears gather in her companion's eyes. She enveloped his hand in hers and gave it a squeeze.

"What's wrong, Liam?" she asked gently, her own woes forgotten.

"Nothin'," he said, dashing at the tears with his free hand.

"Liam," the girl intoned sternly, "do not dissemble with me. Be truthful. You would wish the same of me."

The blond man sniffled but refused to say a word.

"My dear Liam," she said softly, stroking his hand as she knelt before him. "Please tell me what bothers you. You have been in such low spirits of late. Was it any deed or word that I have done or said?" She turned earnest gray eyes to the priest and searched his face. "Is it b-because of that evening, the night of the ball?"

"Jackie, rest at heart, me love, fer it be nothin' that ye've said nor done. Don't trouble yerself, dear. It be no concern o' yers."

Indignation flared through the girl, and she rocked back on her heels, fists balled at her hips. Her gray eyes flashed as she spoke in a firm tone.

"Father Liam Dougherty, listen to me. What concerns you concerns me. Just as anything that happens to me concerns you. Now tell me."

Liam stared morosely at the cracked leather of his boots. He sighed and scratched the side of his head.

"Ye remember that night o' the ball?" he asked.

She nodded. "You know that I could never forget," she said softly.

Blood rushed to his face, and he remembered the weeks that had passed in agony for the girl, who had gone to the earl, and pleaded with him not to reveal her true identity. Laughing, he had pinched her chin and assured her that all would be right and that she should have nary a concern. But, of course, she did. What if she were carrying his child? She had shuddered at that thought. Then a few days later she had awakened in the night, as she had when she was thirteen, and, seeing the rust-colored stain, had known that she no longer need fear a child, and she had quietly informed Liam. And she had further told him that she believed the earl would keep his word and not betray her.

"Go on, Liam."

He opened his mouth, then closed it and put his head in his hands. "I cannot go on."

Jackie wrapped her arms around him. "Of course, you can, Liam. Now try."

He inhaled raggedly, and his body shuddered. "I left ye when ye be asleep that night. So young ye be lookin' then. I came out here, an' I prayed long, Jackie, long fer strength an' guidance. An' finally it came. I got out me pistols an' I left. I went lookin' fer that cad. I be aimin' to blow off his dastardly head.''

"Liam, Liam," the girl said, "if there was to be killing, I could well have done it myself.''

"An' ye bein' a babe that never killed nobody," Liam said.

"And neither have you," Jackie pointed out.

He sniffed and resumed his narrative. "I found him. I found him in a corridor, dallyin' with some girl, some poor child that probably ended up like ye, dearie. An' I leveled me pistol an' I cocked it an'—'' The priest's voice wavered, then broke. "I couldn't do it. I be not man enough to murder the bastard. I be a coward, Jackie, an' I let ye down!'' The tears ran down his reddened cheeks, and he turned miserable eyes toward her. "I be a man without a spine," he finished softly.

Immediately Jackie's heart went out to the tortured man. She squeezed him tighter and patted his back reassuringly.

"Come, Liam, you're no coward. You could not have killed that man. You're a priest, not a destroyer. It was only right that you couldn't bring yourself to shoot Lord Malvern. They would simply have captured you before you could escape, and then you would have been tossed into prison. That would have done me no good, nor you. Now don't castigate yourself, silly one. It doesn't signify.''

"But ye be so upset," he said, rubbing his nose across his sleeve. "An' so unhappy, an' he hurt ye bad.''

"Yes, that night," she replied calmly. "But what is done is done. I cannot change the past. I am no longer a virgin, and I have had to face that. After that . . . episode, I've decided that I can never marry. I have put aside any thought of that sort of life. I have vowed to love my God, my king, and my country.''

"Oh, darlin'," the priest wailed, "I be so unhappy fer ye. What a miserable life ye'll be havin'. Ye'll be fair goin' on to be a saint!''

"Hardly, Liam!'' She laughed. "I shall simply be a soldier, and I shall lead the spartan life of one. That is all.''

"But, Jackie, I don't be wantin' ye to be dressin' as a soldier all the time. I want ye to be in pretty dresses an' fine jewels an' such. 'Tis not right fer a young colleen to live the life o' a solider. We be savin' all that money fer our retirement. What will we be doin' with it if yer to lead a plain life?"

"Liam," the girl said, "I shall be all right. Please don't worry about me."

"Aye," he pointed out, "but ye yerself said that yer concern be mine. I be mightily concerned fer ye, Jackie. Ye need some sort o' life ye can look ferward to. Ye need a proper home, with a proper roof over yer head. Ye need someone to look out fer ye an' to love ye. Ye need someone to love."

"I have you. You look out for me, and we love each other."

"Ye know o' what I be speakin'," Liam said wistfully. "Ye need a husband."

"Come, how am I to get a husband when I am spoiled goods and have dressed as a boy all my life? I would certainly be no bargain, Liam. Hush now, and say no more." She stood and looked down at the unhappy priest, huddled in his misery. "I have you, Liam. That is enough for me." She patted him on the arm.

"Mayhap—"

"Yes?"

"Mayhap a miracle will happen," he said, his face lightening with the thought.

She smiled. She could not destroy his hope. "Mayhap," Jackie agreed.

"It is time," Victorée said, brushing back her long silver hair, "that you began earning your way." She smiled at her reflection in the mirror. Behind her, candles gave the sybarite's room a golden glow. The scent of cinnamon and musk permeated the room.

Random, lying on the bed, rolled over on his stomach and stared at the Frenchwoman.

"What do you mean?"

She smiled at him, but it was an icy smile that stabbed him. "My sweet, do you not remember our conversation—and agreement—the night of the coronation ball?" She yawned behind one white hand. "Do cast your mind back, Michel."

He frowned. "Oh yes, I remember now."

She rose from the vanity and moved across to the bed. As

she walked her black silk robe, loosely belted, came open.
She wore nothing beneath it, and Random licked his lips.

She sat on the bed next to the prone man. "Michel," she
cooed, trailing a hand down his back and over his buttocks.
She stroked their plumpness, then traced the line of his spine
upward. Suddenly she grasped a hank of his hair, twisted it
around her fist, and jerked his head back. He gasped, and she
laughed. She roughly shook his head, then released him,
pushing his face into the soft coverlet.

She sprang up and walked to the window.

"Victorée!" he called, once he had recovered from the
shock of the moment.

"*Oui, mon cher?*" she answered without turning to face
him.

"About our bargain—what would you have me do?"

"In a week's time, the king hunts. You go with him, is
that not correct? You surely must understand the rest, *mon
cher*. Or must I explain everything to you, *mon enfant*?"

Random stepped across to his mistress and slipped his arms
around her body, hugging her tightly to him. One hand crept
inside her robe to caress the firm flesh, but she stopped it,
pinching the soft skin on the back of his hand with her
fingernails. Pained, he withdrew the hand.

"No. Business first. Then—perhaps—pleasure."

He nuzzled her neck and nibbled at an earlobe. "I am *très
stupide* today, love. Explain to me—what do you expect of
me?"

She sighed. At times there was something to be said in
favor of a handsome but not highly intelligent lover; unfortunately, this was not one of the times.

"You are to hunt with the king. It will be very convenient,
mon cher, for you to slip away and arrange an 'accident.' If
he should be shot, I am sure that it will be blamed on
poachers or bandits. You *must* prove successful, Michel. You
know that I chose you because you are close to the king. One
of my henchmen could not get within range of him. And,
besides, no one in his right mind would ever accuse you."
She sighed. "Poison would be simpler and more effective,
but, alas, he employs a food-taster and has since his youth,
when Louis tried to poison him. Ah, let us hope you do not
fail, *mon cher*. Especially if you wish to receive that promised dukedom. I like my men to succeed in all they do."

Victorée turned and, reaching down, grasped his manhood and tugged at it, then laughed as he grunted with pain.

"You were not successful earlier, Michel. Be careful." She moved away and sat down again at the vanity. Picking up her gold brush, she pulled it through her long hair. In the candlelight her hair shone like newly minted silver coins, and her eyes were but a pale glimmer. The only jewels she wore were ruby earrings that gave her cheeks a rosy glow.

Oui, she must soon look for a new lover. This one was growing very tiresome, very tedious. As soon as he had dealt with the Dutch prince his usefulness would have ended and he could be removed. The girl could be removed. Until then, though, the woman reflected, she must not discount the child, for the girl/boy must be considered a backup if Random should fail.

"What sort of reassurance will I have? My dukedom is sometime in the future. What will I get *now*?" Random asked. He stubbornly refused to be dismissed until she had completely sealed their bargain. He stood behind her and watched as the gold brush flashed through her silver hair.

"Reassurance?" the Frenchwoman asked, raising a silver eyebrow. "Do you seek words or monetary reassurance, Michel?"

"Money," the young earl replied flatly. "Now."

"I suspected as much." She crossed over to the wardrobe and opened the doors, then drew out one elegant shoe. Inside was secreted a small brown bag which she flung to Michael. It struck him in the stomach before he could catch it, and she grinned as he grunted from the impact.

His fingers trembling with greediness, Michael loosened the drawstrings of the purse and dumped the contents into his hand. He began counting the money.

"Ten . . . twenty . . . thir—" He paused, staring at the silver coins in his hand. Random whirled, faced the faintly smiling woman, and flung the coins away from him. Like a silver shower they rained onto the carpeting.

The earl of Malvern, a scowling expression upon his plump face, stormed from the room. But he could hear her laughter like burning devils prodding him, and it followed him the length of the hallway, dogging his footsteps.

For weeks now, like a wolf tracking its prey, he had hunted

for the old woman. Sometimes he would gain her scent; other times the trail was cold. But he persisted. He would find her; he had been so directed.

When he had last seen her, it had been many years ago. He had been younger; she had been younger. Perhaps she no longer lived; perhaps she did.

But he must find her, at all costs.

How long had it been? He moved stiffly from the filthy straw pallet resting on a wooden frame. He brushed his hand across his face, feeling the beard, the bite marks of vermin and . . . rats? His clothes were the stinking breeding grounds of lice and fleas, his hands shook, palsied with an age he had not achieved, and there was a rank odor about him.

But his overwhelming desire now was, first, to eat, for his stomach grumbled painfully with hunger, and then, second, to obey his mistress.

He searched the room with his eyes, looking for any evidence of food. But there was none. It was an empty hovel, except for. . . . He blinked in the gloom of the room and stared.

A huddle of filthy rags lay along the hearth of the fireplace, the remnants of a wood fire evident but long cold. He nudged the heap with the toe of his soiled boot, and the heap groaned and shivered.

Carel pulled his cloak around his broad shoulders and stared down at the miserable human being who remained nothing more than a pile of rags.

He could not remember properly, but he had snatches of memory. Scenes floated across his consciousness like spirits.

Hands like claws plucking at him, pushing him onto his back, spooning thin gruel into his mouth. A face, haggard with hardship, staring down at him. And then the fever had risen, sweat had poured from his body, and he had seen a devil, horns sprouting from its forehead, leering down at him. He had screamed, then reached out to defend himself, grabbing the devil's neck with both hands. He had twisted and twisted, the devil shrieking all the while for its very life, and he had shoved it aside with what little strength remained in him. It had landed on the floor and had not bothered him again.

The fever had broken that night, and he had slept. But where had the devil gone? This heap was nothing, not a

demon sent by the Evil One to plague him. He prodded it
again with his boot, but the heap did not move. He shrugged.
It was not his concern.

He left the room, strength flowing back into his contorted
body as he walked. He squinted as daylight struck his unused
eyes. He peered, trying to find his bearings.

It was a large city, teeming with a large populace. Dirty
faces leered at him. Every other face had devil horns, and
some had tails. He brushed away the nightmares and stumbled forward. The cobblestoned way rose up to meet him, but
he put his hand down and so did not fall.

He gathered himself and walked, searching for food. At
last he came to an open-air stand displaying overripe fruits
and rotting meat crawling with flies.

He looked quickly up and down the alley. No one was
staring at him. With quick thick fingers he grabbed some of
the fruit and meat and stuffed it inside his shirt. Then with
affected unconcern he moved off, closing his eyes at times to
shut out the grinning devil faces.

When he had left the food stall far behind, he pulled the
meat from the sweaty confines of his shirt and began gnawing
on it. He grinned as the meat juices ran down his chin. He
wiped them with the back of one beefy hand.

He would conquer the devils. He knew they had been sent
to dissuade him. They were a test. He would beat them, and
he would find Her, for She had sent them. Oh, yes, of that he
was certain. He would find Her and wring Her neck like that
of a chicken, and he would toss Her in the bog, and that
would be the end of it.

He grinned, revealing wide gaps between his teeth. But it
would not be quite the end, for he would return to his lovely
mistress. Grinning even wider, he scratched at his groin with
one hand. Then he would get his reward.

With renewed relish, he gobbled at the rank meat.

She swept away the ashes with one hand, then thoughtfully
stroked her chin. That pattern was not correct. It would do no
good. Her face covered with soot, she applied herself once
more to the Pattern That Would Destroy.

She had so many who deserved what her Lord would mete
out to them. She brushed away a fly from her face, and,
biting her lip, stared down at the tracing of soot on the flat rock.

It was a special rock, which her Lord had directed her to find in a dream long years ago. She had searched through the marsh until she discovered it, half-covered with slime, half-embedded in the earth. She had found sticks and dug around the stone until, her hands cracked and bleeding, she had recovered the rock. She had rolled it back to her hut, to the open space before the fire. And she had used it in her spells, just as her Master had directed her to do.

She sighed, for her Master had not visited her often in the past few years. He had other favorites now, that much was apparent. Yes, old Ulrica had fallen into disfavor in her Lord's eyes because she had allowed the Black Boy to take away Angel. She was being punished for that.

So many years ago. Angel would be grown. Her silver hair, mischievous gray eyes, and pointed chin were but dim memories to the old woman, but she could still recall the shrill piping of the small girl.

Every year since the discovery of the stone Ulrica had tried different spells to bring back the small girl to her. She had poured the blood of a still-living rabbit onto the rock in the slight depression on top and bathed her hands in it. Cupping her hands, she had touched the red liquid to her lips. She had smeared the blood upon her withered cheeks and cracked lips until she looked like some half-crazed parody of the great ladies at court. She had taken off her rags and washed the blood over her aged body.

But it had not worked.

She had sacrificed chicken after chicken, wringing their skinny necks, silencing the desperate squawks. She had watched afterward as the headless torsos flopped around. Then she had set them upon the stone, her altar, and she had with her own hands torn into the flesh of the birds, pulling the still-warm entrails out. She had draped them around her neck like primitive ropes of pearls.

She heard faint footfalls, a scrabbling, the striking of a pebble knocked loose and rattling down a slope.

She licked her cracked lips and wiped back the strands of her greasy hair with one hand. She ran both hands down the ruined bodice of her dress in an effort to straighten herself. If it were her Lord returning, she must not appear unseemly.

Her breath catching rapidly, Ulrica waited expectantly.

She heard a grunt, then a cough, the crackling of bending

vegetation. The years slipped away, and Ulrica could remember waiting before.

Ano, he was coming. Her husband, home from the fields, and behind him would come, laughing and skipping and jumping, the three children.

She rose. She could not meet them without a meal. She tossed a handful of herbs into the black pot boiling over the fire and stirred it with a large stick. She stuck a finger into the mixture, but withdrew it when pain seared her skin.

Nursing the finger, she waited excitedly, like a little girl, like an expectant bride.

He was there. She smiled, her cheeks creasing.

"Anton," she croaked happily.

She stumbled forward, grabbing his hand with her claw.

"Dinner awaits," she said fondly.

She led him before the fire and pushed him into a sitting position. She knew he would be hungry; he always was when he labored in the fields. Eh, but the fields worked up an appetite!

She heard the high voices of the three children now, calling to her as they came up the path. She rushed to them and hugged each one in turn.

Carel stared as the old woman hobbled away and embraced empty air three times. He scratched his head, then his side.

"Come," she said, leading two of the children by the hand to the fire. The third she leaned down and kissed upon his soft child's cheek.

"Food is ready," she declared and reached for bowls. But she found only one.

"There are no more," she told Anton apologetically. She ladled out the boiling liquid into the wooden bowl and handed it to him. She watched as he sipped at the soup, then waved his hand in front of his lips.

"Hot, eh?" She cackled, pleased with her culinary efforts. "Eat hearty now."

When the bowl was empty, she took it from his hands and filled it again with the gruel. She watched eagerly as he drained the bowl, then refilled it.

She talked to the children, telling them that each would get his turn after their father had eaten. She apologized for having only one bowl, but they must remember that most everything had been destroyed in the fire. When he indicated that he was finished, she took the bowl from him and ladled in more soup and handed it to Stefan, the eldest. But his appetite was off, as were those of the other children, for they would not touch the soup.

"Are you sick?" she asked, concern in her voice. The little ones were so susceptible to the ill humors. She hoped that nothing was wrong.

But they were strangely silent and just looked at her with great hollowed eyes, sockets that were empty, black holes in their pinched faces.

Ulrica screamed and stumbled backward. Carel, startled, stood up and looked around to determine the cause of the old woman's agitation.

Moaning, she fell to her knees and began swaying back and forth. Carel wiped his mouth on his sleeve and walked in front of the gibbering woman.

She could smell the fire . . . see the flames . . . hear the awful cries. She could not allow them to go by themselves! She wanted to help them, to hold them one last time, but she could not.

She sobbed, her cracked hands over her wrinkled face, and shuddered with misery.

Carel flexed his fingers, cracking each joint. Then he rubbed his hands together.

He reached down and placed his hands gently around the scrawny neck of the old woman. She whimpered and looked up into the face of the mute man.

The tears fell from her bleary eyes, and she could hear her children calling to her, hear her husband's voice murmuring to her.

"Come with me, Ulre," he was saying. "Come, we have missed you all these years. Come to us, my love." And then he began sobbing, the sound mingling with her own loud weeping.

She raised her head to the sky and waited for Death to take her. She would soon be home, be at rest, be with her loved ones. . . .

It did not take long. One sudden wrenching of her neck, and the old woman moved no more. Carel grinned down at his handiwork. He released her, and she crumpled to the ground.

He looked around and, seeing the fire, saw a way of

disposing of the body. He picked her up, light bundle that she was, and dumped the hag inside the rickety hut. Then he stuck a piece of wood into the fire and watched as the flames tickled the wood. Soon the end of the wood was alit with flame. He thrust it under the roof of the hovel and watched as the sparks flew to the dry material.

He walked around the hovel, torching it here and there. .Soon the entire hovel was immersed in flames.

He grinned and tossed the piece of wood into the flames, then stepped back to admire his handiwork. He moved further back to get a better view and stumbled over the rock that Ulrica had found long ago. He lost his balance and, arms flailing, attempted to regain his feet. But he continued lurching back, and when he could once more upright himself his feet were encased in the mire of the marsh.

He grunted, trying to pull his feet out of the mire, but they only made a horrible sucking noise and sank a little deeper.

Calling out of his ruined throat, Carel attempted to move out of the invidious bog, but he could not free himself. He reached out, trying to touch his hand to firm ground, but the tips of his fingers reached only loose soil that crumbled beneath his grasp.

Time after time he cried out in his suffering, seeking help. But there was none in the silent marsh.

Chapter
Eighteen

THE HUNTING PARTY was small, a handful of men selected by King William himself. With him rode his good friend William Bentick; Michael Random; Jackie McKier; the duke of Avalon; Shrewsbury; and two of William's favorite courtiers. John Churchill was not included, for while he admired the man's ability and competence, William little liked the man privately.

Blade, guiding his horse to trot close to the flank of the king, frowned as the man coughed harshly. The beaters moved on ahead of the riders, hitting the bush with their sticks for birds. Suddenly a quail shot from the underbrush, skittering across the path of the horses. A fit of coughing seized the king, and his horse reared as he fought for control.

At precisely the same time Jackie and Blade flung themselves, from opposite directions, at the reins of his mount. Jackie ran her velvet-gloved hand down the muzzle of the frightened horse, while Blade patted the horse's flank.

"*Dank U wel,*" the king gasped. Both the young girl and the duke nodded briefly. Bentick, who had ridden ahead, spurred his mount quickly toward the king.

"Your Highness?" the Dutch man inquired solicitously.

"I . . . am fine," William said, embarrassed at the attention. "Please . . . let us go hunting now."

"But only if Your Highness feels he should," Random said, speaking for the first time.

"*Ja.* I am good now."

Blade said nothing. He was uneasy, and he could not say precisely why. Jackie, too, said nothing. Random, on the other hand, appeared overly concerned, more so than he would have expected, for Blade recalled that the blond earl had sat on his horse, never attempting to come to the monarch's aid. And for that reason something in the back of his head nagged at him.

"Your Grace?" asked a quiet voice beside him.

"Yes, child?"

"I think His Highness should ride no more today," the young girl said as she played with her mount's black mane.

The duke glanced back at William. The short man's face was white and pinched. "Perhaps you are right, but he did wish to hunt this day."

"I think he is more affected than he will say," Jackie murmured. "London is not healthy for him, and he feels it even now. The smoke from the fireplaces, the mist off the river—none of it helps him."

"No," Avalon said, his blue eyes filled with amusement as he surveyed the child before him. "And what concern is it of yours? Are you a gentleman of the bedchamber?"

Jackie's face took on a look of puzzlement. "I—I do not understand, Your Grace."

"Never mind, child." He swerved his horse and rode back to the king and Bentick. Random stood next to his horse, to the right of the king.

"Your Majesty." Blade bowed from the saddle.

"Help me, Avalon," Bentick appealed. "I have been attempting, with little success, to convince His Majesty to return to the city."

"Ah, sir, 'tis the very reason I approached." He fixed his bright blue eyes upon the king. "I think, sir, 'twould be wise for us to return to London and to hunt another day."

"No, no," William insisted. "We have come for enjoyment."

"Sir," said a voice behind Blade, "there can be no enjoyment for us if you are ill."

Blade recognized Jackie's low voice and watched as William smiled slightly.

"Master Jackie is correct, sir," Random said. "Your well-being is on our minds at all times. Pray go back, sir."

"You are both right. I shall return."

"Then, sir, allow me to fetch the carriage," Random said.

"Very well, Michael," replied the king. "Stay with me, Jackie."

Bentick's eyebrows rose in surprise, and Blade flashed the Dutch aide a cynical smile. Bentick understood the unspoken comment and frowned in thoughtful silence. Quickly Random mounted and rode away from the group.

The hunting party continuing riding for some distance, the king having insisted on riding to meet the carriage. Jackie followed the chestnut-haired monarch, while to one side of her was the silent duke of Avalon.

Avalon covered a yawn with the back of one hand, and Jackie glanced over at him. In the bushes behind the riders a sudden movement caught the girl's attention. Something inside the greenery gleamed metallically.

"Your Majesty!" the girl shouted and spurred her horse abreast of the king. She threw herself against the small man, knocking him to the ground at the same instant a loud report sounded in the air. Instantly the men around the king were shouting.

William's horse shied and bolted. Avalon, stirring from his lethargy, leaped from his mount. Jackie knelt over the king, who lay on the ground.

"Your Majesty, are you all right?" Her face was filled with concern. The small man lay with his eyes closed and did not move. Jackie directed a worried look at Avalon, who frowned at the still monarch.

Bentick and Shrewsbury directed their horses to the bushes, and the two other courtiers followed. In a few minutes they returned.

Bentick knelt beside the king, then looked at Jackie, then Avalon. "What happened?"

For once, the handsome duke was at loss for words. But Jackie willingly supplied an explanation. "I happened to look off to the side and saw something suspicious, and, without thinking, I rushed to the king, fearing some sort of treachery."

Bentick looked at her astutely. "It would seem, child, that your fears were well-founded." The Dutch man's hands ran lightly down the king's limbs, searching for broken bones. He listened to the monarch's chest, then tapped him around the ribs. William moaned softly.

"We must return him at once to the city."

"Here's the carriage," Avalon said, finding his voice at last.

Michael Random dismounted and hurried to them, in an obvious state of agitation.

"What has happened? Tell me!" he cried repeatedly. His voice rose higher and higher, until finally Jackie cautioned him, "Quiet, sir, you are noisy enough to wake the dead!"

"I hardly find that an appropriate image!" Random snapped angrily.

Avalon stepped between the two. "Calm yourself, Lord Malvern, for the king is not dead but merely stunned."

Without replying, the earl of Malvern pushed past the tall duke and knelt beside the king.

Carefully Bentick and Shrewsbury lifted the shaken monarch and gently deposited him in the carriage. Both climbed in with him, and Random followed.

"We shall follow on horseback," Avalon said, and the girl made no protest.

They followed the carriage along the road to London, and neither spoke during the journey.

After the king had been taken to his rooms and Dr. Bishop had been sent for, Avalon turned to the girl. "I would remain here if I were you."

She turned angry gray eyes on him. "I had planned on that, Your Grace. I do not intend to run away while the king is ill."

"I meant—" Avalon began, then a dull flush crept over his face, and he turned away.

In a few minutes Dr. Bishop came out, shaking his head.

"Is His Majesty all right?" the girl asked anxiously. Avalon's face, too, mirrored concern for the monarch's well-being.

Edward Bishop laughed shortly. "Hardly. He's awake now, and irritated that he has to stay abed for a while. He appears to simply be bruised and to have no broken bones. I would trust that he will rest for the remainder of the day, but well do I know the man.'' He turned to Jackie. "He wishes to see you, Master Jackie.'' Churchill had sworn the doctor to secrecy concerning the girl's true identity, explaining that to say anything of it would upset his wife, Sarah. And he had implored the doctor to remember the virago Sarah could become once she had been crossed and her temper was loosed. Bishop had quickly agreed.

Jackie, aware of the man's knowledge, blushed slightly and dropped her eyes. "Is he angry with me?'' she asked.

Bishop chuckled. "No, my child. It would not be the king's way.'' Yet as he uttered the remark he glanced across at Avalon, who looked away, aware that the doctor was subtly referring to the duke's banishment from the English court. Jackie entered the room, with Avalon behind her.

William was propped up with pillows on the expansive bed. His upper torso was bandaged, and a nightshirt had been thrown across his shoulders. His face was paler than usual, but otherwise he looked fit.

An obviously upset Michael Random paced, like a guard dog, the length of the room. When they entered the young earl stopped and faced them, a serious expression on his face.

"Come here, my child,'' the king said to Jackie. She approached the royal bed and bowed low. "Thank you, Master Jackie, for saving my life. The doctor says that I would no doubt have been killed had it not been for your quick thinking.''

"You are most welcome, Your Majesty,'' she replied earnestly. "I only wish that you might not suffer the bruises you have received.''

"Better,'' said the king, a slight smile playing about his thin lips, "to suffer bruises than a musket wound in my chest.'' His eyes shifted to those of Avalon. "Was there any trace of this assassin, Your Grace?''

The man shook his head. "None, sire. Bentick and Shrewsbury combed the area, and later Churchill sent a detachment of troops to search the district. They found no musket, nor any trace of the man or men, although the bushes had been beaten down in that area. 'Twould indicate someone had knelt there for a considerable length of time.''

The king groaned suddenly as he shifted his weight. Random rushed forward to help the man.

"Perhaps we should leave," Avalon suggested. "The king needs to rest."

"I think that only too good advice," Jackie said.

William, fatigue evident in his pinched face, waved a hand. "Wait, Master Jackie."

"Sir?" she inquired.

"What would you have of me?"

She felt Lord Malvern's eyes on her, and the color drained from her face. "Only to continue serving you, sire. That is all I ask."

"Very well, child." Again a slight smile played about the monarch's thin lips.

Once outside the royal rooms, Blade and Jackie walked along the corridor without speaking. Finally Avalon broke the silence.

"I am little surprised that no trace of the assassin was discovered," the duke said, his blue eyes narrowing thoughtfully.

"Oh?" the girl replied, lifting one winged eyebrow.

"Oh yes, for I have little doubt that the assassin may be found in this palace," the man murmured.

Jackie's astonished gray eyes met the cynical blue ones of the duke of Avalon, and she could think of nothing to say. Avalon nodded.

"Too convenient," he said.

"What can we do?" the girl asked.

"I am afraid that nothing can be done. We have no proof whatsoever," the man replied. "However"—and his eyes met hers again—"we can watch."

She smiled.

The Frenchwoman knew the Sun King would be most displeased with her report on the attempt on William's life. Why had her lover bungled this? Oh yes, she had heard his excuse—that Jackie McKier had pushed the king away. She glared at him, and he ducked his head, as if sensing what she thought.

She stretched amid the rumpled silk sheets, and ran an indolent finger down her young lover's chest. Random shivered and rolled onto her, trying to kiss her.

"No," she said, pushing him off. He pouted, but the woman ignored him.

Random watched as what appeared to be good humor returned to the lovely visage of his French paramour.

"It is time for a celebration, Michel," she murmured.

"Oh?" he inquired casually.

"*Oui*, I have decided how we shall get out of this tangled web."

The young earl propped himself up on his elbows and traced the line of her jaw. He kissed her neck, but she pushed him away. He rolled over onto his back.

"How?" he grunted.

The silver-haired Frenchwoman smiled—a most unpleasant expression.

"We shall enlist the aid of 'Master' Jackie McKier," she replied and collapsed upon him, laughing.

"Oh," Random replied slowly, giving it thought. " 'Twould solve two problems at once."

"You are such a bright boy today," she said, her words heavily laced with irony. "*Oui*, the problem of what to do with this impish lad and the problem of the king's assassin. I should have perhaps used that child from the beginning."

"Perhaps," the blond man said, kissing her bare shoulder, "you had other things to do."

"Perhaps." She looked down at his light-colored head, then up at the mirrors. She grasped his hair, pulling his head toward her, and kissed his lips. Then she rolled away quickly and stood, stretching.

"Enough of this, Michel. We must get to work now." She walked to her wardrobe and stared thoughtfully at the contents.

"Dress first," she commanded, and he obeyed his mistress.

The woman pulled the bell cord for her servant, then slipped on a cherry-colored satin dressing gown. The low-cut bodice revealed the swell of her white breasts, and Michael Random watched, licking his lips, as her bosom rose and fell with each breath she took.

"Ah, Griselle," she said, when the maid entered, "I wish to dress in a half hour's time for dinner."

"*Oui, madame*," the girl said, bobbing a curtsy.

"But first bring us some hot chocolate," the noblewoman directed.

The maid curtsied again and left the room.

Victorée seated herself in a scarlet velvet chair close to the window and eyed her young lover. She crossed her legs and the dressing gown fell back, revealing the gleaming length of her perfect limbs. Random licked his lips again, then forced his mind away from the sight of her body. "What would you have me do in this?" he asked.

"Ah, *mon cher*, you must first bring young Jackie to me. And then my people shall take over from there," she replied sweetly.

The earl of Malvern looked with interest at the Frenchwoman. "Might I ask what will then be done? How will you persuade her to help us?"

The silver-haired woman stretched languidly and crossed to the fireplace, the light silhouetting her form in the dressing gown.

"You might ask, dear boy, but it would be better if you attended the session."

"Session?" he asked with a sinking feeling.

The Frenchwoman looked up as someone scratched at the door. "Come in." Griselle entered with a tray and set it on a table in front of Random.

"Thank you, Griselle."

The girl bobbed her head and left again. Random watched with interest as she did, for he had been thinking for some time that the little brunette would prove to be a tender morsel.

"Give up that thought," Victorée admonished as she sat to pour the chocolate.

"Eh?" he said startled.

"Griselle. Leave her alone, *mon cher*. I do not wish my servants to be toyed with by those outside my household."

"I could be inside your household permanently, my love," the earl said in amost ingratiating tone of voice.

She restrained a smile and handed him a steaming cup of chocolate. "Do drink, Michel, before I laugh at you."

He frowned, sipping at the hot liquid. "I don't understand what you have to laugh about," he said sullenly.

"Of course not, *mon cher*," she replied languidly, leaning across the table and flicking his round cheek with one finger. "Now, do be a good boy and drink it all."

"You still haven't answered my question, Victorée."

"Nor do I intend to do so at present, *mon cher*. Simply bring her to me at my country house in . . . hmmm"—she stared thoughtfully into her bone-china cup—"three days. That shall provide me with sufficient time."

"I still wish you would trust me and tell me your plan," the young man grumbled.

"Do not worry, Michel. My plans shall soon become clear to you. Now drink your chocolate," she admonished, "for I have much to do."

What to wear? It was a formal dinner tonight, and she must dress well for it. For many minutes she stared at the breeches and embroidered coats, and at last she selected a plum coat decorated with silver thread and dove-gray velvet breeches embellished with plum lace forget-me-nots down the sides of the legs.

Dressing quickly, the girl stared at herself in the full-length mirror as she metamorphosed from young woman to young man. Then she hurried to the great dining hall.

"Where is your lesser half?" the exquisitely turned-out Avalon asked, viewing Jackie through his quizzing glass. Chance, and whoever had arranged the seating, would have it that he sat across from her. The Englishman wore a gold and cream outfit, embellished with pearls so thickly sewn over his brocade coat that it was hard to see the gold material underneath. His dark hair had been powdered, and he had a star-shaped *mouche* on one cheek.

She frowned at him crossly. "Master McKier has been tired these past few days," she replied loftily, "so I let him sleep. He's getting old, you know," the girl said, dropping the tone of superiority.

"Yes," the duke replied in an amused voice.

Ignoring the man who constantly filled her thoughts, she turned to the young woman on her left and began chatting about the new Purcell opera.

This evening the duke sorely missed Jasmine. He had visited Sarah Churchill earlier in the day, ostensibly to pay a morning call on her but in reality to inquire after her beautiful cousin. Sarah had slyly informed him that Jasmine was now away from her country home and could not be reached. That was all Sarah would say concerning the girl, and the duke had left with a most unsatisfactory feeling.

When the meal was finished, the music was struck up, and the two left the table without speaking, going off in different directions.

Jackie looked around, but there was no one with whom she

wished to dance. This evening, if she danced, she would be
tempted by all the sparkling jewels to steal, and that would be
dangerous. No, better not to put that temptation in her path.
Besides, she felt more in the mood for conversation.

She saw Avalon talking heatedly with Simon Martin and
the earl of Shrewsbury and thought of approaching that group,
then discarded the idea. *He* would little like her intrusion.

How should she spend her evening? She considered the
various possibilities, and none seemed attractive enough to
divert her. Tonight she felt strangely at odds, bored and
restless.

Jackie's mind was made up for her when a strong hand
clasped her elbow forcing her to turn around.

"Random!" she exclaimed, a scowl crossing her face.

"Ah, yes, Jackie boy," he replied, giving the last word a
wicked turn. "How do you fare this evening?"

"Well, sir," she responded coolly, attempting to extricate
her elbow from his firm grip without appearing too obvious.
She was unsuccessful, and his grasp only tightened.

"I am well-pleased to hear that." His blue eyes mocked
the girl's discomfort.

"Why do you detain me, sir? Pray, allow me to go my own
way."

He chuckled, a not very pleasant sound, and slowly drew
her from the room. All she could do was go with him, for
otherwise she would create a disturbance. Outside in the
corridor, the young earl stared thoughtfully at the girl.

"You are alone this evening," he said, smoothing the
wine-colored brocade of his coat. He flicked back the lace
that fell luxuriously about his wrist and, his head tilted,
peered through his long blond eyelashes at the girl.

"Yes."

Michael Random chuckled again, and the sound of it grated
on Jackie's nerves, causing her to lose her temper.

"Sir, release me at once!" Her face was warm with anger.
"Else . . . ," she said slowly, forcing a smile on her face
that bared her teeth, "I shall doubtless find it necessary to
incapacitate you."

The blond earl laughed again, and Jackie gritted her teeth.

"Leave 'lone, sir," and the young girl jerked her arm away.
She turned to go back to the festivities but paused when he
uttered her name softly.

"You may be more alone than you realize, dear child," he added and began walking away.

She frowned. "What do you mean by that?"

But Random did not answer, preferring to give the girl a mocking bow and then leave with quick steps.

Jackie looked after him for a few moments with a thoughtful expression on her face. What did he mean, alone?

It could be only one thing.

Liam.

She raced through the halls of Hampton Court and up the back stairs. She threw open the door to their sitting room and called the man's name.

The priest did not answer.

Perhaps he's soundly asleep, the girl thought frantically, her heart thumping wildly against her ribs. He had been tired. Perhaps he was in a drunken stupor. That must be it.

She lit a candle and held it aloft, and in five strides the silver-haired girl reached Liam's bedchamber and knocked on the closed door. Then, not waiting for an answer, she threw it open and entered, looking around. The candle cast a yellow glow on the walls.

The bedclothes were rumpled, and a dagger lay beside the bed.

The room was empty. Liam was gone.

Chapter

Nineteen

LIAM HAD BEEN kidnapped—or worse!

The realization struck Jackie hard, and she slowly sank to the floor on her knees and rocked back and forth. She stared with mounting horror at the empty room, at the stained sheets.

No, think, she told herself, *don't feel.* She must force her mind to work logically.

First, why would anyone wish to kill Liam? He was simply a harmless old man. Second, if he were . . . dead, why would his murderers take his body away? Wouldn't they have left it behind? Why—and where—would they have dragged off a corpse?

No, that made no sense. And yet the other alternative—abduction—seemed just as improbable. But it had to have happened . . . unless the priest, injured, had wandered off somehow.

Why would anyone wish to abduct Liam? He owned not a single item of value to anyone; he posed no threat to a flea, much less a person; he knew nothing at all. He was just a happy drunk, nothing less, nothing more.

Why? the girl asked herself repeatedly, seeking an answer to the most difficult riddle she had ever encountered.

She paced around Liam's room, and with each step her despair mounted. Where could she even begin to find Liam? And if she found him, how ever would she rescue him? For a moment she thought of appealing to the duke of Avalon for aid in this matter. But the girl quickly dismissed that foolish notion from her agitated mind. No, Jackie swore, she would sooner die than go begging and whining to that cynical Blade.

She ran her hands through her hair, then stopped. Someone was rapping on the outside door of the sitting room. Who was it at this hour? Could it be Liam? No, she told herself, he would have a key, wouldn't he? Not if he'd been abducted in his nightshirt. Maybe . . . maybe it was the priest. . . .

Jackie ran into the sitting room and flung open the door. Her joyful expression faded when she saw who stood there.

"You." The single word was filled with contempt.

"Yes," said the earl of Malvern, lounging in the doorway. He walked into the room past the young girl.

"What do you want, Lord Malvern?"

He strolled around the room, examining the various items of furniture, then turned back to her.

"Why, I thought you knew, Jackie."

"No." She frowned, nibbling at her lower lip.

"How is your companion tonight?" he asked cheerfully.

"You did it!" she cried. She leaped across the room and grabbed him around the throat with both hands. Random gasped, then choked as her hands tightened and she shook him.

"Where is Liam? What have you done with him?" she demanded harshly.

Only strangling noises arose from the blond man's throat. Suddenly her hands fell away.

"Tell me," she threatened darkly, reaching for the knife she always carried.

"I would not do that, my dear." A most efficient-looking pistol had appeared in his hands.

Jackie dropped her dagger and looked at the young earl with disgust.

"Come along, my dear, and be casual, I wish no attention drawn to us." He gestured with the pistol for the girl to leave the rooms. He concealed the pistol inside a pocket of his coat and followed her.

A black carriage, the crest on its black door concealed, waited outside Hampton Court. Soon it was moving, its two new passengers rocking with the rhythmic swing of the coach.

"Is this how you nabbed Liam?"

"No," he replied easily, "your companion needed a small amount of persuasion. We had to bag him."

"Bag him?" she repeated dully, her mind numb.

"Oh, yes. First a burlap sack was tossed over his head, then the man was placed in a larger sack and sewn in. Two lackeys carried him out through the servants' quarters. And perhaps you've never noticed, but no one ever gives a lackey a second glance."

"Why did you steal us away? Of what possible use can we be to you? She said, keeping her voice calm and cool.

He did not reply. They rode in silence for what seemed hours, but she did not think it was that far from the palace. Finally, the coach halted. With a firm hand on her upper arm he helped her from the carriage. Her legs buckled under her when she reached the ground, and he roughly pulled her to her feet.

"Don't try any tricks," he hissed.

Jackie shrugged, not denying that she had planned a ruse. She was pushed along a gravel walk, then down some steps. Along a cool passage, their footsteps echoing on stone, they passed, his hand still clasped tightly on her arm, the pistol jabbed into her side.

For several minutes they walked in silence, then Random stopped the girl. "Enter here." He directed her through a door, which he closed after them.

She squinted in the sudden light. When her eyes had focused, she saw that she was in a narrow room. One wall was an ornate iron grille from floor to ceiling. The room was sinful in its luxuriousness, but the silver-haired girl noticed no details, for at that precise moment a groan sounded from the other side of the grille, and, curiosity overtaking her, Jackie stepped closer so that she might peer through it.

Liam was here! He hung cruelly by his arms from chains attached to the walls. He had been stripped of all clothing and his body was crisscrossed with red welts.

"Liam!" she called, thrusting her hands through the iron grille, seeking to reassure him with her presence. "Liam!"

The blood- and sweat-specked man raised his head weakly and peered vaguely toward the sound of her voice.

"Jackie?" he croaked. "Jackie, be that ye, child?"

" 'Tis me, Liam. What have they done to you?" She whirled on Random and raised her clenched fists to strike him on the chest.

Alarmed by the girl's violent expression, Michael Random hastily moved back a step and waved the muzzle of the pistol at her. Before he could say a word to the girl the door opened, and a woman swept in. She surveyed the two and paused, fanning herself delicately with a painted fan.

With shock Jackie stared at the newcomer. It was the woman whom she had seen at the masquerade at Versailles the night Jack had died, and later at the English court.

Confused, Jackie weakly sought a chair and sat down.

Victorée chuckled richly at the girl's apparent bewilderment, and yet she studied her daughter with fascination.

A lovely girl, the Frenchwoman told herself, with large gray eyes, a pointed chin that gave her face a piquant quality, and high slanted cheekbones. Exquisite. But she felt no maternal urgings. She simply appraised the girl's physical appearance as she might study the confirmation of a fine horse.

"You might well wonder why I have had you brought here, Master Jackie," the woman said, smiling at the young girl.

"It has crossed my mind," Jackie replied laconically.

The Frenchwoman laughed at the girl's attempt at bravado. "Ah, why do we not show Master Jackie why we have brought him here today."

She nodded to Random, who called through the grille, "Jean-Pierre."

"*Oui, monsieur*?" a French voice asked.

"Bring the Spaniard in once more."

"*Oui*." A minute later he escorted in a dark man.

The Spaniard bowed from the waist to the man and woman from behind the grille, then opened a polished box. He withdrew two thumbscrews and placed them on Liam's thumbs.

Jackie's eyes widened in horror, but she forced herself not to cry out.

A twist was applied, and Liam moaned in pain.

Jackie gritted her teeth but stubbornly refused to make a

sound. She vowed that not even the tiniest noise would issue past her lips.

Another twist; more screaming.

Idly fanning herself, Victorée shot the girl a sidelong glance and wondered how much persuasion would have to be used before they could thoroughly convince the girl to help them.

"Will you aid us?" the Frenchwoman asked.

"What do you want of me?" the girl said through gritted teeth, her fists tightly clenched.

The Frenchwoman smiled at her, then at Random. "Do you not see how easy it can be, *mon cher,* when the appropriate amount of . . . pressure is exerted?

He grinned at her pun.

"Well?" demanded the girl.

"You must kill the king."

Jackie swung around to face the woman, astonishment sending her black eyebrows up even higher. "What? The king of England? William? You're insane!"

"Of course, the king of England," the woman replied scornfully.

Jackie opened her mouth to tell the woman she would sooner rot in hell than murder the king, but Liam's voice stopped her.

"Jackie, please, fer the love o' Mary, help them!" he said in a hoarse whisper. He screamed suddenly in pain.

The girl shuddered at the priest's cries. If she refused to help them, they would go on torturing him. She had to say yes . . . had to pretend to play along with them. She would agree, and then somehow she would get away from them and go to the king and tell him what this woman's plans were. He would send his guardsmen to rescue Liam, and all would be well.

Yet—what if she could not get away from them? the girl asked herself. She frowned in concentration.

"Do not delay, child," the woman said. "Again," she called to the torturer.

He splashed a bucket of salt water into Liam's face, and the priest whimpered softly, tears falling from his eyes. The Spaniard moved in front of Liam and applied another thumbscrew. Liam's screams rose in volume, filling the room so that Jackie wanted to cover her ears with her hands, to close her eyes, to somehow shut out all traces of her companion's agony. But she knew it would do no good. Too, she must—above all else—present a brave front. She would not cry in front of this woman or Random.

Liam fainted, and Jackie's shoulders shook from the effort to keep herself under control.

The priest was revived, and the torture was renewed.

"Oh, Jackie, do it," Liam pleaded, his eyes filled with tears and pain. "He be only a Protestant, after all. Please, Jackie, don't be makin' me go through this pain." He screamed again. Then, suddenly his body went limp.

She jumped up and ran over to the iron grating and stared, horrified, at the priest. She turned to the Frenchwoman. "Is he dead?" she whispered. Then a red fury rose up inside her, and she flung herself at the woman. She would kill the bitch. She would strangle her, would cut the very life and breath from the woman's throat.

Random leaped up from the chair and, grabbing her shoulders, shook her until her head wobbled back and forth.

"Silly fool," he hissed. "The man's not dead." His tone cut Jackie like a blade. Like a blade, she thought, and she saw those sardonic blue eyes. To think that she, in her stupid innocence, had thought the duke was cruel. She could almost laugh or weep, she was not sure which, given the chance.

She whirled to face the woman. "I'll do it."

"Good," Victorée said. She signaled for Random to approach her. He bent and she whispered in his ear, then indicated the man on the other side of the iron screen.

"Jean-Pierre," Random, a sly smile on his plump face, called. "Come here."

The stocky man entered and waited for Random to speak. The earl turned to the henchman, speaking to him in a low tone, Jackie could not make out the words. The man smiled, an oily expression that Jackie mistrusted. What new devilment were they up to? she wondered.

The henchman beckoned to the Spanish torturer, and they departed from the room.

Jackie frowned and looked at the Frenchwoman, who was sipping a glass of wine.

"Oh sweet Mary, me shoulders," Liam, who had returned to consciousness, moaned. Jackie stared down at the tips of her shoes.

At that moment the Spaniard and the Frenchman returned

with a metal brazier which they set down on the stone floor a few feet away from the priest.

Jackie could see the red-hot glow of coals. The Spanish man placed an iron rod in the brazier so that the tip was buried in the coals. He waited.

Liam screamed at the sight of the brazier.

"What are you doing?" Jackie yelled. "Didn't I agree to your plan? I'll murder the king for you, if that's what you want!" She looked angrily from the earl's eager face to that of the woman, whose features were so close to those of the girl yet so alien in their cruelty and inhumanity.

No one replied.

"What are you doing?" she screamed again, jumping at the Frenchwoman. Startled, Victorée rose hastily, backing away from the snarling girl.

Random stepped between them once more, but this time he swung his fist into Jackie's abdomen. The young girl doubled over, then crumpled onto the floor from the blow. The earl picked her up and set her in a chair.

He left her there, bent over at the waist.

The Spaniard picked up the hot iron, its metal tip glowing with intense heat. Advancing on Liam, he placed the rod on the priest's private parts.

"Oh God, no!" Jackie screamed, jumping up from the chair.

"Oh, yes," Victorée said. "This is an . . . inducement, Master Jackie."

"But I told you that I would kill the king!"

"And do you not suppose that we think you might try to play us false?" the woman asked archly.

"I give you my word," the girl said strongly.

"The word of a footpad—pray tell me, what that is worth? Nothing. That is why I shall further convince you." She smiled. "Now your priest shall sacrifice his manhood. It is a bothersome thing, many say. I am sure he'll be far happier without it."

Unconsciously, Random's hand went to his groin. He shivered at the inhuman tone in the voice of his French mistress.

"No!" the girl cried, staring with horrified eyes.

The Spaniard moved the iron, and the tip merely touched Liam's tender flesh before it was removed. The foul odor of burning flesh filled Jackie's nostrils, gagging her.

The priest screamed and screamed. Tears of anger and frustration at her inability to do anything filled Jackie's eyes.

"Now," Victorée said to the man, "castrate him."

"*Si, señora*," the man replied, and once more applied the hot iron.

"No!" the girl cried and, grabbing the screen, rattled it. "You don't need to persuade me! I'll do it! Please don't castrate him! Please!"

"Good, I believe you. Now," Victorée said, snapping her fingers, "enough."

The Spaniard appeared disappointed, but he pulled the iron away. He glanced over at his subject, who hung insensible in the chains. No great damage, this. Just a little burned skin, that was all. Perhaps he could finish the job later, after everyone had departed. It could be that his mistress would wish the man flayed. That he would eagerly do.

"Now," the Frenchwoman said briskly, "Random will accompany you on your return journey to the palace. In fact, Michel will be with you at all times. You see, we still do not trust you, Master Jackie, and we must ensure that you will keep your word, *n'est-ce pas?* The king trusts you, or so Michel reports, and it would be so very easy for you to get close to him and then—then, child, lean near to his ear as if whispering to him—at that point, stab him in the heart with a dagger."

The girl shivered and stared at the woman whose pale eyes gleamed with an unholy light. She sipped again at her wine and took a deep breath. As she talked, Victorée fondled the emerald ring on her hand.

"One smooth stab should do it," the woman said. "And to speed things up, so we do not risk being discovered, each hour that you delay you shall receive some part of the priest's body. A finger here, a toe there, perhaps one of his testicles. It will be sent by a special messenger, and I think," she smiled, "that you will not take overlong for the deed."

The disguised girl looked at the smiling woman, then at Random, who sat watching her with an expectant air. They would be paid in full for this someday, she vowed. How, she did not know at present. But she would kill them. She would try to escape . . . but how? He was to be with her at all times. Now, she could send no message to the king, nor even one to Simon Martín. Little hope existed for either Liam or her.

But still there must be some way . . . perhaps she could jump Random . . . knife him instead. How she would relish that deed! She would drive the dagger deep into his throat and watch with satisfaction as fright seized his plump features. As for the woman . . .something slow would be appropriate, the girl thought savagely to herself.

Something of her turn of mind must have been conveyed to the earl of Malvern, for he gulped nervously, then said, "Don't try any of your tricks, Master Jackie, for I shall be watching you like a hawk."

"Then it is agreed," the Frenchwoman said, standing and fanning herself gently. "You will kill King William for me. Good. Come, Michel." She turned to leave.

"How will I know you just won't kill Liam when we leave?" Jackie asked, scowling.

"You cannot know, *mon enfant*. Random!" The woman snapped her fingers and he followed her out, flashing a grin at the girl as he departed.

I have agreed to kill the king. They may kill Liam. No, they will. Then they'll turn around and kill me. There's no hope, no hope at all.

And, for one of the rare times in her young life, Jackie felt despair fill her soul completely, and tears streamed down her cheeks. It would seem that this was one time when there would be no escape for them.

None.

Chapter
⋙ • Twenty • ⋘

THE JEWISH SWORDSMITH, who had stepped outside for some fresh air after a heated political discussion with Shrewsbury and Avalon within the stuffy confines of the ballroom, frowned at what he saw.

He watched as the two people stepped into the carriage and the coach pulled away from the grand driveway of Hampton Court and drove down the long lane.

How strange that the girl should be getting into a coach with the earl of Malvern. Although she had never told him her reasons, he was well aware that she loathed and feared him. Strange, too, had been the girl's face—it was white and strained. He frowned.

Slowly Simon walked through the great doors of Hampton Court and paused. All was not well here. Perhaps he should go to Master McKier and see what the old man had to say.

When he knocked upon the door, it swung open by itself. "Hello?" he called, then walked in when no one responded. Odd, he thought, for Jackie had said to him earlier that Liam was resting and staying in his rooms that evening.

He glanced around the sitting room, then noticed almost

underfoot a dagger on the carpet. Squatting to examine it, Simon picked up the blade, turned it over once, and then, rising to his feet, placed the knife on the table.

Perhaps Liam was sound asleep. Both bedchambers were empty however, and in the second room he saw signs of a struggle.

The swordsmith quickly walked down to the kitchen level and looked around at the various servants, who were running back and forth on royal errands. If anyone knew of subterfuge, the servants would.

"You," Simon said, signaling to a stocky footman in the royal livery.

The man paused, his hand over the lid of a silver bowl. "Sir?" he inquired politely.

"Have you seen anything odd this evening? Perhaps another man being escorted out by one or more others? I thought they might have come this way."

The footman wrinkled his brow in concentration. "No, sir, I don't remember anything like that."

Disappointment stabbed at Simon. He glanced at the other servants.

"Sir," said a tentative voice.

Simon looked around, then down into the periwinkle-blue eyes of a young servant girl. "Yes?"

She bobbed a curtsy, flashed a dimple at him, then blushed.

"What is it, child?" Simon pressed gently.

"I saw somethin' odd, sir," she said in a soft Irish brogue. " 'Twas a carpetin', mayhap a bag. Man shape it be, an' the two fellas carryin' it be the furtive sort, if ye take me meanin', sir."

"I do," Simon smiled. "Go on."

"They come through here like nobody be seein' them. I seen them because they knocked into me, an' I dropped a load o' eggs. They all be thinkin' we be blind," she said. "I be fair angry then, sir, as ye might expect, an' then they go out the door an' put the carpetin' in a carriage."

He glanced at her sharply. "Not a wagon?"

She shook her head. "No, sir, it be a coach. Big it be, with four black horses. Black coach it be, with no crest on it."

Black horses, black coach, no crest—the coach that he had seen Jackie and Random enter. It could be none other. "Thank you—" He paused, looking at her.

"Katie," she supplied.

"Thank you, Katie." Simon reached into his pocket and drew out a coin, which he pressed into her hand. She started to demur, then stopped when she saw the gold profile of the king.

"Thank ye, sir." Her eyes wide, she bobbed a curtsy and scurried off, leaving Simon to his less-than-pleasant thoughts: Liam forcefully taken from the room. Signs of a struggle. Jackie in the company of a man she loathed. And that mysterious dark coach, unmarked so that no one could easily identify it.

Leaving the kitchen area, he returned outside. He shivered in the night air, although the September night was not cool.

Jackie was in danger. He felt that. And he could not allow her to come to harm. Quickly the swordsmith hailed a groom and ordered the man to saddle a mount for him.

The groom led out a gray horse, and Simon swung up into the saddle. He glanced down at his evening outfit of brown velvet and smiled wryly. But it was of little importance that he was not dressed for riding; he must follow that carriage.

"Your knife, man," he said to the groom. The man stared blankly up at him, and Simon, impatient to be away, snapped his fingers. Reluctantly the man handed him the dagger, and Simon tucked it into his belt.

Simon rode in the direction he had seen the unmarked carriage take. Before long he spotted a carriage, one lantern swinging in the darkness. This must be the coach he sought, for it was still early enough in the evening that few had left the court's festivities to return to London—and this carriage, too, traveled in a direction away from the city.

Simon rode on for what seemed hours, keeping far behind the coach so that no one could hear the hoofbeats of his horse, nor spot him in the moonlight. Unexpectedly the coach made a turn and disappeared behind a line of trees. He followed down the long lane.

Ahead he could see the lights of a large country house. The lantern on the carriage had stopped swinging, so he assumed that the carriage had come to a halt. He waited, but he did not see the front entrance open. Odd, he thought, unless the occupants of the carriage had gained entrance to the house elsewhere.

He urged his mount closer, then dismounted. He tied the

horse to a tree close at hand but out of sight of the lane in case someone should leave that night. Keeping to the bushes and trees on the lawn before the house, Simon maneuvered his way quickly to the house's gravel drive. Quickly looking about, he saw no one approaching. He dove across the gravel and ended close to the house, on his stomach. He smiled wryly at the absurd position, then got to his feet. Brushing the gravel from his coat and breeches, he reflected that a new outfit would be in order after this night.

He moved nearer the house. The carriage now stood empty, and there were no signs of anyone about the house. He circled to the right side of the mansion, seeking another entrance. Suddenly he paused, in midstride, cocked his head, and listened.

Faint and muffled through the walls of stone came the sound of a scream, an outcry filled with terror and pain. Simon started to put his hand to his sword, then stopped, for he had not worn it that evening, weapons not being allowed in the presence of the king. He groped for the knife in his sash.

He moved around to the back and there before him was a door. He approached it, still glancing around to see if anyone might spot him. He tried the door, and it opened without a sound. As he proceeded down the stone corridor, the horrible screaming increased in volume. A door opened at the end of the corridor, two men stepped out, and a heartrending moan could be heard clearly. Simon quickly stepped into a doorway, and, his heart pounding, hoped fervently that they would not come his way. He withdrew the knife and held it ready for attack.

The men moved in the opposite direction. The moaning continued, and presently the two men came back, carrying a brazier between them. The door slammed shut. There was silence for a few minutes, then a piercing cry. "What are you doing?" Jackie's voice shouted. Simon started, dropping the knife. He groped for it in the darkness of the corridor, and at last his fingers found the cold metal.

One dagger, he thought bitterly, against two men, maybe more. He was no coward, but if he were imprisoned or killed, no one would know the location of Jackie or Liam, and there indeed would be no hope for their rescue.

He turned and ran back lightly down the corridor. Once

outside he paused, looked around, then ran for the cover of the bushes. He rolled into a bush and landed hard against a sturdy stem, momentarily stunning himself.

Grunting with pain, he heaved himself to his feet and hastily returned to his horse. He was preparing to mount when a side cellar door opened and two cloaked figures appeared. Simon paused, one hand on the horse's neck.

The figures slowly walked toward the carriage. They could be seen outlined against the light of the torches set on either side of the house's doorway, but the swordsmith could discern no further details.

"I have misgivings on this matter," a man's voice said.

"*Mon cher*, you fret far too much," a woman's voice replied caressingly in a French accent. "What choice does the girl have? She must do it."

"Aye, or the man will be far less than he is."

They both chuckled in appreciation over some unknown joke, then she spoke again. "Do not worry, Michel. Our sweet Jackie will kill the king. And then you, *mon cher*, must kill her after she murders him. That way she will not talk. *N'est-ce pas?*"

Her companion chuckled, and Simon thought it not a pleasant sound. "What of the prisoner, Victorée?"

"When Master Jackie has succeeded—and is dead—then the old man will be eliminated."

"Good," the man said. "We shall follow in a few minutes." He helped the woman into the carriage. "What was that?" He paused suddenly and looked around.

She gazed down at him in the dim light. "What, Michel?"

He frowned. "I heard a noise."

"An animal," the Frenchwoman replied lazily. She chuckled, a low rich sound. "Do you permit your guilt to hobble you, Michel? To possess no guilt is a most marvelous thing. You must cultivate it, as I have done. Now, *bonne nuit, mon cher*."

"Yes. Give my regards to the king," he said mockingly.

He moved away, the coachman gave a crack of the whip, and the four black horses pulled the coach down the lane.

Simon was already halfway down the lane, heading for the road back to Hampton Court. All thoughts of saving Jackie or Liam had been pushed from his mind. A plot to kill the king was afoot, and he must warn William!

* * *

"Yes, sir?" Cornelius Snodgrass asked deferentially when a disheveled Simon Martín set upon him in the halls of the palace.

"I must needs send a message to your master, Corney. Tell him that the Frenchwoman and her lover Random plot against the life of the king, and that they have captured Master Jackie."

His face turning red, Corney sputtered speechlessly.

"Find him at once, Corney," the swordsmith urged the servant. "I go to warn the king and his guardsmen."

"Yes, sir!" The man turned and ran from the corridor, leaving Simon to wonder where the king might now be found.

The manservant shook his head ruefully as he skittered along corridors searching for his master, inquiring of all he met if they had seen His Grace. He saw a dark head down the corridor, ran up to the man, bowed, and, quite out of breath, inquired of Shrewsbury if he had recently seen his master, the duke of Avalon.

"Why, yes," the noble replied. "I saw him leave the grand ballroom a scant hour ago. He was on his way to visit with Lady Marlborough."

Puffing and panting, the plump manservant reached the apartments of the Marlboroughs and knocked frantically on the door. " 'Tis the most awful thing, Your Grace," Corney blurted when he saw his master. " 'Tis that Frenchwoman and Master Jackie!" the man said, in his flustered state confusing the names. "They are aiming to kill the king! Master Martín sent me to tell you, sir. He has found out somehow and goes now to inform the king!"

Avalon jumped to his feet. He stared thunderstruck at Sarah.

Jackie? she said to herself. It could not be so. Then quickly aloud, "There must be some mistake."

"Oh no, Your Ladyship," the manservant said. " 'Tis the Frenchwoman, her lover—that Random fellow—and Master Jackie. I distinctly heard Master Martín tell me those names." He touched the side of his head. "With these very same ears, sir."

"Indeed, I have no doubt of that Cornelius," his master replied wryly. "Did Master Martín say where these people might be or when they would make their attempt?"

"Oh no, sir, that he did not, for he did not appear to have time to fill me in, as it were, on the intimate details of this nefarious plot!"

Sarah rose, a most perplexed expression on her face. "I cannot believe . . . not Jackie," she said.

"Believe it, madam," Avalon said roughly. "Come, Corney, we must find the traitors." Sketching a bow to the perplexed woman, the duke departed with his servant.

"Corney, find Simon and tell him that I shall handle these people. But be discreet, for God's sake," the duke said. The short man rushed off, leaving Avalon to his thoughts.

The devil of the problem, was that they must proceed carefully with the Frenchwoman. If she were an agent of Louis XIV, her detention by the king's guards could cause a serious diplomatic incident. Louis would welcome an excuse to declare war upon his old nemesis, William, and such a war could only aid the cause of the deposed James.

Tact and diplomacy were tools Avalon would need in handling this affair and this woman. And he was expendable, he told himself with some amusement.

Avalon strode through the silent hallways of the palace in search of the woman and the boy. He knew that the king would have been in bed when Simon reached him, and even now they would be in the monarch's study. They were safe there, and yet William, being no coward, would chafe at the necessity of being hidden away. He would wish to go among his people, Avalon knew—as did the Frenchwoman. And Simon would have to prevent the king from such a rash action, for surely there was no safer location than where the king was already closeted.

Stopping, Avalon peered down a hallway, pondering whether he should go down it. He heard the whisper of a silk skirt and, without thinking, he stepped back into a doorway so that he would not be seen.

Along the hall lined with gilt-edged mirrors, unconcern upon her lovely face, glided an unescorted Victorée L'Este du Plessis. Waiting until the Frenchwoman had almost passed the doorway where he stood, the duke reached out, and firmly grasped the startled woman by the arm. "In here, French bitch!" he growled, forgetting in a moment all his vows of diplomacy, and, thrusting her into the room, slammed the door behind him.

Their eyes grew accustomed to the gloom of the chamber, and Avalon turned to survey the woman, whose bland expression had been replaced by one of amazement.

"Your Grace?" she said, dropping a curtsy. "What is the meaning of this?" Her hand crept to her bosom.

"Oh no, none of your French tricks!" Avalon snarled. He reached out for her, but Victorée ducked behind a sofa with a silky whisper of skirts and petticoats. Then her hand found what it had sought within her bodice: a slim stiletto, evil in its highly polished surface and its hollow tip, in which was concealed a most unpleasant poison. She grinned at him—a savage look that transformed her face into a feral mask. In response he lunged toward the woman, grabbing at her skirt. The material gave way, ripping until below the waist she was clad only in her petticoats.

He did not wish to kill the woman, so he had not yet drawn his sword. He paused, his hand hovering at his side, and an expression of dismay crossed his face. His sword . . . he had not worn it that evening. What a fool he had been not to have Corney fetch it for him, or to have taken one of Churchill's.

The Frenchwoman laughed when she saw his hand move to his side from which hung no weapon.

"Come, Avalon," Victorée said, thrusting her hips forward slightly. "Come to me," she purred, brandishing the dagger.

He vaulted over the sofa. The sudden action caught the woman unprepared. Victorée fell back, the high heel of her satin shoe catching on a rug. She stumbled, and Avalon was upon her. Victorée thrust at him with the poison-tipped dagger. Seeing the discolored tip of the dagger move in exorably toward him, he drew back his arm barely in time, so that the blade passed harmlessly through the sleeve of his coat and shirt.

He could no longer afford to be a gentleman. Since there was no other way to subdue the woman, he hit her hard on her pointed chin. Her head snapped to one side. Her arm fell, and the dagger flew from her limp fingers.

Drawing in a deep ragged breath, he stared down at the fallen woman. He bent to her chest, listening for a heartbeat. Satisfied that she was still alive and that he had not broken her pretty neck, Avalon moved quickly to tie her hands and feet together with one of the curtain restraints, and to gag her with a wad of cloth torn from her overskirt. There was unfortunately no way in which to lock the door to this room, but he thought it highly unlikely that the Frenchwoman would be able to free herself.

Now he would go in search of Random and Master Jackie and take care of those two villains, who, he was sure, could not be far away.

Victorée returned to consciousness, frustration growing within her as the minutes passed and she could do nothing to free herself. She must warn Random. If the girl did not soon kill the king, their plans would be ruined once more. And Louis would not care to hear of two failures to rid him of William. She must escape somehow.

Rays of the rising sun streamed faintly through the windows and reflected on the objects in the room. Something gleamed, commanding her attention out of the corner of her eye. She turned her head carefully to stare, her pale eyes widening in surprise at what she saw.

Smiling the Frenchwoman began inching toward her dagger.

Simon raced through Hampton Court toward the royal apartments. Outside were posted two armed guards, who had been instituted after the attempt on the king's life at the hunt.

"Hold to," one commanded. Simon slowed to a walk and drew in a deep breath. "What is your errand?"

"I must see His Majesty. It is a matter of life and death," Simon said urgently.

"The king is not well," the second guardsmen said. "He sees no one tonight."

"I must see him," Simon pressed.

"No one sees him, *Jew*," the first man said, turning the word into a sneer.

The swordsmith flushed angrily. What sense was there in attempting to plead with the man? Who was he, Simon Martín, to demand to see the king at this early hour? No one, the swordsmith thought bitterly, a man without a title, a *Jew* with few strong connections at court. Yet he must make some attempt.

"Come, man, let me see your master," Simon said in a reasonable tone of voice. "It is of utmost importance to the king."

''And I think, Jew, that it is of 'utmost importance' that you depart these halls and find your satanic master,'' the man said with a derisive smile.

His fists tightly clenched, Simon whirled and strode from the royal apartments. If he could not see the king, could not warn him, then there was left but a single alternative—he, Simon must stop the would-be murderers from carrying out their plan.

And, as he came to that firm resolution, his hand strayed to the dagger which he had secured earlier in the evening. Fight them, yes, he would do that, and kill them, too, if necessary.

But stop them he must.

Chapter

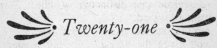 *Twenty-one*

THE RETURN JOURNEY to Hampton Court through the darkness and stillness of the early morning hours was interminable, and Jackie felt as though time stood still for her. Her head throbbed, and her eyes stung painfully from her crying earlier.

Yet while she might feel despair that there was no escape for either Liam or herself, she must not give up completely. If she could somehow stop this hated earl, kill him, then race to the king and warn him . . . somehow she must do it.

As if sensing her violent emotions, Random stirred opposite her. "Soon we will be there, 'pet,' " he said, his voice filled with condescension.

She growled at him but said not a word.

True to the earl of Malvern's word, the carriage soon rolled to a stop. He tightly gripped Jackie's upper arm and escorted her into the palace, so that it would seem, to the uninformed eye, that the man steadied a slightly tipsy friend. In this manner they walked down the hallways of the palace and upstairs to a neglected suite off a corridor.

Random shoved her into the central room of the suite and

eased the door shut behind him. He walked across to an old
scarred desk, pulled open a drawer and handed the girl a knife
hilt first.

She slipped the dagger into a pocket within her coat and
stared at him.

"Now," he told her, "we shall both go to the royal
apartments, and you alone shall go to the king's bedroom.
You will demand to see him privately, and because it is you
who makes the request, you will be allowed to enter into His
Majesty's presence. And then, 'pet'?"

"I am to rush across to him as though seeking his protection from something." She paused. "And then I . . . I am to
do it."

His only response was to nod, and his mouth formed a sick
smile.

Simon recognized that distinctive waddle "Corney!" he
shouted, rushing forward.

The plump man started visibly, then turned.

"Have you given the message to your master?" Simon
demanded.

"He goes to find the conspirators, sir."

"Good." Simon drew his brows together in a frown of
concentration. "Here, Corney, come with me." He indicated
that the small man should follow him, and he walked into a
room and approached a desk. He rummaged through it until
he found what he needed: a quill, ink, and parchment.

"Master McKier must still be rescued. He is in grave
danger, Corney. I am writing the instructions on how to get to
the Frenchwoman's estate. Give this to Santu and have him
take the house by surprise." He sanded the paper, folded it,
and gave it to the servant. "Now, for God's sake, man, hurry!"

After his departure, Simon walked slowly out of the room,
still frowning.

He glanced over at the stairwell as he heard footsteps, then
moved back into the room. It was Random with Jackie, and
the man had a firm grip on the girl's arm. He listened as they
climbed the stairs, then cautiously moved out of the room to
follow.

The couple was nowhere to be seen. Simon walked quietly
down the hallway, pausing to listen at each door. Finally, at
the door at the end of the corridor, he was rewarded.

Both Jackie and Random turned in his direction as he entered.

"Simon!" the girl called. "Warn the king! They're—" But she could say no more, for Random had pulled back his fist and slugged her.

Simon leaped forward, brandishing his dagger, only to look into the muzzle of the silver-plated pistol the earl had pulled. He saw as if in slow motion a belch of flame and smoke, and then he was knocked back by the impact of the ball. It entered his chest, and slowly, oh so slowly, his body slumped to the floor, and he could feel his lifeblood draining out of his body.

Then he knew no more.

Random chuckled and turned his attention back to the girl.

"Ah, little pet," the blond man cooed, "as you're so enamored of dressing as a boy, perhaps you would care to be treated as one."

Her gray eyes widened in horror. "Damn you, Random, I'll kill you, I'll kill you." She started to yell, and his fist brought blood to her cheek.

"You'll see what it means to be a boy at court. I shall teach you the ways, as they were so gently taught to me."

He rolled her onto her stomach, then threw himself onto her back. Releasing her hands, he gripped her shoulders roughly and, before the girl could even realize her hands were free, thrust his manhood deep inside her. Pain seared through the girl, and though she struggled and clawed at the floor, there was no surcease. Each time she struggled, her effort was rewarded with a stunning blow. She cried out and banged her fists on the floor, but Random only laughed.

Avalon paused in the palace corridor and listened. From whence had the cry come? There it was again. He looked around. It was too far away to be along this corridor. He walked swiftly down the hall and turned a corner, and he could hear the noise more clearly.

Avalon rushed to a door and threw it open. What he saw made him stop, shocked into inaction.

In front of an immense desk, Random and that traitorous child had paused . . . paused to make love, while a few feet beyond them lay the body of his friend Simon. With horrified eyes the duke gazed at the blood staining the swordsmith's waistcoat, his coat, the floor.

"Goddamn you both!" he yelled, leaping toward them. Startled, Random moved off Jackie, and Jackie hastily pulled her breeches up and closed her coat.

The duke knocked Jackie flat with one blow from his fist, then rounded on Random. Random backed up hastily and tripped. Avalon leaped toward the earl, grabbing the young man by the arm and neck. Snarling, Random brought his hand up to the duke's throat and thrust his fingers into the hollow of his neck. Avalon, choking, released Random and fell back.

The younger man laughed and circled the duke, then quickly kicked him hard in the stomach. Unprepared for this assault, Avalon bent over, then his body arched up as Random followed up with a vicious kick under the chin.

The nobleman exhaled sharply as he fell back against the door. He shook his head in an effort to clear it, then launched himself across the room toward Random, who met the assault with a rain of blows to the other man's face and chest. Then they were down on the floor in a wild tangle of flailing arms and legs, grunting and groaning as they struggled.

Jackie slowly drew herself to her feet and watched the men. *He* had hit her. After all this, he had hit her. Just as Random had. Anger built within the girl.

First Avalon was on top, then Random, then Avalon again. She stared as they continued fighting, until suddenly Random was on top once more. He grabbed the duke on the side of his head and began pounding it against the floorboards. The duke cried out hoarsely once, then there was no sound.

Something inside her twisted, and her breath caught. Random would kill him. *He hit me. But, he can't die. Not by Random's hand. Nor by mine. Fool,* she told herself bitterly. She railed at herself for never realizing it before. She did not hate Avalon. She loved him. And now he would die . . . unless she did something.

Painfully, her breath rasping, she dropped to her knees and found the knife. Random was too intent upon his deadly business to hear the young girl's approach.

A white fire suddenly struck between his shoulders, then again and again. Then, blood spurting from his back and spreading in an immense red stain across his shoulders, Michael Random gave a hoarse cough and slumped forward.

Viciously she drew back her foot and kicked him, and he

rolled off the duke. Then she knelt beside Avalon, the bloody dagger clutched in her hand.

Gently Jackie touched his face. He did not move. "Wake up," she said, and yet she knew he would not. She watched to see if the man breathed, but she saw no movement.

Inside her the pain exploded, and her world slid sideways. Tears stung her eyes, and she dropped the knife. He was dead.

"No," she moaned. "No." She rocked back on her heels. She had been too late. Random had finished his murderous business.

Her face contorted, she turned to Random's body. She would slash him, rip his soft round face, cut from the sockets those pale blue eyes.

But no, Liam and Jack had not raised her to be a defiler of the dead. Pain rippled through her. She slowly rose to her feet, and, looking around, saw Simon's body. Her gray eyes filled with tears again. Another death . . . her friend, too.

All this death . . . and pain . . . and waste, she thought, looking at Simon and Avalon. She glanced down at the duke, and the knife she had used to kill Random lay just inches from Avalon's outstretched fingers. She shuddered and wiped the blood from her forehead that was dripping into her eyes.

Jackie drew in a ragged breath and felt the pain radiate throughout her body. She was still alive—she must go to warn the king. Where would he be? What time of night—or day—was it?

Stumbling from the room, not stopping to look back, she paused in the hallway and looked around, dazed. Voices sounded from the stairwell.

"Search well. His Grace said the boy could be hiding anyplace. Said he's a particularly slippery one, making his living as a footpad!" a man's voice said.

"To think that that boy gained the ear of the king, too!" a second man's voice said gruffly.

The first man murmured assent, then said, "I'll look down this corridor. You go the opposite way. Be careful, as His Grace said the boy is armed."

"Aye, I will be."

She drew back into the room, her heart pounding, her sides heaving as she tried to breathe.

They were wrong! She wasn't trying to kill the king! She

was trying to *prevent* his murder! Avalon had told the guards she was involved, that she was one of the conspirators. She put an unsteady hand to her bruised head. But then how had the duke known of the plot?

There was no way of knowing now. What she must do was reach the king. But it seemed impossible, now that she was suspect.

She waited until their footsteps receded down the corridor, then opened the door carefully and peered out. No one was in sight. She stepped outside the room and ran lightly down the hall to the stairway. She would go above stairs, to the floors as yet untouched by the renovation, and there she would hide and wait until she could come out . . . and warn the king.

The pain tore at Liam's body and chewed his flesh. It ate through his skin, his sinews, his bones, until he dully wondered if there was anything left of him.

"Take, eat of my body," came the phrase into his mind. "Drink of my blood. . . ."

I be havin' no blood, no body left, the priest thought feverishly. *I be burned an' cut an' torn an' me fingertips be all burst an' . . . an'. . . .* He wanted to cry, but there was nothing left inside of him. The pain had devoured even his tears.

He prayed for the swift deliverance of death. Death would set him free, and he would be happy once more, whether he went to heaven or to Limbo. Jackie was captured; he was captured; she was being forced to kill the king and would, no doubt, in turn be killed herself.

'Tisn't fair! he cried to himself. *I be not that bad a sinner. Not really, Lord,* Liam hedged. *Take me, but don't take me poor Jackie, poor darlin' that she be.* He sobbed, but it was a dry, racking coughing that seared his throat and brought even more pain to his tortured body. Sweat dripped into his eyes, and he blinked them rapidly.

There was a noise outside the torture chamber. Shouting and yelling and the sound of muskets.

Rescue, Liam thought, his heart thumping. *Rescue. Me Jackie's come back fer me. I knew she be gettin' out o' this fix.* Gladness filled his heart. He waited eagerly, able to bear the pain, knowing that his own true Jackie was without the room.

Thunder sounded at the door, over and over and over, then the door gave way. The Spaniard stumbled in, knocking the brazier over, and the coals flew out, some of them striking Liam on his legs. He cried out in renewed pain and stared down at the red coals that lay in a heap just beyond his feet. He could feel their heat prickling his skin, could see the shimmering air above them.

The Spaniard screamed and Liam looked up, and the hope that had sprung up in him faded.

He was doomed. Jackie did not stand there.

What filled the doorway, what approached was . . . the devil. Large and black and menacing . . . it came toward him, came for him.

He was damned. He would not be going to heaven, nor even to Limbo.

He had gone to hell. Stark terror seized the priest, and, commending his soul into the hands of his Maker, he opened his mouth to scream, then knew no more as black oblivion slid over him.

Chapter
Twenty-two

THE LARGE NUBIAN servant reached the unconscious man hanging in chains and, with two mighty tugs, ripped the chains from the wall. He gathered the priest in his arms and turned.

"Oh, dear, oh me," said Cornelius Snodgrass as he hurried in, gingerly skirting the bodies on the floor. What a scene of carnage it was . . . terrible, terrible . . . and wahtever had happened to Master McKier? "Is he dead?" he asked Santu.

The black man shook his head.

Corney peered at the priest's body, noting the burns, the whip marks, the bruises, the terrible condition of the fingernails.

"I . . . I think I shall be ill," he murmured faintly but, catching the eye of the Nubian servant, decided that on second thought he might be able to carry on.

"Come, Santu, bring him along. We shall return him to Hampton Court. "Dear me," the flustered man remarked as the tall Nubian followed him. Avoiding the bodies of the Spaniard and Frenchman, they left the house behind.

Carefully Santu put Liam's body into the carriage in which

he and Corney had arrived and the two servants climbed in. Snodgrass tapped on the roof, and the coach rolled forward.

"How dreadful it was back there," the plump man breathed. "Absolutely frightful . . . so heathenish . . . so un-Christian. N-not," he added hastily, "that that is necessarily a bad thing . . . . Er, what I am trying to say, well, it—it far surpasses any wickedness I have ever seen!" he finished triumphantly, confident that he had not indelicately trod upon the religious toes of this impassive Nubian.

Still Santu said nothing, so Corney, sighing loudly to himself, lapsed into silence until they reached Hampton Court.

"You take him upstairs and call for a doctor. I shall endeavor to find His Grace."

Santu moved swiftly up the stairs, carrying his burden, and Corney, running a hand distractedly through his hair, ran off to find his master.

Little drummers energetically thumped their tiny timpani beside his ear, and Avalon opened his eyes carefully so that he might shoo the small interlopers away. But he saw nothing and, with a start, realized that the hideous noise was *in* his head. With a groan he propped himself up on one elbow and, looking around at the room, remembered.

He had found those two, Random and McKier, making love, had interrupted them, had hit both of them. Random, though, had gotten the upper hand and had beat his head against the floor. The source, no doubt, of the pounding in his skull.

The boy had left, that much was obvious. But where was Random? The duke frowned.

There. The earl of Malvern lay face down on the floor, a giant bloodstain marring the cloth of his coat. There was a bloodied dagger at his side.

Avalon drew his dark brows together in concentration, trying to put the puzzle together. Somehow, he had found a dagger and thrust it into the blond man's back. And then . . . then he must have fainted, for he remembered nothing after that—in fact, recalled nothing after having his head pounded into the floor.

But he must have killed Random. Who else would have committed the deed?

Slowly, and with great difficulty, the duke of Avalon rose

to his feet, making his unsteady way toward Simon's body. He half-knelt, half-fell beside his friend.

"Simon," he whispered, taking the man's hand in his own. "Friend." He frowned. It was still warm. He touched Simon's wrist, feeling a pulse, a slow one, to be sure, but a pulse nonetheless!

"Thank God," Avalon murmured and gently swung the swordsmith up in his arms. Carrying Simon, he left the room.

He walked until he came to the rooms he sought. Avalon stopped outside a door, then kicked it. After five good blows it flew open, and the nobleman entered the front room of the suite.

"What's that?" Sarah Churchill whispered, startled out of her sleep, to her husband, who was snoring softly by her side. John stirred, murmured something inaudible, then turned over, his head tucked under his arm. The noise outside their bedroom continued. There was a sharp crack, silence, and then:

"Sarah!" came a great roar. "John! Wake up!"

"John!" Sarah cried, jabbing a sharp elbow into her husband's side. "Wake up! Something is amiss!" She leaned over and quickly lit a candle.

John struggled groggily out of the firm and tender embrace of Morpheus and, sitting up, rubbed his eyes and looked about the bedchamber with confusion. His eyes blinked from the light of the single candle.

"Hsk, John!" Sarah called, pulling a gossamer dressing gown on and cinching it about her waist. She pushed back her blond hair with one hand.

John Churchill was reaching for his wig, set upon its stand alongside the bed, when the door to their chamber flew open, and a man holding another man stood framed in the doorway.

"Blade!" Sarah exclaimed.

Churchill scowled. "What the devil?"

"Master Martín!" Sarah exclaimed, recognizing the other man, and rushed toward them. Then, noting the condition of both, she demanded, "What goes on here?"

"Sarah, hush," Churchill said. "It would appear that there has been some sort of . . . fight. Is that not so, Blade?"

"Yes," the duke replied, "but allow me to put Simon somewhere, for he grows heavy."

Sarah Churchill's expression softened, a look of concern

crossing her face. "Here," she said indicating the bed, "put the poor man down." Sarah quickly rang for a servant.

"Where are those shiftless lazybones?" she asked sharply, her arms crossed, her foot tapping impatiently. A hastily attired maid, yawning and rubbing the sleep from her face, entered, then recoiled at the sight of the man. "Come, come, do not be afraid, girl," Sarah said, although Avalon admitted privately that if he were standing in the shoes of the servant girl at that moment he would be less than reassured by her mistress's stern tone. "Fetch Dr. Bishop at once, and don't be a laggard. Also bring up brandy, water to wash wounds, dressings for bandages, and something to eat. Be quick about it, girl."

Sarah narrowed her eyes as she surveyed the tall duke. I think you are not overly hurt," she remarked.

"I believe I shall not die of my wounds," he said dryly, ruefully rubbing the back of his skull. He withdrew his fingers and studied the blood upon them. "Although 'tis highly likely that I shall slowly seep away my lifeblood."

A second servant girl brought in a tray and set it down. Sarah poured a goblet of brandy and handed it to the duke. As he sipped at it he could feel the strength returning to his limbs, and his head throbbed less than before. Still, he continued to hurt . . . and it was not a physical hurt alone.

How could the boy have become a traitor? Why? He slowly made his way out to the drawing room and lowered himself onto the settee.

The Churchills followed Avalon to the other room, John remembering to pick up the liquor bottle.

The bandages and water arrived, and Sarah left them to check on Simon. She returned in a few minutes. "He seems to be resting more easily. Where is that doctor?" she fretted.

Churchill shrugged. "He had to get dressed, no doubt, Sarah."

"Well, he should have come in his nightshirt!" she rejoined indignantly.

John smiled at Avalon, who rubbed his eyes with one hand. He tossed down his drink and held his glass out for more.

"Tell us what happened, Blade," Sarah said. "We are waiting."

Sipping at the invigorating liquor, the nobleman began with

the message brought by Corney and ended with his own lapse into unconsciousness.

"But, Blade—" Sarah began.

But Avalon was on his feet, his glass having dropped from his hand. "My God," he said. "I had forgotten the French-woman. I must go."

"In your condition, Blade? Your wound has not been treated, nor are you properly dressed." She glanced significantly at the smear of blood upon his crumpled cravat.

Avalon brushed aside her concern with a wave of his hand. "'Twill simply have to do. I am well enough. Now, I bid you two a good night—morning—" he corrected, then stepped quickly to the door.

As he left Churchill turned to his wife. "Why didn't you try to tell him that Jackie could not have been one of the conspirators?"

She shrugged. "I tried. You saw that, John. But he's convinced the 'boy' is involved, and nothing will change his mind." She paused, frowning. "I wonder where that poor girl is. Quick, John," the blond woman said, punching him lightly in the arm, "get dressed!"

"Why?" he asked.

"You're to follow Avalon and look for Jackie so that she comes to no harm!"

"I am?"

"Yes, yes. Now go on!" she said impatiently. "I shall stay here and wait for the doctor to arrive. If he should ever deem it possible to show his face!" She turned to her husband, her foot tapping. "Well, John, what are you waiting for?"

Sighing, he left the room to follow the command of his lady.

Searching for the room where he had left the Frenchwoman trussed up like a game bird about to be served as a main course, Avalon was vaguely aware of the quizzical looks given him by the various people now out and about their errands. Yet he cared not at all. Propriety could hang.

Finally, after a few false turns in the rabbit warren of the royal residence, he reached a familiar bend, rounded it, and located the proper doorway. Taking a deep breath, he twisted the knob of the door and entered.

Yes, this was the room, although it looked far different in the daylight. It was a shambles, with the tables overturned and crushed glass underfoot.

It was the proper room all right, but it was an empty room. The French bird had flown her cage.

She crept along the hallways, keeping to the shadows. She must not be discovered. Slowly she moved, hiding in rooms when she heard voices approach along the corridor.

Her careful plans had been wrecked. But not all was lost. No, not all. Victorée smiled bitterly. It would seem that the distasteful task of assassinating King William of England had, in the end, fallen to her.

Random had failed; Jackie had failed; that was apparent now. So, the Frenchwoman told herself, somehow, she must gain admittance to the king's innermost chambers. . . . She must appear to be someone well trusted.

The albino woman drew back into a room as someone approached. She watched the man pass and her pale eyes narrowed.

Feeling for her dagger, Victorée smile unpleasantly, for it would seem that the solution to her dilemma had just presented itself to her.

Pursuing the man, she quickly jabbed the knife into his back before he could utter a sound. She dragged his body into a deserted room, where she stripped the man of his clothing.

Dressing quickly, she secured the dead man's wig on her head, then stuffed her clothing and black wig under a cloth covering a wing chair.

She approached a mirror and smiled at her reflection. What was good for the daughter was excellent for the mother, and now she would make her way to the king.

No one would stop a servant.

Blade ran down the corridors toward the royal apartments.

"Halt!" a guardsman cried as the duke approached. He stopped.

"I must see the king at once," Avalon said. "Let me pass," and he attempted to shoulder past the two sentries.

"Here now," said one man. "What's your rush?"

"It's a matter of life or death," Blade said anxiously.

"That's what the other fellow said," the second guard commented.

"Other fellow?" Avalon inquired. "A man of medium height, slight build, brown hair?"

The first guardsman nodded. "That's him, all right. A Jew."

"Did he talk with His Majesty?"

"Of course not, man! We sent the beggar packing!"

"Fool!" Avalon said angrily. "That man was sent to warn the king of a plot against his life!"

"What seems to be the problem here?"

"Sir!" The two men snapped to attention, and Avalon turned to see John Churchill approaching.

"Come," said Churchill. He walked past the two men, and Blade followed him. They stepped into the room, and a servant sitting outside the door leading to the king's writing closet stood and opened the door for them.

"Your Majesty." Both men bowed, and William looked up from his desk, where he had just dipped his pen in the inkwell. Although feeling ill that night, the king had risen at his usual early hour to begin another long day of work. The only concession to his sickness was that the curtains to the room had been drawn against the harsh light of the day, and his desk was lit with a cheering candlelight.

"Marlborough," he addressed John Churchill. "Avalon. What brings you here?"

"Grave news," the duke said. "There has been a plot against your life—and even now you are not out of danger."

"What? Explain yourself," the monarch demanded.

"Simon Martín has discovered a plot instigated by the Frenchwoman, Lord Malvern, and Jackie McKier to kill you. He warned my servant, who brought me the message. I found Simon seriously injured and those two making love. I killed Random, but the boy eluded me. I had the Frenchwoman subdued for a while, but I fear I must report, sire, that she has escaped."

The quill pen fell from William's hand, splattering his paper with ink. The color drained from his face. "Michael. And Jackie. Both." He gazed with stricken eyes at the duke.

Churchill opened his mouth to respond, but Avalon made a sharp gesture. "I took the liberty of informing two of your guardsmen earlier, and they have been searching for the boy since. Simon attempted to warn you, but he was turned away by the guards at the door.''

"What?" William's brows drew together in a frown. "Why?"

"He told them that it was a matter of life and death, but it would appear that they taunted him because of his religion."

The king turned to Churchill. "Deal with them immediately, Marlborough. I do not wish them in my service any longer."

"Your Majesty—" the man began.

"Now," the small man said.

"Very well." He bowed and withdrew from the room.

"I believe," Avalon said, "that the boy will still try to kill you. I would suggest organizing a massive hunt for the boy and the woman."

"Yes," William said slowly. "Yes, do that, Avalon." He rose to his feet and walked to a window, where he pushed aside a curtain to look at the rain-drenched garden. For days now the rains of the English fall had come, soaking the grounds and his spirits, and this news did little to revive them. The world was gray, and the dampness permeated his body, his lungs, his brain.

Was there no one he could trust?

A sharp pain went through him, and he sighed. Turning from the gray garden, he looked with saddened eyes at the tall duke, then said, "Find them, Avalon. And do what you must do."

In the darkness she waited. Sometime someone would walk down the corridor. And then . . . then she would leap out from her place of concealment, knock the man to the floor, and steal his clothing. If she could not approach the king as herself, she would do it as someone else.

A noise sounded down the hall, and she peered out of the room.

And what she saw almost made her shout with joy. It was Avalon! He wasn't dead, after all! She wanted to rush out and tell him how glad she was that he was alive, but some sixth sense stopped her. After all, he thought she was one of the conspirators . . . he had started a manhunt for her. . . . No, she would have to wait until after the king was safe, then she would tell him . . . what? How could she speak of her true emotions when he thought she was a boy? No, there could be no words between them.

She quickly withdrew back into the room and looked around. Where could she hide? She had seen the pistol in his hand. What if he came into the chamber? She rushed across the floor and dove under the cover on a settee and made herself into as small a bundle as she could manage.

The doorknob turned. She shook, for she had no way of defending herself.

The door opened, and she heard footsteps. They came closer and closer, and she could feel his presence near the settee. She trembled as she imagined his hand coming down to pull the cover off—he would find her, and he would smile that mocking smile of his. And then he would shoot her with that pistol, and the last thing she would see would be his cynical blue eyes.

"Your Grace!" a man called from the hallway.

"Yes?" Avalon asked, his hand poised over the settee cover.

"There's a body down the way. Come and see."

"Very well." His hand dropped to his side, and he left the room.

Slowly, ever so slowly, Jackie eased out of her hiding place, then walked quietly to the door and peered out into the hallway. She saw no one. She tiptoed down the corridor toward the back staircase. Then she heard whistling.

She was doomed now. There was no place to run. If she ran upstairs now, she would attract notice. No, she must make her stand here.

"Jackie!" a voice exclaimed.

It was Dickon, the king's page, and he was still in his livery.

"Jackie, there's a hunt going on for you! Where have you been? What's happened to you?" the boy asked, his eyes large with concern as he glanced at the blood and bruises on Jackie's face.

"I'm sorry, Dickon," she said softly.

"What?" His expression was puzzled.

Drawing back her fist, she drove it into his face. Dickon's head jerked back, and he slumped to floor. Quickly the girl knelt and pulled his clothing off him. Inside one pocket she found a piece of parchment and drew it out, scanning the lines written on it.

It was the poem written to Jasmine Jennings. Smiling faintly, she folded it and slipped it between the fingers of Dickon's hand. Then she patted his hand.

She dressed quickly in the boy's clothes, then ran a hand over her wig, smoothing it. She was ready. She would find the king and warn him and explain to him that it was all a mistake, that she wasn't trying to kill him but instead was trying to save his life.

She drew in a deep breath and calmly began walking down the stairs toward the royal apartments.

Kneeling, Avalon examined the body. It had been stripped of its clothing, inner and outer. Gingerly, he turned the corpse over . Below the ribs was a neat slit made from a knife's blade.

"It was murder," the duke announced, rising to his feet. He looked at the faces of the guardsman who had discovered the body. "Anything else?"

"Aye," the man said, pointing to a bundle.

Avalon moved to it and stared down. Clothing and a wig. Black. Woman's attire. He knit his brow in puzzlement.

"Do you know who this man is?" the duke inquired.

"Aye, a servant, Your Grace."

"A servant," he mused, turning to look at the body. "What sort of a servant?"

"Footman."

Perplexed, Avalon studied the bare corpse. He thought of the missing underclothes, royal livery, and wig.

Suddenly, the pieces of this puzzle fell into place. The color drained from his face. "I know where we can find the Frenchwoman," he said. "Come at once."

He raced from the room with the guardsman close upon his heels.

"John!" he called, passing Churchill on his way back to his apartments. "Come with me! To the king!"

Down the stairs they hastened, past long rows of portraits, past silent windows, until they reached the royal apartments and finally the king's writing closet, where earlier in the morning Avalon had conferred with the monarch. The servant who had patiently waited outside the room was no longer at his post.

His face set in grim lines, Avalon approached the door. "Inside," he said softly, a murderous glint in his blue eyes, "we shall doubtless find the Frenchwoman."

He twisted the knob to the door.

The door was locked.

Chapter

Twenty-three

KING WILLIAM OF England, wearying of his writing at last, sighed deeply, his spirits being so very heavy, and pulled the cord for a servant.

The door in front of him opened, and a liveried footman came in and bowed low to him.

Then the door behind the monarch opened, and a page entered and bowed low to him.

"Come," he said, indicating the footman. The man lingered in the shadows, and William frowned. He peered past the circle of light. "Jackie!" he exclaimed softly.

The footman reached behind him to lock the door. "What is the meaning of this?" William asked.

"Simply this," the footman said, pulling out a pistol and pointing it at the king's chest. The page boy stepped forward, and for a moment the pistol swung in his direction.

As the footman came closer, William said, "There is a hunt on for you, child. Why are you doing this?" he asked, bewilderment reflected in his face. "I do not understand. Why did you turn against me?"

The Frenchwoman only smiled and remained silent. She

329

could not fail her French master now. She could not meet with disaster at the hands of the English. She would succeed, then return to France in the glow of triumph.

"Jackie," the small man pleaded softly, "do not do this. Consider what you did before. You saved my life. Why have you changed?"

Victorée, a smile playing about her lips, advanced on William. He stood his ground, for he was no coward and would not turn to run. Cocking the pistol, she raised it.

"No!" the page boy cried, leaping into the circle of candlelight.

William stared with amazement at his face, then that of the footman in front of him.

The two were mirror images of each other!

"Who are you?" Jackie demanded.

The woman laughed. "Do you not know? I am Jackie."

William looked first at the footman, then at the page, and wondered if his mind might not be touched by a fever. He was ill, after all, perhaps more ill than he had realized.

"Jackie?" he inquired.

"Yes, Your Majesty?" Victorée and Jackie said as one.

His confusion deepened, and he shook his head to dispel the phantoms. But when he looked once more, the two mirror images remained.

William slowly rose to his feet. "Jackie," he said, holding out his hand, "do not turn against me. Please. Give me the pistol."

The Frenchwoman raised the pistol toward the man, and, with a burst of flame and sound, it fired. Without thinking, Jackie flung herself in front of the king, pushing him back. He lost his balance and fell to the floor. Jackie's body jerked as the pellet entered, and the impact flung her against the wall, where she crumpled into a heap on the floor. The king rose to his feet.

"*Petite bâtarde* that you are," the woman said, calmly reloading the pistol. "Ghost from my past. You should have died seventeen years ago. I paid the woman, but she failed me. Well, she has paid for her treachery." The woman's pale eyes gleamed in the candlelight. The man before her seemed paralyzed. "Now you will pay for your treachery, little man," she said softly to the king.

Suddenly a thump sounded behind Victorée, and she whirled.

The door flew open, and three men tumbled into the king's writing closet.

"No!" Victorée shouted. Avalon and Churchill rushed toward her, and Churchill grabbed at the pistol. Avalon drew back his fist and slammed it into the Frenchwoman's jaw. Her head jerked back, and she released her hold on the pistol.

Noticing Jackie for the first time, John Churchill rushed to where she lay and knelt beside her.

"How does he fare?" the king asked hoarsely. "He—he tried to save my life."

"I think she's dead," John Churchill said slowly.

"She?" Avalon asked and stared blankly at the girl, at the bruises on the pale face.

"Yes, she," Churchill replied shortly. "Jackie is a girl, not a boy. Sarah and I have known it for some months now."

"A girl," the duke repeated dully.

"Yes. Don't you recognize the face of Jasmine Jennings?" Churchill asked bitterly.

Avalon looked down at the girl's tranquil face, and the world turned to ashes. His knees suddenly weak, he reached out to the king's desk to steady himself.

Silence fell over them, and then the duke of Avalon saw a blurred movement out to the corner of his eye. He whipped his head around. It was the Frenchwoman, closing in on the king, who, unaware, was staring down at Jackie. In her hand was a knife with a wicked blade, the tip of which was discolored. The dagger she had tried to use on him, Avalon knew.

"Watch out!" he yelled, then jumped across the intervening distance. He grabbed at her hand, trying to wrest the dagger away from her. Curving like a cat's claw, her hand reached toward him. Down the knife arched toward him, and he leaped aside. The dagger cut harmlessly through the air. Avalon jerked her arm, and she whirled away from the king. Victorée's arm snaked around Avalon, and there was a frenzied movement between the two, who seemed to be locked in some devilish embrace.

Someone screamed.

Avalon staggered back, and Churchill leaped to his friend's side.

Shrieking, Victorée clawed at her breast, where the hilt of the dagger protruded. She writhed, whimpered and then slumped to the floor. No further sound came from her.

Avalon stared down at her, her beautiful face twisted into a mask of pain. Then he looked at William. "Are you all right, Your Majesty?" he asked.

"Yes," William replied wearily, groping for, then sitting in his chair behind the desk. "But send for a surgeon quickly."

"He may be found in my quarters," Churchill called after the guardsman who rushed from the room. He looked at Avalon, then down at the pistol in his hand, and slowly eased the hammer into place. "Dr. Bishop arrived not long after you left. He has removed the bullet from Master Martín, and says that, if an infection does not develop, Master Martín should soon be on his feet."

"Good." Avalon stared down at the body of the French-woman, then that of Jackie. Jackie and Jasmine . . . he had been attracted to both, and now they were dead. It was too late, for her, for him. Jackie . . . Jasmine was dead . . . and with her went his heart.

"Sit down, Blade," Churchill said, seeing the lost expression on the man's face.

Avalon sat, lost in silence and the agony of his private thoughts, while Churchill ordered the remaining guardsmen to secure the area.

William looked up at the captain fo the guardsmen. "Remove the body," he commanded. "And call off the search—the Frenchwoman is dead."

The guardsmen picked up the body of the woman and departed the king's writing closet.

"Here, let me through," said Dr. Bishop, pushing his way through the men. He brushed past John Churchill, gave a sharp glance to the seated Avalon, then knelt by the girl's body. He checked for pulse and opened her coat and ripped the front of her shirt. Laying his head on her breastbone, he listened intently.

"She's not dead," he declared at length. Churchill and the king exchanged relieved glances, but the doctor's next words turned those expressions into ones of dismay. "But she is dying. I don't think she can make it."

Avalon stared at him, as though having difficulty in understanding the man's words. "W-what?" he stammered.

"She will soon die. We must remove her from here," Dr. Bishop said.

"Take her to my apartments," Churchill said quickly.

Bishop indicated that two of the guardsmen should lift the girl, but Avalon pushed past them. He picked her up, the blood from her chest staining his coat, and walked with her from the writing closet. Bishop following close behind.

The king looked at Churchill. "When . . . if she heals, when Master Martín has healed, when everyone who has been wounded heals, I wish to see all of them in the audience chamber. Without fail. Do you understand?"

"Entirely, Your Majesty," John Churchill said, executing a most proper bow to his monarch, and, being dismissed, left the room.

She saw the circle of faces again: Jack, and Liam, and John Churchill, and the little page Dickon, and Simon, and Avalon, and they smiled at her and laughed at her.

"So you are a coward," said a familiar mocking voice. "Think you will die now, eh?"

She turned her head to escape the cynical voice, that voice that penetrated her being . . . but she could not get away from it.

"Devil . . . hell's spawn," whispered another voice, unknown to her.

"I always thought you were fainthearted," the hard voice pursued ruthlessly. "Craven, base coward. Little coward . . . 'Tis easy to die, far harder to live. . . .

Go away, she crossly told the voice. *Go away. I don't want to listen.* But she had not spoken, simply said the words in her head.

"A sneak, as well," the voice continued in a lazy drawl. "Timid as milk. Soft. Spiritless."

The irritating voice faded, and she smiled to herself. *Good.* She would just drift here in this nothingness, this void, where it was so comfortable, and she felt no pain, and she didn't have to worry or think or hurt. . . .

"Oh no, child, you're not going away," the voice said loudly.

Why didn't it leave her alone? Didn't it . . . didn't he know . . . that she wanted this?

She heard a deep sigh. "I cannot imagine that your foster father would be very proud of you. In fact, I am sure he would be red-faced with shame."

"No!"

"Yes," the voice insisted. "He would wonder if this were the child he had loved and raised, and I think he would have to conclude there must have been an exchange of children at some point, that you are a changeling . . . a spineless one, at that."

"No, dammit!"

"Yes, dammit." The voice chuckled. "Well, if you continue thusly, you will die, and when you are but rotting flesh in the ground none of us shall remember you. The memory of you will soon pass, as quickly as the passing of the day into night."

"NO!" She wanted to put her hands around the throat from which issued that provoking voice, and she would squeeze and squeeze and squeeze until there was nothing left . . . .

"The king has already declared that he is much better off without you. Truly it must have been by accident that you saved His Majesty's life. I cannot imagine how it could have been otherwise." The voice chuckled.

Up through the darkness she swam, and it seemed to part like water, and she saw a faint grayness above her. "No, I—"

"You what, coward?" the voice sneered at her.

"I—"

"Yes?" the voice demanded.

"I did it."

"Did what, child? Saved the king's life? Ha! Or perhaps it was a matter of arranging—something was planned between you and Lord Malvern. Is that not correct?"

The darkness broke, and she saw light, and she yelled, "No, no, no, dammit, I hate you, I hate you!" And she turned her head to glare at the source of this terrible voice.

Blue sardonic eyes gazed down at her.

"Hello, infant."

"Only your third day up," Sarah Churchill said, watching the girl, "and already you are commanded to a private audience with the king."

"Aye," the girl said, nervously fingering the lace on her cuff. "Sarah, I need another drink."

The woman poured the girl a glass of wine and handed it to her. "Be careful, or you'll be as drunk as Liam!" she chuckled.

"Hardly." Jackie tossed her drink down, then scowled. "Where is Liam?"

"Gone on ahead," the woman said.

"What can the king want?"

"That I do not know," Sarah replied. She turned away, picked up some embroidery, and studied her stitches.

Taking a deep breath, Jackie rose unsteadily to her feet. She reached out and grasped the back of the settee.

"Perhaps you shouldn't go," the woman said.

"I can manage," Jackie replied shortly.

"Umm."

She walked to the mirror to take one final look at herself. Sarah had persuaded her to wear white and silver and then had helped her dress. Her breeches were a white satin, her coat a white brocade embroidered with silver thread. Diamonds twinkled in her cravat and on the buckles of her shoes.

All that spoiled the effect of this gallant courtier, the girl thought, was her left arm in a sling. Ruefully she stared down at the material. How it ruined the line of her coat!

She sighed.

"Oh," Sarah remarked casually, "there are some letters here for you." The woman reached into her desk, pulling out a small packet of letters secured with a silver ribbon.

Jackie glanced at the packet with some interest. "Who are they from?"

"The duke of Avalon."

She stared at them but did not take them. "You'd best burn them," the girl said at length.

"Now, don't be so hasty," the woman said.

"What does he want?" Jackie asked slowly.

"How should I know? I've not read the letters."

"Hmmm. I thought he only wanted catamites around him," the girl said bitterly. "Why should he send missives to Jasmine?"

Sarah's look of astonishment was genuine. "Why, Jackie, whatever gave you that absurd notion? Catamites, indeed!"

"It's not absurd," Jackie replied, her chin rising stubbornly. "It was most reasonable when I first met the man that evening. Simon mentioned something about the duke's 'pets,' and the duke kept boys' clothing in the upstairs bedroom. Then I heard all those horrible tales about him, and even Liam has told me, as a child, of the family of Blade. So what was I to assume, Sarah? When we left by deception that night, he clearly said that others had departed by the same route. And when he was banished to his country estate, he took a boy with him.''

''Need you think the worst of the duke?''

''I admit that 'Satan' Blade has little impressed me with his kind and generous behavior.'' Why must they talk of the man when it only hurt her inside? He liked boys; she loved him; it wouldn't work—that was that. ''I have little cause to love him for the foul way in which he has treated me,'' she said, in an attempt to lessen the pain. It did not work.

''As foul as Random?''

For a moment, Jackie teetered on the edge of anger, then she was able to control herself. ''There is no comparison,'' the girl said.

''You should be more charitable.''

''Why? He didn't come to see me when I was ill.''

Sarah smiled. ''Oh, but he did.''

''No.''

''Yes.''

There was the memory of the mocking voice, making her angry, calling her a coward . . . the voice in the fever.

''I—I thought that his voice was a dream,'' she said, looking down at her shoes, ''from the fever.''

Sarah simply smiled, and the girl scowled. ''I'm leaving.'' She carefully placed the white velvet hat upon her brown wig. She curled the plume around her face and decided she looked quite good . . . despite the cumbersome sling.

''Wish me well,'' she said sourly.

He wouldn't come to see me, she told herself as she walked down the hallway, away from the Churchills' apartments. *It couldn't have been the duke's voice.* But she knew that it had been.

Why had he done it? she wondered. He didn't care for her; he hated her; he thought the worst of her; he even thought she had planned to kill the king.

Perhaps he wants me as a pet, and that thought only filled her with misery.

''Well,'' said King William III, dourly surveying the nervous quartet as they stood before him in his audience chamber.

The somber colors of the room seemed to reflect the king's

mien. Everywhere he looked Simon saw only shades of brown, gray, and black. It was a most unsmiling chamber, he thought. And the very day itself had dawned ominously, with thick cloud-laden skies that threatened a deluge of rain.

William was wearing his royal dress, as a proper monarch should, and Simon realized that he had never seen the small Dutchman so stern and unbending. It boded ill for their futures.

Simon noted as well that no sign of fever now touched Jackie's cheeks, and she appeared to have begun the process of mending, but her shoulder was still bandaged, her arm supported in a sling. Simon's own wound, unlkie Jackie's, had developed no complications, and he had soon been on his feet.

The swordsmith had tried to visit the girl, but Sarah Churchill had refused, saying that she was to have no visitors.

Except one, Simon thought wryly, looking at Avalon. The man had never left the girl's side while she tossed in her fevered sleep. Unto death, the phrase came into his mind, and he remembered how they had all thought she would die. Distressed by the girl's illness, Avalon had asked his friend how he, too, had come to know of the girl's true identity. Simon had simply said that over the months he had learned it, deeming it not the time to give a detailed explanation.

Simon glanced at Jackie and thought of Jasmine, for the white and silver she wore this day, evoked memories of Sarah's country "cousin."

After she had recovered from her fever, she had begun to quickly heal, but Sarah and Avalon had thought it best not to inform Jackie that the monarch was aware of her true sex, and so she was in a happy state of blissful ignorance, although apparently puzzled by the serious nature of this audience with the king.

Avalon, attired in a heavily embroidered blue brocade and lace outfit, waited for the king to speak. His nervousness displayed itself in his fingers, which toyed with a sapphire ring on his hand. His handsome face showed the lines of exhaustion from the ordeal of the past few weeks.

Liam, agitated for a number of reasons, wished with all his heart that he could pull out his rosary and tell his beads so that he might help ease his concern, but the duke had sternly forbidden such papist nonsense on the part of the priest.

Simon, apprehensive, simply waited.

"What would you have of me?" the king finally asked, directing his gaze to Jackie. "A title? An estate? A fortune? Tell me, Master Jackie, what will you have?"

She shook her head. "I need nothing from you, sir. 'Tis simply enough that I serve you, as I said once before to you." She raised her right hand, indicating the ring upon it. "This is present enough from you."

"I cannot make you an earl?" he pursued quietly, with a slight quirk to his lips.

"No, Your Majesty, I do not desire that. There can be no earthly reward. . . . Well. . .," she said, dropping her eyes to the tiled floor.

"Yes?" William asked.

"Perhaps a small monetary reward would not be out of order," she replied with a slight smile.

William laughed, an open appreciative sound that somehow reassured the concerned Simon. "Yes, Jackie, you may have your 'monetary reward.' Ask what you will."

"Oh no, sir," she said demurely, "I cannot attach a price to your life. You must decide."

"That is very true. Still, I thank you again for saving my life." He turned his hazel eyes to the others. "I thank all of you."

"Master Martín." The swordsmith looked up. "You shall receive an appointment to the court and be our armaments merchant, and so the duke of Avalon will no longer be your greatest patron."

He inclined his head. "You are most generous, sir. Thank you."

"And Your Grace—what would you have of your king?"

The tall nobleman moved in front of the others and bowed low before the king. "Sire, I would ask only one thing—that I may have the hand of this commoner in marriage," and, thus saying, he took Jackie's right hand in his.

Liam gaped, and Jackie, who thought the duke had lost his senses, tried to loosen her hand from the man's grip, but she could not.

"What!" the girl cried. What sort of man was he, to perpetrate such a horrible joke? Asking the king to marry her when the man thought she was a boy!

"What do you say to this, Jackie?" the king asked gravely.

"Why, why, 'tis the most horrid—" she began, but Avalon interrupted her smoothly and with a smile. "We know your true sex, Jackie."

She blinked owlishly several times at him. "W-what?" she faltered.

"We know, all of us," he said, gesturing to the other men, "that you are a girl and not a boy."

"Oh." The single word was flat. The girl turned accusing eyes on Simon.

"No, Simon did not betray you," Avalon replied dryly, seeing her glowering expression, "nor did Liam. Liam would rather face certain death than reveal your secret. Is that not so?" he asked the man. Liam nodded hastily, his eyes fixed on the girl's face. "How then did I learn?" the duke asked, anticipating Jackie's question.

"John Churchill accidentaly revealed it in the king's writing closet when we thought you had died."

"Oh," she said faintly, blushing. She would not allow her gaze to move from the tip of her toes.

"I—I cannot," she muttered to the duke.

"Why?"

Her face turned a deeper shade of red. "I am not pure, Your Grace." Her voice had lowered to a husky whisper. "I am . . . no virgin," her voice slowly sank. She wavered, as though she would faint, then seemed to recover. "Hell's spawn," she whispered.

"You? Surely not," the duke said. He gazed at her with deep regard in his blue eyes. "Think you, Jackie, that that is all marriage is? It matters little to me; I would make no demands of you," he said softly. "I would wait until you came to me."

She raised her startled eyes to meet his blue ones.

"What do you have to say for this deception?" William suddenly asked, his voice stern, intruding into the intimate moment.

"I say, sir, that it was no deception," Avalon replied evenly.

"No?" William asked, one eyebrow raised. He tapped his fingers on the arm of the throne. "Then tell me, Your Grace, what would you call it?"

"I thought at first it was a deception, too, sir, but it would seem that Jackie was dressed as a boy by her father and the

priest so that she would not be harmed as she grew to
womanhood. They traveled about the Continent, and a young
girl of such rare beauty, you must admit, would have been
ready bait.'' The monarch nodded silently. ''They were concerned for her safety.''

''If they were concerned about the girl, they should have
found her a good home,'' the king replied crossly.

''She not be an abandoned puppy or kitten,'' Liam said,
speaking up for the first time. ''She be our own Jackie, an'
we loved her from the very first. I found her in France where
an ould hag had her livin' in a horrible marsh, an' I took her
to Jack an' I be wantin' to put her with the good sisters, but
he talked me out o' it, fer he said she would be losin' all her
spirit behind walls, an' that it be like cagin' a bird.''

The Dutchman frowned and tapped his fingers.

''She received a good education,'' the priest continued
eagerly. ''I taught her her letters, an' she learned to be a right
proper lady.''

''As well as a proper gentleman,'' Avalon remarked dryly.

''That be true,'' the Irishman said with animation, nodding
his head. ''Aye, that be a right fine description.''

Avalon and Simon chuckled, and they were joined by the
king, who could not maintain his sternness in the face of
Liam's enthusiasm.

''Too,'' Avalon said, ''I must point out one further fact. If
Jackie had not been disguised as a boy, she would not have
been here with us. Moreover, and most important, sir, she
would not have saved your life. Twice,'' the duke drolly
emphasized.

The king cleared his throat self-consciously. ''Yes, that is
true,'' he admitted.

''You must allow,'' Blade pursued, ''that the element of
fate entered and directed the girl to this spot in time.''

''Still, in the end, that does not solve your problem, Avalon. I say that naught can be held against the girl,'' the king
said. ''But what shall you do, Jackie?''

She scuffed her toe along the tiled floor. ''I—I don't
know,'' she replied truthfully. His words had sounded sincere
enough. Yet . . . was this the man she had once vowed to
kill? She raised her head and gazed intently into his clear blue
eyes, and what she saw helped her not at all in her trouble.

"Why not say yes?" Avalon asked, a smile playing about his lips.

Why not? she wondered, for she did love the man, and had for some time. Yet he was a duke; she was no one. She could harm him in the eyes of the world, for all would mock a great man married to a common vagabond without name or title. She was sullied, not pure, and while he said it mattered little he was after all a man, and he would have a man's passions, and he would come to her, demanding. Or would he?

Smiling, Liam moved past them, patting Jackie reassuringly on the shoulder as he passed her. "I think I be havin' the key to the hopes o' these young folks," he replied smugly.

"Oh?" The king raised a skeptical eyebrow, and Simon and Avalon exchanged glances.

"Aye." He reached into the folds of his clothing, and when his hands were once more out in the open, he clasped an object that caught the candlelight, reflecting it with a gold light.

"Our insurance!" Jackie cried.

"Oh, aye, darlin', it be what Jack stole—er," Liam said somewhat nervously, eyeing the king, "borrowed—years ago, an' I took it so that he not be spendin' it all at one time." Liam handed it to the king, who gently turned it around and stared at it.

In the monarch's hands was a frame of beaten gold. In its sides were gaping holes where once, he assumed, jewels had resided. Only a single gemstone remained. A pearl, somewhat scuffed, still lodged in the bottom of the frame.

William studied the frame, then looked at the beaming Liam. He turned the frame upside down, peered through its center, then set it down in his lap and folded his hands.

"What is it?" the king asked finally.

"How remarkable," Avalon said, irony heavy in his voice as he surveyed the frame through his quizzing glass, "but what exactly does it prove, Master McKier?"

"Oh," the priest said, his face falling for just an instant. "I be fergettin'—the picture be taken out fer years. I be returnin' in but an instant." And he turned and ran from the audience chamber.

"I believe this to be yours," the king said gravely, handing the empty frame to Jackie. Grasping it, she stared down at the gold.

As she gazed at the golden frame and tuned it over in her hands, Jackie's thoughts tumbled in her head. What should she do? To whom could she turn for advice? To Sarah? To Liam? To Simon? No, there was no one from whom she could seek counsel. She would have to turn to her own heart.

Liam, desperately out of breath, one arm clutched to his heaving side, came running back to them and stopped in front of the king's throne, waving his missal excitedly.

"How timely," Avalon murmured, "we shall now have a sermon read to us."

"Devil," Simon said, smiling.

The priest continued waving the missal as he caught his breath. The book, Avalon decided, looked quite new, and he suspected the cause to be its general disuse. When he had recovered, Liam carefully opened the book and withdrew something.

"I put this in me book fer safekeepin' years ago," the priest explained. "I be thinkin' that when the frame be sold at last, we might get a pretty penny fer the picture." He rolled an apologetic eye at the king, then gently handed the item to Avalon and Simon, who studied it for a few minutes, then in turn gave it to the king.

It was a miniature oil portrait of a woman wearing an emerald gown. Her silver hair was caught at the nape of her neck and flowed in ringlets across her shoulders. She had a heart-shaped faced, high cheekbones, and eyebrows that swept up like the wings of a startled bird.

It could have been Jasmine, Avalon thought. The eyebrows were a different color, yet. . . . Another face came unbidden into his mind, and he frowned.

It could have been Jackie, the king thought, but for the hair color. It could have been the Frenchwoman's face when she was younger.

Liam, seeing the monarch's mounting confusion, said, "Take yer wig off, Jackie girl."

The young girl obeyed quickly, pulling off the brown wig that she had adopted so many months ago and by which most people at the English court knew her. She plucked the pins from her hair, and down past her shoulders fell lock after lock of silver hair, matching that of the woman in the miniature.

Simon caught his breath at such perfection, and, pain stabbing at his side, all the more regretted his loss. She was an exquisite beauty, of that there could be no doubt. Avalon would, indeed, be a lucky man.

Jackie took the miniature from the king and stared at it, her hands trembling. It *was* the Frenchwoman who had tried to kill the king, who had directed Liam's torture, the woman she had seen two years ago at Versailles.

It was almost her mirror image, as she had fancifully imagined. Where had Liam come by this portrait, and why had he never before shown it to her?

Immensely pleased with himself, Liam beamed, his face wreathed in smiles.

"Do you care to explain?" William asked after some moments of profound silence. "Who is this woman in the portrait?"

"Ay, that be Jackie's mother."

"But that is the face of the Frenchwoman," Avalon said, confusion crossing his face.

Only Simon said naught, unable to wrench his gaze from the girl's heart-shaped face.

"Oh, aye," Liam said. "This portrait be stolen from a French household o' noble blood," he emphasized, "eighteen years ago. Jack be visitin' that woman one night when he be takin' the frame, an' here she be comin' later to England. It be Jackie's mother, o' that I be sure," he concluded happily.

"Then . . .," Jackie said slowly, the color draining from her face, "that means that Jack is . . . was . . . my. . . ."

Liam smiled fondly, a tear coming to his eye. "Aye, it be meanin' that Jack be yer father fer real, darlin'. I just be figgerin' this out meself a few months ago when I be seein' her at the coronation ball."

Tears filled the eyes of the young girl, and she clasped the frame close to her breast. "Did he know, do you think, Liam?" she asked, hope in her luminous gray eyes.

There had been many women and many more drunken nights between that night in March, 1671, and the day when Jack first saw the face of his adopted daughter, and Liam doubted greatly whether Jack O'Connell had possessed the insight to see the resemblance between Jackie and a French paramour of five years before. But he did not say so, for he really could never be sure, and he would not for the world hurt the girl. "I think he be knowin' it, darlin'," the priest said gently. "He loved ye as his own, that be fer sure."

"That's true," she said, sniffling softly. "But if my mother were that wretched woman—" *Hell's spawn*, said the voice inside her.

"You were not raised by her," Avalon replied smoothly, "so there can be no worry on that score. I am convinced that the good, er, influence of Master McKier and your father far outweigh any effect of bad blood that you may have received from her."

"Are you sure?" Jackie asked, her gray eyes searching his handsome face.

"Convinced," he replied with great confidence, and the girl heard the inner voice grow fainter and fainter until she could no longer hear it.

"Now," William said clearly, "Jackie, will you answer the duke on his proposal?"

A great weight seemed to have been lifted from the girl, and she felt a peace come over her. She smiled first at the king, then at Avalon, for her heart knew what it wanted and her mind had been made up. She spoke only a single syllable.

"Yes."

Avalon's handsome face creased into a joyful expression, as did William, who felt himself in the singular spot of royal matchmaker.

Simon attempted to smile but failed, sunk in his own misery, and knowing that he would soon have to master it in order to help his friend . . . his friends, he corrected.

Liam beamed, for this was precisely what he had wanted for so long for the girl, and he couldn't have asked for a better—But wait. His smile faltered, then slipped from his plump features. Be that man a devil? Didn't they call him Satan? He turned to speak to the girl but stopped when he saw that she had eyes only for the handsome duke. He might be a devil, but she be an imp, for sure, and that might be a match, if not made in heaven, at least one that be equitable.

"Now, priest," the king said severely.

"Aye?" Liam quavered, his knees knocking together in fright. Oh, he be in mighty bad trouble, that he be seein'. Mayhap if he skulked out now, no one would be the wiser.

"I would have you put aside your rogue ways and become either a true priest, or—"

"Oh, Yer Lordship," Liam said, his voice shaking, "I be good from now on, sire, I be. I be"—his face brightened—"I be the tutor in Jackie's household fer all the good children she be havin'.''

"An you'll be able to go to Rome at last!" the girl exclaimed.

"Er, aye," the priest replied tentatively, not at all sure he wished to finish his pilgrimage begun so many years before.

William nodded. "I think that would be a suitable occupation for you, Jackie?"

"Yes, Your Majesty?" she asked.

He beckoned to her. "Come closer, child." He studied her youthful face and the outfit she wore, and she hung back slightly, for upon his thin face was a most disapproving expression. Gradually it faded, to be replaced with a kindly smile that lit his hazel eyes.

"Put aside your men's breeches, Jackie," he said gently. "Become a lady and a woman, and a good wife to the Duke. Your days of intrigue, I suspect, are over."

She smiled at the king, then at her future husband. "Oh, my days of adventuring are of the past," she declared, but Avalon, seeing the minxlike expression on her face, was not totally convinced.

"I shall be so good," Jackie cried, and, forgetting the presence of the others in the audience chamber, threw her arms around Avalon's neck. He smiled down at her and circled her with his own arms.

"I shall be his true angel," the silver-haired girl averred earnestly, her warm dove-gray eyes sparkling with suppressed laughter.

"Satan's angel," the mocking duke of Avalon gently corrected as he bent his head to kiss her.

Turn back the pages of history...
and discover

Romance

as it once was!